THE GATHERING DEAD

Stephen Knight

ISBN: 978-0-9871044-2-7

1

The dead had risen.

McDaniels heard the fragmented reports over the radio, and he could glimpse the reality of it through the Humvee's thick, bullet-resistant windows. The dead had risen, and they swarmed through New York City like a plague of locusts, consuming every person they could find. The gates of Hell had opened, and the dead were the vanguard of Satan's army. Every now and then, the .50 caliber mounted in the Humvee's cupola would bark, and red-hot cartridges would roll into the vehicle's passenger compartment, tinkling to the floor between McDaniels and the slightly stooped man cowering in the armored seat beside him. Whenever the soldier manning the .50 fired, the gray-haired man flinched. His pale face grew even more pallid.

"Shooting them really doesn't help," he said to McDaniels. "It takes a head shot to make them fully dead again. And the noise is just giving us away."

McDaniels shifted the M4 carbine in his lap. "A few rounds from a fifty don't really leave all that much, doctor. I'd rather deal with a couple of stiffs that are blasted into several different pieces than a couple that are still whole and able to give chase."

"But the noise..."

McDaniels shrugged. "The city's falling apart. A little gunfire isn't going to make any difference, sir."

From the front right seat, First Sergeant David Gartrell glanced back at McDaniels. "Zeds in the street ahead. Looks like they busted through the NYPD cordon. We have a choice of deviating or going through 'em. For what it's worth, top cover says we're on the most direct route." The grizzled senior noncommissioned officer hesitated for just a moment before dropping the bomb. "There are lots of civilians still in the area, so it's going to get messy no matter where we go."

"Keep on going," McDaniels said. "Doctor, you'd better prepare yourself—this won't be pleasant."

Doctor Wolf Safire shrunk even further into the seat's hard contours. His big blue eyes brimmed with terror, but there was a defiant set to his jaw.

"My daughter," was all he could get out. His voice was barely a choked whisper above the roar of the Humvee's diesel engine and the sporadic chatter of the .50 caliber overhead.

"She's right behind us. We won't leave her behind, doctor. I promise."

Safire nodded and ran a hand through his thick gray hair. He opened his mouth to talk, but the Humvee bounced on its suspension as it drove over something. The bouncing continued, and McDaniels knew the vehicle had rolled over *several* somethings. He looked up as a distorted face flitted past the window to his right, then another. A smear of blood splashed across the window. Above, the .50 caliber opened up again, this time with a vengeance as the trooper manning it let loose salvo after salvo. McDaniels leaned past the trooper's legs and looked at Safire again. The thin scientist had his hands clenched into fists and pressed them against his eyes.

"Holy shit, is it thick out here!" the gunner said over the din of his weapon.

He wasn't kidding. Through the windshield, McDaniels saw dozens—maybe hundreds!—of the walking dead surging onto West 58th Street as they overwhelmed the hasty barricades set up by the NYPD and New York Army National Guard. The barricades weren't totally ineffective; constructed from garbage trucks, fire engines, squad cars, and any other vehicle that could be driven into position, they still held a mass of stinking dead at bay. But the dead just piled up on each other, trampling each other as they formed great writhing dunes of bodies that loomed over the barricades. That was how they crashed through. Undeterred by the firepower arrayed against them, they closed upon the barricade defenders and slammed into them like a tidal wave. The single-minded desire to feed was what drove the legion of the dead to swarm out of lower Manhattan like a vicious, malignant cancer. No matter what they had been in life, in death—or the *new* death—all that was left for them was incessant, never-ending hunger. And all the food was pulling away from them, headed to the north. Out of the city.

Why the dead needed to eat live human flesh was beyond McDaniels.

He slapped the trooper's right leg. "Ritt, button it up! Secure your weapon, *now!*"

"Hooah." As the Humvee plowed into the first of the walking dead, Rittenour dropped back into the Humvee's passenger cabin and closed the cupola's hatch. Just in time; the vehicle was jarred by a sudden impact.

"Looks like we got some jumpers," Gartrell said from the front right seat. "I don't believe this... the damn stiffs are actually jumping off the buildings to try and get at us." He adjusted his helmet's strap slightly as the Humvee slammed through two other shambling corpses, sending them flying. McDaniels watched as a New York City Police officer ran toward the convoy, a pack of the dead on his heels. He stumbled, and that was all it took; some of the faster ghouls fell upon him, nails slashing, teeth tearing. McDaniels turned away from the sight.

Gartrell glanced at the driver as the armored vehicle drove over another clutch of the dead, its big, knobbed tires spinning momentarily as they crushed bone and pulped desiccated flesh.

"No need to try and go around them or anything, Leary."

The driver kept his eyes riveted on the chaos before them. "First Sergeant, you can kiss my—oh God!"

The Humvee skidded to a sudden halt, throwing everyone against their harnesses before they could brace themselves. Sergeant Rittenour flew into the back of Gartrell's seat and rebounded pretty much right into McDaniels' lap before McDaniels could restrain him. He hadn't had the time to buckle up.

"Leary, what the fuck?" Rittenour yelled.

And then McDaniels saw what had prompted Leary to stand on the brakes. Standing next to the Humvee's left fender was a slender woman with curly red hair. She wore a white terry cloth bathrobe, and clutched a small toddler to her breast. The toddler's eyes were big, blue, and beautiful, much like her mother's would have been had they not been so full of terror.

"Please! Please help me!" the woman screamed. She pounded on the driver's window with one well-manicured hand.

"Oh God," Safire whimpered.

"Major," Leary said.

"Drive, Leary!" McDaniels said.

Leary twisted in his seat and looked back at McDaniels. He compressed his lips into a thin, bloodless line.

"Major," he said again, his voice soft but the plea was unmistakable. *Please major, don't make me leave this woman and her kid to these things.*

"God damn it, troop!" Gartrell reached across the wide vehicle and rapped his knuckles across Leary's Kevlar helmet. "Drive!"

Leary glanced back at the woman, and she must have seen it in his eyes. She pounded on the bullet-resistant glass as the dead swarmed toward her, some at a slow run, others at a limp.

"My daughter, take my daughter!" she screamed. Leary finally stomped on the accelerator, and the Humvee's diesel engine roared as the vehicle pulled away just as the first of the ghouls slammed into the woman and ripped the child from her arms.

"Oh fuck," Rittenour said.

"God forgive me," Leary muttered. There was no mistaking the sob in his voice, and McDaniels' heart went out to him. None of them had ever thought they would be abandoning defenseless American citizens to the ravages of a brutal and uncaring enemy like this. If they had, McDaniels knew none of them would have signed up to wear the uniform of the United States Army.

"God's not here today," Gartrell said. "But I am. Just do what you're told to do, troop—drive. Straight down 58th until we're told to turn. Got it?"

"Got it," Leary said. He got a semblance of his game face on and sped up, weaving around the odd abandoned vehicle here and there. But when the dead shambled into view, he drifted toward them and let the Humvee's reinforced bumper and brush guards deal with them. The heavy vehicle swayed as it crashed through the corpses.

"You're not hurting them," Safire said.

"Sir?"

"You're not hurting them, soldier! They can't feel pain! They can't reason, they can't feel fear, all they know is hunger!

Going out of your way to run over them isn't hurting them *at all!*" Safire said, his voice nearly a high-pitched shriek.

Leary kept his eyes riveted on the street before him. "That may be, sir. But it sure is fun."

McDaniels' radio headset came alive. "Terminator Six, this is Two-Six, over."

"Terminator Two-Six, this is Terminator Six, go ahead."

"Six, keep on 58th. Don't turn toward Columbus Circle. That area was a mess before the quarantine, and it was being used as a staging area for the fire department before they were stood down. A lot of the tankers and ladder trucks were abandoned, I saw it on the flight in," said Chief Warrant Officer 3 Walter Keith. He was the real commander of the Special Forces Operational Detachment, not McDaniels. McDaniels didn't know Keith well, but he had immediately impressed upon the major and First Sergeant David Gartrell that he was a hard charger who wasn't about to shrug off a mission.

"Roger Two-Six, good copy." To Gartrell: "Verify that with top cover."

Gartrell spoke into his headset's boom microphone, talking directly to the pilots of the MH-6 Little Bird that paced the convoy from overhead. He listened to the response.

"Keith's right. The Night Stalkers verify what he said, but it's not their intention to send us that way. We'll drive through the intersection of 58th and Eighth Avenue, then across Broadway. We turn north at Seventh Avenue and enter the park there."

"Got that, Staff Sergeant Leary?" McDaniels asked.

"Hooah," Leary said.

McDaniels relayed the information to CW3 Keith, who rode in the Humvee behind them. "If we get separated, take that route. Over."

"Roger, Terminator Six. We'll be with you, over."

The convoy broke through the infested area and charged past a manned barricade. McDaniels was surprised to see two M2 Bradley Infantry Fighting Vehicles mixed in amidst the M1114 Humvees. Army National Guard soldiers wearing full MOPP IV gear—the accoutrements a soldier would don in the event of a nuclear, biological, or chemical attack—stared down at the three Humvees from atop their own vehicles.

"Poor bastards," Gartrell said. "They feel safe because of the hardware, but it's not going to help them."

"Maybe we ought to tell 'em," Rittenour said.

"Maybe you ought to sit back and enjoy the ride, troop. This vehicle is not stopping," Gartrell said.

Ahead, a fire raged unabated as a fashionable Midtown West apartment building burned, filling the street with pungent, thick smoke the color of coal. Unarmed civilians stared at the Humvees as they tore past, but the dead hadn't made it this far yet. Despite the uncontrolled fires, the uniformed soldiers manning the corners, the perpetual songs of sirens mixed with the throbbing basso beats of helicopter rotor blades, the residents of this part of New York City thought they were safe for the moment.

McDaniels shook his head. A moment was about all they had.

***

The dead hadn't made it to Central Park yet, at least not in sufficient force. Still, the fair citizens of New York City had heard the helicopters, and they knew the jig was up. As the three Humvees roared through the park, armed soldiers and NYPD were using all the tools at their disposal to keep the citizens at bay. They were using non-lethal force, McDaniels saw. No one wanted a rising to occur here, not in the middle of an evacuation. Just a few members of the walking dead could spawn dozens of fellow walking corpses.

A television news van was off to one side of the intersection of the 72nd Street Transverse and East Drive. The Humvees were a mess, having driven over and through pretty much everything the dead could throw at them, and judging by the viscera smeared across the windows, McDaniels was certain the convoy was not a pretty sight. The TV cameras immediately swung in their direction, broadcasting the image out to millions.

The Humvees accelerated through the intersection and past the news crew without slowing down. They wound their way through the vast park that sat at the heart of one of Man's greatest cities, a city that was slowly being consumed by a kind of nearly untreatable cancer.

And the only thing that kept it from being completely untreatable sat in a Humvee not more than three feet from one Cordell McDaniels, Major, United States Army Special Forces. Doctor Wolf Safire, the brilliant biochemist that had started the renowned pharmaceutical company InTerGen over two decades ago. McDaniels' bosses said that Safire might have a cure, or a vaccine against whatever it was that caused those bitten by the dead to turn into one of them. That was why McDaniels had been pulled out of his normal work at Army Special Operations Command and dispatched with First Sergeant David Gartrell to link up with Operational Detachment Alpha OMEN in New York City. He would oversee the rescue of the scientist and his thirty-something daughter, and ensure they were placed on a dedicated transport that waited for them in one small portion of Central Park's Great Lawn. McDaniels hadn't even thought to ask why him. Not only was it against the heritage of service he embraced, but one did not question lawful orders—especially in the special operations community. And if there was a man who said he might be able to stop the rising tide of the dead, then McDaniels would run through an erupting volcano naked if that's what it took to get him to deliver. And McDaniels had his own family to worry about. Though the Big Apple was the general nexus point in the United States, there were catastrophic infestations in Europe. No one knew exactly where it had started, but all indications seemed to point to somewhere inside Russia. McDaniels had been on the task force assigned to determine the outbreak's etiology. The best the threat team could determine, it seemed that someone had come across some long-forgotten relic of the Cold War and tampered with it. True or not, what had been released was first reported in Russia, and within weeks, Russia went dark. Satellites showed the legions of the dead moving across the nation, heading for both Europe and China. It was the double attack on capitalism the old Soviet guard might have dreamed of, but this time, the attacking foot soldiers had an entirely different perspective. They weren't in it to destroy capitalism. They were in it to eat people, and it didn't matter if those people were Russian, German, French, Polish, or Chinese.

The sky overhead was dark with smoke from gigantic fires. South of 14th Street, New York was an inferno, an intentional blaze started by the military in hopes that it would contain the army of the dead and prevent it from advancing north. And in a small measure, it was a successful gamble; even the dead couldn't soldier on when all their flesh had been burned to a crisp and tendons and ligaments could no longer move muscle and bone. But there were gaps between the fires, gaps filled with soldiers and policemen that were being overwhelmed by the sheer numbers of the walking dead. There were tens of thousands of them in lower Manhattan, and they avoided the flames by using the subway tunnels, by massing at roadblocks in such numbers that they overpowered the defenders, and in some instances, by walking into the East and Hudson Rivers and marching upstream. McDaniels had heard reports on his way in that a group of stenches had emerged from the East River and was headed for the United Nations building. He had chuckled at that. Finally, something would devour the United Nations before it could envelop the world in leftist glory.

But the fires had also blackened the skies with thick smoke, smoke that was driven northward by the prevailing winds. This had curtailed aviation operations. Even though McDaniels' convoy had a helicopter escort, it was by sheer chance that the proper flight crew from the 160th Special Operations Aviation Regiment had been in the area and was available for the tasking. The pilots flew their small MH-6 Little Bird without doors and usually operated at an altitude of 40 feet above the deck, at night, in all weather, so flying in smoke wasn't a show stopper for them. But for the rest of the aviation community, the smoke was thick enough to hamper many general aviation missions. That was why the assembly area at Central Park had been set up. VIPs and their dependents were to make it to the Park and, upon identity verification, they would board a helicopter or tiltrotor bound for greener pastures.

That was the idea, anyway. McDaniels looked out the window at the smoke-tinged afternoon and wondered just how many aircraft would wind up burying their noses in the dirt because their pilots couldn't fly by instruments.

Shapes moved amidst the trees as the Humvee sped up East Drive. McDaniels straightened in his seat and looked out the gore-smudged window, trying to make sense of what he saw. Were those people, or...?

"Holy mother of God," Gartrell said. He'd seen them as well. "Freaking stiffs in Army BDUs!"

McDaniels felt a deep chill envelop him. "Leary, step on it. We're way out of time."

"You got it, major."

2

Dozens of helicopters of all shapes and sizes had landed in the Great Lawn, from massive CH-47F Chinooks to small, aged OH-58 Kiowas. There were even some MV-22 Ospreys, big tiltrotor aircraft that had been flown in from North Carolina by the U.S. Marine Corps. McDaniels shook his head when he saw the gigantic, odd-looking aircraft. He knew the Osprey was a capricious aircraft, and something of a maintenance nightmare. The saying was the Osprey couldn't decide if it wanted to be an airplane or a helicopter, so it just failed at both.

As the Humvees drove around the Great Lawn, McDaniels heard sporadic gunfire from the south. While distant, it grew in intensity.

"Sounds like there's a party going on," Gartrell said.

"I'm going to switch over to the common net, Gartrell. You stay on our private network and keep an ear open, all right?"

Gartrell nodded. "Roger that."

McDaniels switched his radio to the common frequency. Whereas the private frequency being monitored by OMEN team was quiet, the common net was a storm of traffic. Most of the transmissions were disjointed and overlapping, as troops in contact frantically tried to give updates or request reinforcements. At the same time, area commanders tried to coordinate troop repositions and fire support for those units that were danger close and had ringside seats to the havoc. McDaniels heard more than a few transmissions ending in agonized screams.

Yep, the world's going to Hell in a handcart.

McDaniels switched back to the private frequency, which was still blissfully silent. He fidgeted in his seat and looked out the grimy window. It was an early afternoon in October, and the leaves in Central Park were starting their colorful transition. This was the time for horse-drawn carriage rides and lovers strolling hand in hand, while dogs dashed about, chased by small children. That picture had gone out of focus days ago.

McDaniels wondered if the Big Apple would ever be able to recover. If it was allowed the chance. While at U.S. Army Special Operations Command, he had overhead some possible plans to deal with the threat in New York City, and some of them consisted of essentially turning Manhattan Island into one giant brazier.

"Terminator Six, this is Rapier, over."

The voice over the radio jarred McDaniels back to the here and now. He keyed his headset's push-to-talk button. "Rapier, this is Terminator Six, over."

"Terminator Six, Rapier. SITREP, over."

"Rapier, Terminator Six. Package in transit, heading for assembly area ROMEO. We are in the Park, and are no longer in immediate contact with any zeds at this time, over." McDaniels' situation report was brief and succinct, just the way the Army brass liked it.

"Terminator Six, Rapier. Roger that, and good work. The Black Hawks are spooling up and will be ready to break deck the second the package is aboard, over."

Another volley of gunfire caught McDaniels' attention. Much closer this time. Even thought he couldn't see any immediate threat, he clicked the fire selector on his M4 from SAFE to SEMI. They were so close to getting out of this shit that if something were to go down, now would be the perfect time.

"Terminator, Rapier. Did you copy that last, over."

"Rapier, Terminator Six. Roger, good copy across the board. We'll come back to you when we're airborne, over."

"Roger that, Terminator Six. Rapier, out here."

"Coming up on the assembly area, major," Gartrell said. "Looks like there's some serious activity on the far side, where ROMEO is." ROMEO was the two MH-60M Black Hawks that were tasked to transfer Safire, his daughter, McDaniels, Gartrell, and the rest of OMEN Team to MacArthur Airport on Long Island. From there, they would board an Air Force jet and fly to Fort Detrick, Maryland, where McDaniels and Gartrell would escort Doctor Safire to the U.S. Army Medical Research Institute of Infectious Diseases. Once that transaction had been completed, McDaniels didn't know what lay in store for him.

He hoped that being reunited with his family in North Carolina was on the short list.

"How far are we from the ROMEO aircraft?" McDaniels leaned forward and looked through the Humvee's windshield. Civilians streamed across the road in tight, panicked groups, despite the throng of soldiers and police trying to hold them back. Leary had to slow down to keep from running people over.

"I'd guess about five hundred meters." Gartrell glanced back at McDaniels. "I know what you're thinking, major. We should get closer before we try and hoof it."

"We might not have much of a choice if this doesn't get under control, first sergeant." McDaniels pressed his radio button. "Two-Six, this is Six. Get ready to abandon the Humvees. We might have to go the rest of the way on foot, over."

Keith answered immediately. "Six, Two-Six, roger."

They stuck with the Humvees for as long as they could, but after having traveled no more than a hundred meters in almost ten minutes, McDaniels decided to dismount. The security situation was clearly deteriorating more quickly than the forces on hand could handle. If they were going to get out of New York City before it fell to the ravenous ghouls that charged through its cold concrete canyons, they would have to leave the comparative safety of the armored Humvees.

"My daughter. I'm not leaving without her," Safire said obstinately as Leary brought the Humvee to a halt.

"She's still coming with us, doctor," McDaniels said. "Now let's get going."

The pall of smoke had grown thicker, and it filled McDaniels' nostrils with a sharp, acrid odor as he flung open the Humvee's heavy, up-armored door and stepped out into the hazy autumn daylight. Gartrell stepped out from behind him, his Atchisson AA-12 autoshotgun already shouldered and ready. The first sergeant's head panned from side to side like a tank turret as he took in the sights. While they were safe for the moment, all around them New Yorkers were rushing into the park, thousands of them. The few soldiers they encountered tried to stop them, but the flow of refugees was too great. Just the same, gunfire broke out, and people screamed and whimpered.

"My God, are your people shooting innocent civilians?" Safire asked.

"These aren't 'my people', Doctor Safire. But there's definitely some shooting going on, but I don't want to guess at whom." McDaniels ran a gloved hand over his face, then pulled his goggles over his eyes. The smoke had started to make them burn.

CW3 Keith rolled up with the rest of his team in tow. In the center of the formation was a tall, raven-haired woman with tanned skin and the biggest green eyes McDaniels thought he had ever seen. She didn't look much like her father, which was probably a bonus. McDaniels saw she was tense, but not frightened.

"Regina!" Safire called.

Regina Safire hurried toward her father and embraced him immediately. She fairly towered over the stooped scientist, and McDaniels saw there was more to the embrace than just filial piety. The look in Regina's eyes hardened as she scanned the area, taking everything in. She was determined to protect her father as best as she could, and McDaniels had to appreciate her grit.

"We're ready to roll," Keith said as he stopped beside McDaniels. "I figure we should keep you, the first sergeant, and the Safires in the center of the formation while the rest of us make up the bleeding edge." As he spoke, Keith didn't look at McDaniels or First Sergeant Gartrell. His eyes were cast outward, surveying the chaos that threatened to swallow them up whole. The rest of OMEN Team took up defensive postures with their weapons charged and ready to fire.

McDaniels nodded. "We need to get to the ROMEO aircraft, which Gartrell says are about four hundred meters that way." He pointed into the hazy day where the collection of aircraft sat. A nearby CH-47 Chinook came alive, its gigantic rotors slowly turning as its turboshaft engines shrieked.

"Roger that. Let's move out," Keith said over the rising din. Without waiting for the major's agreement, Keith barked orders to the rest of his men. They formed a loose phalanx around the civilians and the two soldiers from Army Special Operations Command, and led the way toward the helicopters.

"I like his can-do attitude," Gartrell said, half-shouting so McDaniels could hear him over the Chinook. "I also like how he automatically determined that we're a pair of PUNTS." PUNTS was the acronym for Personnel of Utterly No Tactical Significance, or more simply, individuals who were of no operational use. McDaniels shrugged. He was a field grade officer, much higher up the food chain than Keith. But if the solidly-built warrant officer wanted to try and assert his dominance in the middle of the end of the world, McDaniels couldn't give a damn. He had his own job to do.

"Let's hit it," he said, taking one of Wolf Safire's thin arms in his left hand. Gartrell did the same to Regina, and the two of them tugged their charges along as CW3 Keith and the rest of OMEN Team set out at an aggressive pace. They trotted through the smoke-filled park, shoving people out of their way. Most didn't protest the harsh treatment, not when they were fighting to get to a helicopter and get out themselves. But one group of toughs—apparently gang-bangers from Harlem—elected to try and go to guns on one of the Special Forces soldiers. The soldiers didn't hesitate. They killed each gang-banger with headshots.

Because only headshots would keep them from turning into zeds.

"Good God," Safire groaned, sickened by what he had just witnessed. "With everything that's going on, do we need to be killing each other as well?"

McDaniels shook the smaller, frailer man. "Snap out of it! Those pricks wanted to kill us and take our guns, and then try and hijack a chopper. No one's wearing any kid gloves today, Doctor. We might have to kill a lot more people to get out of this."

"Stop hurting my father!" Regina shouted. She slammed her fist into McDaniels' upper arm with enough force to hurt, but he favored her with what he hoped was a sufficiently grim smile.

"That's the spirit," he said. Her eyes flashed and she drew her hand back to strike again, but then Gartrell jerked her forward.

"Come on, let's keep moving, miss. You don't want to fall behind here," the first sergeant said, his face unreadable behind his big goggles and the boom microphone of his headset.

"Get your—"

Whatever Regina Safire was going to say was swallowed up by the sudden shrieks that erupted from the team's right. People ran from the trees separating East Drive from the Great Lawn like rabbits spooked from the brush by hunting dogs. And behind them came the walking dead, about forty or fifty of them. Some wore the woodland green battle dress utilities of Army soldiers. They fell upon any civilian they managed to catch and tore into them savagely. Blood glistened in the afternoon sunlight.

"Keith!" McDaniels shouted. "Let's pick up the pace!"

Keith signaled the rest of the team to run.

The assembly area erupted into pandemonium as the zeds poured into it. They overwhelmed the ground security forces stationed at the perimeter and attacked helicopter crews inside their aircraft. Some of the zombies met rather ignominious fates as they charged headlong into spinning tail rotors, where the vanes slashed them to pieces before fragmenting and whirling through the air. The fusillade of gunfire that met the zombies was ferocious, but it failed to stop those that were not hit in the head. And the gunfire had a secondary effect, as several civilians and other soldiers were cut down in the melee. In a matter of minutes, they would rise again and join the other zeds in their quest for human flesh. It was a cycle the military had been exposed to, but had not had the time to train for.

As bullets snapped past McDaniels and Safire, the major pulled the older man along as if he were no more than a child. When one of the SF troops to his right suddenly went down, he forgot all about the high-value civilian in his left hand and released him, bringing his M4 around. The soldier screamed as two zombies slammed into him, taking him to the ground like a pair of NFL linebackers sacking a quarterback. The soldier got off a quick burst from his M4, but it was too low; the volley passed right through one zombie's center of mass and did no substantial damage. McDaniels shouldered his own weapon and fired a single round through one zombie's head. It dropped to the verdant green grass of the Great Lawn like a sack of potatoes, its dull eyes knocked askew by the impact. But the second zombie sank its teeth into the screaming soldier's cheek even as he beat at it with his fists. His blood was bright and red in the diffused sunlight, a sudden splash of Technicolor in an otherwise black and white scene. McDaniels stared, transfixed for an instant, as the zombie ripped a huge chunk of flesh from the soldier's face and chewed it hungrily, its face blank, expressionless, its rheumy eyes vacant and without any sign of intelligence. The corpse wore the remains of an expensive blue suit. Its white dress shirt was dappled with blood, and it had lost one expensive loafer. McDaniels had the impression the zombie had been a successful man in life.

The soldier continued to struggle beneath the zombie, and he jerked his M4 into position as the corpse spread its jaws wide for another bite. A burst of gunfire blasted its skull apart, and the soldier tossed the grotesquerie aside as it collapsed on top of him. He then reached up to his mangled cheek with one hand, and explored the ragged hole torn there with his fingertips.

"Oh Jesus," Regina said, her voice small and barely audible above the din of combat and helicopters.

The soldier looked at her, then at her father. His molars were visible through the rent in his face.

"Can you help me?" he asked Safire, speaking as clearly as possible despite the wound.

Safire shook his head. "No. I'm sorry. No."

The soldier's face collapsed as a burst of bullets tore through his helmet and pulverized the skull beneath. McDaniels turned. Keith held his weapon at his shoulder. He walked toward the corpse, knelt, and pulled the rubber-edged dog tags from around its neck. He pocketed them, then rose to his feet and looked at McDaniels.

"Let's go, we're pretty close now," he said, before resuming his jog. If he was at all remorseful, he did not allow it to show. McDaniels followed, tugging Safire along.

The two MH-60M Black Hawks were surrounded by six ground security experts from the 160th. Several bodies lay around the two aircraft, some in uniform, most in other dress. Not all were zombies.

"OMEN Team," Keith told the first Night Stalker he came across. He jerked a thumb over his shoulder. "We've got two AMCITs that need to be hauled to MacArthur, on Long Island."

"Took you guys long enough, chief. Are any of you injured? Have any of you been bitten?" The tall, rawboned sentry looked from person to person, his Heckler & Koch MP5 held in both hands.

"Negative. We're all good," Keith said.

The sentry spoke into his helmet's boom microphone and waved them toward the waiting Black Hawks. Keith turned to McDaniels.

"Major, you go with the Safires in one ship," he shouted over the roaring jet engines and slashing rotor blades. "You take your first sergeant and Leary and Rittenour. The rest of us will be in the second chopper. In case anything goes south, we'll come in and extract you guys."

"Roger that, chief. *Sine Pari*, huh?" McDaniels said, throwing in the Special Forces Latin motto of Without Equal. A ghost of a smile flickered across Keith's face, then he pointed to the men he wanted to accompany him and led them toward the second helicopter.

"Let's saddle up!" Gartrell shouted, and he pushed the Safires toward their Black Hawk. One of the crew chiefs helped them aboard and strapped them into the hard seats that ran the width of the helicopter's troop compartment. Before returning to his own seat and the six-barreled M134 minigun mounted on an articulating cradle before it, he handed McDaniels a headset that was hardwired to the helicopter's intercom system. McDaniels removed his headset and donned the new one.

"This is Major McDaniels," he said.

"Major, this is Chief Warrant Officer Five Cox. We'll be pulling pitch in just a moment, but I want to let you know that we'll have to keep it at about 100 feet above ground. Our FLIR is messed up, and we can't get it operational. Without it we can't see through the smoke, so we'll have to fly below the layer. Understood?"

"Roger that, chief. Do whatever you need to do, this is your aircraft. We're only along for the ride."

"That guy with you—they say he might have a cure for this... this plague or whatever the hell it is. That true?"

"That's what they say. Any more than that, I don't know." McDaniels turned and checked Safire's safety harness. He then placed his own helmet on Safire's head and drew the chin strap tight.

"Keep that on," he said, shouting over the Black Hawk's twin engines. He didn't know if Safire heard him or not, but the scientist nodded, and that was good enough for McDaniels.

The security perimeter collapsed as the ground control personnel retreated to the helicopters and climbed aboard. The timing was unfortunate. As they mounted the helicopters, another incursion of zombies cut through the assembly area. McDaniels saw them approach the second helicopter that carried CW3 Keith and the rest of OMEN Team.

"Zeds to the right! Zeds to the right!" he shouted over the intercom while pulling his M4 into position. If he had to start shooting, he'd have to push the rifle past Safire and fill his lap with red-hot shell casings. He needn't have worried; the crew chief leaned forward in his seat, grabbed his M134's A-frame handles, and ripped a burst at the oncoming zombies. They literally exploded as the salvo of rounds ripped through them. McDaniels saw one decapitated head bounce across the grass and come to a rest face-up. Like a scene from a cheap horror movie, the dull eyes still moved, and the mouth repeatedly opened and closed.

"We're out of here!" the pilot said. He reached up to the overhead panel and advanced the engine condition levers. The Black Hawk's twin turboshaft engines went from wail to a full-on scream as the helicopter's main rotor picked up speed. The helicopter clawed its way into the air as the last members of the security team threw themselves aboard. McDaniels watched as the second helicopter made to follow. As it grew light on its wheels, several shapes darted toward it from its left rear. The door gunner stood and spun his M134 to bear, but he couldn't get it zeroed in time. Before McDaniels could do more than key his microphone button, the zombies threw themselves into the helicopter as it lifted off. After a moment, its nose suddenly rose and tracked to the right before its main rotor lost thrust. The Black Hawk's tail rotor disintegrated as it struck the ground, and the big helicopter rolled over and slammed back to the earth. Its spinning rotors slashed at the ground before they broke apart, throwing sod and earth into the air. The helicopter spun around in a circle as its tail boom fractured into three different pieces. It came to a sudden rest, and smoke rose from its engine cowlings.

In the tree line, a ragged line of figures shambled toward the downed aircraft. More zombies, coming in for the kill.

"We lost ROMEO Six-Two," the pilot said over the intercom. "We're a solo flight now, major."

"Roger that," McDaniels said. He looked at Gartrell, who returned his somber glance. The first sergeant's shotgun was between his legs, its butt planted against the helicopter deck between his boots. Beside him, Regina Safire had also seen the helicopter crash. Her gaze met McDaniels', and for a moment she looked less like a hard-charging New York City professional and more like a frightened child. Her dark hair flew about her head, courtesy of the rotor wash that entered the troop compartment through the open doors.

McDaniels turned to Wolf Safire, who sat motionless beside him. His eyes were shut, and his jaw was set. McDaniels squeezed the smaller man's wrist. Safire nodded slightly, but didn't open his eyes. McDaniels faced forward, looking out through the canopy. He sat right behind the air crew, so he had a good view.

The smoke was dense and roiling as the sun edged closer to the western horizon, now to the helicopter's tail. Other helicopters launched, and the MH-60M banked from side to side as its pilots threaded it through the pattern with a cool, almost mechanical proficiency that McDaniels found admirable. These were people who had just seen their wingman burn in, and there was little doubt what was happening to the flight crew and their passengers. The Black Hawk charged on, flying over the treetops of Central Park, just south of the city's historic Metropolitan Museum of Art. McDaniels had visited the museum three years ago with his family on one hot, muggy summer day when the city had been besieged by seemingly never-ending thunderstorms. He had been impressed not just by the displays, but by the architecture of the museum itself. He wondered how it would fare in the near future, and he wondered if zombies were tearing through its corridors, hunting and killing. And in the process, swelling the ranks of their army.

The helicopter thundered on, staying as far below the smoke layer as possible. McDaniels was discomfited to see the pilots flew the big chopper directly down one of the streets (was it East 79th?), as if it was the most natural thing in the world. Buildings rose up on either side of the aircraft, and the major knew that the rotor tips had to be perilously close to making contact with cement and glass. The Black Hawk charged across Madison Avenue, clogged with traffic. Figures ran through the halted mass of cars and trucks and buses, and in some places, more figures gathered in what looked like free-for-all fights. They were zeds in the middle of feeding frenzies, and McDaniels suddenly remembered the woman standing outside his Humvee, begging for the soldiers to save her child.

My daughter, take my daughter!

He gritted his teeth and forced the memory away.

The helicopter continued on its eastbound track, rotors thumping, vibrating slightly as any odd-ass aircraft that flew like a helicopter would. They crossed the multiple lanes of Park Avenue, and it was similarly blocked, a city artery clogged with automobiles instead of placque. More smoke billowed, this time from a burning bus.

As the helicopter approached Lexington Avenue at sixty knots, something fell past the helicopter, startling the crew chief sitting in the right gunner seat. McDaniels didn't have to see it perfectly to know what it was: a human shape. It had been a zombie, and it had tried to land on the helicopter.

"Pilot, climb out!" he said over the intercom. "The zeds, we saw them diving out of buildings to get to people—"

Something exploded above his head and the helicopter started bucking like some crazy carnival ride. Alarms went off, and McDaniels saw rotor alerts on the pilot's multifunction displays. The helicopter dipped to the left as the pilots fought against it.

"We're going in, make sure everyone's strapped in!" the pilot shouted. "Mayday, mayday, mayday, ROMEO Six-One, twelve souls aboard—"

The pilot didn't finish his transmission and the rotor blades scythed through a treetop at the corner of Lexington Avenue and East 79th Street. The Black Hawk continued its apparently uncommanded left bank and turned up Lexington, slowing, its nose rising as the pilot fought to chop its airspeed and bring it into something approximating a hover. It seemed to work, as McDaniels noticed the aircraft suddenly slowed to a crawl, still crabbing to the left but no longer flying along at 70 miles an hour. As the helicopter descended, the miniguns on either side barked as their gunners fired on nearby targets.

Jesus, we can't be landing here! McDaniels thought.

The pilot resumed his mayday as he and the copilot fought to regain control over the Black Hawk. The alarms continued to sound, and as the aircraft lazily spun to the left, something fractured overhead like a thick bone. McDaniels saw the blurred remains of an entire rotor blade fly away from the aircraft and disintegrate as it smashed into the brick façade of a nearby office building, disappearing into a spreading cloud of shattered carbon fiber and broken glass. The pilot screamed something unintelligible over the intercom system as the helicopter flounced from side to side as if in some sort of mechanical epileptic seizure.

Then it rolled to the right and crashed into the traffic-choked street.

3

McDaniels curled up into a ball in his shock-absorbing seat as the helicopter slid across the rooftops of several cars, crushing them flat before it suddenly catapulted back into the air and rolled upright. The entire airframe lashed from side to side for an instant as if fighting to remain in the air. Both pilots wrestled with the cyclic and collective pitch sticks and managed to keep the aircraft right side up before it came back to earth, this time with its landing gear in the proper position. The wheels folded up as they were designed to do, absorbing a goodly amount of the G forces. McDaniels' seat stroked, sliding along gas-filled struts, diminishing the remainder of the forces, and the major had just enough time to hug his knees up against his body armor. His head struck his kneepads with sufficient force to make him see stars for an instant as the wrecked MH-60M slid forward, tearing through automobiles as if they were as insubstantial as paper. The sound of metal being torn asunder was all McDaniels heard.

And then, the helicopter slammed into the back of a garbage truck. The pilot screamed as the right side of the cockpit imploded, driving the instrument panel into his armored seat and pinning him in place. The aircraft jerked to a halt, and the only sounds left were those of the engines winding down and the metronomic *beep-beep-beep* of an alarm.

An eerie buzzing filled McDaniels' head. He slowly sat up in his seat and fumbled with his harness's quick release, but couldn't quite make it work. He looked to his right and saw Safire was still strapped to the seat beside him, leaning forward against his own harness. A trickle of blood ran from his thin nose, and his eyes were glassy, disoriented. McDaniels shook his head, trying to clear away the cobwebs.

Something clattered to the floor of the helicopter, and he saw Gartrell slip out of his four-point safety harness. He grabbed onto the left gunner's seat and pulled himself to his feet, standing bent over at the waist in the Black Hawk's troop compartment. He looked at the door gunner in the seat before him, then sidestepped over to McDaniels.

"I got this, sir," he said, and he reached out and hit the quick release on McDaniels' harness. McDaniels slipped to the floor and fell to his knees. The Black Hawk was tilted to the right, lying across the crumpled remains of abandoned cars. The rear of the garbage truck intruded into the right side of the cockpit. He saw no sign of the pilot inside the twisted mass of metal and plastic.

The crew chief unstrapped himself and eased out from behind his now-useless M134 minigun. His visor was fractured, and he reached up and shoved it back under his SPH-5 helmet's visor guard. He had a beefy face and a thick mustache, and his eyes were still sharp despite everything he had just gone through.

"Who's injured?" he asked, after glancing toward the destroyed cockpit. He grabbed McDaniels by the arm and looked at him. "Major, are you hurt?"

McDaniels slogged to his feet as Gartrell and the crew chief held him steady against the incline. "I'm fine," he told them. "Are we on fire? I smell smoke!"

"The fuel tanks are self-sealing, rated to stand up to 23 millimeter fire," the crew chief said. "You're smelling transmission fluid burning up. The tranny box must've been sheared off the mount." He looked past the seat Safire was still strapped into. "Ground control, you guys alive back there?"

"Still here, but Jimenez is hurt," was the reply. "His back's all fucked up."

"Rittenour and Leary?" Gartrell asked as he turned to tend to Regina Safire. She looked stunned but unhurt.

There was movement in the back of the compartment. "We're good," said Rittenour.

In the front of the helicopter, the copilot stirred. He groaned and fumbled with his straps. The crew chief pushed between the door gunner seats and went to him.

"Mr. Goggins? You all right, sir?"

"I think I'm caught beneath the instrument panel." The copilot looked around the aircraft and grimaced when he saw the devastation encasing the pilot's station. "Is he...?"

"He's dead," Gartrell said. He put his fingers against the neck of the man in the left gunner's seat. "This guy's dead, too." He reached forward and pulled the dead man's straps as tight as he could.

"What are you doing?" the copilot asked as he shrugged out of his harness.

"We need to get out of here," Gartrell said. "We need to find someplace we can hole up in and call for an extraction." He finished with the gunner and picked up McDaniels' rifle from where it lay on the floor between the two gunnery seats. He handed it the major, and McDaniels checked it quickly.

"He's right, we do need to get the hell out of here," he said. "Gartrell, see to Miss Safire." McDaniels turned and looked at Wolf Safire critically. "Doctor Safire? Can you travel?"

The older man wiped at the blood trickling from his nose. He pulled a handkerchief from inside his dark suit jacket and dabbed at his nostrils gingerly.

"Yes, but where will we go?" he asked.

"We'll find that out in just a moment." McDaniels unstrapped Safire and helped him to his feet. "We'll have to go out the left side of the helicopter. The right side is blocked." And he was right, the Black Hawk had come to a rest with its right side pressed against several cars.

In the near distance, more gun fire rang out and helicopters buzzed through the area. There was a rending crash, and McDaniels knew another helicopter had gone down somewhere nearby. He found his tactical headset, slipped it on and switched to the common net. It was filled with urgent, overlapping radio calls. It was difficult to determine who was saying what.

"Any station, this is Terminator Six, come in." McDaniels transmitted while pulling Safire toward the left side of the helicopter. Gartrell preceded him and hopped out, then turned back to help Regina out of the wreckage. "This is Terminator Six. ROMEO Six-One is down on the hard on Lexington, just past East 79th. We need immediate evac, over." He repeated the calls as he helped Safire step out of the open cargo door in the Black Hawk's left side. Gartrell and Rittenour waited to help him navigate the crushed car and twisted landing gear assembly that was directly below the door. Regina looked up at her father with wide eyes, standing right behind them. Leary and the Night

Stalker security crew had already exited the aircraft, and they provided overwatch cover, weapons oriented down either side of the street. Leary fired twice, and McDaniels saw a figure collapse to the ground.

"We gotta boogie," he said.

As McDaniels clambered out of the wrecked helicopter, a voice crackled over his headset, barely discernable in the electrified chaos: "Terminator Six, this is Uniform Six... you read..."

The transmission quality was horrible, but McDaniels knew that Uniform Six was the overall ground element commander at Central Park, a colonel from the 10th Mountain Division's 2nd Brigade Combat Team. McDaniels pressed the earphone tighter against his right ear as Leary opened up again, this time joined by one of the Night Stalkers who released a full automatic burst downrange. Gartrell slapped the Night Stalker on the shoulder.

"Conserve your ammo, troop!"

"Uniform Six, Terminator Six, we need immediate evac, over," McDaniels said. He saw shapes climb over the cars in the near distance, and he slapped Rittenour on the shoulder and pointed them out. Rittenour nodded and aimed his rifle at them but did not fire. McDaniels realized the Special Forces trooper was waiting for the zeds to get closer, so he could be certain to deliver head shots.

"Terminator... Uniform Six... —ative on evac... overrun. I say again, we are overrun... all aircraft are..." The voice was drowned out by a fusillade of heavy weapons fire from somewhere inside the park, and McDaniels recognized the detonations as were from 70 millimeter rockets. Apparently, the Night Stalkers' Little Bird gunships were going into overdrive and using all the munitions at their disposal. "... someplace high and hole up, we'll try and..."

The transmission was overwhelmed by a frantic, fragmented report from an infantry unit that was in close contact with the zombies. The report was almost undecipherable over the sound of small arms fire, but McDaniels heard total fear in the voice of the soldier trying to make the broadcast, just one amidst dozens. It cut out suddenly. Was the unit overrun? McDaniels wondered. It didn't matter; another frantic report filled its place, just as garbled and unintelligible as all the others.

"Uniform Six, this is Terminator Six. Say again on status of evac, over." Something moaned to McDaniels' right, and he turned to see a small, ghoulish figure emerge from beneath a car. It had been a toddler, perhaps a three-year-old boy with straw-blond hair and an aquiline nose that resembled Regina's. In life, the boy would have been almost beautiful, full of life and vitality. In death, it was anything but, its blue eyes open and unblinking, already marred by motes of dirt. The zombie was missing most of its right arm, and its movements were slow and imprecise as it clambered to its feet. It wore dirty pajama bottoms, and the knees had already been worn through, exposing scraped flesh the color of alabaster beneath.

McDaniels fired one round through its head as its moan turned to a hiss and it charged toward him. The bullet blasted through the top of the zed's skull, removing it along with a good portion of the brain, splattering it across a nearby white BMW. The zombie was knocked back into the car, then fell to the street face-first. It did not move.

Regina's steely façade cracked suddenly. She shrieked and buried her face into her father's shoulder.

"Uniform Six, this is Terminator Six, come in, over!" McDaniels looked around the street. There were far too many hiding places for the zombies to stalk them, and down on the street, visibility was limited. Overhead, a Chinook hurtled past, fading in and out of the roiling black smoke that rose into the air.

He heard nothing further from Uniform Six.

McDaniels slapped the side of the helicopter. "Flight crew, are you guys coming out?"

The copilot leaned out of his open doorway. The aircraft flown by the 160th always had their doors removed to increase visibility. "One of my fucking legs is trapped under the instrument panel," he said. "And to top it off, I think it's broken..."

McDaniels swore and pulled himself up onto one of the cars the MH-60M lay across. He peered inside the cockpit, and for sure, the pilot's right leg was pinned beneath the instrument panel overhang. If the entire console hadn't been shifted back in the crash, he could have been simply crawled out the doorway to his left, but that wasn't an option.

"Can we lower the seat?" McDaniels asked.

The crew chief was already trying that, pulling a control at the base of the pedestal and shoving down on the seat with all his weight. He shook his head.

"Seat's stroked all the way down. There's no way to depress it further. I might be able to remove the back, but we'll have to figure out a way to lift the panel off—*oh shit!*"

The crew chief was yanked toward the right side of the cockpit. McDaniels leaned inside to see what was going on. He saw an arm had reached out through the wreckage on that side, and fingers had grasped a handful of the crew chief's flight suit.

"Mr. Cox is still alive!" the crew chief shouted. He grabbed onto the pilot's wrist.

"No, he's not!" McDaniels said. "Sergeant, stay away from that man, he's not Cox anymore!"

The crew chief hesitated, and when he did, the zombie sitting pinned inside the wreckage moaned and pulled again, this time harder. The crew chief made a strangled sound in his throat and ripped the hand off his flight suit. The arm flailed around blindly, trying to find its target again. The crew chief fell against the copilot's seat and pulled his Beretta pistol from its holster.

"Fucking *shit*," he said, his voice barely more than a strangled whisper.

"Sergeant, pay attention... help me figure out how we're going to get your copilot out of this seat, all right?"

"No time for that, major." Gartrell's voice was a flat deadpan. "Multiple targets inbound from both sides. We don't have the manpower or ammunition to make a stand out here in the street." McDaniels straightened and looked up and down the street. Gartrell was right. Dozens of figures shambled, ran, or crawled toward the crash site from the north and the south. More gunfire sounded from Central Park, but the sounds of helicopters were fading now. All the aircraft that could lift off were on their way out.

Glass exploded nearby as a ghoul crashed into a car. McDaniels looked up in time to see several more boil out a window in a nearby apartment building. All of them reached for the humans in the street as they fell, as if trying to grab them. All of them crashed to the street or sidewalk below, and all of them stirred after impact. Though bones had been broken and flesh shredded, the walking dead were still capable of movement... and they remained hungry.

"But what about Mr. Goggins?" the crew chief asked. "We've got to get him out of here!"

"Gartrell, take everyone into that office building there." McDaniels pointed toward an office building at the corner of the street. Through its thick glass lobby doors, he saw the marbled lobby was empty. "People are still holed up in the apartments and residences, but the chances of people being in an office building are a hell of a lot less likely. And with less people—"

"Fewer zeds. Roger that." Gartrell barked orders to the rest of the men and pointed to the building. The Special Forces soldiers immediately did as instructed, but the Night Stalkers were reluctant to leave the helicopter.

"Sir, we don't leave one of our own behind!" one of them said to McDaniels.

"I'm staying with him, soldier. Move your ass!" McDaniels turned back to the Black Hawk and looked at warrant officer Goggins. The younger man's eyes were full of fear. The ghoul trapped in the pilot's seat moaned and struggled against the metal that kept it pinned in place, and McDaniels saw the top of its helmet moving.

"Sergeant, try and help me lift this console off his leg," McDaniels said.

Gartrell tapped McDaniels' right boot. "You've got about thirty seconds, major." And with that, the first sergeant disappeared, loping toward the office building.

"Come on, sergeant!" McDaniels snapped. He pushed upward against the instrument panel with both hands. His M4 hung from his side by its patrol strap; if he needed to use it, he'd never get to it in time. The crew chief bent down to help him, pulling upward on the panel at the same time. Metal flexed and plastic squeaked, but the instrument panel didn't move enough for Goggins to pull his leg free.

"Fuck," was all the pilot could say. He looked through the shattered windscreen. McDaniels followed his gaze, and his heart started hammering in his chest. More dead shuffled toward the crash site.

This guy's not going to make it.

"Come on, major! Let's get this done!" the crew chief shouted. He saw the approaching zombies as well.

"Get out of the aircraft, sergeant. And watch out for the other door gunner. It's... awake." McDaniels nodded toward the corpse in the left gunnery seat. It was sluggishly moving, hissing slightly, its unblinking eyes fixated on him. McDaniels was thankful Gartrell had had the foresight to strap it in tightly, otherwise there would have been nothing to prevent it from attacking the crew chief.

"Are you going to leave me?" Goggins asked. There was no rebuke in his voice. He pulled his pistol from its holster and looked at it speculatively before turning back to McDaniels. "I can't do myself. I'm Catholic."

McDaniels grabbed his M4 and fired at the approaching zombies. Three shots, and only one went down. Not a great hit ratio.

"Sergeant, get out of the aircraft," he said. "This is your last chance." Behind him, more gunfire sounded as Gartrell and the others engaged the zombies. A ghoul crashed to the pavement right behind McDaniels, half its skull missing.

The crew chief looked at the pilot. "Mr. Goggins..."

"Go on, Terry. Go with the major. This is the end of the road for me." Goggins looked at McDaniels imploringly. McDaniels nodded and raised his M4.

"NSDQ," he said before pulling the trigger. *Night Stalkers Don't Quit* was a legendary credo in the special operations community, and McDaniels had seen it in action once again on this day. His M4 barked once, and Goggins sank into his seat. McDaniels pulled the pistol from the pilot's dead hand and jumped off the car.

"God damn!" the crew chief said. His voice was high, almost a panicked shriek. "You shot Mr. Goggins! You fucking *shot* him!"

"Cap off those zeds in the helicopter and get the hell out here!" McDaniels snapped. More gunfire from behind, and more zombies fell. Something moved atop the wrecked helicopter; the only warning McDaniels had was the lazy bobbing of one broom-strawed rotor blade. He raised his rifle as a female zombie leapt toward him, its jaws spread wide, its filthy dark hair trailing behind it like the tail of some ebony comet.

McDaniels' first round passed through its neck, and the zombie's head lolled sickeningly to one side as it crashed to the street. It scrambled to its hands and knees, and its head fell downward, hanging from its neck by skin alone—it was obvious that McDaniels' errant shot had severed its cervical vertebrae. McDaniels fired again and this time dropped the grotesquerie to the pavement.

Inside the Black Hawk, the crew chief swore in total panic as he fired several shots at the reanimated corpses of his flight crew. He then half-jumped, half-fell from the aircraft and slammed into a smashed SUV. If he hadn't still been wearing his flight helmet, he might have knocked himself unconscious against the vehicle's stout A-pillar.

"Let's go, major! Last chance!" Gartrell shouted from the corner. He was already backing toward the office building with Rittenour while the rest of the soldiers held the lobby under guard.

McDaniels grabbed the crew chief's arm and pulled him along as he ran toward the office building. A zombie crashed to the ground ten yards from him; another jumper, and its skeleton was pulverized by the impact, yet it still tried to make its jellified extremities work so it could pursue. Something cracked past his ear—a bullet—and he heard it strike something fleshy only a few feet behind him. Without turning to look, McDaniels knew the ensuing clatter was a zombie collapsing against a car.

The crew chief screamed, and his wrist was torn from McDaniels' grasp. He looked over his shoulder and saw the young sergeant taken to ground by no fewer than three zombies; one of them tried to bite his skull, but the flight helmet saved him. The crew chief writhed and struggled beneath the weight of the zombies, and he fired his weapon into one of them at point blank range. The rounds passed through the ghoul's thorax without causing any real damage. McDaniels dropped it with one shot, then took out the one trying to chew its way through the crew chief's helmet. It fell upon him, and for a moment, the younger man was trapped beneath the dead weight of two corpses.

The third ghoul grabbed up the crew chief's left hand and ripped off all his fingers in a single, vicious bite. The crew chief screamed and struggled to throw off the ghouls, but it was too late. McDaniels knew that once bitten, the man was as good as a zombie. He fired two rounds, one through the zombie's skull, the second through the crew chief's. The young sergeant collapsed to the street, motionless.

"*Major!*" Gartrell shouted.

McDaniels ran for the office building as fast as he could, his pack jerking from side to side on his back, his feet slamming into the asphalt. He hopped over the curb and fired blindly at the zombies closing in on him from the right. One of the rounds was lucky enough to strike a stench in the femur, and it collapsed to the sidewalk. The rest of the zombies tripped over it and fell into a writhing pile. It was only a momentary respite; all of them clambered back to their feet and continued to pursue him, whatever injuries they had accrued ignored.

But then he was at the open lobby door. McDaniels threw himself across the threshold and slid face-first across the cool marble floor as Gartrell yanked the heavy glass door shut.

4

The ghouls rammed into the door with their entire weight, but it couldn't be budged. Just the same, Gartrell and Leary hung on to it for dear life. Even though the door only opened one way—outward—they didn't have the key to lock it. And while the zombies had the cumulative intellect of the average pen holder, they might eventually get lucky and pull on the handle as opposed to trying to push their way inside.

McDaniels got to his feet, shocked to see dozens more zombies stumble toward the building. All of them catapulted themselves against the windows of the glass-walled lobby with a single-minded fixation that was almost awesome to witness. Even though they only succeeded in breaking their own bones and leaving smears of gore across the glass, they immediately got to their feet and charged again. And again. And again. The lobby was filled with the din of bodies smashing against glass.

A nearby door popped open, and McDaniels spun, rifle at the ready. It was Rittenour and one of the Night Stalker security troops, emerging from a stairwell.

"Stairway is clear, first sergeant! We checked the first five landings, and there's no one inside!"

"You got it ready to go?" Gartrell asked, still holding onto the lobby door.

"Roger that, ready to go," Rittenour said.

"Gartrell, you have something in mind?" McDaniels asked. He joined the NCO at the door.

"I figured if we couldn't get this place locked up, we'd have no choice but to go up. And if we did that, we'd have to blow up some of the stairwells to make sure those things can't come after us. Ritt's the demolitions NCO in OMEN team, he's got enough of the goods on him to make it happen."

"Has anyone checked any of the floors above?"

Rittenour shook his head. "No time. Some of the doors are exit only, so the first floor that's open to us is the fifth. I opened the door and looked in, but didn't see anything other than cubicles and offices."

"Jimenez, have you found a damned key yet?" Gartrell asked. McDaniels turned and saw the Night Stalker with the bad back going through all the drawers in the lobby security desk. The young soldier's face lit up like a Christmas tree.

"Affirmative, I got the key!" Jimenez said suddenly. "At least, I think I do—"

"Get over here!" Gartrell said.

Jimenez started toward the door, but his gait was slow and stiff. The tall, rawboned Night Stalker snatched the key ring out of Jimenez's hand and dove toward McDaniels, Gartrell, and Leary. The door locked in two places, at the top and the bottom. The soldier fell to his knees and inserted a key into the bottom lock. The cylinder wouldn't turn. The soldier fumbled about and tried another key. It also wouldn't turn.

"Finelly, what the fuck are you waiting for?" shouted a small, wiry Night Stalker as he pounded up and helped hold the door as well.

"Fuck off, Maxi!" the soldier on the floor said. He tried another key, and this time, metal snapped home as the lock set. The soldier jumped to his feet and repeated the process with the top lock. After some hesitation, Gartrell and Leary stepped back from the door, but the other soldier kept pressing against it, his face blank. McDaniels saw the soldier was on total autopilot, terrified out of his mind. He grabbed the soldier's backpack and pulled him away from the door.

"Keep it together, soldier," he said, right in the soldier's ear.

"Hooah," the soldier replied automatically, his gaze rooted on the glass door.

The zombies continued to batter it, but the door held. Gartrell examined all the doors in the lobby critically, then nodded to himself.

"Locked up tight," he said.

"Good work, guy," McDaniels said to the aviation trooper who had locked the door. He let go of the soldier's backpack and turned to the rest of the soldiers in the lobby. "You've *all* done great work. Now let's keep doing it, and hope to high hell we can all get out of this alive. And the beers are on me at Campbell and Bragg."

There was a chorus of "hooahs", the Army term that could be anything from an affirmation to a zoological classification. The crashing against the glass increased, and McDaniels estimated the number of zombies outside the lobby had swollen to several hundred.

"We should get upstairs, major," Gartrell said over the growing din. "We're attracting a hell of a lot of attention, and even though this glass is pretty thick, it might give eventually."

McDaniels nodded. "Yeah, let's do that."

***

Rittenour took the lead as the seven soldiers and two civilians mounted the stairs, leaving the din of the lobby behind. The building still had power, which was a blessing, as the stairwell was brightly lit. The stairwell was all gray-painted concrete, with florescent tape marking the edges of each step, so they could be navigated in a lights-out situation. As they climbed, Rittenour pointed out the plastic explosives he had planted at various intervals. He explained to McDaniels the charges were strong enough to blow out two sets of stairs and one landing. McDaniels believed him.

"Any chance of the explosion screwing up the building structurally?" he asked the demolitions expert.

"Don't believe so. Looks like the core support is in the center of the building, around the elevator shafts. The stairwells are close to them, but not too close, if you get what I mean." Rittenour kept the butt of his M4 tucked against his shoulder as he walked up the stairs, eyes scanning each landing for a threat before stepping onto it.

As they passed by one of the re-entry doors leading to the third floor—the lobby below was two stories tall, so the first floor available was the third—McDaniels tried to push it open. It was locked. There was a card reader next to the door, where he presumed an employee would swipe his card to gain access to the floor.

"Locked, like I told you it would be," Rittenour said.

McDaniels leaned against the door and pressed his ear against it. He heard nothing.

"Might be a good idea to try and get inside anyway. See what we might be sharing a building with."

Gartrell patted the key card reader. "Tall order, major."

McDaniels nodded. "Still, something to think about, if we're going to be here for a while."

They made it to the fifth floor. Rittenour and Leary took positions on either side of the stairwell reentry door, while the short Night Stalker readied to pop it open. McDaniels motioned for Gartrell to remain behind with the Safires. The first sergeant gave him a grim smile, and then stepped forward, his sidearm in his right hand.

"Sorry major, you're the designated adult. You hang back with the Safires, I'll back up Leary and Ritt."

McDaniels glared at him. "Excuse me, first sergeant?"

Gartrell's expression was remote and inscrutable. "I'm still a lot closer to where the rubber meets the road, major. I've got this." There was no apology in the senior NCO's voice, and only the bare minimum of required deference. McDaniels clenched his teeth together and prepared to tear Gartrell a new one.

Leary broke in before things got out of hand. "You sure you're still ready for this kind of stuff, first sergeant?" He looked back at Gartrell from over his shoulder.

"Sergeant Leary, I'm a plank-holder with Delta." Gartrell raised his pistol. "And I'm still able to double-tap a man in the right eye with this at fifty meters."

Singularly unimpressed, Leary grunted and turned back to the door. Gartrell looked at the two uninjured Night Stalkers.

"You aviators come in after we secure the immediate area on the other side. Depending on the lay of the land, we'll probably split up into two groups and do our recon. Jimenez, with your back I don't want you moving any more than you have to, so you stay here with the major and civilians, understood?"

"Roger that, first sergeant."

Gartrell rolled his head from side to side, loosening up. He conspicuously avoided looking at McDaniels as he moved the Safires down a few steps. Gartrell firmed his grip on his pistol and nodded to the short Night Stalker.

"Open it on three, son. One. Two. Three!"

The soldier yanked open the fire door and stumbled to one side, wincing in pain. Rittenour and Leary surged inside, followed closely by Gartrell who held his pistol in a double-handed grip. The soldiers from the 160th moved to the open door and took up their overwatch position, assault weapons at the ready. They all held Heckler & Koch MP5K Personal Defense Weapons, modified variants of the time-tested H&K submachine gun that was heavily favored by most of the American special operations community for close-in work. As he watched them form up, McDaniels realized that other than Jimenez, he still didn't know their names. Jimenez fell back from the doorway and leaned against the concrete wall, his own MP5K held in both hands. The Safires stood with their backs against the opposite wall.

After a minute or so, Gartrell drifted back into sight and waved the Night Stalkers forward. They shoved their way into the brightly-lit office space beyond. McDaniels grabbed the door and softly closed it, then kept it covered with his M4. For a long while, the only sounds he heard were the breathing of those in the stairwell with him.

"How long will this take?" Regina asked after a moment. She watched Jimenez slowly pick his way past them, his MP5K's barrel oriented toward the stairwell they had just ascended.

"It'll take as long as it has to," McDaniels said. "Now please, keep quiet." He looked back at Jimenez. "What's up, sergeant?"

"Don't like having the back door unguarded, sir," Jimenez responded. His hair was cut short on the sides in the medium whitewall fashion that a lot of Army grunts favored with a semi-Mohawk on top. His eyes were dark and dwelled deep in his head, and he blinked often as beads of sweat ran down his face. McDaniels reached back and grabbed his shoulder firmly.

"Hang in there, soldier," he said.

Jimenez nodded. "I will, sir. This is just a totally FUBAR situation, you know?"

McDaniels smiled as easily as he could. Fucked Up Beyond All Repair definitely fit the circumstance. "I definitely know that." He turned back to the closed door and glanced over at Safire after a moment. Safire looked back at him with expressionless eyes. His daughter put her hand on her father's arm and looked at McDaniels herself, her eyes full of both terror and annoyance. McDaniels found that combination almost laughable under the circumstances.

The minutes passed, and they waited in the stairwell as patiently as they could. McDaniels listened to the sounds that entered the stairwell: machine noises from HVAC, the gentle gurgle of water in pipes, the soft susurration of air cycling past. There were no sounds he could attribute to the walking dead. No moaning, no banging on doors, no footfalls. As far as McDaniels could tell, they were alone in the stairwell.

When the reentry door slowly opened, it was still a shock. McDaniels pointed his rifle at the door as it swung open. Gartrell was on the other side, and he waved them in.

"We're clear inside."

McDaniels motioned the others forward while he hung back, covering the stairways leading to the landing. The Safires entered the office floor, followed by Sergeant Jimenez, who moved gingerly. McDaniels could tell by the set of his jaw that he was in no small amount of pain. Once the Night Stalker had crossed the threshold, McDaniels backed into the office and silently closed the door behind him.

"We should probably figure out a way to block this door," he said to Gartrell.

Gartrell nodded. "We're already looking into that. Lots of heavy file cabinets and credenzas we could use, but this seems to be the only exit. Would be a shame to block it off and not have a way out."

McDaniels sighed. "Well, let's have one of the troops stand guard, then. What's the lay of the land around here?"

"Typical office environment." Gartrell waved to the virtual sea of cubicles that made up the office. "Cube farm, with offices on the far side that have windows overlooking Lexington. They'll probably rename it to Dead Avenue, though—tons of stenches everywhere." The older NCO sighed and adjusted his backpack. "You might as well walk the floor, and take a look around. I've got the rest of the troops poking around. Latrines are that way"—he pointed to his right—"along with a pantry. Vending machines, coffee, hot chocolate, even a refrigerator with that Parmalat milk. Tastes like crap, but you can drink it and it won't kill you. I think." He paused. "Radios work out here, since they're not cut off by the stairwell walls, but they're pretty much useless. Our private freq is blank, but there's still some activity on the common net. All fragmented. Some of our guys are still alive, but they're on the run, I think." His face hardened a bit, and McDaniels knew the first sergeant had heard some things he didn't like.

McDaniels flipped frequencies on his radio. The private frequency USASOC had allocated for them was indeed silent, nothing but a vague hiss of static. The common tactical frequency was a mish-mash of static broken every now and then by pleas for assistance or other units trying to reconstitute. Most of the calls were unintelligible, and some of them carried with them the sounds of distant combat.

He looked at Gartrell. "We need to keep focused on staying alive, first sergeant. Once we get established here, we should make sure the civilians are safe, and then take an inventory of our gear and ammo. We'll also need to break out the sat phone and see if we can get a hold of anyone at Bragg."

"Satcom's not going to work in here, sir. We'll need to be up on the roof. And this building is 27 stories, so we're going to have to go for a walk, unless you want to consider taking one of the elevators. Which are in a locked bay over there." Gartrell pointed to his left. McDaniels turned and walked over to a nearby reception area. A set of glass doors separated the elevator bay from the office floor. When he tried to pull them open, he found they were locked.

"Magnetic lock, major." Gartrell hadn't followed him, and remained near the fire exit. "To get out, you press that button on the wall there. To get in, someone either swipes an entry card or is buzzed in from that receptionist's desk, there."

McDaniels saw the illuminated red button on the wall beside the glass entry doors. It was clearly labeled EXIT, and he pressed it. A loud metallic click sounded, and he pulled open one of the doors easily enough. He listened, but heard no evidence that any of the elevators were in operation. He let the door close, and the click sounded again. The doors relocked automatically.

"I wonder if it'll still work when the power fails," he said.

Gartrell said nothing. They would deal with that when it happened.

McDaniels looked around. "The Safires?"

Gartrell pointed to over his shoulder. "In the pantry. No windows, single point of ingress. Seemed to be the safest place to put them for the moment. Jimenez has guard duty." As he spoke, the remaining two Night Stalkers appeared, carrying a heavy wooden credenza by either end.

"Put that here," Gartrell ordered, and stepped aside while the red-faced soldiers pushed the ornate piece of furniture against the fire door. It only blocked half of it, and the door opened into the stairwell anyway, but it was a start.

"I'm thinking one of us should be on the other side of that door," one of them said. McDaniels couldn't see his nametape, as the ballistic vest he wore covered up the blouse of his battle dress utilities. He didn't know any of these soldiers at all, and they didn't know anything about him, other than the gold oak leaf insignia on his uniform lapels.

"I'm Major McDaniels, with USASOC J-2," he told them, "and this is First Sergeant Gartrell. Who're you guys?"

"Staff Sergeant Dane Finelly," said the first, a tall, broad-shouldered man who spoke with a subtle twang. "Alpha Company, First Battalion, 160 SOAR." Finelly's face was almost as broad as his shoulders, and he had the ruddy, rawboned look of a farmer's son.

"Sergeant Eugene Derwitz, Alpha Company, First Battalion, 160 SOAR," said the second, a smaller-framed man with dark eyes and a hooked nose. The way he truncated his Rs spoke of somewhere on the Jersey Shore.

McDaniels nodded to both men. "Keep doing what you're doing, troops. Any problems taking orders from a couple of ground pounders for a while?"

Finelly shook his head. "Negative on that, sir. If you're Special Forces, then this is your show." Derwitz offered nothing further, so McDaniels presumed Finelly spoke for both of them.

"All right. Keep bringing over stuff to form a barricade. When you're done, one of you relieve First Sergeant Gartrell at the door. The other will inventory his ammo and gear. Once that man is finished, he'll stand overwatch while the other man does his own inventory. Count every bullet, every MRE, every NVG battery you have. And fill your canteens. We don't know how long the water will hold out."

The soldiers murmured their assent and set off to gather more furnishings to use as barricades. McDaniels looked back at Gartrell.

"When they're done, come join me in the pantry. We'll need to plan our next step, and we should get that done sooner rather than later." He nodded toward the floor-to-ceiling windows overlooking Manhattan's Upper East Side. "It'll be dark soon, and I don't think things are going to get any better."

5

"How long will we be here for?" Regina Safire asked. Her green eyes had taken on what McDaniels supposed was their usual predatory cast, and they followed the tall black Special Forces officer as he stepped into the pantry and slowly removed his Kevlar helmet. McDaniels made her to be about thirty-five years old, a few years younger than he was. He knew she had been a medical doctor before joining her father's company as a medical consultant, but he didn't know what her specialty was. He hoped her bedside manner was a bit more refined than what she presented now.

Just the same, beneath the hard exterior, there was a certain softness that was visible whenever she looked at her father. She was a Daddy's Girl, as incredible as it might seem. She was also very attractive, McDaniels thought. Her dark hair and tanned face were complemented by what seemed to be a trim body beneath her sturdy jeans and long-sleeved work shirt. Her denim jacket lay across the top of a nearby Xerox copier.

"Major?" she prompted.

McDaniels set his helmet on the counter next to the sink and allowed his radio headset to hang around his neck. He looked at the Safires for a moment, then focused on the woman. He held out his hand.

"I'm Cordell McDaniels. I'm afraid we were never properly introduced."

She looked at him for a long moment, as if his sudden politeness was something alien, untrustworthy. Then she finally extended her own manicured hand and shook his.

"Regina Safire. But I'm sure you know that already?"

McDaniels nodded. "But an introduction is never something you should waste." He looked at Safire, who sat on a pile of copying paper boxes next to two softly-humming vending machines. He didn't meet McDaniels' eyes; instead, he kept his gaze rooted on the industrial-looking white-tiled floor.

"Doctor Safire?"

Safire looked up at him. In the pantry's harsh overhead light, he suddenly looked like Andy Warhol, only not quite as swishy. "I already know who you are, major. There's no need to waste time with pleasantries. Are they coming for us?"

"Is *who* coming for us?"

Safire frowned. "The military, of course."

McDaniels turned to the sink. There was a Keurig coffee machine next to it, the kind that used the single-dose K-cups that McDaniels was so fond of. He opened one of the overhead cabinets and found several boxes of coffee. He sorted through them and pulled one down.

"We're having communication problems at the moment. Our uplink to the communication satellite was at the assembly area in Central Park, and it seems to be offline. The helicopters had satellite radios built into them, but we obviously lost access to those as well." He opened the coffeemaker and dropped in a K-cup of extra-bold coffee. After positioning a cup beneath the spout, he pressed the brew button.

"So you mean we're *stranded* here?" Regina asked.

McDaniels watched the dark liquid fill the paper coffee cup. "Not at all. Once the men have this floor secured and we take an inventory of our consumables, I'll go up to the roof with my satellite phone. I'll be able to reach my component command and arrange for another extraction, probably by helicopter."

"How long will that take?" Safire asked. "Shouldn't you do that now?"

"I'll attend to it as soon as we can fortify our position, Doctor. As far as how long it will take, I can't tell you. I would imagine we lost a lot of aircraft back at the park. I don't know what resources are still in the area, so it could be some time until we see any kind of rescue mission mounted. Which is why we have to fortify our position. Coffee?"

Safire rocketed to his feet, and his pale face flushed with sudden color. "No, I don't want any fucking coffee! I want you and your people to do your job, which is to *get us out of here!*"

"Dad! Take it easy," Regina said softly.

McDaniels stirred a serving of light cream into his coffee. He brought the cup to his lips and tasted it, noticing for the first time his hand was trembling slightly. Was it from fear, or just the aftereffect of what seemed to be a gallon of adrenaline wearing off? He couldn't tell.

"Doctor Safire." McDaniels kept his voice low and level, striving to at least sound calm and collected, though in truth giving the scientist a nice shiner sounded good at the moment. "You might have noticed that no fewer than fifteen men have died trying to get you and your daughter away from... those things out there. We're now down to seven gunslingers against probably thousands of the walking dead. The precariousness of our situation is hardly lost upon me. I think maybe you can cut us a little slack?" He stared at Safire as he took another sip of his coffee. Right now, it tasted better than a cold beer on a hot day.

If Safire was moved by McDaniels' comment, it did not show. "You need to get us out of here," he said.

McDaniels sighed. "As I tried to tell you, that's pretty much what I'm all about right now." He leaned back against the counter and crossed his arms over his chest as looked at Safire.

"Tell me who else knows what you do, doctor. Because if things go any further south, we're going to need a contingency plan."

"What do you mean by that?" Regina asked. She walked over to Safire and put a hand on his arm.

McDaniels ran a hand over the stubbly bristle on his head. Even though he wasn't required to keep his hair as short as it was, he found a tight crew cut suited him just fine after fifteen years in the Army.

"He means that in case I get killed, someone else will need to know what I do," Safire said in an acidic tone.

"I mean we might need to spread the wealth a bit," McDaniels countered. "Who else knows what you do, Doctor? Who else knows how to stop the walking dead?"

"No one," Safire said immediately.

"So you're telling me that all of your research is—what? In your head?"

"I'm the only person who knows what RMA is, and what it does to a living human host."

"RMA?" McDaniels asked.

Safire loosened up a bit, now that he had something else to occupy his thoughts other than fleeing from the walking dead.

He straightened his navy blue dress jacket by pulling on its lapels.

"RMA. *Rex Articulus Morte.* Essentially, 'the moving dead', the name I assigned to the bioengineered virus that started all of this."

"Bioengineered? So whatever's causing this is man-made?"

"Without question. The signature in some of the precursors that I was able to find in the bug's building blocks definitely point to something from the old Soviet Union. I learned all about Soviet biological weapons when I was working for the government in the 1970s and 1980s." As he spoke, Safire drifted toward the vending machines behind him and regarded their wares through the glass in their doors. "How it can reanimate the dead is still something we don't know. There's obviously some components that make up the virus which we've never dealt with before. But I have developed a method for preventing humans who are bitten by the dead from becoming one of them, and if the drug is administered while the individual is alive, even their death won't result in them rising again."

"But why would the Russians develop a weapon like this in the first place? It's not like they could ever deploy it."

"Perhaps," Safire agreed. "Or perhaps they had a therapy that would prevent their troops and citizens from turning into ghouls after exposure. Maybe they lost the records for the therapy over the decades, or maybe they never had one to begin with, and what was released was only a test study. Whatever the case, the U.S. most certainly experimented with some rather esoteric weapon systems. Did you know we worked on a weapon that was designed to make all the Russians go mad and attack each other? What we face now is much the same, only ours was chemical, this is biological."

McDaniels sipped some more of his coffee, then poured it down the sink. "But the question remains, doctor... with all the research that went into creating this process you're speaking of, you're the only one who knows what it is? No assistants, no researchers, no laboratory partners, no one at all?"

"Just me, major." Safire smiled grimly. "You see, if you had been a little faster in getting to us, you might have been able to save two colleagues who could have replicated my work, and who in fact contributed to it greatly. But doctors Walsh and

Vinjamuri were taken by the dead, like so many others before them."

"Our... tardiness was hardly our fault, doctor. It took a while for your message to make its way through the command structure and get to someone with the horsepower to actually do something about it."

Safire waved the explanation away as he turned away from the vending machines and sat heavily on the cardboard paper cases again. "Whatever. The end result is the same. I'm the only one who knows how to do what needs to be done, and I'm just *thrilled* to be trapped here in the city with the rest of you. Truly."

McDaniels put his helmet on and walked to the door. "Then maybe you can make yourself useful? Get off that skinny ass and take a look at Jimenez, he's hurt bad. And since he's one of the people who will be saving you and your daughter, maybe you might want to do something to start returning the favor ahead of time." He put his hand on the door knob and turned back to the Safires. The daughter looked at him with anger in her eyes; the elder couldn't be bothered with such a useless emotion. His expression was totally blank.

"We have to save you whether we like you or not," McDaniels said, as much to Regina as to Safire. "But it might be better for all of us if you didn't act like such a prick, doctor."

"I'll take that under advisement," Safire said sarcastically.

6

"We have about six hundred rounds of five-five-six per man, and around half that in nine millimeter. I have one hundred fifty-five tungsten cored magnum rounds for the AA-12, and one drum of high-explosive minigrenades for a total of 25 shots. Three hundred and ninety rounds of .45 ACP for our sidearms. Every man still has five M67 frag grenades, four M8 smokers, night vision goggles with two spare batteries, enough MREs to get through the next five days—more if we ration ourselves—and water, which we can replenish here. Personal radios with two spare batteries. One satellite phone, three PRC-90s..." Gartrell had written everything down on a yellow legal pad in block letters that were so neat McDaniels thought the list had been printed. He read the list as Gartrell recited it from memory. The Night Stalkers had less gear to lug around, as all of their equipment was mostly defensive, for protecting forward area refuel points where their helicopters would refuel and rearm. The assembly area in Central Park's Great Lawn had been nothing more than one gigantic FARP, and the 160th ground control teams had been outfitted accordingly. While their load-out was consistent with the mission they were to accomplish, it wouldn't sustain them for long if bad things started to happen. The three Night Stalkers had only Heckler & Koch MP5K Personal Defense Weapons, which fired 9mm rounds but were limited by a fairly short range. And besides basic soldiering skills, they weren't especially proficient in military operations in urban terrain, which is what street fighting zombies in New York City most assuredly was.

The Special Forces troops—which included McDaniels and Gartrell—weren't really all that much better off. The heavy weaponry, such as the M249 machine guns, had been lost when CW3 Keith's helicopter had crashed during takeoff in Central Park. Not that the weapons were a key concern. The loss of the lion's share of a Special Forces Alpha Detachment and all the skills associated with it were what weighed heavily on McDaniels now. As things stood, he just didn't have enough manpower to go around.

"Major?"

McDaniels looked up from the list, a little annoyed. After what had happened between them in Afghanistan, Gartrell consciously avoided calling him "sir" whenever he could. It was always "major". And that bothered McDaniels more than he would like to admit, even to himself.

"I got what you said, it's all here." McDaniels tapped the pad. "Sounds like we're good for the time being, so long as we don't get decisively engaged. But we need to start making some noise and see if we can't get the hell out of here."

Gartrell nodded, and waved toward the cube farm behind McDaniels. The two men stood at a long row of filing cabinets while the rest of the troops sat near the reception desk on office chairs. There was no need to keep them on their feet the entire time, and everyone's dogs were already tired to begin with.

"We tried several phones, but there are no working lines outside. We can dial extensions inside the building, though, so the PBX is still up. But there's something up with the connection outside the building. Cell phones don't work either— I tried mine. Could be anything, so I doubt we can fix it ourselves. SATCOM is going to be our only bet."

McDaniels snorted. He had his own cell phone in his pocket, and he hadn't even thought of it. He pulled it out from behind his body armor and checked it out. He had signal, but when he tried to place a call, all he got was a quick beep followed by silence. CALL FAILED flashed on the display.

"How inconvenient," he said. He cleared the display and caught the time. He verified it against his watch.

"We went down in ROMEO fifty-three minutes ago," Gartrell said. McDaniels smiled slightly. While all Special Forces soldiers were nicknamed "Jedi Knights", there was no doubting First Sergeant David Gartrell was Obi-wan Kenobi himself.

"Good to know one of us still has his head in the game," McDaniels said. "Thank you for staying frosty, first sergeant."

"Someone has to provide timely adult supervision, sir. That's why USASOC sent me."

McDaniels couldn't tell if Gartrell was being insulting or if it had been an offhand quip. He decided he didn't want to deal with it, either way. "We need to get on the SATCOM. And I also want to know what the hell is going on downstairs. It's great that Rittenour rigged the stairs, but someone still has to detonate the charges before those things make it upstairs."

"Roger that. You want that done now?"

McDaniels shook his head. "Negative. Let's get someone to take a peek downstairs." Through the windows, he saw that the sun was setting, and the concrete canyons of New York City were growing dark and cold. "I don't want to attract any more attention than necessary, but it might be worthwhile to see if the zeds have forgotten about us."

"One of the doors was open downstairs, major. There could be some of those things in the building with us. Maybe we should send some more guys with you? Just you and another swinging dick can take out a few deadheads, but what if you hit the mother lode and you run into a few dozen? Or a few hundred, even?"

McDaniels shrugged. "Not much anyone can do about it," he said. "We can't leave the Safires unguarded, and even if I did bite the big burrito, that doesn't mean all chances at rescue come to an end. Hell, for all we know, the Air Force and CIA are moving every satellite and UAV they have over Manhattan right now, just looking for us."

"For him, you mean."

"Yeah. For him."

Gartrell nodded. "I'll take care of checking the lobby personally. Leary should go topside with you. I'll take Rittenour. We'll leave the Safires here with the Night Stalkers—they should be able to keep them out of harm's way for the time being."

McDaniels frowned. "I don't want all the SF troops off the floor, just in case there's a breach." He looked over at the gaggle of soldiers sitting before the barricaded glass entry doors. "Night Stalkers, any of you guys up for a run to the roof?"

Finelly got to his feet. "I am, sir."

"Then hit the latrine or whatever it is you might need to do now, because we're going to be gone for a while."

"Roger that, sir."

Gartrell unslung his big AA-12 and handed it to McDaniels. "Since it's only two of you, take the shottie. It's got tungstens loaded up, so you should be able to blast anything that comes your way to hell and back. I'll take your M4 for the time being."

McDaniels hefted the AA-12. It had been a while since he handled one, and he liked how it felt. Especially now. He handed his assault rifle to Gartrell.

"Not really a fair trade, but I'll take it. Thanks, Gartrell."

"I'll go over the detonation sequence with Ritt to make sure I can do the job in case the zombies get inside," Gartrell said. "I still remember my demo training, but it's been a while. It would be a shame to mess it up after not being up to bat for so long."

McDaniels nodded. "If anyone can do it, you can, first sergeant. Lord knows you like blowing stuff up."

Gartrell gave him a wan smile, but that was it. McDaniels gathered up the SATCOM and looked at Finelly.

"Are you ready, sergeant?"

"Yes, sir."

"Then let's get this done and get the hell out of here." McDaniels waved for the other soldiers to remove the barricade in front of the fire door.

***

The stairwell was still brightly illuminated. McDaniels checked the landing above, while Finelly checked the one below. Gartrell and Rittenour stepped out onto the fifth floor landing, weapons at ready. McDaniels, Gartrell, and Rittenour conducted their radio checks, with Leary serving as their primary point of contact. As he was from a different unit, Finelly couldn't communicate on the same frequency, and used his handheld PRC-90 radio to maintain contact with the other Night Stalkers. If something went down, they would relay that to Leary, who would reach out to the other SF troops.

"Take it easy down there," McDaniels said to Gartrell. He nodded toward the stairwell leading down.

"Hell sir, our climb's nothing like yours. And besides, if we're not getting any heat, we're not near the target."

"Hooah, first sergeant." McDaniels turned and started up the flight of stairs. "Let's get on with it, Finelly."

"Right with you, major."

The two men climbed steadily upward. Finelly took the lead, as McDaniels was both the commanding officer and carried the satellite communications phone. He set an aggressive pace, and McDaniels found he had to work to keep up. As a field grade officer, he hadn't been required to do more than just the usual morning PT to stay in shape. However, staying in shape was relative when comparing an officer to an enlisted man who still had to go on field marches, even if he was with a special operations aviation unit. After ten flights, McDaniels was breathing hard.

They paused at each landing and listened at the fire door. Again, many were non-entry doors and were locked. Some were unlocked, but neither McDaniels nor Finelly were interested in checking the floors beyond. There was no telling what they might find.

"Terminator Six, Terminator Five, over." Gartrell's voice was all business over the radio. McDaniels looked up at Finelly, but the big sergeant kept on walking. Of course, since only McDaniels could hear the first sergeant.

"Finelly, hold up." As Finelly stopped and turned to face him, McDaniels pressed the transmit button on his radio.

"Five, this is Six. Over." He kept his voice low, just in case. They were between the sixteenth and seventeenth floors, which meant there was still a lot of unexplored territory ahead and just as much behind. Zombies could be anywhere, and all it would take for the dead to get at them was as much luck as it took to turn a door handle.

"We're in the lobby stairwell. Just cracked open the door and took a look without exposing myself. Dozens of stenches are outside. Looks like they're still interested in the building. Bad news is that they're using objects to try and get through the glass. Over."

McDaniels was alarmed. "Say what kind of objects, over."

"Nothing too credible at the moment, Six. Cell phones, blackberries, notebooks, soda bottles. Looks like items a lot of them might have had on their person. But if one of these things has enough smarts to get a sledgehammer—or maybe start up a car—things're going to get very interesting. Over."

"Understood, Five. Break. Terminator Three, you get that? Over."

Leary's voice came back immediately. "Roger Six, I copied that. Over."

"Pass that intel over to Safire, see if it's of any use to him. Break. Five, this is Six. How are the explosives? Over."

"Explosives have been checked and verified as still operational. We can blow the stairwell at any time, over."

"Roger that. You think you're good to stay put for the time being, and keep a watch on the lobby?"

Gartrell's voice was firm and matter-of-fact. "Roger that, Six. We're ready to camp out and keep an eye on things all night. Over."

"Well, maybe not all night, Five. We're on our way to make our call, so we'll get back to you soon. We're on sixteen, moving up to seventeen. Over."

"Roger that, Six."

"Terminator Six, out." McDaniels released the transmit button and motioned Finelly forward. The big sergeant had questions in his eyes, but he did not pause to ask them. He just turned around and continued his advance up the stairway.

By the time they reached the twentieth floor, Finelly stopped on the landing. He held out a clenched fist and raised his MP5K slightly. McDaniels froze and firmed his grip on the AA-12. He watched Finelly as the bigger man slowly crept forward and peered up the next stairwell. He stopped with one foot on the first step and placed his back to the wall, and stayed there for a moment. McDaniels was about to prompt him when he heard something. It was a rhythmic, repetitive banging in the distance, very faint and barely discernable above the soft noises of building machinery doing whatever they did. The two men listened to it for a time, keeping silent, trying to decipher what might be making it.

Finelly turned back to the major finally and leaned toward him. "Sounds like someone banging on a door," he whispered. "Not real close, but definitely above us."

McDaniels moved forward and slowly pressed his way up the stairs past Finelly. The rawboned sergeant didn't protest, but McDaniels knew he wasn't happy with McDaniels taking the lead. To mollify him, McDaniels stopped on the next landing, which was a no-reentry door.

"If that's what it is, it's not a human doing it," he murmured to Finelly. "Too regular. Too mechanical."

Finelly didn't know what to make of that. "You think it's a machine?" he asked, and McDaniels almost laughed at the comical expression of confusion on his broad face.

"No, sergeant. I think it's a zombie."

"Oh." Finelly leaned to his left and slowly looked up between the hand rails. McDaniels did the same, and mentally kicked himself for not doing it sooner. They saw a small slice of the distant ceiling, still ten stories away, and other than being able to tell the lights were on, there was not much else to see. McDaniels looked down and saw pretty much the same.

"So what's the plan?" Finelly asked. "I gotta tell you, major, I'm not too keen about getting into a firefight. If we open up on these things in here, every freaking zed in the building will hear us."

"Understood. Let's keep moving. Maybe it'll turn out to be something else." McDaniels looked up the stairwell, then back at Finelly. The soldier didn't look happy.

"I'll lead," McDaniels said.

Finelly shook his head. "No, sir. I'll do that." He shouldered his MP5K and advanced up the stairs, keeping the weapon ready at all times now. If anything happened to pop out in front of him, it would get a face full of nine millimeter steel jacketed rounds. He kept his back to the far wall as he ascended, and McDaniels did the same. At the landings, Finelly would halt, and McDaniels advanced to the base of the next stairway and secure it before Finelly pushed past him and continued on.

The banging sound grew louder as they climbed. Its rhythm did not alter. *Bang. Bang. Bang. Bang.*

At the 25th floor, McDaniels grabbed the back of Finelly's uniform blouse and brought him to a halt. The big enlisted man looked down at the major and waited for him to tell him what's up.

"You smell something?" McDaniels whispered.

"I think I smell a deadhead," Finelly whispered back.

"No, not that. Something else. Cigarette smoke." As a reformed smoker, McDaniels could detect cigarette smoke at what seemed like one part per one hundred billion. It drove him mad, because the scent almost always triggered a bout of craving before revulsion could make its appearance.

Finelly glanced up the stairs. The banging sound continued unabated, so the zombie—or whatever it was—hadn't heard them just yet. He looked back at McDaniels and just shrugged. McDaniels motioned for him to stay put, then retreated down the steps to another landing.

"Gartrell, this is McDaniels, over."

"Terminator Six, Terminator Five... are we going dress casual with the commo? Over."

"There's no one on this frequency to hear us, though I'd love for us to be proven wrong. Listen, we have a deadhead up here on twenty-seven. We haven't put eyeballs on target, but if I'm right, we'll have to go to guns on it. Over."

"Roger that. We'll keep an eye on things down here, over."

"Roger. McDaniels out." McDaniels took a moment to put yellow foam hearing protectors in his ears. They were good for preserving one's hearing during gunnery practice and while riding helicopters; McDaniels hadn't put them in before as there just hadn't been enough time before the Black Hawk crashed.

"Hearing protectors," he whispered to Finelly, then took up a guard position while Finelly dropped back and did as instructed. The Atchisson AA-12 assault shotgun was heavy in McDaniels' hands. Above, the rapping noise continued unabated. Finelly joined him again, and McDaniels waved him to the rear.

"I've got more firepower. I'll take the advance."

Finelly looked appropriately stressed that a field grade officer should be leading him into danger. "Uh sir, I know you're Special Forces and all, but maybe I ought to be the guy who does this? A lot of difference between our pay grades."

McDaniels shook his head. "I got this one, troop—you'll just have to owe me one." He handed over the sat phone. "But you can hold this."

Finelly accepted the phone with a shrug.

"Let's go," McDaniels said, and he pushed himself up the stairs. The muscles in his thighs were burning, and he had no doubt he would be feeling some pain tomorrow.

Up the stairway leading to the landing below the 27th floor. McDaniels flattened against the wall, AA-12 trained up the last remaining stairway that led to the final landing. Sure enough, someone stood at the gray fire door, dressed in a still-pristine blue pinstriped suit that looked expensive even from where McDaniels stood. It banged on the door with a hand that was nothing more than a mass of bruised, split flesh that suppurated viscous fluid; the door was smeared with gore. As McDaniels watched, the figure slammed its right fist against the steel door again and again, totally ignorant of the damage it was doing it itself.

It was a zombie, and it grunted every time it slammed its hand against the door.

Kind of whistling while you work, zombie-style, McDaniels thought.

He glanced back at Finelly. The big soldier stood next to him with his back pressed as flat against the wall as his packs would allow. He looked up at the zombie with a vaguely sickened expression, and McDaniels knew why. This zombie must have turned a few days ago, as it was getting pretty ripe. He slowly advanced up the steps, keeping his right shoulder against the wall while training the AA-12 on the zombie's head. The zed continued pounding on the door, oblivious to the two men creeping up behind it. McDaniels mounted the steps one at a time, moving as quietly as he could. With each step, more of the zombie came into view. The suit was indeed doubtlessly expensive, as were its Gucci loafers.

McDaniels stopped three steps from the landing and aimed at the zombie's head. At the last moment, the ghoul must have sensed his presence. It pivoted, turning to face him with milky eyes that had once been pale blue. Its dark hair was a mass of tangles, and in life, the suit had probably been one of those well-coiffed metrosexual types that knew nothing beyond business and the phone numbers of the five star restaurants stored in its PDA. It moaned when it saw him, and lurched toward McDaniels with outstretched arms. McDaniels suddenly reached up to his helmet, found his goggles, and yanked them over his eyes. He then firmed up his aim, and pulled back on the AA-12's trigger.

The sound and muzzle flash were tremendous, almost overwhelming the hearing protectors and the light polarization of the goggles. The 12-gauge antipersonnel round did its job quickly and efficiently, and from McDaniels' perspective it seemed that the zombie's head simply disappeared into a smear of gore that was plastered against the gray cinderblock wall behind. McDaniels was pelted with pieces of cinderblock, and he looked down at his body as the headless corpse collapsed to the landing. He was revolted to discover his uniform was peppered with bits of dark gore.

A small stream of blackish liquid flowed from the ragged stump of the zombie's neck. McDaniels stepped to one side as it trickled past his feet and down the stairs. Finelly did the same, and leaned against the metal handrail as he looked down the center of the stairwell.

McDaniels' radio crackled. "Major, this is Gartrell. You guys all right up there? Over."

"Roger that, Gartrell. One shot, one kill. Zed is down on the 27th floor landing. Over."

"Roger that. Situation remains the same down here, no change. Stenches still hanging around outside, but no longer actively trying to get inside. Not sure what that's all about. Over."

"Roger. I'll get back to you in a bit. McDaniels, out." To Finelly: "Let's get this thing out of the way, and watch your step." He let the AA-12 hang from his shoulder by its patrol strap and mounted the landing, stepping across the rivulet of ichor that ran across the painted concrete. Finelly did the same, and they each grabbed the zombie's ankles and dragged it across the landing and set it parallel to the wall.

"Wonder what the hell the thing was doing here," Finelly asked.

McDaniels looked around. Above the stench of the corpse on the floor and acrid odor left by the AA-12's discharge, something still tickled his olfactory system. And there they were: three crushed cigarette butts, lying in the corner next to the fire door. McDaniels grabbed the gore-smeared door's knob. It moved easily enough in his hand, but when he tried to open it, it would move only a fraction of an inch.

"Locked?" Finelly asked.

McDaniels shook his head. "Negative. Held back on the other end, somehow." He pointed to the cigarette butts. "Someone's still alive up here. Probably on the other side of this door."

Finelly looked in the corner and nodded. He then looked at the placard next to the door. McDaniels followed his gaze. The placard read CAFETERIA.

"Well, if they have any gumption, at least they won't starve to death. And whatever they have in there probably tastes better than our MREs."

McDaniels nodded, then turned. Behind them was one more set of stairs, which terminated at a heavy, green door. Painted on the door was the message:

ROOF ACCESS
AUTHORIZED PERSONNEL ONLY

"And here we are," he said. He bolted up the stairs and pushed on the door. It was locked. McDaniels sighed, but with the AA-12, he was prepared for this eventuality.

"I'm going to have to shoot the door off its hinges," McDaniels explained. "I could use a grenade to do it, but for all I know, there's a gas main in one of these walls, and I don't want to get blown into orbit. So I'm going to shoot it off instead."

"Guess you Jedi Knights have a lot of fun on your gunnery range days," Finelly said. He jerked a thumb over his shoulder at the entry door to the cafeteria behind him. "What about whoever's still in there?"

"Later. We have a call to make. You better step back. This is going to be pretty freaking loud."

Finelly retreated to the lower staircase and took position there. McDaniels lowered his goggles and shouldered the AA-12. He fired two shots. The first round tore through the locking mechanism in an explosion of sparks and shredded metal that ricocheted off the cinderblock walls. The second round blasted the remains of the latch assembly into oblivion, and the roof door flew open as if it had been kicked. The tepid remains of daylight entered the stairwell.

"We're good," McDaniels said to Finelly. He reported the current events back to Gartrell, who informed him the situation near the ground remained static, but that the zed count seemed to be increasing.

"They might have heard those last shots," the first sergeant opined. "HE rounds can be pretty loud, you know. Over."

"Got that, Five. Time to make the call, I'll get back to you."

McDaniels edged out onto the roof. Finelly was right behind him. The building they were on was by no means the tallest, but there weren't many huge skyscrapers this far from midtown; Manhattan's Upper East Side was mostly residential. The two men checked the rooftop for any ghouls, but they had it to themselves.

Glass shattered in the near distance. Both men looked toward another office tower on the opposite block. This building was mostly dark; apparently, it was without power. It was also completely infested with zombies. McDaniels and Finelly watched as one zombie pushed itself through a plate glass window, reaching toward them as it did so. Of course, it fell thirty stories to the ground below. Another zombie replaced it, then another, and another. They boiled out of the building like a sudden rush of maggots, moaning and writhing as they tried to walk across thin air to the neighboring rooftop. If it wasn't so gruesome, McDaniels thought it would be hilarious.

"Those things are pretty stupid," Finelly opined.

McDaniels felt the mindlessness of the zombies was frankly horrifying. There was no chance they would ever give up their pursuit of human flesh. They were already dead and had nothing else to lose. He walked to the edge of the roof, watching as the zombies kept walking out of the shattered window. How many of them were there?

A chorus of moans from the street below rose up to meet him. McDaniels looked down from his vantage point over the corner of Lexington Avenue and East 79th Street. What he saw took his breath away.

Below, thousands of zombies milled about. The ones falling from the building landed on those walking on the sidewalk and street below, but the fall didn't kill them. Even though a great many of their bones had to have been turned into pulp upon impact, they still twitched and shuddered and tried to return to the building they had fallen from. One, a half-naked woman, rose from the ground with a horribly mangled arm and severely fractured leg. Her head hung over her shoulders so her face was pointing backwards. The zombie merely turned and hobbled toward the building... backwards.

No stopping these things, McDaniels said to himself. *No stopping them at* all...

He turned and faced downtown. Fires still raged there, casting a ruddy orange glow across the skyline. The smoke was just as thick and heavy as before, and even on the roof of the building, he saw its taint hanging in the air. It was like looking out over Los Angeles on a smoggy day. At least half of the city was dark now, and many of the tall, elegant skyscrapers of midtown Manhattan stood a silent watch over the burgeoning walking dead. In the distance—was it from uptown?— McDaniels heard sirens, and the occasional gunshot. But other than the whisper of the wind, the moaning of the dead, and the whirring of the building's HVAC systems, the city was as quiet as it likely had ever been over the past two centuries.

And the dead. There were *thousands* of them. As McDaniels watched, they slowly marched mostly uptown, away from the flames, toward the still-lit horizon. They were hungry, and they were following their food source.

He turned away from the vista and pulled the satellite phone from its holster. According to the display on the transceiver, it had signal. McDaniels punched in the access code and placed the phone against his right ear.

"Rapier, this is Terminator, over. Rapier, this is Terminator, over."

"Terminator, this is Rapier, over." The response was so sudden that it was almost overpowering. McDaniels felt the relief shoot through him, and it must have shown on his face, because Finelly started smiling. The action seemed uncharacteristic for him.

"Rapier, this is Terminator. Just calling to let you know that we are still above room temperature, and still in possession of our packages. We were wondering if there's any chance for an extraction, over."

"Terminator, this is Rapier. Give us your pos, we'll see if we can work something out. We got the word ROMEO burned in, so we're kind of surprised to hear from you, over."

"Rapier, this is Terminator. Roger that. Position is: latitude, forty point seven seven five two. Longitude, minus seven three point niner five eight seven. Total of nine souls looking forward to getting the hell out of the Big Apple. Over."

The operator at Fort Bragg read back the GPS coordinates, which McDaniels verified. The operator then told McDaniels to stand by.

"So what's the story?" Finelly asked. He squatted on the rooftop next to McDaniels, but could only hear his part of the conversation. He looked up at the darkening sky. Twilight was almost upon them, but it didn't seem to worry the big sergeant. McDaniels knew that was because he was a Night Stalker, and was used to operating at night. A daytime op like what they had undergone in Central Park must have been an anomaly for him.

"Put on hold. They're probably looking for an asset to hand the air tasking order to," McDaniels said.

"Here's hoping it'll happen soon. I don't want to stay here overnight." Finelly watched the zombies as they continued to spill out of the office across the street. McDaniels turned and looked as well. It was an unsettling sight, something he hadn't dreamed of watching in person.

"Terminator, this is Rapier, over."

"Rapier, Terminator. Over." McDaniels squatted opened the kneeboard on his right leg. He found a blank sheet of paper, pulled out the pen, and stood ready to start writing down the details.

"Terminator, this is Rapier. We're scrambling trying to find a vertical lift asset that can pull you out of there, but almost everything we had in the zone was lost at Central Park. We don't have any 160th resources available to us right now, though we do have units moving up from Georgia, over."

McDaniels blinked, but avoided looking at Finelly. "Roger that, Rapier. So what do you think you can send our way? I want to make sure you know we have the package, and that our situation isn't as great as it could be. Over."

"Terminator, this is Rapier. Roger on that last, we know you have the package and we're trying to coordinate an extraction with available resources. We'll have to go outside the family on this one." McDaniels winced a bit when he heard that. Going outside the family meant that a regular line unit would be tasked to make the extraction, which shouldn't be a big deal, but he had no idea who would be doing the flying. "So we're calling contacts on the leader board trying to find someone who has something they can throw your way. Uh listen, Terminator, there's no chance you could get out of there by heading over land, is there? Over."

McDaniels almost laughed. "Rapier, negative. Terminator can't make it out over land. There are about ten thousand stenches between us and Harlem, over."

"Roger that, Terminator. Stand by, we're still looking. Over."

"Rapier, Terminator standing by, over." McDaniels adjusted the boom microphone connected to his personal radio earpiece and pressed the transmit button. "Five, I'm in touch with USASOC now. They're seeing what they can do for us. What's your SITREP? Over."

Gartrell came back immediately. "None too good, major. We've got a lot of activity outside... looks like the deadheads are more active at night. You hear anything about that during the mission briefings? Over."

McDaniels shook his head even though Gartrell couldn't see it. "Negative on that, Five. I don't think anyone really knows that just yet, but I'll run that by the doctor once we get back down. Over."

"Roger that. I'm going to send Rittenour up to check on things, and he'll send Leary down to me. Shouldn't be solo down here for very long, but I've got my eye on things, over."

"I trust your judgment on that, Five. How many stenches are outside, would you think? From up here, it looks like over ten thousand. Over."

There was a pause before Gartrell responded. "Ah major, did you say 'ten thousand'? Over."

"Roger that, Gartrell. At least ten to twelve thousand zeds in the streets that I can see. Lexington is full of them, over."

"Good to know... I guess. You might want to give USASOC a poke and find out if they know of any other units in the area. I've been flipping over to the common net, and there is some sporadic activity on that, I was briefly in contact with an operator who had holed up in a coffee shop with a couple of NYPD guys and some civilians. They had one guy turn on them, had a bite on his arm and he went over to the dark side, over."

"Terminator, this is Rapier, over."

"Five, roger that last on the radio contact, I'll pass that on. McDaniels, out." McDaniels spoke directly into the sat phone. "Rapier, this is Terminator. Go ahead, over."

"Terminator, Rapier. We have a lot of resource contention, but we're working to free up an asset to head your way. I'm sorry, but it's going to take some time. Lots of commands are fragmented right now, over."

McDaniels felt a sinking sensation start to form in his stomach. "Roger that, Rapier. We're secure for the time being, but that can change in a heartbeat. We don't have a lot of guns available, and the numbers aren't on our side. And the package says he's got some important research to farm out, so I hope that gets us kicked up the list. Over."

"Terminator, Rapier. Good copy on all. We're trying to move mountains on this side, but there just aren't enough aircraft to go around right now. We have lots of assets repositioning, but there's just no one out there who can jump out. I know you don't want to hear it, but we need more time. Over."

McDaniels sighed. He heard the sincerity in the operator's voice, and even if he hadn't, there wasn't any reason for USASOC to push him off. He had Safire with him, after all.

"Rapier, Terminator. How long do you think you'll need? Over."

"Terminator, stand by."

"Roger." McDaniels looked at Finelly, and shrugged. "They're trying to see who they can send our way. I guess New York's not the only place where there's trouble."

"Right before we left Campbell, we heard about zeds showing up in Louisville. No idea how many, and the local PD was dealing with it. And some of the Air Force guys and jarheads mentioned 'em being in Florida and North Carolina, too."

McDaniels frowned. "How long ago did you leave Fort Campbell, sergeant?"

Finelly checked his watch. "Almost three days now, major."

McDaniels clenched his teeth and watched more zombies march out the busted window on the 30th floor of the building across the street. They didn't seem terribly put off by the fact they had a rapid fire date with the concrete below.

"Three days," he said. "I was deployed a day ago, and I never heard anything about an infestation other than in New York."

Finelly shrugged. "I guess maybe you were in a rabbit hole or something."

McDaniels snorted. "Working for USASOC's J2 directorate is just about that. Funny, I thought I was supposed to be up to date before jumping out."

Finelly was silent for a long moment. "Major, when they come back to you, maybe you can ask about our families."

"Give me the full names of all your troops." McDaniels opened his kneeboard and flipped to his notebook. Finelly gave the full names of the Night Stalkers, and McDaniels wrote them down, including ranks and unit. He then added the names of the Special Forces soldiers, as well as Gartrell and his own. At the end, he added the Safires. He didn't know if they had any relatives in the area, or if USASOC would even know anything about them, but it wouldn't hurt to ask.

"Terminator, this is Rapier Six."

McDaniels straightened up a bit when he heard the voice. Rapier Six was the call sign for Lieutenant General Josiah Abelson, the commanding general in charge of the United States Army Special Operations Command. Even though McDaniels knew Abelson personally—the general was actually a fairly affable individual, as far as three star generals went—a commanding general almost never interacted with field personnel during an operation, which meant this was something of a precedent. And a damned spooky one, at that.

"Rapier Six, Terminator Six. Go ahead, over."

"Terminator, Rapier Six. Good to hear your voice again, Cord. When we got word that ROMEO had gone in, we'd thought the worst. How's the package? Over."

"Rapier, the package is good for the time being, but I can't guarantee that's going to continue to be the case. We're in the middle of dead central, and the only thing that's keeping them from us is that they don't have the collective intelligence to turn a door knob. Over."

"Understood, Terminator. Listen, Cord... I have to be honest, things are falling apart quicker than we can put them together again. We never thought the lines would be overrun as quickly as they were, and we didn't anticipate we'd lose the entire assembly area. We surged every airframe we had available into Central Park, and only a few made it out. From what we can see on the satellite displays, a lot of our aircraft are still on the ground. Hell, some of them still have their rotors turning. Over."

McDaniels didn't know what Abelson expected from him, so he merely said, "Understood, Rapier. Over."

"Big Army is putting together a land movement to the city. The entire 10th Mountain Division is already on the move. I've tried to get a CH-47 from them, but all their assets are tied up supporting the movement. They've been encountering issues on the way... not just zeds, but citizens are evacuating in their direction, and slowing up the advance. But we haven't forgotten you, major. We intend to get you people out of there, any way we can. Over."

"Roger that, Rapier. Sir, I'd like to give you the names of those who are here with me, and we're all hoping someone on your side can take a moment to verify the well-being of our dependents." McDaniels felt an undercurrent of black dread forming in his breast when the images of his own family arose before his mind's eye, unbidden. "We'd probably get along better if we knew how they were doing. Over."

"Understood, Terminator. I'll be turning the mike over to operations now, they'll take the information. You keep things together up there. We really are coming for you, Cord. Rapier Six, out here."

In other words, Onward Christian Soldiers, McDaniels thought sourly. General Abelson's intentions might have been in the right place, but if a three-banger in charge of all the Army's special operations forces couldn't tell you what was going to happen and when, then it was dire time indeed.

"Terminator Six, Rapier, over."

"Go ahead, Rapier."

"Let me have those names, Terminator. We'll try and get some info out to you."

McDaniels read off the names in a flat monotone. Across the street, zombies tumbled from the building in a seemingly endless stream. For all he knew, some of the less-battered ones had crawled back up for another round.

The operator heard the tone of his voice even through the compression algorithms that made up secure satellite communications. "Uh listen, Terminator... you heard what Rapier Six said. We're moving all the pieces trying to build a bridge your way. Sorry it's not an instant-on kind of thing, but we really are trying. Only thing left for you guys is to keep low and camp out for a while. Over."

"Rapier, Terminator Six. I know the routine, no need for the pep talk. We're all big boys and we know what we have to do. When do we call you next? Over."

Finelly rose to his feet and walked a few steps away. It didn't show on his face, but McDaniels knew the NCO was disgusted at the wait. And, to no doubt, frightened.

"Give us an hour, Terminator. Over."

"Roger, we'll be back with you at"—McDaniels checked his watch—"1910 hours. Terminator out." With that, he powered down the phone and placed the unit in its holster. He rose to his feet and adjusted the AA-12 and his backpack.

"Let's go see who's on the twenty-seventh floor, Finelly."

7

The body still lay against the wall at the base of the stairs, and the wall was still covered with gore. The heavier chunks had slid down to the floor, but a wide swath of dark, meaty particles clung to the gray paint. McDaniels wondered how long it would take for it to turn ripe. Already, a fly was happily buzzing about.

McDaniels tried the door again, and found he still couldn't open it. Using his knuckles, he rapped out shave-and-a-haircut on the door while Finelly covered the stairs leading up to the landing.

"Hey, open up in there! U.S. Army Special Forces!"

McDaniels removed his helmet and placed his ear against the door. He couldn't hear much of anything through it, so he stood straight and pounded on the door again, this time with his gloved fist.

"Come on, open up! You must've heard us kill the zombie out here!" He twisted the door knob and pulled again, but the result was the same: the door would open only a fraction of an inch, not even enough to get a finger inside.

"Maybe there really isn't anyone in there," Finelly said.

"Then how do you explain those?" McDaniels asked, pointing at the cigarette butts in the corner.

"Hell, major... someone could've smoked those days ago. Corporate America is hardly without its malingerers, you know."

McDaniels only grunted and pounded out shave-and-a-haircut again, trying to ensure whomever was on the other side of the door knew he wasn't a zombie. He stopped and listened. Still nothing. With a sigh, he took a hold of the AA-12.

"I guess we'll just do it the old fashioned way."

"If that door really is tied down on the other side, shooting away the bolt won't help."

"I'll blow off the hinges."

"Why not just pull the hinges?" Finelly asked. "I mean, they're right there, sir. That way we get access, and we save a couple of shotgun rounds."

McDaniels thought about it. Since the door opened out into the stairwell, the hinges were on their side. It wouldn't take much doing with a knife to pull them free and pop the door out of the frame. He looked back at Finelly with a raised brow.

"Hmph. Guess they do teach you Night Stalkers some things after all."

"We may be sheltered, sir, but we do have our moments."

McDaniels snorted and pulled his knife. Just as he started getting to work on the lowermost hinge, he heard a voice through the door.

"Who dat?"

"U.S. Army Special Forces," McDaniels said, straightening up. "Mind opening the door? Otherwise, we'll just take it off its hinges."

"How many a them are you?"

"Two here, nine total, spread out on the ground floor and the fifth floor."

There was no reply. After some moments, McDaniels and Finelly heard something hit the floor on the other side of the door. Then the door opened just a crack. A figure peered out at them from the darkness beyond.

McDaniels slowly pulled the door all the way open. "You mind if we come in?"

A short, wiry black man stood on the other side of the door, blinking against the light of the stairwell. His tightly-packed afro was dusted with gray, and a small scar ran across his broad nose. His brows knitted as he regarded McDaniels with narrowed eyes.

"Well, well. You a brother. And in uniform, even." He looked at the insignia on McDaniels' lapels. "And an officer?"

McDaniels nodded. "I'm a major."

"Damn. You come to take us out of here? I guess not, since we saw your helicopter crash in the street."

"'We'? How many of you are there?"

The man looked from McDaniels to Finelly, then back again. "You better come inside. I got the lights off in here, so they can't see us. Least, I hope they can't."

McDaniels nodded to Finelly, and stepped through the door. Finelly followed him, still covering the stairway with his MP5K until the door was closed.

The darkness on the other side was not absolute. Some lights were still on. McDaniels saw they were in a corridor that ran along one side of the building with doors at either end. The door to the stairs had been tied shut with a fire hose that was stored on a reel on the wall opposite the stairway. In the center of the corridor was another elevator bay, just like on the fifth floor, although minus the glass entry doors. He worried about that, and the short man beside him followed his gaze.

"Don't worry bout the elevators. I got em turned off."

McDaniels looked back at the man, and saw he wore a green uniform. The nametape on one breast read EARL in red embroidered letters on a white background. His shoes were scuffed but sturdy, and on his belt were a huge key ring and a large flashlight in a holder. At his kidney was a walkie-talkie.

"You must be Earl," McDaniels said.

"Earl Brown. I work here. Used to work here. Well, whatever." Earl extended his hand.

McDaniels shook the proffered hand. "I'm Cord McDaniels, and this is Sergeant Finelly."

"How you doin, sergeant," Earl said, and shook Finelly's hand. Finelly smiled and nodded, trying to look as friendly as possible since he practically dwarfed the man.

"You a maintenance worker, Earl?" McDaniels asked.

Earl nodded. "Yessir. Been workin here at Verbatim for almost twenny years."

"'Verbatim'?"

"The name of the hedge fund group that was in this building. One of the oldest ones in the city. Used to be an investment bank, but got bought out by another bigger bank and the principals started a hedge fund. This was their building. One of the partners lived here in the Upper East Side, and he didn't want no long commute downtown." Earl smiled. "Me, I come across from Queens, and it takes me an hour to get here." The smile suddenly vanished from his face, and he looked at the two soldiers before him.

"Sorry. Guess I was ramblin."

"That's okay," McDaniels said. "So, the cafeteria's on this floor?"

"Yessir, that's right. You gen'lmen hungry?"

McDaniels smiled. "You know Earl, now that you mention it, I think I'm *damned* hungry."

Earl smiled, revealing a large set of nicotine stained teeth. "Den you came to the right place."

***

The lights were on in the kitchen, and they were bright and antiseptic. The main serving area was empty, but there were stocked refrigeration units filled with soda, tea, milk, and specialty drinks, as well as ready-made sandwiches and takeaway meals that the sign declared were "Grab-N-Gos". On both sides of the area were serving stations with refrigerators under the counters; Finelly walked behind one and notified McDaniels he had found the sandwich station.

"Complete with roast beef, salami, tuna, turkey, you name it," he said.

"Bread too," Earl added. "An all the condiments a man might want." He swung an arm wide, indicating the rest of the kitchen. "We got a grill, we got a pizza station with ovens, we got a sushi station if you like eatin dead fish, we got Fryolators, we got gas ranges, we got ovens big enough to cook turkeys in, we got chips, cakes, pies, fries, cookies, gifelte fish... whatever you want, it's here."

McDaniels nodded appreciatively. "You certainly have everything laid out, Earl."

The praise seemed to please the small maintenance worker, and he smiled and nodded. McDaniels caught a whiff of tobacco clinging to the man's green uniform.

"So who else is up here? You said 'we saw your helicopter crash'."

Earl shuffled his feet a bit, head held low. For a moment, McDaniels wasn't sure he was going to answer, and he wondered why that was.

"Just me... and my two daughters," he said finally, his voice so low that McDaniels barely understood the reply.

Daughters. Ah. That explained the reluctance on the maintenance worker's part, and McDaniels didn't blame him for being cautious. After all, it seemed the world had just ground to a halt, and a responsible father had to be mindful of his children. Always.

"I see. Well, at least you have your kids with you, Earl. Might not be the best place in the world for them, but at least you know they're safe for the moment, right?"

Earl didn't look up, only shrugged. "If'n you can call this safe."

"It's definitely better than being on the streets," Finelly said, walking out from behind the sandwich station. "Take it from us, we drove from the west side to Central Park, and look where we wound up."

Earl looked up at Finelly and favored him with a thin smile. "Yeah, I guess so. You boys hungry? I can start the grill or somethin', I guess."

McDaniels' radio crackled. "Six, this is Gartrell, over."

"Excuse me for just a second," he said to Earl, then half-turned away from him and pressed his microphone button. "Five, sorry about that. We're on twenty-seven, and have made contact with an individual who is up here in the cafeteria. He says he's with two dependents, though I have not seen them yet. What's the SITREP from your end? Over."

"Zeds are still massing outside, but they don't seem very directed at the moment. Can't really keep eyes on them all the time, but it appears they're just milling around in the street. Maybe attracted by the lights, Lord knows the lobby is bright enough with all that white marble. Any news from USASOC? Over."

"Roger, news from USASOC. Break, Leary, you listening in?"

Sergeant Leary transmitted after a brief delay. "Yessir, listening in. Over."

"Good. Here's the deal: Rapier is looking for an aviation asset that can haul us out of here. The assembly area at Central Park was completely overrun by the zeds, and all the aircraft are a write-off. Lots of aviation units are repositioning, but no one's in reach right now. I'm supposed to get back with them in an hour. Leary, how are the Safires doing? Over."

"About as well as can be expected, major. Scared stiff, like the rest of us, but coping for the moment, over."

"Five, the twenty-seventh floor seems pretty defensible. The maintenance man up here says he has the elevators turned off, and the cafeteria seems to have its own controlled exits separate from the fire escape door. We might be better off up here, over."

"Roger that, Six. We should still keep someone on overwatch in the stairwell, though. Wouldn't advise we keep them on the ground floor, since support would have to cover twenty-seven stories in case something goes bad, over."

"Understood. Let us check out the rest of this floor up here, and we'll figure out how to play it. McDaniels, out." McDaniels turned back to Earl. "Mind showing us around the rest of the floor, Earl?"

"Sure, no problem. Follow me."

The small maintenance worker led them through the serving area and into the kitchen in back, where everything seemed to be made from stainless steel. Cooking ranges sat dormant. There was a walk-in freezer built into one wall, and a walk-in refrigerator in the other, both well-stocked. Cookware had been put away neatly; whatever had befallen the city had done so when the building was shut down for the day. McDaniels realized it was Sunday, and the order to evacuate Safire hadn't come to him until Saturday morning. So the building was very likely unoccupied.

As Earl led them out of the kitchen, McDaniels asked, "Earl, what were you doing here over the weekend?"

"My shift is Wednesday through Sunday nights," Earl said. "When things started to go bad, I was already here. Had no place else to go, and it was just me and Artie Johnson and the two security guys in the lobby. Everyone else left. I stayed back."

"Why was that?"

"Because my family was nearby, and they came here when I called 'em. We was gonna go north, but we got caught here."

Beyond the kitchen was the dining area itself, a fairly expansive area that took up most of the available space on the floor. Dominated by floor-to-ceiling windows that overlooked the city (parts of which were still lit up, McDaniels noticed) and dozens of tables and long booths, the cafeteria could easily hold almost 300 people. After coming from the brightly-lit kitchen, the cafeteria itself was dark and gloomy, illuminated only by a few lights. Earl turned to McDaniels and Finelly and held one finger to his lips as they walked through the semi-dark area. McDaniels saw why. Sprawled across one booth were two figures beneath coats, their legs and feet visible in the tepid light. Earl's daughters.

"We're going to take a quick look around, if you don't mind," McDaniels told Earl. He nodded to Finelly, and the big sergeant turned and headed for the far side of the cafeteria, his feet whispering across carpet and linoleum tile alike.

"Sure, go ahead," Earl said.

McDaniels smiled and nodded, then headed off in the opposite direction Finelly had taken. There wasn't a great deal to see. The cafeteria had been closed, cleaned, and readied for a working week that would never come. McDaniels checked around for any indication someone other than Earl had been on the floor, and there was nothing to say that there had been. McDaniels slowly walked toward one window and looked out over the city. The windows faced Central Park, and he saw the glow of fire there, and more noxious smoke roiling into the air. It looked to him that one or more of the helicopters at the assembly area had caught on fire, and the jet fuel that propelled them was burning bright and strong. Several buildings in the area still had power, and if he looked hard enough, McDaniels saw survivors had hung signs outside the windows:

4 TRAPPED, PLEASE SEND HELP!

SINGLE MOTHER WITH TWO YOUNG CHILDREN, PLEASE HELP!

SOS SOS SOS WE'RE TRAPPED SOS SOS SOS

GOD IS PUNISHING US

Through the windows in some buildings which were still illuminated, figures moved. McDaniels didn't reach for his binoculars to get a better look. From the shambling, roiling gait most of them exhibited, he knew the figures were deadheads moving about aimlessly in their search for human flesh. Hundreds in the buildings and, when he looked down, thousands in the brightly-lit streets.

He finished checking the rest of the floor, including the restrooms. The lights flicked on automatically when he stepped inside, blinding him momentarily. He checked the stalls and found nothing. On impulse, he checked for running water by waving his hand under the sensor in one of the sinks. Warm water came forth immediately. At least that hadn't changed.

He rejoined Finelly, who stood near the table Earl sat at. His daughters continued to sleep in the booth across from where he sat, and Earl looked at them with sad, weary eyes.

My daughter, take my daughter!

Again, the image of the woman on the street, clutching the toddler to her chest. If he had reached across Safire and thrown open the door, could he have saved mother and daughter before the zeds got them? If he'd allowed the hard curtain of discipline he hid his emotions behind to drop for just that one instant, could he have made a difference?

My daughter, take my daughter!

Stop it, lady.

Finelly turned and looked at him oddly. "Sir?"

McDaniels realized he'd whispered the last thought aloud. He rubbed his eyes tiredly and waved the comment away.

"Never mind, sergeant." He looked at Earl. "Earl? The zombie in the stairway?"

Earl nodded. "Yeah... that was Mr. Walsford. He was the CEO. Hard-workin' cat, always here late at night and early in the mornin'. I went out to the stairway to have a smoke, and all a sudden he comes runnin' up the stairs lookin' to eat some brains." Earl snorted humorlessly. "Course, mine wouldn't be more'n a snack."

"You're a lucky guy," Finelly said.

Earl shrugged. "Don't know 'bout dat. I was already done and heard his footsteps when he started runnin' up from the 25th floor. That's where his office was. Musta just pushed open the fire door there and got into the stairway. Guess he smelt the smoke and came up."

"So they still have all their senses, then?" Finelly looked at McDaniels, who shrugged.

"I don't know. Some of those things are in pretty bad shape... burned, rotted, chewed up. I would guess the ones in better shape still have all five senses, but not all of them." McDaniels glanced at the two shapes sleeping on the booth, then reached down and put a hand on Earl's shoulder.

"You did good, Earl."

Earl sighed and reached into his pocket. He pulled out a pack of Marlboro Lights cigarettes and something else. A photo. He handed it to McDaniels.

"You see her down there?"

McDaniels frowned. The photo was of a mildly-attractive black woman, probably in her very late thirties or early forties. She had lighter skin than Earl did, and teeth that were so white they could only be described as brilliant. There had been laughter in her eyes as well as on her face when the photo had been taken. McDaniels sighed softly and handed the photo back to Earl.

"Your wife?"

Earl nodded. "She was coming in separately from the girls. Was right outside the doors when the first one of those things grabbed her. I was right at the lobby door, and couldn't get out—they'd shoved her against it when they piled onto her, then dragged her off and started to try and get to me. I ran for the elevators and got up here. Guess I forgot to lock that door, otherwise you guys wouldn't be here." Earl's eyes clouded behind his glasses. "We'd been married for over twenny years. And I just turned and ran like a little girl when those things fell on her."

"You have any weapons? Any specialized defense training?"

"Nossir."

"Then you did the very best thing you could have done. You survived." McDaniels pointed to the two girls sleeping nearby. "And they're depending on you."

Earl nodded, but said nothing. McDaniels motioned for Finelly to stay put, then walked back toward the windows. He keyed his microphone button.

"Five, this is Six, over."

"Go ahead, major."

"Let's start thinking of moving everyone up to the cafeteria. I'm headed back for the fifth floor. Why don't you meet me there. Over."

"Roger that, Six."

8

"Your soldier has more than just a back that's been thrown out," Regina Safire told McDaniels when he returned to the fifth floor. "He has rather serious spinal compression fractures, and he needs medical attention."

McDaniels looked to where Jimenez lay curled up on the floor. His armor and backpack had been removed, and his flight suit had been pulled down, exposing his torso. He wore a white cotton T-shirt underneath. Leary was nearby, leaning against the wall, arms folded across his chest. Jimenez looked up at McDaniels with pain-filled eyes.

"It's not so bad when I'm curled up on my side, major," he said.

"Because his spinal column is unloaded and isn't carrying much weight," Regina said. She knelt beside Jimenez with the contents of the building's first aid kit strewn about her. McDaniels knelt beside Jimenez.

"You father examined him?" he asked.

Regina shook his head. "I did. My father's skills are mostly in research now. Up until a few years ago, I had my own practice. I'm a pediatrician."

"Ah." McDaniels looked up at Leary. "I need you on the ground floor. Take Derwitz"—McDaniels pointed to the enlisted man guarding the barricaded glass doors leading to the elevator bay—"with you to relieve the first sergeant and Rittenour. You know how to detonate the charges in the stairwell?"

Leary looked wounded. "Of course I do, major. I'm still operational, you know." The implication behind the statement was clear: *I'm not a staff weenie like you, major.*

McDaniels ignored the potential jibe. He jerked his chin toward the fire door.

"Hop to, troop. Report once you're in position."

"Hooah." Leary straightened and tugged on the straps of his backpack, repositioning it on his shoulders. He walked toward the door and snapped his fingers at Derwitz.

"Off your ass, specialist. We got work to do."

Derwitz clambered to his feet with a weary slowness and joined Leary at the door, tightening his helmet strap as he walked. Leary slowly opened the fire door and stepped into the stairwell, scanning for threats. Derwitz pushed in after him, and gently closed the door behind him.

McDaniels looked down at Jimenez. "Can you still move?"

Jimenez swallowed and nodded. "Yes sir."

"He shouldn't," Regina said. "Without a set of X-ray to refer to, there's no telling how bad the compression fractures are. If any of the disks are severely compromised, the injuries could increase. He could even be left paralyzed."

"I can still fight, major," Jimenez said. "I might not be able to run or march, but I can still point my weapon at a stench and shoot it."

"I don't doubt it, Jimenez. But if there's a way we can try to make you comfortable, then we'll do it." He patted Jimenez on the shoulder. "You just hang in there, troop. We'll be relocating to the twenty-seventh floor. So you just rest for the time being, all right?"

"Yes, sir."

McDaniels rose to his feet and turned toward the unguarded fire door. "How is your father doing, Miss Safire?"

She gathered up the contents of the first aid bag she'd gone through and put them back inside the red backpack. "He's doing as well as anyone could under these circumstances. He's stressed, and wants to get out of here. When *are* we getting out of here, by the way?"

"As soon as my commanding officers can get a resource available, we'll be pulled out," McDaniels said. "Until then, we're on our own. But we seem to be secure."

"I heard a gunshot a while ago. What happened?"

McDaniels debated on whether he should tell her, then opted for the truth. It was probably less risky that way. "There was a zombie in the stairway. It was one of the people who worked here. I guess at some point he was bitten, and he crossed over. It was trying to get at some people who are barricaded on the twenty-seventh floor, and we put it down."

Regina kept packing the bag. "And that was the only one you saw?"

"Yes."

"But if there's one, there's more, right?"

"It makes sense to live life like that's how it is." McDaniels walked closer to the fire door, the AA-12 cradled in his arms like a favored child.

Regina finished packing the bag and got to her feet. She put the backpack on a nearby file cabinet. Jimenez slowly rolled into a sitting position, and she knelt down to help him.

"You shouldn't be moving around," she chided.

"Gotta do what I gotta do. Major, I can cover the door from here easy. You go ahead and hit the latrine or whatever," Jimenez said.

"I'm good, Jimenez."

"Seriously, sir. I can do this." Despite his obvious pain, there was a set of commitment to Jimenez's face. McDaniels considered this for a moment, then shrugged.

"Okay, Jimenez. You've got the door. The first sergeant and Rittenour will be coming up in a moment, so don't shoot them, all right?"

"Roger that, sir."

McDaniels took the opportunity to visit the men's room and relieve himself and washed up at the sink with hot water. He wondered for how long their good fortune would last? Heat, power, hot potable water, food... realistically, if nothing changed, they could hold out for months. They weren't in that tight of a spot. Of course, no wanted to stay and watch the Big Apple fall before the walking dead. As soon as they could, McDaniels wanted everyone out.

He regarded his reflection in the mirror and noticed the bags forming under his eyes. He held his hands up and watched them. They weren't quaking, but they weren't rock-steady, either. He resolved to ensure the soldiers all got some rest once they relocated to the 27th floor, starting with the two Special Forces troops, Rittenour and Leary. They'd been on the sharp edge for days, and they doubtless needed recuperative sleep.

The restroom door opened, and McDaniels automatically grabbed the AA-12. First Sergeant Gartrell walked around the privacy wall that separated the restroom proper from the doorway. He held up his hands and cocked a brow.

"Don't shoot, major."

"Stop fucking around, Gartrell. What are the circumstances down below?"

Gartrell strolled over to the row of urinals and did what he had to do. "Same as before, only with Leary and that poindexter from the 160th keeping an eye on the door. Leary's got what it takes, but not so sure about the other guy. Oh well. If he doesn't, he'll be the first to go, I guess. Looks like Jimenez is royally fucked up?"

McDaniels nodded. "Safire's daughter thinks he has spinal compression fractures."

Gartrell grimaced. "That guy's got to be in a world of hurt, but he's holding up pretty well. Hard core, if you ask me." Gartrell finished his task and flushed the urinal, then headed for the sinks. He washed his hands and took quite some time doing it, soaping them up mightily and using water so hot it turned his hands red. He looked up at the mirror and caught McDaniels watching him.

"It's like I can't stay clean enough," he said, as if confessing some grievous sin. "I've been out in the field for weeks without a shower, and I can't tell you how bad I want one right now. I don't think I've come into real contact with any of those things, but I still feel filthy. Like I've got bugs crawling all over me." He stood up straight and looked away from McDaniels' reflection, turning his blue eyes toward the man himself.

"Jesus, major. You got someone's brains all over your armor and BDUs."

McDaniels looked down at his front. True enough, he was speckled with small, rust-colored droplets of dried blood and gore. He snorted and shook his head.

"From the zed up on twenty-seven," he explained. "It was the company CEO, I'm told. Guess he did work himself to death."

Gartrell unstrapped his helmet and placed it on the marble countertop. He attacked his face and scalp with hot water, rinsing himself off thoroughly.

"How'd you like the shottie?" he asked while working his fingers across his scalp.

"Awesome weapon. Great to have handy when going up against deadheads or locked doors. Glad I had some hearing protectors on hand, though."

"Listen, you think USASOC's going to be able to pull us out of here? Because I'm having some trouble coming up with a Plan B." Gartrell straightened up and pulled a handful of paper towels from the dispenser to his left. He dried off his face and head, then handed the damp towels to McDaniels.

"Use these to wipe down the front of your uniform. Go on, I don't have any cooties that haven't been treated already."

McDaniels took the damp towels. "Thanks." He turned toward the mirror and started wiping down his battle dress utilities and body armor. "USASOC's going to do whatever's necessary to get us out of here. After all, we have Safire, and he's the genius."

"Oh hell yeah, they'll come for *him*. It's the rest of us dogfaces I'm worried about."

McDaniels shrugged. "I'm sure they'll take all of us if they can get to us." He paused, and looked up at Gartrell's reflection in the mirror. "Gartrell. We need to bury the hatchet. We've got a lot of people who are depending on us, and I'm going to need all the help I can get. I need you to respect my rank and fall in line."

Gartrell finished drying his face and tossed the paper towels into the waste basket. He put his hands on his hips and regarded McDaniels critically for a moment, then moistened another handful of towels and handed them to McDaniels. The ones he had been using were stained a dark russet.

"I'm always mission first, major. You know that."

"I do. I just want to make sure we're going to get along. The rest of the troops need to know who's in charge."

"Yeah, I get that." Gartrell's eyes were hard, and he kept his gaze locked with McDaniels'. "Here's what I'll do, major. You stay focused on the mission and don't do anything dumb, I'm cool. But you fuck things up like in Afghanistan, I'm going to insert my twenty-five years of experience leading soldiers in the field. How's that?"

McDaniels thought about it, then nodded. "Thanks, first sergeant."

"No problem, sir. So tell me more about this cafeteria on twenty-seven?"

"If we have to hole up here in New York City, it would be tougher to find a better place. Maybe inside the Federal Reserve or Rikers Island, but even those wouldn't be a hell of a lot better than what we have here. The building's big, but it's not like it's the Chrysler Building. We can still move from top to bottom if we need to. And there's enough food upstairs to keep three hundred folks going for a week or so. I figure that we've got at least two months of provisions, and that's with the power going out and half of what's upstairs spoils in a week."

Gartrell grunted. "I like the way that sounds. But if no one gets us off of Manhattan island in the next couple of days, they never will."

McDaniels sighed. Gartrell was right. Whatever caused the dead to reanimate wasn't going to remain localized. Infected people would travel before they sickened and died, then rose again from wherever they had succumbed to the disease. And the cordon sanitaires that had been erected hadn't been put in place in time, nor were they very effective in the first place. He had seen how the dead had overrun the barricades and attacked the officials manning them. To think the communities to the north would have better luck was asking for a bit much.

"Let's try and stay positive," he said anyway.

The skin around Gartrell's eyes crinkled as he smiled. "Optimism wasn't part of my advanced individual training, major."

"Then adapt to the circumstances."

"Roger on that. When do we move topside?"

"ASAP. I have to put in a call to USASOC in less than forty minutes. We have to figure out how we're going to get Jimenez up there. He's not going to be able to walk twenty-two flights of stairs, and I doubt we can carry him that far and not knock ourselves out."

"Elevator?"

"Too risky. Plus Earl the Maintenance Guy shut them down. Would be very off-putting to have the doors slide open a few floors too low, and find about a dozen stenches waiting."

Gartrell picked up his helmet and regarded it idly for a moment. "Hey, what about a freight elevator? Less chance of it making an unscheduled stop, right?"

McDaniels frowned. "There's a freight elevator on this floor?"

"Oh yeah. Right past the elevator bay, there's another door, across from the mailboxes. Locked from our side, but we checked it out during the initial recon. The bay was empty, but there was an elevator there. Judging by how wide the door was, it must be the freight elevator. It's got to go all the way up."

"Show me," McDaniels said.

***

The freight elevator was in a smallish room off the corridor that was accessible through a set of double steel doors. They were supposed to be locked, but one of the doors had been left slightly ajar; McDaniels figured this was done by the nightly cleaning crew so they wouldn't have to swipe in and out. And like the other elevators, it was switched off.

He called up to Finelly on Jimenez's radio and told him to ask Earl if the elevator went all the way to the 27th floor, and if it was in a secure area. It was in the same corridor as the fire escape, and Earl confirmed that it could go straight up. And he was in possession of a fire key, which meant he could summon it directly if required.

But the question remained, was it empty?

"Only way to find out for sure is to call it up," McDaniels told Gartrell.

"So do we bring it here, or to twenty-seven?" Gartrell asked. "If we want to bring it here, we need to get the key, call the elevator, wait for it to open, then blast the living shit—or un-living, I guess—out of whatever's inside. Once it's clear, we all pile in and ride it upstairs."

McDaniels considered that. "Or I can head upstairs and have Earl call it up, Finelly and I do the same if it's occupied, then come down and pick up you guys."

Gartrell shrugged. "Either way. One of us would probably have to go up anyhow, I don't think we can let that maintenance guy come downstairs without an escort. If this man has his kids up there, we don't want to leave them alone." He smiled crookedly. "At least your way, one of us won't be quite so tired."

"So very true, first sergeant. All right, I'll hoof it upstairs. You get Jimenez as ready to travel as possible."

"Roger that."

The climb back to the 27th floor was uneventful, but McDaniels' thighs were on fire by the time he knocked on the fire door. Finelly and Earl let him in.

"You're looking pretty peaked, major," the tall sergeant observed. "Thought you Jedi Knights were immune to things like, you know, physical exertion and all."

"It's been a tough day, sergeant."

"Tell me about it, sir."

McDaniels clucked his tongue at the NCO's insouciance, but he killed his reply when he sniffed the air. He looked at Earl.

"You smoked?"

Earl looked chastised. "Uh, that a problem?"

"Hell no, Earl. But I'd love to bum a smoke off of you, if you don't mind. Later," he added, when Earl immediately reached for his breast pocket. "Let's call up that freight elevator, clear it, and then head down to get the rest of our group."

Earl led them to the freight elevator bay, and like its twin on the 5th floor, it was empty and silent. He slid a red key into a receptacle on the elevator door frame and turned it, then pressed the DOWN button. A motor started, and McDaniels heard the elevator come to life.

"Step outside, Earl. We'll call you when the coast is clear," he told the small maintenance man.

"Okay. You guys be careful."

McDaniels shouldered the AA-12. "No need to worry about that." He looked at Finelly, who formed up to his right, his MP5K at the ready. Both men had had the foresight to leave their hearing protectors where they belonged: in their ears. Earl scuttled out of the brightly-lit vestibule and slammed the metal door closed behind him.

"Safety off, booger-hook on the bang lever?" McDaniels asked Finelly.

"Hooah."

Ding. The elevator had arrived. McDaniels held his breath as the door slowly slid open.

It was empty. Just the same, McDaniels slowly stepped inside and visually cleared it. The elevator was vacant and cool.

"We're good," he reported to Finelly. The elevator door started to close, but he stopped it with his foot. He pressed his radio button as Finelly knocked on the door and told Earl to join them.

"First sergeant, the elevator's clear. We're on our way down."

"Roger that, major."

9

The massive MV-22's rotors were winding down as the Marine aircrew went through their post-shutdown checklist. Their landing platform, the USS *Wasp*, rolled gently from side to side in the Atlantic as she came about, her bow pointing to the south. There was some heavy weather moving in, with winds approaching seventy knots and bands of rain so dense that the leading edges had been plainly visible on the MV-22's weather radar. The *Wasp* was getting the hell out of Dodge, and the Marines that crewed the Osprey were thrilled. Theirs was the sole surviving aircraft Marine Medium Tiltrotor Squadron 263; the rest of the squadron had been lost to the stenches in Central Park. The two pilots and two enlisted crew chiefs kept their conversation all business as they secured the mammoth aircraft. Watching friends and coworkers die was not usually conducive to witty repartee, especially when they died after being overrun by fucking flesh-eating *zombies*.

Still, the Marine aircraft commander was a little put out when one of the crew chiefs broke the monotony of the checklist. "Hey, we've got fuel coming aboard."

"Say again," the aircraft commander said over the intercom.

"I said we have fuel coming aboard. Hose has just been attached to the fast transfer port."

The aircraft commander saw his frown was mirrored by that of the pilot sitting beside him as he rapidly shut down the Osprey's main electrical bus. "Generator on standby, batteries on," he reported.

"Reset speed selectors forward and apply rotor brakes," the aircraft commander said as he checked the parking brake handle between his seat and the pilot's. While the MV-22's rotors had lost a substantial amount of energy already, their rotor wash could still blast a man off the deck of the *Wasp*.

"Big Eye, this is Thunder Three, what's with the fuel transfer, over?" he asked over the ship-to-ship.

"Thunder Three, Big Eye, we've been told to top off your tanks. Stand by."

"Top off our tanks?" the pilot asked. He looked across the cockpit and out the windows on the AC's side of the aircraft. Darkness reigned, but in the distance sporadic ripples of lightning flashing about inside the approaching cloud front. "Man, we're not going *anywhere* tonight."

"Let's get back on the checklists," the AC ordered, and the aircrew went back to work. They were almost done anyway, and it took only a few minutes to secure the aircraft. The crew was ready to egress, and the AC notified the *Wasp*'s air boss.

"Big Eye, Thunder Three is ready to dismount."

"Ah, negative that, Thunder Three. You're clear to disembark your PAX, but then you need to start turning cycles. You have to head back to New York, over."

"Oh man, what the *hell*?" one of the enlisted crew chiefs moaned.

The AC wasn't having any of it. "Get those civilians off the aircraft! Once they're clear, we get on the cockpit pre-start and engine start checklists!" He depressed his microphone button. "Big Eye, Thunder Three. This crew's run out. Going back to New York City's going to bust us, over."

"Thunder Three, high value targets are still in the city barricaded in a skyscraper on the Upper East Side. There's no one else in the area that can pull them out, so you get the job. ENAV is on its way out to you. This comes straight from the top, over."

A sailor rushed into the Osprey, pushing his way into the aircraft through the right entry door. The few civilians who had managed to get aboard the aircraft before it lifted out of Central Park were deplaned by the ramp at the rear. The sailor carried a plastic case, which he handed to the pilot. The pilot accepted it with a grunt and opened it. The case contained a flash card and a USB thumb drive. He pulled a flash card from the navigation panel between the two pilot seats and replaced it with the new one. He punched a code into the system via the soft keys on its panel, and the new route and target destination appeared on a moving map display.

"Good ENAV," the pilot reported.

"Big Eye, Thunder Three has the ENAV. Who is it we're supposed to pick up, over?"

"Thunder Three, Big Eye. You're picking up someone who has key information to stop whatever the hell's going on. Not to add any more pressure, over."

The pilot chuckled mirthlessly, but the AC didn't pay any attention to it. He turned and looked out the canopy windows as heavy, wind-blown rain droplets slammed into it.

"Big Eye, is this storm headed for New York? Over."

"Thunder Three, this is Big Eye. You know it is, Marine. Now pull pitch and get the hell out of here, over."

"Oorah," the AC replied, then started the communication display unit checklist. The sooner they broke the *Wasp*'s deck, the faster they could start outrunning the storm.

***

Gartrell and Rittenour had loaded Jimenez onto a leather office chair and wheeled him into the freight elevator, then brought the Safires out of the pantry. Regina looked expectant; her father's expression was blank and vacant.

"Are we getting out of here?" Regina asked.

"We're leaving this floor," McDaniels told her.

"I don't understand," she said.

"We're going up. To get further away from those things on the street. There are other people on the twenty-seventh floor, and we're going to join them while we wait for exfil."

"'Exfil'?"

"Short for exfiltration, Regina." Safire's voice reflected his weariness as he leaned against the elevator's metal wall and rubbed his eyes. "An exfiltration is a military term for a stealthy pickup."

"So... so someone's coming for us?" she asked, puzzled. "That's why we're moving?"

McDaniels considered explaining things completely, but settled for expediency. "Yes." He nodded to Earl. "This is Earl. Earl, meet Doctor Wolf Safire and his daughter, Regina. The man in the chair is Sergeant Jimenez, and the other two are First Sergeant Gartrell and Sergeant First Class Rittenour."

Earl ducked his head. "Pleased to meetcha," he said meekly.

McDaniels clapped him on the shoulder. "Twenty-seventh floor, if you would."

Earl smiled and twisted the fire key. The elevator door slid shut and the lift ascended.

"On our way," Earl said quietly.

They rode upward in silence for a moment before Safire spoke.

"You've checked the rest of the building, major? Are we alone?"

McDaniels shook his head. "I have not. I only know that the twenty-seventh floor is more defensible, and it's well stocked with supplies. It's the best place in the building to barricade ourselves."

"Really. Eating old cheese sandwiches out of a vending machine, are we?"

"Oh, it's not like that at all, sir," Earl said. "We got a little bit of ever'thin' up there. Fresh fruit, veggies, bread, meat... hell, we even got some jerk chicken and spicy meat patties. That's what they usually serve on Tuesdays. Jamaican Tuesdays."

Safire didn't quite roll his eyes. "Really."

Earl heard the sarcasm in his voice and looked at him directly, suddenly no longer so meek.

"Kiss my black ass, motherfucker," he said.

Gartrell smiled. "That's the spirit, Earl."

The elevator arrived, and the door opened. Earl yanked the key free and marched into the loading vestibule, where Finelly stood watch with his MP5K in his hands. Earl pushed past him and disappeared past the double metal doors. Finelly watched him go quizzically.

"What's up with that?" he asked McDaniels.

McDaniels waved the question aside. "Help us get Jimenez inside and get the Safires squared away. Then get Earl to shut down the elevator again. I have to get topside and call the taxi service."

***

As soon as McDaniels stepped onto the building's roof, he felt the certain electric quality in the air that signaled a storm was coming. The moon had already risen into the darkening sky, illuminating a dense line of storm clouds on the horizon, still many miles distant.

"Holy fuck, would you look at that," Gartrell said as the clouds flashed with internal lightning.

"Yeah, looks like we have some weather coming in," McDaniels said. He broke out the sat phone.

"Was talking about the window divers, major." McDaniels looked up at Gartrell. The first sergeant pointed across the roof, where the zombies had started surging out of the broken window in the building across the street. They reached for the two Special Forces soldiers as they fell. McDaniels shook his head. He was already used to them.

"Window divers, huh? Pretty creative."

Gartrell didn't say anything, just continued to stare at the line of zeds spilling out of the building, a look of revulsion on his face. Then he snapped out of it and took an audit of the roof, his AA-12 ready. Even though he hid it behind years of discipline, McDaniels saw the man was spooked.

"Rapier, this is Terminator, over," McDaniels said into the phone. "Rapier, this is Terminator, back with you on the hour, over."

"Terminator, this is Rapier. Good to hear from you. Give us your SITREP, over."

"Situation remains pretty much the same, Rapier. We've relocated to the top floor of the building to get some distance from the zeds. One in our party has some fairly serious injuries, and he needs better medical care than we can give him. But for the moment, we're holding out. What've you got for us? Over."

"Terminator, Rapier. We have an MV-22 headed your way, should be on-station in less than two hours. Asset is equipped with a rescue hoist, so you'll be uploaded that way. You'll be taken back to the Marine operational platform until we can arrange for a transfer, over."

"Roger that, Rapier, and that's great news. It does look like we have some weather moving in, over." He gave Gartrell a thumbs-up and a smile. "V-22 in about two hours."

"Now that's what I'm talkin' about," Gartrell said.

"Terminator, Rapier. Roger on the weather, the aircrew is aware. The weather guys down here say you can expect some rain with moderate gusts up to thirty miles an hour, but those conditions shouldn't arrive until after you're on your way back to the boat, over."

"Rapier, Terminator. Good to know. Do you have any information on our families, over?"

There was a lengthy pause, and the elation McDaniels felt when given the news about the inbound MV-22 faded. He waited, but there was no response.

"Rapier, this is Terminator, over."

"Terminator, Rapier. Sorry, we haven't been able to get anything conclusive with regards to your families. We just don't have the resources to track that down. I know it's not what you want to hear, but it is what it is. Sorry about that, Terminator. Over."

In the distance, McDaniels heard sporadic gunfire, vague and ghostly. It didn't last for long.

Is that what my family is going through now? Are they being attacked by a horde of zeds while I'm here?

"Rapier, Terminator. You're right, it's not what I want to hear. You need to figure out how you're going to get that intel our way, because we've been busting our balls trying to accomplish this mission. You can give us a little peace of mind by determining the disposition of our families. Any other answer is bullshit, over."

"Terminator, Rapier. We get it. We really, really get it. We're doing our best. Over."

"Outstanding, Rapier. What about that troop movement north of us?"

"Terminator, Rapier. Movement is underway, but not in your vicinity yet. You should consider that element a total dark horse solution. They still have a lot of miles to cover before they can get to where you would want them, over."

McDaniels sighed. Was anything going to go right tonight? He stood up and stretched, cracking his back as he did so. To his right, more zombies tumbled out of the building. The sight was almost comical, if it didn't rather finely underscore the desperation of their situation: the stenches would do anything to get to them, and there was absolutely no way to reason them out of it.

"Rapier, Terminator. Roger that last about the troop movement from Drum. How much of New York City has gone to the zeds? Over."

There was a long pause before he got his reply. "Pretty much all of it right now, Terminator. That's why the 10th is heading your way. They're going to try and quarantine Manhattan Island and then start systematically exterminating every stench they can find. I'd say it promises to be quite a show, but you'd probably want to be gone by then. Over."

McDaniels shook his head. "Rapier, how can one light infantry division possibly kill over a million zeds? Makes no sense, considering they'd need to make head shots for every kill, or use some pretty intense burning agents to raze them. Over."

"Terminator, Rapier. We get that. This is a Big Army plan, not something USASOC is onboard with. The opinion here is that the 10th Mountain guys are gonna go under, but there's no way to put a stop to it. Looks like the National Command Authority wants to do something, and this is it. But not our problem, Terminator. As far as you're concerned, the Marines are on their way, and they're your ticket out of the Big Apple. Over."

McDaniels checked the horizon again, and saw the line of clouds had moved closer. "Roger that, Rapier. Keep an eye on the weather... it would totally suck if we get closed out because of a little rain and wind, over."

"Taken care of, Terminator. The Marine call sign is Thunder Three, flight of one, and will be calling you on frequency seven, one-three-two megahertz. You'll have the frequency all to yourselves, and the Night Stalkers should be able to monitor it as well, over."

"Roger, Rapier. Anything else?"

"Negative from this end, Terminator. Hope that the next we hear from you is that you're feet wet and heading for the boat with all souls, over."

"From your lips to God's ear, Rapier. Terminator Six, out."

McDaniels powered down the satellite phone and folded up its antenna. As he packed it away, Gartrell ambled over, his AA-12 held loosely in his hands.

"So it sounded like USASOC was blowing a lot of sunshine your way," he said.

"I get that they're a little busy."

Gartrell nodded. "I'd figured that as well, sir."

McDaniels finished packing up the radio and rose to his feet. He looked at Gartrell and shrugged after a moment.

"Don't know what to say, Gartrell. I guess we're both in the same boat. I'm hoping our families are smart enough to get out if they can, or to shelter in place until they can get rescued."

Gartrell nodded again. "Laurie and the girls should be good to go if things are getting out of hand in their area. We have guns, and everyone knows how to use them. And if they have to evacuate, they can overland with the ATVs." The first sergeant paused again. "What about your wife? Paulette, right? And what's his name, Lenny?"

"Lenny's at school in Texas. Paulette is at home, alone. And she hates guns. I have two of them in the house, but she won't touch them. She doesn't even know how to load them."

Gartrell said nothing.

McDaniels nodded toward the roof door. "Let's get back downstairs before things get any more maudlin," he said.

Gartrell grabbed his arm as he stalked past the first sergeant. McDaniels stopped and looked at him, and Gartrell's blue eyes shined in the tepid light given off by what remained of New York City.

"You need to cultivate some faith, major," he said. "And real fast. Your family will need it."

McDaniels nodded after a long moment. Gartrell slowly released him, and McDaniels continued toward the door. Gartrell took one last look at the falling zombies as they tumbled through the night, on a date with pavement kissing. He shook his head and pressed on after McDaniels.

10

Regina Safire looked around the darkened cafeteria as she slowly walked back to the booth where her father sat, brooding over a bottle of water. She had checked the wounded soldier again, and found his condition unchanged, though his pain had increased. There was nothing for her to prescribe for him other than Advil and Tylenol, which had been found in the kitchen first aid kit. She'd given him more than the maximum doses of both, but of course they were too weak to really put down the pain. The poor man would just have to suffer until he could be delivered to a real medical facility. She ran a hand through her dark hair, and hoped that would be soon.

Her father barely looked up as she slid across the bench facing him. She reached across the table the put her hand over his, but he didn't react to the contact.

"Dad?"

Safire sighed lightly, that perpetual indicator of impatience she'd grown accustomed to while growing up. "What is it, Regina." His voice was flat, expressionless, like it always was when he was stressed. The light pouring in through the big windows overlooking Lexington Avenue illuminated his hair, surrounding his head with a nimbus of gray and white.

"We're going to be all right," she said, voice low. "We're going to get out of this. These guys, they seem pretty well connected, and they obviously know what they're doing."

Safire smiled thinly, his gaze rooted on the surface of the table between them. "You think so, Regina?"

"These are some pretty tough hombres, dad."

"And you think that toughness is enough to get us out of this?"

"They have resources. They can communicate with people outside of the city, or at least they say they can. And the government wouldn't send just anybody to get you out of here. They'd send the best they had."

"That man, McDaniels... do you know what he was doing before he was sent to New York?" When she shook her head,

Safire grinned widely, like some sort of jack-o-lantern. "He was putting together PowerPoint presentations for generals to use in their briefings. Not exactly a signal they sent the best they had, is it?"

Regina frowned. "How do you know that?"

For the first time, Safire met her eyes. He looked at her for a moment, and she suddenly felt stupid and childish. It was obvious that her father knew what he did from a trusted source, otherwise he wouldn't have said what he had. She was about to apologize when he suddenly turned and jerked his chin toward one of the soldiers, sitting at a nearby table. They had assembled a veritable feast of thick sandwiches, chips, soda, slices of cake and pie. She had heard them discussing the merits of some beer they had found in the kitchen as well, but oddly enough, they weren't drinking any. Only soda and water. She presumed that indicated they were disciplined enough to resist the charms of alcohol, even during a nightmare like the one they were all living.

"One of *them* told me," he said.

Regina frowned again. "Why would they do that?"

"Perhaps they don't like the major. I understand they normally work for someone else. I really don't know why I was told that, unless it was an attempt at humor."

Regina ran both hands through her hair. "Well, not too funny if it was."

Safire only shrugged and went back to contemplating the tabletop. Regina touched his hand again.

"I'm getting hungry. Do you want anything to eat?" she asked.

Safire shook his head silently. Regina patted his hand and slid out of the booth and headed toward the kitchen. She walked past the maintenance worker, sitting with his two daughters, both of whom were now awake. They regarded Regina with blank expressions as she walked past, and she smiled at them. The older girl, who was maybe 19 or 20, smiled back; the younger one, perhaps 10, kept her expression neutral.

The kitchen was spectacularly bright compared to the dining area, and she had to blink against the light for a few moments before her eyes adjusted. When they did, she opened the refrigerators and freezers until she found what she had been looking for: one of the walk-in refrigerators did indeed contain several cases of beer of various brands. She pulled a bottle of Corona Light from one, found a bottle opener, and uncapped it. Lifting the cold bottle to her lips, she relished the taste of the chilled beer as it raced past her tongue. Despite everything they had gone through, a cold beer was still welcome. Maybe because of the hardships they had endured, it tasted better than ever.

"Now that's what I was talking about!"

The sudden voice cut through the air in the sterile kitchen like a knife. Startled, Regina turned to see two soldiers standing inside: the tall one she knew as Finelly, and the shorter, darker one whose name she couldn't recall. Markie? Maxie? Finelly looked at her openly, a smile on his big, country-boy face.

"And what were you talking about?" she asked.

"About drinking a few damned beers, but we all know the first sergeant would land on us with both boots." Finelly stepped toward her, still smiling. He had removed his helmet, and his straw-blond hair was shorn so short on the sides of his head that it reminded her of a whitewall tire. His eyes dipped down, taking in her figure. She presumed it was an automatic thing for him to do—he was a soldier, after all—but she was surprised to discover that beneath her initial sensation of disgust, her nipples had hardened and her cleft had grown moist.

Jesus. Of all the times to get horny!

"And why would he 'land on you with both boots'?" she asked, and tipped the bottle back to her lips again.

"Because he's an all work, no play kind of guy," Finelly said, drifting closer to her. "He lives life by the letter of the law, like all senior noncoms do. I don't work for the guy, but you can tell it just by looking at him."

"He's a little bit on the stiff side," the other soldier offered, trying to get into the conversation. Regina looked at him. To her, he looked like just another goofy Jersey Shore guido trying to strike a pose, even under all the Army gear. But this guido wasn't as in your face as most of his civilian counterparts were. If it was because of his training or because his personality wasn't in it, she couldn't tell which.

"Like you'd know anything about that, Maxi." Finelly walked past Regina without touching her and opened the walk-in refrigerator she'd pulled the bottle from. She watched as he regarded the beer wistfully for a long moment.

"Is your name Max?" she asked the other soldier. His name must have been DERWITZ, it was printed on the left side of his uniform. "They keep calling you Maxi."

Finelly laughed as he slammed the walk-in door shut. "Yeah, go ahead, tell her why we call you Maxi," he said, chortling.

Derwitz looked embarrassed. "Kiss my ass, Finelly."

"Never mind," Regina said. She looked around the kitchen. It was time to rustle up some grub and rejoin her father.

"It's short for maxi-pad," Finelly said, rather indelicately. He looked at her directly, searching for any embarrassment. "We call him that because he's a constant complainer, as if he's on his monthly or something. But with Maxi, he's never *not* on his monthly, you know what I mean?"

Regina snorted humorlessly. "That's sweet," she said with as much venom in her voice as she could muster. "You guys have a remarkable sense of humor. I'll bet your IQs are off the charts as well."

"I doubt that," Finelly said earnestly. "But we *did* save you guys from the stenches, so maybe we do have some smarts after all, Miss Safire."

She found some Italian bread more sandwich fixings: cheese, salami, lettuce, tomato, peppers and onions, pickles, the works. And every condiment she could have hoped for, all in an under-counter refrigerator. In another under-counter refrigerator she found even more sandwich meats. The place was stocked.

"I don't doubt you know how to do your job," she said, poking through the refrigerator. "And you do it well. But the humor's a little lost on me. Sorry, I guess I'm not into the whole 'boys will be boys' scene."

"Well, maybe that'll change." There was something else in Finelly's voice, something that tickled the edges of her persona. He was clearly coming on to her. And oddly enough, Regina was surprisingly receptive to it, even though she usually favored what her father disparagingly referred to as "thoroughbreds": moneyed traders or corporate chieftains, men who made millions with their brains and on occasion, their brawn. Finelly obviously didn't do much with his brains, but the brawn, oh he had that, in spades.

She turned to him, and hit him with her patented wilting smile. "Oh, I wouldn't worry about that, Finelly." As in, *You don't have a snowball's chance in Hell of ever seeing me without my clothes on.*

"That was just plain cold," Finelly said, without a trace of remorse in his voice. He'd either been teasing, or had expected to go down in flames from the get-go.

"Hey Finelly, let's get what we came for and get back outside," Derwitz said. "The major and the first shirt should be back any second now, and I want to hear what they got to say."

"Yeah, yeah, yeah," Finelly said, rolling his eyes. He grabbed some salt and packets of mustard and mayonnaise, while Derwitz grabbed bread and roast beef. He then headed for the door, followed by the taller (and infinitely sexier, Regina thought against her will) Finelly. Finelly turned and looked at her as he backed through the door.

"Don't go far," he said. "No one's really supposed to go anywhere alone, but if you plan on stepping outside of the kitchen, let one of us know."

"I will," Regina said. She started to thank him for his concern, but he stepped out of the kitchen, and the door swung shut.

She went ahead and made herself a zesty salami sandwich with oil and vinegar and black pepper, grabbed another beer, and headed back for the dining area. She sat down across from her father again.

"The soldiers were right, there is beer," she said.

Safire merely grunted, apparently totally uninterested. Regina shrugged mentally and started eating. She was surprised at how utterly ravenous she was, then she realized she had had nothing to eat for almost twelve hours. She consumed her sandwich rapidly, punctuated with draughts from the beer bottle. It was definitely low on the class scale, but the meal was one of the enjoyable she'd had in a long time.

And then, McDaniels and the first sergeant were there, striding across the room. Everyone perked up when they saw the major, and Regina knew exactly why. The man exuded confidence and calm, even though he must have been infinitely more tired than he appeared. And he was clearly educated, much more so than, say, Sergeant Finelly by a long shot. The fact that he was black was not lost upon Regina either. She wondered if his race had made life in the Army easier or harder for him. She'd known many people in the corporate and medical arenas who had experienced a little bit of both, but she imagined the Army was more of a vacuum-sealed environment. Maybe things like color didn't mean anything in the military.

"All right folks, listen up," McDaniels said. "In about two hours, we'll be getting out of here. The Marines are coming for us in one of their V-22s and will upload us from the roof. We just have to keep alive until then." He looked around. "Where are Rittenour and Leary?"

"Back on the first floor," Finelly said. "They hit the latrine, grabbed some chow, and headed downstairs. Wanted to keep an eye on whatever's going on down there."

McDaniels glanced back at Gartrell. "First sergeant...?"

"Not my idea major, but makes sense. If anything goes down, those two can handle it long enough to pull back, blow up the stairway, and then fight a rear guard if necessary." Regina noticed the first sergeant met McDaniels' eyes squarely. There wasn't much respect and absolutely no obsequiousness in his demeanor. She could almost see the undercurrent of tension between the two men.

Are they enemies? she wondered.

McDaniels turned to the two soldiers who sat at the table, still eating. The third, Jimenez, lay on his left side on the floor, some distance away. He hadn't moved much since Regina had last examined him.

"Finelly and Derwitz, I want the two of you to head topside once you've finished eating," McDaniels said. "The Marines will be looking to get in and out as quickly as possible, and I would guess you Night Stalkers can help them out on the ground, correct?"

"Hooah," both soldiers said in unison. Finelly went on to add, "We have IR strobes and radios that talk on their freqs without any problem, sir. What's the call sign?"

"Thunder Three," McDaniels said.

Finally nodded, smiling. "Heh, the Thunder Chickens. Yeah, that's their real unit des, sir. We worked with them just about a month ago when they got back from Iraq."

"I'll consider that to be a good thing, then." McDaniels nodded to the two Night Stalkers. "Check in with us before you leave for the roof. The first sergeant and I are going to get some chow." With that, McDaniels turned to leave.

"What about the weather," Safire asked suddenly.

McDaniels turned back to him. "I'm sorry, Doctor?"

"The weather, major, the weather!" Safire twisted around in the booth and pointed toward the windows that looked out to the east, over the rest of Manhattan, the East River, and the borough of Queens. The dark clouds were still stacking up, and had definitely moved closer than the last time Regina had looked.

"The Marines can handle it," McDaniels said. "The MV-22 Osprey is one of the most sophisticated airframes in the service today. It's an all-weather transport, Doctor. Please don't worry."

"Fifty dollars," Safire said.

"Sorry?"

"Fifty dollars that the weather gets in the way," Safire said. "Fifty dollars says we're here throughout the night, at the very least."

McDaniels snorted and looked around the room. Everyone seemed a little bemused by the sudden impulse wager.

"Sure, fifty bucks it is," McDaniels agreed with a shrug, before he turned for the kitchen. Gartrell headed for the wounded soldier, Jimenez, and knelt beside him. They talked softly.

"Why did you make that bet with the major?" Regina asked her father.

"To keep him honest," Safire said. "I'm not sure he's been thinking of alternatives. Maybe fifty dollars will jumpstart his mind."

11

The hours passed slowly, moving like molasses on a cold January day. Despite the tension of the situation, McDaniels felt bone-weary after eating a light meal; his eyes burned, and his ears buzzed. He felt as if he hadn't slept in a week, and that was not a good thing. He needed to have all of his wits about him now, up until the Marines extracted them and they were on their way out of the city. If his mental faculties weren't up to par, then mistakes could be made, threats overlooked. It would suck to have made it so far for so long, only to have defeat snatched from the jaws of victory due to his carelessness.

So he brewed some rather fine gourmet coffee he found in one section of the kitchen (where there was hard liquor as well; apparently, Earl's bosses knew how to get their drink on when the circumstances warranted it). The coffee was sharp and bitter and strong, and cut through the veil of lassitude that had descended upon him like a fisherman's net. It was a temporary situation, he knew. Caffeine was a godsend to most soldiers, but McDaniels' body processed it quickly, leaving him just as tired and moribund as before. He brewed an entire pot, just in case.

He checked in with the two Special Forces troopers watching the front gates down on the first floor. They reported nothing particularly unusual, beyond the fact the street was full of a bunch of walking dead people. McDaniels filled them in on the coming exfiltration, to which Sergeant Rittenour said he didn't care was conducted by the Corps or the Civil Air Patrol, so long as their butts were pulled out of the city. McDaniels told them to remain in place until the MV-22 was closer, then he would have them withdraw to the roof with the rest of them.

He also ordered them to report in every fifteen minutes, and the Green Berets agreed.

For a change of pace, McDaniels walked through the cafeteria again, checking it out, making sure their security condition hadn't changed since his last jaunt to the roof. There was very little to see that he hadn't noticed before. He edged toward one of the windows and looked out over Lexington Avenue. The view hadn't changed much either since the last time he'd taken it in. Parts of the city were dark due to power loss, and the orange glow from Central Park had diminished as well. The growing breeze had cleared away most of the smoke, and he could now see in all directions. Below, zombies shambled about in the lamplight on Lexington Avenue, moving this way and that in an aimless fashion. Or was it? McDaniels wondered if the dead actually patrolled the street like a shark might swim through its territorial waters, using all of their senses—whatever they had left—to search for signs of prey. He had no doubt that the zeds below would do anything they could to reach him; most certainly, the "window divers" as Gartrell had called them proved that point. There simply was no negotiating with the dead. Trying to parlay with a Great White shark was likely to be more fruitful.

"'Scuse me, major?"

McDaniels was startled out of his reverie by Earl's whisper. He turned away from the city and thoughts of the walking dead and swimming sharks, and refocused his attention on the cafeteria. Earl and his two daughters stood nearby, watching him.

"Hey, Earl. What's up?" McDaniels kept his voice low, even though no one was sleeping. There was just something about the situation that warranted whispers.

"These're my daughters," Earl said, not without some pride. "My eldest, this is Kenisha. Kenisha, say hello to the major. He's an officer in the U.S. Army, and he's in charge of these men here."

The girl rolled her eyes. "I can see that, dad." She was about twenty years old, McDaniels guessed, and was quite the beauty. With skin the color of dark chocolate and bright, inquisitive eyes that held the light, he was certain she was popular with the boys. She extended one finely-boned hand in his direction, and McDaniels clasped it gently.

"Pleased to meet you, major," she said. Her grip was firm and strong. She was no wallflower, this one, so McDaniels firmed up his own grip a bit. "Thanks for everything you're doing."

McDaniels smiled and nodded to Earl. "Call me Cord, if you would. And you should thank this man here, Kenisha. He's the one who saved you and your sister, right?"

Kenisha glanced back at her father and smiled gently. "Yeah, he did great."

Earl beamed, then motioned to his second daughter, who looked to be about ten or eleven. Her demeanor was different from her sister's, more standoffish, more reserved. She had the same intelligence in her eyes, but not the same bravery. She was the kind who preferred to hold back and take in a scene before stepping into it.

"This here's Zoe, my youngest." When she didn't offer anything, Earl nudged her forward. "Go ahead, Zoe, say hello to the major."

"Hi," was all she said.

"Hi back, Zoe," McDaniels said.

Earl frowned. "Well, shake the man's hand, baby girl!"

McDaniels shook his head. "No need to push her, Earl. Really. It's no big deal." McDaniels smiled at the girl again, and sipped his coffee.

"Are we going to fly on an airplane?" Zoe asked. Her voice was soft but sonorous, and McDaniels wondered if singing might be in her future.

McDaniels smiled. "Well, sort of. The Osprey, it can be a helicopter and an airplane. It can move its engines like this." He held his hands before him and bent them upward at the wrist, trying to mimic the motion of the MV-22's tilting engine nacelles.

She seemed to consider this for a moment. "We've never been on an airplane before. They look like they might be fun."

"Well, I think it'll definitely be different, that's for sure. I don't think very many little girls like you have been on a V-22 before, so it's something you —" McDaniels stopped himself before he said *it's something you can tell your friends about,* because there was very little chance most of her friends were still alive.

"It's something you can look forward to," he amended.

"My daddy says there aren't very many black men in the Army," she said suddenly.

"Well, that's not exactly true. There are plenty of black men in the Army."

"Will you be a general like Colin Powell was?" Zoe asked. "He came to our school last year and gave a talk. He was the leader of the Army, I think."

McDaniels snorted. "Yes, he was the leader of the Army for a while. Actually, he was the head of all the military chiefs for a time. And I'd be glad if the Army made me a general like him, but I think I need to get past being a major first."

"Are there a lot of black generals?" Kenisha asked.

"Some." He tapped the U.S. Special Operations Command patch on his shoulder. "Very few black guys in special operations, though. Even fewer in the Army's Special Forces, which is where I'm from. Not sure why, but I think the promotion rate might have something to do with it," he finished with a grin.

Kenisha nodded. "I see," she said, though McDaniels could tell she wasn't so sure she did. She did seem sharp, and he detected the undercurrent of an activist in her. Hopefully, she wasn't about to try and engage him in a conversation on the state of the racial equality inside the U.S. Army.

Earl apparently felt that way too, and put a hand on her arm as he spoke to McDaniels. "I just wanted to introduce 'em to you, major. Seein' as how they was asleep and all when you were up here before."

McDaniels nodded to the girls. "I'm glad you did. Nice to meet you, ladies."

"Kenisha, why don't you take Zoe into the kitchen. Maybe find some of that nice sweet potato pie. Should be some left, unless those Army guys ate it all."

Kenisha started to argue, and it was obvious she thought the idea of fetching a piece of cake for her sister was far, far beneath her.

"Come on, now," Earl persisted.

When Kenisha looked at her father's smiling face, she relented with a sigh. She reached out and took Zoe's hand.

"Come on, Zoe, let's get some more pie."

Zoe nodded and allowed herself to be led away, then suddenly turned back to McDaniels. "Bye," she said.

"Bye, Zoe. See you later. Save some pie for me, okay?"

She sniffed haughtily. "*Maybe.*"

McDaniels chuckled as the two girls disappeared into the dark cafeteria and looked over at Earl. Obviously, Earl got what he wanted from his girls' smiles. McDaniels hadn't figured Earl had much going for him. Obviously, he was wrong.

"Beautiful girls," he said. "Really top notch, Earl. You should be proud."

"I am, I am. I wanted them to meet you, you know, before anything else happen. I wanted them to see a black man who's *successful*, you know what I mean? Not one a them bond traders or somebody like that, but a man who will put it all on the line for people he don't even *know* and not even blink an eye."

"Well… thanks, Earl."

"We comin' with you guys, right?"

"What?" The question surprised McDaniels.

"I said, we comin' with you guys, right?"

"Of course you're coming with us. We're all getting out of here."

Earl shrugged and looked past McDaniels, out the window behind him. "I just gotta be sure. I can't have my kids here. If somethin' happens and we all can't go, I'll stay behind, and you take my kids, okay?"

"Earl, the V-22 can lift like ten tons or something like that. Don't worry, we're all going."

Earl nodded slowly, then stepped toward the window. He pointed toward it. "Can this thing fly in the rain?"

McDaniels suddenly became aware of rain being flung against the window. He turned and saw small droplets smash against the pane of glass as they were driven into it by the wind. He heard the wind whine slightly as it wrapped around the building. Below, the street—and the deadheads that prowled it—were becoming wet. The zombies didn't seem to pay any attention to the rain or the wind.

"It can fly in rain just fine, Earl," McDaniels assured him. He put what he hoped was a comforting hand on the smaller man's bony shoulder and squeezed. "After all, if it couldn't take a little rain and wind, then the Marines probably wouldn't be flying it, right?"

"I guess. I'm just thinking about your helicopter crashin', that's all."

"We crashed because a—a window diver landed in the Black Hawk's main rotor. The V-22 isn't going to have that problem, it's going to hover over the building and hoist us up with its winch, one at a time, until we're all aboard."

Earl frowned. "That sounds kinda dangerous. And in this rain 'n wind? It can do that?"

"Well, it certainly beats the alternative, doesn't it?"

Earl chewed on that one for a while, then turned back to McDaniels. "My kids. Please save my kids."

Please take my daughter!

"We will," McDaniels promised him. "Now, let me ask a favor of you, all right?"

"Sure. Name it. Anything."

"Let me have one of those smokes. I'm going to step out into the stairwell and have one, if it's the last thing I ever do."

Earl smiled and handed over a cigarette and his butane lighter. "You ain't worried about any of those things comin' up from down below? Like Mister Walsford did?"

McDaniels patted his M4 carbine. "If they do, I have this. And they tend to move pretty slow, and we should have plenty of warning."

"Then I'll go with you. I ain't had no cigarette in almost half a day!" Earl said with a smile so bright that it bordered on being positively radiant.

12

"We should kill the kid," Sergeant Racine said for the fourth time.

McDaniels looked at the young sheepherder sitting nearby. His eyes were full of fear, and his face was still bereft of even the most nascent whiskers. McDaniels figured he was maybe eleven, possibly twelve; he looked much older because the Pashtun lived hard lives in the mountainscapes of Afghanistan, where the terrain was so hostile and forbidding that humans seemed to age a year to the month. The boy looked from Racine to McDaniels almost pleadingly, as if he understood what the reedy Special Forces soldier had said. McDaniels knew that was impossible; the boy didn't know a lick of English, and the valley in which he lived hadn't seen a foreigner since the Soviets had pulled out decades ago. Hell, he probably hadn't seen much of the tribe that lived in the next valley over, as the tall, craggy peaks that separated the geological depressions were so high that the locals called them the spine of the world. The boy's sheep bleated forlornly, looking up at the Special Forces Operational Detachment (Alpha) that surrounded them and their herder, weapons always close at hand, their eyes both hard and soft. McDaniels wondered if the boy knew exactly how much his presence had upset them. His arrival was almost as disturbing as Racine's apparent willingness to sentence a young boy to death merely for walking into their hide site, a place he had come to for years.

McDaniels looked at Master Sergeant David Gartrell, his team senior NCO. He knew Gartrell was a man of quiet religion, and he felt he could count on him to back him up when he pushed Racine back into line. He was surprised to see Gartrell's eyes were flat and expressionless, and that caused McDaniels some worry.

My God, is Gartrell actually going to suggest we kill a kid? he wondered to himself.

Gartrell stirred uneasily on the rock he sat on, glancing up at the peaks overhead, then down at the small village that lay almost two miles away. There was no real activity there, though the intel guys had said it was an al Qaeda rally point. There were Taliban there, that was for sure. But the Taliban weren't what they were after. It was the followers of Osama bin Laden that ODA PHANTOM hunted. Taliban were just poseurs, pretenders when it came to combat. To the

Taliban, warfare was a thing of ritual, something that started when the sun rose and ended when the sun set. If it had been any other way, then they would have ousted the Northern Alliance years ago. At their core, the Taliban were no more than children playing with guns. They claimed they lived and died for Allah, but the reality was they were just as afraid of death as anyone.

Gartrell rose to his feet and dusted off the seat of his battle dress utilities. He looked at McDaniels with those strangely hooded eyes, like a poker player trying to determine just what he was up against in the final hand of a high stakes game.

"We kill the kid, we buy ourselves some time," he said. "Of course, we'd have to kill the kid's goats too. We can't have them ranging around. But if we do that, we'll have to dispose of the bodies and hope we can hide 'em well enough that the rest of the villagers don't find them."

"This kid already found our hide site," said Abood. He was one of the only troopers in the entire branch who spoke and understood Pashto, Dari, and Arabic. A small man with narrow shoulders and an expression that made him seem to be in a constant state of disapproval, he had been against the notion of harming the boy from the start. He kept his eyes riveted on Racine as he spoke. "We kill this kid, we lose any traction we might be able to develop with the villagers down there. I guarantee you, captain, they don't want anything to do with al Qaeda. They probably hate them as much as they dislike the stinking Talibs." Abood's gaze came to rest on McDaniels, transferring the entire weight of the situation onto his shoulders. McDaniels sighed and rubbed his face. He understood now why there were so few African Americans in Army Special Forces. No one wanted to deal with this shit. Shooting Afghans wasn't a problem for McDaniels; they were giving al Qaeda their cover, and for that, a lot of them would pay. But double-tapping a kid just for leading a flock of mangy goats past their hide site? That seemed a little harsh.

"So, Master Sergeant." McDaniels locked his gaze with Gartrell's. "You think killing this boy is the right thing to do?"

Gartrell's expression didn't change. "We have a mission to preserve, sir."

"That's not an answer, Gartrell." The team had been debating what to do for twenty minutes now. McDaniels knew that calling out his senior NCO was akin to inviting disaster. The two men were supposed to be totally in synch, the glue that held PHANTOM together, the father and the mother who always put on their best faces for the kids. But even among Green Berets, the prospect of intentionally killing defenseless children rarely came up.

For his part, Gartrell finally looked away, turning to gaze back at the village. "No one wants to kill a boy, sir. But I have to wonder if in the context of the big picture, it might be the lesser sin."

"That's a load of bullshit," Abood said.

"Sounds like common sense talking to me," Racine said. He pulled his M9 pistol from its holster, his eyes on the goat herder. The boy began to shake, and he hugged his knees against him. He looked from man to man, searching for some clue as to what was going to happen.

"You're a fucking hypocrite." Abood stood and squared off with Racine, who fairly towered over him even though Abood stood on slightly higher ground. "You run off to the chapel every fucking Sunday, praying to God that he'll save your soul, and here you are getting ready to plug some kid who has to play with goats instead of a fucking X-Box."

Racine's face clouded with anger. "These fucking sand niggers nuked the Trade Center and the Pentagon, Abood. Maybe you ought to remember whose side you're on, huh? Maybe develop a little bit of warrior ethic, now that you're out here with the rest of us steely-eyed killers doing God's work?"

"Sergeant Racine." McDaniels kept his voice low and level as he spoke, his hands clutching his M4 like some sort of weird crutch. "Put your weapon away. Now."

Racine looked shocked. "You're kidding right, sir?"

"Do I look like I'm fucking kidding, Racine? Holster your sidearm or I'm going to land on you with both boots." McDaniels fixed Racine with his patented 'I'm going to fuck you up' stare. Racine seemed to consider debating the issue further, then slowly holstered his pistol. McDaniels pointed at the village.

"Eyes on that village, Racine. They could start looking for the boy at any moment. Make yourself useful and keep an eye out."

Racine unslung his sniper rifle and nodded as the cool professionalism of a Special Forces soldier returned to him. "Hooah," he said simply, then turned away from them and walked toward the line of rocks that would serve as his primary sniping position. He did not spare the boy a second glance.

McDaniels looked at Abood. "Tell him to go home, Abood. Tell him we're his friends, and we're not going to hurt him or his family. He *needs to stay quiet about us, for the safety of everyone. But he's free to go. With his goats," McDaniels added with a smile.*

Abood nodded gratefully. He knelt beside the boy and spoke to him in soft tones, his arm around the boy's narrow shoulders. The boy listened with rapt attention, then nodded a few times. Abood helped him to his feet, and the men watched as he gathered up his goats and shooed them down the rocky hillock. The boy looked at McDaniels with a cautious expression for a long moment, and McDaniels nodded to him, trying to give the impression they were all friends here. The kid didn't buy it, and McDaniels saw that plainly.

Gartrell stepped up beside McDaniels, and together they watched the boy and his goats move down the hill.

"I didn't sign on to kill kids," McDaniels said.

"Neither did I, sir."

"Then maybe next time you'll back me up when it comes to making some hard decisions, Gartrell. You're a soldier in the United States Army, and you wear the patch of Third Special Forces."

"All true. But I represent the men, Captain. I'm the guy who's supposed to keep them alive." He pointed at the kid as he urged his goats toward the village. "That kid's going to get us killed, but it would happen either way. You did what you had to do, and in accordance with the ROE. But the truth is, letting that kid go has just made our lives a lot shorter."

"We'll see," McDaniels said.

The Taliban attacked four hours later. PHANTOM lost five soldiers, and the Air Force had to be called in to decimate the village.

***

"Major? Major, wake up."

McDaniels snapped awake instantly, his hands going for his rifle. He found Gartrell had anticipated him, and held the weapon against McDaniels' body with his free hand.

"Sorry for the wakeup call," Gartrell said. "I tried to wake you by voice alone, but you weren't having none of that. Had to shake you out of it."

McDaniels coughed. He still tasted nicotine in his nostrils, disgusting and bewitching at the same time. He looked into Gartrell's face, and saw the older NCO looked like hell.

McDaniels was embarrassed he'd fallen asleep while Gartrell and the other troops had remained awake and on duty.

"No problem, first sergeant. What's up?"

"Thunder Three's less than thirty minutes out. We might want to start getting organized."

McDaniels cleared his throat and rose from the booth he had been sitting—sleeping!—in. His coffee cup was still on the table, and he picked it up. He needed a refill. "Let's have everyone take a second and do weapons maintenance if they can. If they need light, they can head for the latrines and take care of it there. Someone will have to take care of Jimenez's weapons, I don't want him trying to do that in his condition, but he does need to be able to shoot his weapon if circumstances warrant."

"Understood, sir. I'll see to it personally. You given much thought to the order of egress?"

McDaniels nodded. "Jimenez first, he's injured. Once he's on the Osprey, then the Safires, and then the rest of the troops. I'll go last, of course."

Gartrell frowned. "That would be my position, sir. You being an officer and all."

"And you being someone who actually still knows his way around a combat zone, I'm thinking everyone else would be better off if you were on the Osprey. Just in case and all that."

Gartrell shrugged. "However you want it, major." He pointed to the windows. "Weather looks positively nasty. I quizzed Finelly on the MV-22, and he says that even though the 160th doesn't use them, he thinks they're pretty solid. Saw them in action in Iraq. Says this weather might push it against the wall, though. We should probably come up with an alternative, in case we can't get out of here and can't stay put."

"If we get compromised up here on twenty-seven, not so sure we're going to have a bonanza of options," McDaniels said. "We could relocate to another floor and fortify that, but we can't do anything there we can't do here. And staying out on the roof is probably a non-starter, since all those things can see us. Eventually they'll figure out they can't get to us from another building, and they'll just surge up here in such numbers that we can't hold them off."

"It is a bit of a sticky wicket," Gartrell said. "But that's why you're an officer. I'll see to that weapon detail you wanted squared away while you think it over."

"Thanks, first sergeant."

"My mission is to make you seem even more amazing, major." With that, Gartrell headed off to ensure everyone's weapons received a basic cleaning and check before the MV-22 arrived. McDaniels wondered if that would include Rittenour and Leary, down on the first floor, but doubted it would. No one on the line stripped down a weapon to clean it when the goblins were right outside.

He wandered back into the kitchen and poured himself some more coffee, adding sugar to it to give it a little extra boost. He then found a pastry and chowed down on that as well, giving his body as much reactive fuel as possible. He figured he would need it all in about the next twenty minutes.

Earl wandered inside the kitchen and looked at McDaniels with his customary smile.

"Another ciggie?" he asked.

McDaniels thought about it, then shrugged and nodded. "What the hell."

"Well, let's go, then." Earl started to backtrack toward the door.

"Let's do it here, Earl. No one's going to care, and the ventilation's got to be better than what we have in the stairwell. We can douse 'em in the sink when we're done."

Earl seemed unusually reluctant, and McDaniels had to smile at that. He sipped his coffee and watched as Earl slowly shuffled over, pulling the pack of Marlboros from his front pocket.

"Not really supposed to smoke in the kitchen areas, but I guess it don't matter. 'Specially since we're leavin' soon, right?"

"Sounds like. First Sergeant Gartrell tells me the Marines are almost here. We'll be going upstairs in about fifteen minutes or so."

Earl grunted and held out a cigarette, then lit it with his lighter once McDaniels had parked the Marlboro in his mouth. McDaniels inhaled deeply while Earl lit his own smoke.

"Damn, this is just divine. Thank you, Earl."

"Well, you welcome, major."

McDaniels was content to allow a few seconds to slip past while he smoked and sipped his coffee. But those few moments he allowed himself expired quickly, and he circled back to what Gartrell had suggested. They needed a decent Plan B just in case Plan A went tits up and left them stranded with zeds pounding on the doors.

"Earl, that fire key you have, we can use it to take an elevator to any floor in the building, right?"

"That's right."

"Do you know if there's any sewer connection in the building? Or any kind of, I don't know, run off system that would be big enough for us to use to crawl out of here if we had to?"

Earl considered it for a moment. "Naw, nothin' like that. I saw the sewer pipes before, they ain't big enough for my little girl to crawl through. Not sure about anything else like you asked about. Maybe there's a way to the sewer tunnel in the street, but I don't know where that is. Why you askin'?"

"Well, we need a backup plan. Just in case things don't go so well for us on the roof."

"Oh. I see." Earl fell silent and puffed on his cigarette for a moment. "Could we drive out of the city?" he asked finally.

"How do you mean?"

"Well, like I said. Could we drive outta here?"

"Our vehicles are back in Central Park, Earl. We'd have a hell of a time getting to them and then getting back here to pull everyone out. Besides, we'd need a tank or something real heavy to drive over the stenches when they line up to eat our brains."

"What about an armored car?" Earl asked.

McDaniels did a double take. "Sorry?"

"An armored car. We have stuff like that in the garage. After 9/11, some of the execs got a van or an SUV or somethin' like that and made it all armored and shit. So they can drive around and not get shot, or somethin'." Earl shrugged. "They might not a needed it right after 9/11, but once the economy went into the shitter, there was all sorts of trouble from people wantin' to try and take on some of the investment folks, you know. Some real bad shit for a while there."

McDaniels took another drag off his cigarette and gathered his thoughts. "Earl... are you telling me there's an armored transport in this building?"

Earl rubbed his chin. His beard stubble was gray, and it stood out on his dark skin like feathery strokes of white-out correction fluid from the old days.

"Well, yeah. Somethin' like that, anyway."

McDaniels snorted and finished his cigarette. He turned to the sink and wetted down the butt, then tossed it into a nearby trash can. He looked back at Earl with a thin smile.

"Earl, you amaze me. You manage to hole up in this place and keep out of harm's way, and then you come up with a possible alternative for us to get the hell out of here. Well... at least the first step toward getting out of here, anyway. Thanks for that, you've just helped me save some face with my first sergeant. Now I can at least *pretend* I have the beginnings of a Plan B."

"That's good though, right?"

McDaniels clapped him on the shoulder. "That's more than good. That's just fucking magnificent, man."

Earl beamed.

***

"Holy fuck," Rittenour said. His voice was scarcely more than a choked whisper, and Leary automatically tensed. He pushed off from the cinderblock wall he'd been leaning against and joined Rittenour at the door. Rittenour was bigger than Leary and about thirty pounds heavier, so there was no way Leary could look past him and see anything through the small crack in the fire door.

"What is it?" he asked, voice low.

Rittenour slowly moved out of the way. "Take a look for yourself, man."

Leary stepped forward and pressed his helmeted head against the fire door. He peered out through the small crack between the door and the frame, which allowed him to look across a small sliver of the lobby. Beyond the pale marble floor, he could barely see the windows facing the street—which street it was, he could not remember, nor was it important to him.

Dark shapes loomed in the deepening night. Even though the streetlights were still on, most of the details were lost upon him, but from their aimless, shambling gait he knew the building was still surrounded by the walking dead. Only a few of them pressed against the windows, however; they had probably forgotten about the soldiers and civilians inside, but the lobby was brightly lit, and it doubtless attracted them. Leary wondered if they should work on a way to douse the lights.

Then another shape appeared, and Leary's eyes widened when it stepped into full view, brushing against the thick glass separating the lobby from the street. The figure wore the filthy remnants of battle dress utilities, and still had a helmet strapped to its head. Its eyes were wide and unblinking, and a bloodless gash had been opened across its chin, gaping like a second mouth. The zombie's eyes moved in its skull as it peered in and scanned the lobby.

"It's Mr. Keith," Leary whispered. "Jesus, Mr. Keith's a fucking *zed!*"

"I always knew the guy was a real stiff," Rittenour said, going for humor when none could be found. Leary glanced back at him, and saw the taller soldier was as shocked by this as he was. Death was nothing new to the troops who served in the nation's elite Special Forces branch, but seeing a teammate come back as a member of the walking dead was enough to tax anyone's neurons, not matter how hard core they were.

Leary looked out through the cracked door again. His former team leader examined the lobby with dead eyes, his—its?—bloodless lips moving in a silent cadence. Was it actually saying something? Leary thought not, but the thought that Keith's body might still be inhabited by some sort of residual intelligence merely served to ramp up the creep factor.

And then, to Leary's horror, Keith was joined by another uniformed special operator. And another. And another.

"Oh my God... it looks like the rest of the team is out there!" he said, his voice a strangled whisper. "I think I see Sanchez. And Larrabee. And Meltser!"

"Get out of the way, let me look." The two soldiers swapped places, and Rittenour peered through the opening. He was silent for a few moments as he took in the scene. The muscles of his jaw knitted as he clenched his teeth. Finally, he straightened and stepped back from the door, motioning Leary to take over. As the shorter soldier stepped back into position, Rittenour activated his radio.

"Major, this is Rittenour. Uh, we've got some pretty spooky shit happening down here. Looks like the rest of OMEN Team has found us, over."

13

The news of OMEN Team's arrival at the building caught McDaniels by surprise. He had been on his way to find Gartrell to discuss what Earl had told him when the message came over the radio. It stopped him dead in his tracks and it took a moment for him to process what Rittenour had said.

"This is Six. Say again, over."

"Major, this is Rittenour. Looks like several members of OMEN Team have, uh, reanimated. Leary and I can see them outside, over."

Gartrell appeared then, marching through the cafeteria to stand at McDaniels' side. The two men looked at each other, and McDaniels saw his "What the fuck?" expression reflected in Gartrell's face.

McDaniels chose his words carefully. "Let me get this straight, Ritt. You say you see members of OMEN outside the building... and they're zeds, correct? Over."

"Roger that, Six. That's *exactly* what I'm saying. Over."

"Wow, that's totally off the hook," Gartrell muttered.

"Rittenour, give me a count," McDaniels said.

"Trying to get that now, major. Stand by."

McDaniels put his hands on his hips, his thoughts whirling. Was the arrival of the team significant? If they were zeds, then there was very little chance it was intentional. Once a corpse was reanimated, there was no evidence intelligence remained in the corpse. But the Black Hawk the Special Forces team had been aboard went down right after takeoff. How was it they found their way to the building?

"Interesting that they should show up here," Gartrell said, apparently thinking along the same lines as McDaniels.

"Unnerving, is more like it. What do you make of it, first sergeant?"

Gartrell shrugged. "Well... there *is* a crashed helicopter right outside, after all..."

McDaniels hadn't considered that, and the notion gave rise to a new level of dread in his heart. *Jesus... even after they're dead, do these things still have memories? Is Keith trying to find us?*

"Is there a problem?"

Both men turned to see Regina Safire walking up on them, her hands in the pockets of her trousers. She looked from McDaniels to Gartrell and back to McDaniels again.

"Just a report from downstairs, ma'am. Nothing to worry about, our security posture remains the same." Gartrell used his best "you civilians wouldn't understand" tone, something he had previously reserved for inquires from various reporters during the time he had spent as McDaniels' team NCO in Afghanistan and Iraq. It was usually an effective response, one that almost always resulted in shutting down the civilian interrogator and sending him or her packing.

This was not one of those times. Regina was completely undeterred.

"So if nothing's changed, why do you guys look so spooked?"

"It's a spooky situation, Miss Safire," McDaniels said, a little testily. "We're in a pretty bad spot, and there's a lot going on with the rescue."

"Six, this is Rittenour. I count four OMEN guys outside. They still have most of their gear, but one guy—looks like Larrabee—well, something must've eaten his left arm, it's gone, only a tattered stump left." Rittenour paused, and McDaniels turned away from Regina and Gartrell and walked toward the windows. "This is a little weirder than I signed up for, major. Over."

"It's a little weirder than any of us were looking forward to, Ritt. You guys need to keep eyes on target down there. I don't like that these things just showed up all of a sudden. Not here, not now. Something about it stinks, over."

"Was that a pun, major? If so, it was a bad one, given we're surrounded by stenches. Over."

McDaniels looked down at the rain swept street below. The wind moaned as it hurtled past the corner and curved around its shape. Zeds of all shapes and sizes lingered about, some barely moving, others more active. They continued to shamble about in that mindless way of theirs, waiting with infinite patience for... what?

For food. For us.

"That was unintentional, Ritt, I swear. Listen, that MV-22 is inbound. Should be getting close now. When we give the word, you guys need to haul ass up here. But until we call, you two stay on top of things down there. Understood? Over."

"Got it, Six. We'll stay put until you call us up. Do you want us to blow the stairs when we pull back? Gotta tell you, sir, the concussion might be enough to bust some of the windows down here, and if the extraction gets FUBARed, we could be in a worse spot. Over."

"Roger that, Ritt. Negative on the demo... let's keep that in our hip pocket in case we need it. Over."

"Hooah on that, major. Over."

"That's all for now. Hang tight, you'll be hearing from us soon. Terminator Six, out." McDaniels ended the transmission.

"Is everything all right?" Regina asked. She stood just behind McDaniels. "Sounds like things are a little wobbly downstairs, maybe?"

"No such thing," McDaniels told her. "Everyone's still a hundred percent operational, Miss Safire. Updates do not necessarily mean a change in our circumstances, only additional intel that we have to take into account. Nothing more ominous than that."

She remained unconvinced, and he saw it in her green eyes. She evaluated him coolly for a long moment, then slowly nodded. Gartrell hovered over her right shoulder, automatically attaining an at rest stance.

"If you say so, major. But remember... you need my father alive, and if you hold back something that might interfere with that... well, I'm pretty sure your superiors won't like that, will they?"

"If something happens to your father on my watch, I don't give a damn what my commanding officers think," McDaniels snapped. "Because we'll all be dead. That's what it'll take for anything to happen to your father, Miss Safire. The rest of us will have to die first." He stepped closer to her, all business now, no more Mr. Nice Guy. Her eyes widened a bit in surprise, and she took a half step back.

Good. She gets it, McDaniels told himself.

"I understand, major. Sorry, didn't mean to offend you. I know you're doing the best job you can. It's just that... well..." Words seemed to fail her, and at the end, all she could do was offer an apologetic shrug.

"No offense taken," McDaniels told her, "but the constant needling from you and your father is pissing me off."

She nodded stiffly, and looked away from him. "Yes. As I said, I'm sorry."

"If the situation changes in any way, you'll be notified."

Regina nodded again, and smiled briefly when she looked back at him for an instant. "Thank you," she said, then turned to leave. She drew short, apparently surprised to find Gartrell so near. He stepped aside quickly, and she moved past him. The two men watched her return to the booth she shared with her father. If Safire had heard any of the exchange, he hadn't turned around to watch what was going on. That suited McDaniels fine. The less Wolf Safire said for the moment, the better off everyone would be.

Gartrell leaned toward him conspiratorially. "I don't know if you remember your boom lessons, sir, but if Ritt and Leary are in the stairwell when the charges go off, it'll ring their bells big time. They'll have to retreat to at least the fifth floor and secure the fire door before they can blow the charges."

"Are you recommending they pull back now?"

Gartrell shook his head. "No, sir—they need to stay where they are for now. But they are danger close, and some of those zeds can move pretty damned fast when they think they can get their snack on. I guess what I'm trying to say is, if they can't get to five quick enough, they'll have to blow the stairs, and probably go out doing it."

McDaniels nodded soberly. "I get it, first sergeant. But if we send anyone else into the stairwell, they could get rendered INOP as well. Unless you have an alternative?"

"Yeah. Pray like hell that nothing breaks through those lobby windows until after we're on that Osprey and bitching about the coffee service. Because if things go to shit, we're gonna be in a world of hurt, stairway or no stairway."

McDaniels nodded, but Finelly's hurried approach stopped him from responding any further. Gartrell turned and followed his gaze.

"What is it, sergeant?" he said when Finelly trotted up to them.

"Thunder's on the radio, first sergeant. They'll be on-station in five minutes, and they're requesting we deploy an IR strobe to help them navigate."

Gartrell turned to McDaniels. "And the mighty, mighty jarheads hath arriveth."

"You have them on your prick ninety, Finelly?" McDaniels asked.

"Yes, sir. Requested the strobe set up and number of souls to extract."

"Tell them twelve, and advise we have wounded as well as minors. And get the strobe set up. Hell, use all of 'em if you need to. Take Derwitz with you."

"Roger that," Finelly said, and he turned to go, his mind already on the job ahead. McDaniels grabbed his thick arm and jerked him to a halt.

"Stay in the game," he said, staring into Finelly's eyes. "Practice force protection, and keep your eyes open. We're not out of here yet, and for all we know, there are a dozen stenches in this building who just might happen to find their way to the stairs while we're busy waiting for our ride. It would be professionally embarrassing for all of us if someone get bit on the ass at this point in the game. Got it?"

Finelly nodded slowly. "Got it, sir."

McDaniels let him go. "Get on with it, then. Gartrell and I will get Jimenez ready and bring him and the Safires up to the roof once Thunder's on station. You send Derwitz down to us when they're ready for us. Good copy?"

"Good copy, major. You got it, sir."

"Move out."

Finelly turned and sprinted toward the corridor exit, beckoning Derwitz to follow him. McDaniels checked his watch. If all went well, they'd be uploaded and out of the hell hole New York City had become in fifteen minutes.

"Let's get Jimenez squared away," he told Gartrell.

14

The MV-22 bounced all over the place as it flew up the East River, its big rotors churning as they propelled the ungainly-looking aircraft through the wet night air. From his seat on the left side of the cockpit, the AC had a good view of the city. Parts of it were still lit up like normal, but vast swaths of lower Manhattan had fallen into darkness. Other isolated patches of darkness could be seen throughout the midtown section, as if a malignant cancer had begun to metastasize throughout the city. The lights of the Brooklyn and Manhattan bridges were dark, save for the strobing beacons atop NYPD vehicles and city fire trucks as they maintained cordons to protect the boroughs from the dead. To the right, the boroughs of Brooklyn and Queens were still alight, though for how long, the AC had no idea. Ahead loomed the Williamsburg Bridge, bright and shiny in the rainy night.

"Three klicks to target," the pilot said from the right seat.

"Roger." The AC kept his hands on the cyclic and collective pitch sticks, guiding the MV-22 up the river. Despite the rain and the mounting wind, some fires still burned in the city, and the sky was momentarily set alight by an explosion so brilliant that it overwhelmed the Osprey's forward-looking infrared scanner and the night vision goggles the two pilots wore. The AC swore as he flipped his goggles up on their swing away mount and looked through the MV-22's windscreen with nothing more sophisticated than the Mark I eyeball.

"What the hell was that?" the pilot asked.

"Gas station I think. Or maybe a tanker truck. Not really sure." Below, blue strobe lights flashed. The AC looked down as the aircraft thundered on, and saw the lights belonged to an NYPD launch. At least someone was still alive down there.

"NVGs are back," the pilot announced as he dropped his back over his eyes. The gallium-arsenide arrays had cleared themselves of the momentary whiteout caused by the explosion. He grabbed the FLIR's control yoke and panned the unit from side to side, ensuring its super-cooled optical planar array had not suffered any damage. The AC dropped his NVGs over his own eyes, and in the distance, he saw a metronomic flash.

"I have an IR beacon ahead and about ten degrees off the left nose," he reported. "Raise the Terminator team, tell them we'll be overhead in about thirty seconds. Aircrew, LZ is in sight—prepare the aircraft to transition to a hover!"

"On it," the pilot said, and he made the call.

"Checklist underway," said the senior crew chief from the back. As he and the other crew chief began to prepare the MV-22 for arrival, he turned to the Navy medic sitting on one of the long bench seats.

"We're almost there, so you'll have a patient soon," he said over the intercom.

The medic rolled his eyes. "How awesome."

***

Jimenez groaned when Gartrell and McDaniels helped him get into a sitting position. McDaniels could tell the aviation soldier hated himself for expressing his pain, but no one was superman. McDaniels squeezed his shoulder.

"I'm sorry, son. I know it hurts like a bitch, but the Osprey's coming in." As he spoke, McDaniels heard a rhythmic thumping that steadily grew louder. Right on cue, the MV-22 closed on the building.

"It's no problem, sir," Jimenez said. His voice almost bordered on a scream. McDaniels squeezed his shoulder again sympathetically and knelt beside him.

"You listen to me, soldier. You've been a total stud muffin this entire time. If you have to scream your head off while we carry you up those stairs, then you do it. No one's ever going to be able to convince me you're a girlie-man. Got that?"

Jimenez nodded slightly, and even that seemed to hurt him. "Yessir," he said.

"Major McDaniels is something of an expert when it comes to identifying girlie-men," Gartrell said as he knelt to the carpet on the other side of Jimenez. "Comes from a lifetime of actually being one." McDaniels met the first sergeant's gaze and shook his head. Now that transportation had arrived, people were starting to loosen up. Even Jimenez snorted a brief laugh.

Overhead, the sound of turbine-powered whirling rotors deepened, more felt than heard. McDaniels guessed the MV-22 had transitioned to a hover over the building. He looked out the windows for some sign of where the aircraft was, but there were no indicators, not even the reflection of flashing anti-collision beacons.

"Let's go NVGs for the transfer," he said to Gartrell, and both men reached for the PVS-7 night vision goggles in hard packs they wore on their belts. They clipped the devices to the mounts on their helmets and powered them up, testing them in the still-too-bright tepid lights of the cafeteria. Both units were fully functional.

McDaniels rose to his feet and beckoned to the Safires and the Browns. "Folks, we'll be leaving shortly—you can hear the transport, I'm sure. What's going to happen is that Sergeant Derwitz will come down to let us know when everything is stable upstairs, and he'll lead us to the roof. There will be lots of wind, both from the aircraft and from the storm itself, and rain. You'll want to keep your heads down. Sergeant Jimenez will be uploaded first via a rescue hoist, due to his injuries. After that, it will be the Safires, then you and your kids, Earl. The rest of us will come up after the Marines have you aboard. Derwitz and Finelly will lead you to the extraction point and fit the hoist harness around you. You will not move toward the hoist position until one of them physically takes you by the hand and leads you in. This is for your safety, so please, wait for them to do what they need to do.

"Questions?"

Zoe raised her hand immediately, and with such exuberance that it brought a smile to McDaniels' lips. "Yes, Miss Brown?"

"Can I sit up front?" she asked.

"Zoe!" Earl said, his tone one of scolding.

McDaniels and Gartrell laughed, as did Regina and Kenisha. Zoe looked around, confused by the laughter and the contrasting rebuke issued by her father. Safire, of course, merely sniffed.

"That's up to the Marines," McDaniels said. "And that's something else—once we're aboard the aircraft, they are in command. Follow their instructions to the letter. It'll be very loud inside the aircraft, but they'll give you headsets as soon as they can. In the meantime, once you're seated and strapped in, cover your ears with your hands and open your mouths, like this." He demonstrated the position. "This will help reduce the noise level and save your hearing. Anything else?"

"Where are we going?" Safire said. It hardly sounded like a question.

"We'll be flown out of the city and back to the USS *Wasp*, which is the Marine assault carrier in the Atlantic. After that, I don't know. But we can assume the *Wasp* will be the safest place for us to be."

Before anyone else could say anything, the door leading to the corridor opened. Gartrell and McDaniels turned toward it with weapons raised. Derwitz stood in the doorway, one hand on the door handle, the other on the grip of the MP5K strapped to his thigh. He was soaking wet, and his night vision goggles were flipped up on their mounts. McDaniels saw the green-white glow from their eye pieces as Derwitz faced him.

"We're ready, major," he said. "It's a bitch of a night out, so get ready for it." He released the door handle and darted forward, reaching for Jimenez. "Ready to go, Taco?" he asked.

"Oh yeah," Jimenez said. He gritted his teeth and winced as Derwitz and Gartrell hauled him to his feet. Derwitz went to gather him into a fireman's carry, but Gartrell stopped him with one hand.

"Let me take this, Night Stalker. You get everyone else ready for transport."

Derwitz hesitated for a moment, clearly not comfortable with allowing someone else to handle one of his own, but Jimenez pushed Derwitz away weakly.

"Help the major with the civilians, Maxi. The first sergeant can help me out of here."

Derwitz turned and pointed toward the door. "Everyone, out into the stairwell. The stairs going up will be to your right and straight ahead. You'll see some blood and stuff, but it's nothing to worry about." He turned back to McDaniels. "Finelly and I dragged the body down a couple of flights so they won't have to see it," he said, his voice pitched low.

"Good job," McDaniels replied in kind. Then louder, to the others: "All right, let's move out. Derwitz, you have the lead."

He turned and spotted Gartrell as he folded Jimenez over his shoulder as gently as he could, then hoisted up Gartrell's pack. Holding his M4 in one hand by its pistol grip and Gartrell's pack in the other, he followed the first sergeant as he carried Jimenez out of the cafeteria.

***

In the streets below, the walking dead raised their sallow faces toward the wet sky when the thundering rotor beats reached their ears. Though none of them knew what it was they saw, some primordial instinct that survived even death was able to alert them to it, to suggest with vague promises that it led to food. And this in turn led them to contemplate the building with the bright lobby that sat before them more earnestly. Moving slowly at first, then more hurriedly until they moved as fast as their dead ligaments and muscles would allow, the dead rushed toward the bright lights, drawn to it now like moths to open flame.

And at the vanguard of the dead army were corpses wearing the uniforms of the United States Army, uniforms that were subtly decorated with subdued Special Forces patches.

15

Derwitz had been right, it was a hellish night, made even worse by having an MV-22B in a hover overhead. The aircraft's rotors pounded like thunder even through McDaniels' hearing protectors and his radio headset. He dropped Gartrell's pack outside the open rooftop door and turned to help the first sergeant carry the wounded Jimenez up the stairs. Holding a hand up to at least attempt to ward off the rain from splashing across his NVGs, McDaniels looked up at the aircraft. It seemed higher than he would have liked, at least two hundred feet above the roof. It rocked back and forth in the wind, a dark silhouette against the lead-gray clouds.

"Why are they so God damn high?" Gartrell asked over the Special Forces radio net. He stood next to McDaniels, stooped slightly beneath Jimenez's weight across his shoulder.

McDaniels pointed toward the buildings that surrounded the one they stood on, several of which were taller. "They must be afraid the wind's going to drive them into one of the other buildings. Looks to me like they can just barely handle what Mother Nature's throwing at them now."

Finelly stood several yards away with his back toward them. The infrared strobe lights that marked out the landing zone flashed, illuminating his silhouette through McDaniels' NVGs. Finelly's face was turned skyward, and his hands were held out from his sides. His gear sat several feet behind him; he only wore his body armor and weapons. Behind him, Derwitz lined the civilians against the stairway wall so they would be out of the lion's share of the pounding rotor wash. Then he shucked his own gear and joined McDaniels and Gartrell. He pointed up at the Osprey as it fought to maintain its hover.

"Litter coming down for Jimenez!" he shouted, and his voice was distant and tinny above the rotor noise. "I'll lead you out there, first sergeant. Major, you stay back here with the civilians!"

McDaniels shot Derwitz a thumbs-up. He looked up and saw the Stokes litter descending from the MV-22's side-mounted hoist. The litter swung crazily in the air, and he was thankful he wasn't the one who would be riding it up. He watched as it dropped low enough for Finelly to hold it steady while more cable was paid out. Finelly dropped the metal litter to the rooftop and waved Derwitz forward.

"Let's go, first sergeant!" Derwitz helped Gartrell advance against the vortex of wind-driven rain and mist. When they got to the litter, Derwitz pinned it to the deck while Finelly helped Gartrell with Jimenez. Working carefully but with practiced efficiency, they strapped the injured man into the litter. Finelly motioned Gartrell back, and the first sergeant retreated to the relative safety of the stairwell.

"How is out there?" McDaniels asked.

"It's like a day at Club Med. Only colder. And windier. And shittier."

McDaniels watched as Derwitz and Finelly finished securing Jimenez to the litter. Both men stood up and made hand signals to the MV-22, which continued to sway and bob overhead. Finelly held one hand against his face, shielding his boom microphone from the wind as he communicated with the aircraft's flight crew. The cable grew taut as the slack was reeled in, and then the litter slid across the rooftop before springing into the air. It swung back and forth like a pendulum, and Derwitz had to dive to the roof to miss being clipped across the head. He scrambled to his feet, and both he and Finelly moved back.

Overhead, the MV-22's engines shrieked as they labored to keep the aircraft stable in the storm.

***

In the MV-22, both pilots were on the controls, fighting to keep the aircraft steady in the punishing crosswinds. The wind on the Osprey's nose kept changing with such rapidity that they encountered the control limits several times.

"It's the fucking buildings," the co-pilot said. "They keep breaking up the wind flow!"

"Aircrew, how are we doing back there?" the AC asked over the intercom.

"We're hooked up, patient is on his way," the senior crew chief said.

"Get him aboard as quick as you can. This is becoming a furball!"

"Oo-rah, sir!"

The MV-22 began vibrating suddenly. At the same time, an alarm sounded as both pilots looked at the flight displays on the instrument panel.

"Ring vortex state! Advance the nacelles six degrees, we're settling!" the AC shouted as the MV-22 began a slow, steady slew to the left. He shoved the cyclic to the right and stomped on the right pedal, but nothing took. The aircraft's left rotor, though still operational, had entered a condition known as vortex ring state. The rotor disk passed through its own turbulence wake, which sheared away the lift generated by the whirling blades. As the copilot advanced the nacelles and tilted the rotors slightly forward, the MV-22 continued its slew while descending at the same time. The rotors' angle of attack changed slightly, slicing through more-or-less undisturbed air which allowed them to recover. Though still left wing low, the MV-22's left rotor developed sufficient power to halt its descent.

But at the same time, the winds changed yet again and pressed against the undersides of MV-22B Osprey's wings and fuselage. It was like someone had walked up and given the aircraft a strong shove, knocking it off balance, sending it stumbling toward a building across the street from the LZ.

***

McDaniels knew things were headed south when he saw the MV-22B heel hard over. He had no idea what had happened, but the giant tiltrotor aircraft slewed to the left like an out of control car sliding across an icy highway. The tempo of its rotors changed as its engine nacelles tilted forward, as if the Marines had called it a day and were pulling out. Below the aircraft, the litter containing Jimenez snapped from one side to the other, a victim of runaway centrifugal force.

Finelly and Derwitz turned and ran for the roof door, the latter waving McDaniels back.

"Get down, get down, get down!" he shouted, his voice barely audible above the din of the storm and the aircraft that was fighting for its life overhead. Gartrell stood right next to McDaniels, looking up at the crazing tiltrotor through his NVGs; if he had heard the Night Stalker's warning, he didn't react to it. McDaniels reached out and grabbed Gartrell's arm and yanked him back just as the Osprey's left rotor disk struck the building across the street. Glass, steel, and composite rotors came together in an explosive cacophony of sound. As McDaniels leaped back, he saw the MV-22B suddenly bounce back and right itself, like a drunk who had been fortuitous enough to find a wall to steady himself against. It side slipped back toward their building, its belly now only twenty feet above the rooftop. The rotor wash was intense, and Finelly was blown halfway across the roof. The stokes litter still hung from the rescue hoist on the right side of the aircraft, and the Marine manning it held onto the hoist's frame for dear life. The litter slammed to the rooftop and the line attaching it to the hoist went suddenly slack as the MV-22 descended toward it.

"Everybody get back!" McDaniels shouted as Derwitz fairly flew past him and collided with Gartrell, sending both men sprawling down the stairs. McDaniels watched in horror as the MV-22 settled right on top of the Stokes litter—and Jimenez—crushing it into the roof. The aircraft rebounded again, springing into the air like a cat before it listed once more to the left.

And then, the Osprey rolled over the side of the roof as it turned onto its back, falling to the street below. The litter, still attached to the hoist, followed the big machine like a faithful dog.

"Ritt, Leary, the Osprey's crashing!" McDaniels shouted over the Special Forces net as he stumbled down the stairs. He jumped over Gartrell and Derwitz and grabbed Safire, who stood safe and dry on the landing, and hauled him through the fire door as the MV-22B finally hit the street below.

***

The MV-22B Osprey's flight control computers couldn't read the situation for what it was quickly enough, and the aircraft's level of bank passed through 45 degrees, left wing low.

By the time the feather command had been sent and the right engine's rotor system was rolled back, it was too late. The Osprey slowly flipped over onto its back and spiraled toward the traffic-choked concrete of Lexington Avenue. It crashed into the street with enough force to shatter the fuselage and kill everyone aboard. Though designed to be ballistically tolerant, the machine's fuel tanks couldn't withstand the force of the impact. Fuel ejected from the tanks, atomizing once it hit the air. It was then drawn into the still-running number two engine and ignited. The resulting explosion sent a fireball climbing into the air, incinerating Jimenez's corpse as it fell toward the aircraft, still strapped to the crushed Stokes litter. The explosion was forceful enough to rattle windows and cause several secondary detonations as the fuel tanks of passenger vehicles ignited. The flames reached out against the wind and rain and consumed everything that was flammable, including dozens of nearby zombies.

"Holy shit!" Rittenour screamed, even though he had heard McDaniels' warning. The building shook and rumbled, and when he looked outside past the fire door, he saw the streets beyond the lobby windows as if the sun had risen. There were thousands of zombies beyond the glass. *Thousands.*

And the reanimated corpse of CW3 Keith was still there, looking directly at the fire door Rittenour and Leary hid behind. He—it!—ignored the flaming maelstrom behind as the fire raged on, feeding off the JP-8 jet fuel the Osprey had carried in its tanks.

"Oh man, we are so *fucked!*" Leary said. "What are we gonna do?"

"Shut up, man!" Rittenour kept his eyes on his former commander and keyed his microphone button. "Terminator Six, Osprey is down in the street. It's a total write-off. Can't see how any of the Marines might have survived, over." When there was only silence in response, Rittenour grew slightly agitated. "Terminator Six, can I get a SITREP from you, over?"

Shit, are they all dead? Were they on the Osprey?

"Is it just us now?" Leary asked, apparently thinking the same thing as Rittenour. Rittenour only shrugged.

"Six is still with you, stand by," McDaniels reported suddenly.

"Roger that, Six." Rittenour looked outside as the zeds attacked the lobby windows once again. Obviously, they'd finally determined that Rittenour and Leary were in the stairwell. The zombies swelled against the glass windows, which were still remarkably intact even after the explosion and fire caused by MV-22B crash. It was disgusting to watch, all that putrefying flesh pressed up against the glass, frantically pounding on it with hands, feet, faces. But the ones in the Army uniforms, the ones who had been Rittenour's teammates... they weren't having any of that. They just stood there amidst the crush of the bodies piling up behind them, probing the glass with their hands. They pushed against it, but did not pound it with their fists. Rittenour moved slightly to his left and reached behind him. He grabbed a handful of Leary's uniform blouse and pulled him toward the door.

"Check out what Keith and the other guys are doing," he said. He had to raise his voice to be heard above the ruckus outside.

Leary peered through the crack, eyes narrowed. After a moment, he made a *hmm* sound in his throat and stepped back from the door.

"You know what that looks like to me? It looks like they're trying to remember what glass is," Leary said. "It's like they forgot."

"But it looks like they might figure it out," Rittenour said. "See how the other stenches are going ape shit against it? Man, you'd need a fucking sledgehammer and about four hours to break through that glass, it's thick. But our guys are being more... methodical."

Leary nodded slowly. "Roger that."

"Ground, this is Six. We lost Jimenez, he went down with the Osprey. The rest of us are all right. What's the situation down there? Over."

Rittenour filled in the major as succinctly as he could. McDaniels asked him a few follow on questions, which Rittenour answered as best as they were able.

"Six, it really kind of looks like they know we're in here," he said. "Not just Keith and the others, but all the zeds. They're going hog wild against the glass. Over."

"Understood. Are you sure the glass is holding all around the lobby? Over."

"Roger that, sir—uh Six, stand by, something going on outside." Rittenour released his microphone button and leaned forward, looking through the crack in the door. "What the fuck is going on?" he asked.

Leary squatted and tried to look past Rittenour's body, but couldn't see anything. "I can't see shit, so you tell me."

Rittenour watched as the remnants of OMEN team slowly pushed back through the crowd of thrashing zombies behind them. They acted simultaneously, as if of one mind. Then Keith raised its arm and threw something toward the glass. There wasn't a great deal of force behind the throw, but Rittenour's eyes practically bugged out of his head when he saw the hand grenade bounce off the glass.

"Let's move!" he shouted. He pulled the door closed and bolted up the steps. Leary didn't bother to ask for a reason, he merely followed, taking the steps two at a time.

Behind them, the grenade went off outside the lobby with a loud report that was followed immediately by the sound of a river of glass cascading to the floor. And after that, the moaning rush of zombies picking their way across the debris filled the stairwell.

"Terminator Six, the lobby's been breached!" Rittenour reported as they bolted up the stairs. "OMEN team dropped a grenade outside and took out the windows. We have zeds in the lobby!"

McDaniels came back immediately. "Can you detonate the charges from the fifth floor? If you blow them while you're in the stairwell, you could get zeroed. Over."

"Roger that, Terminator, we'll give it a shot, over." Racing up to the third floor landing, Rittenour stopped and turned. Leary came up the steps behind him, and Rittenour waved him on.

"Get to five," he said. "Open the fire door and wait for me, I'll be right up."

"What are you waiting for?" Leary asked.

"Don't fuck around asking questions, move your ass! Go!"

Leary hesitated for a moment longer, then charged up the stairs.

Rittenour turned away and looked down the stairwell as he heard the door open. The zombies boiled in then, moaning, hissing. Looking down the gap between the handrails, he caught glimpses of them as they mounted the stairs as fast as their dead legs could carry them.

He didn't see any uniforms, and that bothered him. Where were the military zeds? Why weren't they in the lead?

Can zeds practice force protection? he wondered as he pounded up the steps.

Fourth floor. Leary bounded up the stairs for the fifth floor, with Rittenour right behind him. As he climbed, Rittenour pulled the remote detonator from its pouch on his side and flipped open the covered safety switch. The charges were armed now.

"Six, the charges are armed, will be setting them off in less than fifteen seconds!" he screamed into his headset microphone as Leary made it to the fifth floor landing. He darted toward the fire door, ripped it open, and dove inside. Rittenour hurried after him; right behind him, he heard the zombies bolting up the stairs, moving faster than he had thought possible. There was only a landing separating them.

Then when he felt something grab onto his back pack, he realized there wasn't even that. Rittenour stumbled on the steps, and that was enough. The zombie shrieked as it grabbed his back pack and hauled itself onto him. The added weight made Rittenour stumble again, and this time he went down on the fifth floor landing.

Leary knelt in the still open doorway, his M4 shouldered and ready to fire. And fire he did, one round that made a loud *snap!* as it hurtled past Rittenour's head at almost 900 miles per hour. The zed clinging to Rittenour's back pack fell off suddenly, and he kicked at it as he scrambled back to his feet. He looked at Leary as he headed for the door. He heard more zeds rolling up the stairs.

"Going for it now, bro," he told Leary. His thumb moved to the remote detonator's trigger.

Leary threw himself back into the office area as hell exploded into being behind Rittenour.

16

McDaniels was just closing the fire escape door on the 27th floor when the building shook. Gartrell spun around to face him as a whistling sound reached McDaniels' ears; it was the explosion's over-pressure wave, rushing up the stairwell. It hit full force and slammed the door closed, knocking McDaniels off balance. Gartrell grabbed him and steadied him on his feet.

"What was that?" Safire said. There was panic in his voice. He held Regina close to him, and she clung to her father's narrow shoulders, eyes wide with fear. Earl had his arms around both of his daughters, and his youngest had her face pressed against his chest. Her shoulders shook. She was weeping.

McDaniels ignored the question and kicked open the fire door. He and Gartrell stepped into the stairwell and peered down between the hand rails. A cloud of dust was visible far below them.

"Ground, this is Six! Ritt, Leary, give me a SITREP, over!" McDaniels checked his M4 while waiting for a reply. The weapon was still cocked and locked, and he flipped off the safety. Wet wind swirled about in them, spilling in through the still-open roof door. It banged back and forth on its hinges, batted about by the wind.

"Rittenour, Leary, give me your status, over!" McDaniels said after several seconds had passed.

He heard gunshots from below, and a single shout.

"Watch over the Safires," McDaniels said, then bolted down the stairs. Gartrell caught up to him on the next landing and grabbed the collar of his uniform, yanking McDaniels to a halt.

"No way, major. This is my territory. *You* watch after the Safires. I'll see to the men." Gartrell's expression was flat and emotionless—his war face. Movement above and behind the men made him look past Gartrell's shoulder. Finelly and Derwitz stood on the landing. Both of them appeared utterly shell-shocked, still down and out after the MV-22 crash and the sudden explosion in the stairwell. Finelly bled from an open cut on his cheek, probably sustained when he had been blown across the roof. One of Derwitz's eyes was swollen, a prize from falling headlong down the stairs.

"What's the op, major?" It was Derwitz who spoke, not Finelly. A surprising turn of events, McDaniels thought.

"You two are going to stay here with the major and keep watch over the civilians," Gartrell said. "I'm headed down to see what's going on with Ritt and Leary." As he spoke, Gartrell stared straight into McDaniels' eyes, as if daring him to counter. McDaniels outranked Gartrell by miles, but the senior NCO was much closer to where the rubber met the road, and his battlefield skills were beyond redoubt.

"I'm not so sure you should be going alone, first sergeant," McDaniels said.

"I'll be good. Make sure the aviators don't do anything stupid, like have a food fight or something. I have a feeling that any eggs we have in the kitchen are all we're going to have for a good long time."

And with that, Gartrell pushed past McDaniels and bolted down the stairs, his big AA-12 automatic shotgun held before him like a shield. McDaniels watched him go, then turned and trudged back up the stairs.

"Let's get this floor secure," he told Finelly and Derwitz.

***

First Sergeant David Gartrell pushed himself down the stairs as fast as he could go without slipping and breaking his ass. The stairwell was filled with an acrid odor that grew stronger as he descended: the remains of the explosives, cordite from gunfire, and unless he was wrong, the odious reek of the dead. He wondered how many had made it up the stairs before the first few flights were destroyed, and decided it could be anywhere from one or two to a dozen or more. At any rate, he'd find out pretty soon.

"Ritt, Leary, this is Gartrell. I'm on my way down to you guys now. Passing the twentieth floor, over."

There was no reply, and that was worrisome. Gartrell had no idea what he was walking into, but he heard sporadic gunfire from below—not from the stairwell, but from inside the building itself. Which meant Rittenour and Leary were trapped on a floor and had been engaged by the stenches.

He heard something above his own footfalls and stopped on the next landing. Stumbling footsteps echoed in the stairway below him, growing steadily louder. Gartrell checked his NVGs, still on the mount attached to his helmet, then took a moment to pull his light cotton gloves tight on his hands. Peering over the edge of the handrail, he saw flashes of movement below. Whoever they were, *whatever* they were, they had climbed above the slowly-settling cloud of dust below.

Gartrell whistled loudly. The figures climbing up the stairs moved even faster, and one of them looked up the center of the stairwell. A pale, gaunt face with shrunken eyes and scraggly hair turned toward Gartrell. When it saw him, it opened its mouth and released a lingering moan that continued even after it had pushed away from the handrail and took off up the stairs again.

Zombies. Of course, they have to be fucking zombies.

Gartrell keyed his radio switch. "Six, this is Five. I'm on eighteen, have zeds coming up the stairs toward me. Don't know how many, but if it's more than fifty or so, I think we can upgrade our condition from 'totally screwed' to 'absolutely fucked', over."

"How long until they reach you? Can you fall back? Over."

Gartrell peered over the railing again. "Contact in less than ten seconds. I can hear gunfire below me. Ritt and Leary are still kicking. Will report my progress to you as soon as I can—if the shooting stops and you don't hear from me, that's probably not an awesome sign. Five out," he said, as the first zombie mounted the landing below Gartrell and charged up the stairs. Gartrell hadn't expected it to be a child, but there it was, a little girl in her pink pajamas, her neck a ravaged mass of torn flesh that was turning black as the fluids there dried into a crust. Its eyes remained focused on him, and did not blink; when Gartrell raised the AA-12, the zombie accelerated toward him, as if eager to face the weapon and be released from the hell it was confined to. Gartrell obliged, and the tungsten-core round destroyed the zombie's skull. As it sank to the stairs, another zed appeared, and another, and another. These were adults now, not children, and Gartrell dispatched them with mechanical precision. The AA-12 rounds didn't just destroy their heads—it absolutely obliterated them. In a matter of moments, Gartrell had dispatched four zombies without even breaking a sweat. It was much easier engaging them in the stairwell than outside on the street. He pressed on, stepping over the bodies, grimacing in disgust. Not only were they smelly, the shotgun blasts had left pulped viscera all over the place.

"Major, Gartrell. I'm through the first wave, making my way down to seventeen. Break. Rittenour, Leary, come in." Now that he knew that zeds had managed to make it past the stairways rigged with charges, he had to press on with more care. He didn't want to run headlong into a group of stenches because he wasn't paying enough attention.

Just the same, it almost happened. Gartrell came around the corner on the tenth floor landing, and there was a tall, reedy stench with a shining bald head and pale blue eyes advancing up the opposite stairway. When it saw him, it lurched toward him with thin, outstretched arms. It was dressed in a filthy white dress shirt and khaki pants that would have been too baggy and ill-fitting even if the corpse had been a living man. Its bald head was surrounded by a fringe of long, greasy hair, and most of its nose was missing. So was its entire lower jaw, which made Gartrell laugh as he backpedaled from the stench and raised his shotgun.

"Dude, you don't have a jaw! How the hell are you gonna be able to eat me?" he asked. As if in answer, the zed groaned and stumbled across the last step and fell face-first to the landing. It grabbed Gartrell's boot with one hand.

The AA-12 roared once again, and the dead zed count went to five.

Gartrell resumed his descent, trying to reach Rittenour and Leary on the radio after he cleared every landing. Still no response, and the gunfire had stopped. As he pushed past the seventh floor landing, the dust had mostly cleared. He felt a cool breeze whisper up the stairwell. Gartrell moved more cautiously now. Most of the lights had been broken by the blast. Chunks of concrete became more numerous on the steps the closer he got to the fifth floor. When he descended to just above the fifth floor landing, he saw three stenches lying where they had been gunned down. Black ichor leaked from their ravaged skulls.

Gartrell leaned over the hand rail and looked down. All he saw was blackness, broken sporadically by a light here, a light there. The charges had apparently done their job—the stairs were completely *gone*, nothing more than a pile of rubble far below. He straightened and looked toward the fifth floor fire door. It had buckled inward from the blast and the attendant shock wave, and it hung drunkenly in the mangled doorframe by one hinge. He saw several hashes of blood on the door, and more on the doorframe. Zeds had pushed their way inside. That explained the gunfire.

Gartrell slowly moved toward the door and peered inside the office. The lights were dimmed, but he could still see part of the floor. A stench lay face down on the carpet, a wide furrow blasted through its head. A distance away, another one—an obese woman in a loud flowery dress—reclined in similar repose, its chubby-cheeked face turned toward him, its eyes gazing off in different directions below the ravaged skull. Gartrell was about to push through the door when a slow movement caught his eye to the left. Whatever it was, it moved among the shadows on the far side of the office floor. He reached up and dropped his NVGs in front of his eyes. They automatically flipped out of standby mode, and the light amplification tubes powered up.

Walking along the offices on the far side of the floor was a zed. Its mouth was wide open, and a flap of skin hung across one eye, bobbing as the corpse shuffled along the carpet. It seemed that Rittenour or Leary had shot at this one, but hadn't scored a kill. Gartrell could rectify that, but he would want to get closer. The first sergeant slowly eased himself onto the office floor, looking to his left and right to ensure nothing lay in wait. The zombie didn't see him, because the flap of skin hung across its right eye. But if it had the common sense to turn its head, it would be able to zero in on him clearly.

And just as he thought it, the stench did just that. It moaned loudly when it saw Gartrell, and immediately charged down the aisle toward him.

Three other zeds moaned as well, and Gartrell was surprised to see them emerge from several cubes. One of them was fast, real fast. Before Gartrell could turn the AA-12 on it, it sprinted toward him, covering the twenty or so feet that separated them in what seemed to be a blink of an eye. He let go of the shotgun and met the oncoming zed head-on. It leaped for him, and Gartrell grabbed one of its wrists in his hand and flung the corpse over his hip. It crashed into a nearby water fountain, severely denting its stainless steel casing. The zed didn't even seem to care; it clawed its way to its feet. Gartrell was ready for it, and as the corpse whirled upon him again, he sank his knife through the top of its skull. The zed stiffened, then fell to the carpeted floor, where it hissed and kicked and slashed at the air. Gartrell was disappointed the knife attack hadn't killed the thing, but at least it rendered it inoperative for the moment.

He seized a hold of the AA-12 and spun as another zed closed upon him, this one being an entirely nude woman. He didn't have time to aim for the head, so he merely blasted away at the corpse's midsection and blew it ten feet away. It collapsed to the floor with its face and buttocks pointed in more or less the same direction. The shotgun blast had completely severed its spine, leaving the zombie grotesquely twisted. But it was still operational; even though its legs couldn't work, the thing started crawling back to him.

The zombie Gartrell had seen initially bore down on him. An office door popped open then, and Leary stepped out of the darkened room, his M4 shouldered and ready. He took aim and fired once as Gartrell jumped to his left. The 5.56mm bullet found its target, and the zombie's forehead exploded outward in a spreading flower of brackish blood and putrid gray matter. It fell to the floor face-first next to the fat woman in the flowery dress.

Leary pumped his fist in the air. "I GOT YOU, YOU FUCK!" he shouted.

Gartrell turned to the last zed that was still moving, and was surprised to see it was an Orthodox Jew, complete with yarmulke and black suit. It moaned at Gartrell as it hobbled toward him, its mouth a black maw surrounded by a matted gray beard. Gartrell dropped it before it got within fifteen feet of him.

"GOOD SHOOTING, FIRST SERGEANT!" Leary shouted as he ran up. He put a round through the broken zombie crawling on the floor, and its movements stilled.

"GOT THAT ONE!" he reported.

Gartrell said, "Leary, where's Rittenour?"

Leary turned and looked around the darkened office with unaided eyes. His NVGs were still in their pouch on his belt. He advanced down the row of cubicles with his rifle shouldered, and began clearing them systematically.

"Leary? *Leary!*" Gartrell shouted. "Where the hell is Rittenour?"

"Right here, first sergeant." Rittenour appeared then, walking out from behind a file cabinet he'd been hiding behind. He looked down at the zombie thrashing about on the floor. It made no attempt to pull the knife from its skull, nor did it seem to know the men were even there.

"Man, that's some weird shit," Rittenour observed.

Gartrell slapped him on the arm. "Hey dumbass, why didn't you answer the radio?"

"Huh? Oh... I guess it got busted in the blast. I've been trying to transmit our SITREP for a few minutes, in between hosing zeds. You didn't hear me?"

"Negative. Why didn't Leary answer?"

"Because he's —"

Leary appeared beside Gartrell and tapped him on the shoulder. He pointed to the shuddering corpse on the floor when Gartrell turned to him.

"THAT'S SOME STRANGE SHIT HUH, FIRST SERGEANT? WE OUGHT TO SHOOT THAT THING AND GET YOUR KNIFE BACK."

"Leary! Stop shouting!" Gartrell said. "What the hell is wrong with you, you go fucking deaf?"

"He did," Rittenour said. "He wasn't wearing any hearing protection when the charges went off."

"What? Why the fuck not?" Gartrell turned back to Leary. "Where the hell is—"

"SORRY FIRST SERGEANT, BUT I CAN'T HEAR YOU! MY EARS ARE REALLY RINGING, LIKE—" He stopped when Gartrell clamped his hand across Leary's mouth. The first sergeant stared right into his eyes.

"Leary! Read my lips—shut... the fuck... *up!*" When Leary nodded, Gartrell removed his hand.

"SORRY FIRST SERGEANT, WAS I TALKING TOO LOUD?"

Gartrell shook his head and turned back to Rittenour. "Are either of you hurt?"

Rittenour shook his head. "Negative. Some bumps and bruises, but no bites or anything like that."

"Good. Recharge your weapons and get ready to move out. We're going back up to twenty-seven. And you're in charge of Copernicus here." Gartrell jerked his thumb over his shoulder at Leary. "I'm going to check out the damage to the stairway."

"Be careful, first sergeant. OMEN's still out there."

Gartrell nodded as he pushed his way past the twisted door. "Roger that. Get squared away ASAP." He shoved the door open as far as it would go, its bottom scraping across the concrete floor. Cautiously, he picked his way down the debris-strewn stairway that went nowhere. Where there should have been a landing and a return to another set of stairs, there was nothing but gloomy darkness, but the NVGs revealed all in stark green and white imagery. The fourth floor landing and all those below it were gone, a mass of rubble at the bottom of the stairwell. Gartrell slowly looked over the edge. The zombies swarmed about down there; dozens of them had shoved their way into the stairwell. They moaned as if one when they saw him and reached upward, as if they could somehow pull him from his high perch. Gartrell realized that even though the zeds were in almost total darkness due to the lights being blasted out, there were still lights shining above and behind him, which meant he was presented to them as a clear silhouette. Cursing himself for forgetting such a basic soldiering skill, Gartrell climbed back to the fifth floor landing. Rittenour and Leary were waiting for him. Gartrell looked at Leary and held a finger before his lips. Leary nodded. Gartrell pointed to the stairway and motioned for them to start climbing up. As the two soldiers mounted the stairs, Gartrell hung back, wondering what could be done about the zombies massing below.

Nothing, he decided. He followed the Special Forces soldiers instead, and once they were on the tenth floor, he made a quick report to McDaniels. Plan B was looking pretty good right now.

17

Once Gartrell and the rest of the soldiers had returned to the 27th floor, McDaniels gave them some time to rest. Rittenour and Leary looked pretty worn down, especially the latter, who complained about a constant ringing in his ears which was slowly subsiding. Regina Safire examined him as well as she could, and determined that he didn't have perforated ear drums, but that tinnitus might be something he should consider getting used to. McDaniels sent them to the men's room to wash up, then get some chow.

"You too, first sergeant," McDaniels said. "Take a load off for the moment."

"We really need to plan our next move, major," Gartrell said. "Those things are still down there, and if what Ritt says is true, then OMEN is just that—a real bad sign."

"I track that, first sergeant. Just the same, take a few minutes to get yourself squared away."

Gartrell wanted to resist that, but he finally nodded. "Hooah." And with that, he headed for the kitchen.

McDaniels returned to the dining area. He motioned to Finelly and Derwitz, who stood near the door leading to the corridor. When they approached, McDaniels looked at them critically.

"Someone has to keep a good overwatch in the stairwell," he told them. "I need both of you out there with booger hooks on the bang levers. Position yourselves so one is below the other, but stay in sight of each other. Swap positions every ten minutes or so, and keep at least one weapon pointed downrange at all times. Keep your ears open. Those things tend to make a lot of noise to begin with, but who knows... if OMEN team is with them, and if they have any sort of skill retention, they might use stealth."

"Got it, sir," Finelly said.

"Keep it tight, troops. Remember your training?"

"Hooah," both soldiers replied in unison. McDaniels nodded to them, and they stepped out of the cafeteria. McDaniels made to follow them, but Safire's voice stopped him.

"Your dead friends are very interesting, Major McDaniels," he said. He sat at the booth he had occupied earlier, another bottle of water before him, enshrouded by shadow. McDaniels couldn't see his face clearly.

"That's a word for it," McDaniels said, turning to walk away.

Safire rose. "We thought there might be a possibility that the newly dead could retain some memories," he continued. "Memories like where they used to live, work, things like that. But we'd thought that more complex tasks, such as operating machinery, even door knobs, were beyond them. That whatever electrochemical activity remained in their dead brains couldn't possibly process complex actions. But your soldiers threw a grenade through the lobby windows?"

"It does seem that Mr. Keith tossed a live grenade at the lobby windows and blew them open," McDaniels said. "I'm not sure if that equals a 'complex action', as you call it."

"How many moves does it take to use a grenade?" Safire asked.

McDaniels shrugged. "Four, maybe. Pull the weapon, compress the safety, remove the pin, and throw it. Five, if you include stepping back, which Sergeant Rittenour said they did."

"They all stepped back." Safire rubbed his chin and slowly walked toward McDaniels. His eyes narrowed behind his glasses. "So it wasn't just—Keith, his name is?—it wasn't just him who stepped back. Of course, he threw the grenade, so perhaps some sort of muscle memory made him drop back. But the others? That indicates a shared understanding of consequence. They knew the grenade could damage their bodies."

McDaniels nodded. "But the explosion wouldn't kill them, as they happen to be already dead."

"No... but it could damage them. Make them slower. Less able to effectively hunt." Safire looked at McDaniels directly. "This is something we'd never observed before, but we never had trained soldiers to work with. It seems to me that procedural memory is strong in them. I would presume that throwing a grenade is practiced routinely in the military?"

"Somewhat," McDaniels said. "Not as often as gunnery practice with an assault rifle or pistol, but grenade practice is something that's taught in the Army from the very beginning." He paused, considering what Safire was hinting at. "So you think Keith and the others, they'll be able to use their weapons against us as well?"

"More than that, major. They apparently still have the ability to *plan*."

Not what I wanted to hear, McDaniels thought.

"In your estimation... how effectively could they plan their moves against us?" he asked, even though he was sure he wouldn't like the answer.

"I don't know, major. How effectively could they plan before they died?"

"I'm told that CW3 Keith was an exceptional Alpha Detachment leader. I'm not familiar with his service record, but I do know that he and OMEN team carried out complicated operations in Afghanistan against the Taliban and al Qaeda. Seems to me they were a cut above, to a man."

"Better than you, would you say?"

McDaniels shrugged. "Sure."

Safire returned to the booth and sat down heavily. Regina slid in across from him, and looked from her father to McDaniels.

"Then our problems are very likely going to get quite a bit worse," Safire said finally.

McDaniels had nothing to counter that, so he put a hand on the holstered sat phone and stepped into the corridor outside.

***

The rain and wind hadn't eased when McDaniels climbed back to the roof, so he stayed just inside the stairwell to make the satphone call.

"Terminator, Rapier. Good to hear from you. When we got word that Thunder Three's ELT had gone off, we thought the worst had happened," said the USASOC radio operator. The relief was evident in his voice, but McDaniels couldn't bring himself to give a damn.

"The worst did happen, pal. All those Marines and one of the Night Stalkers died. Their airplane is still burning in the street. Pass on to their commander that Thunder Three is down, all KIA."

"Roger that, Terminator. Any other fatalities? Over."

McDaniels took the time to brief the operator on everything that had occurred since their last communication. When he spoke of the appearance of OMEN team's leader and how the zombies had used a hand grenade to blast through the lobby windows, the operator grew very quiet. McDaniels finished with their present circumstances, that they were still trapped in the building but had blown out the stairs so they were safe for the moment.

"Uh... Terminator, this is Rapier... you say that members of OMEN Team conducted forced entry ops against the building. And you're *sure* these guys are zeds? Over."

"Absolutely one hundred percent sure, Rapier. Safire seems to feel that the recent dead can access some parts of their brains... 'procedural memory', he called it. It means not only can our guys can remember drills and the like, they might still be able to recall tactics and skills. Enough to make our lives even more difficult than they already are. Over." There was a long pause, and McDaniels wondered if the connection was still good. "Rapier, you copy all that? Over."

"Roger, Terminator. Rapier's got good copy. We'd like to know what you want to try and do next, over."

"The sixty four thousand dollar question, Rapier. What's the latest on Tenth Mountain's advance?"

"Still en route, the last we heard. They've run into the leading bands of the storm that hit you a while ago. Their aviation brigade was sacked at Central Park, so it's a complete ground movement now. With the storm, it's slow going, Terminator."

McDaniels hadn't expected anything different. "What's the situation in New York? Has the entire city fallen? Over."

"Uh... hold one, Terminator." The line went dead for a moment, and McDaniels took a moment to check around the roof. The flames from the Osprey wreckage were starting to die down, though the faces of the buildings facing the roof were agleam with its ruddy orange glow. The zeds had stopped falling from the building across the street, the one the MV-22 had slammed into. McDaniels guessed they were all on the ground, jockeying for a nice cooked meal.

Or looking for a way to get to us.

"Terminator, Rapier. Yeah, about the city. It's not looking good. Looks like all the federal forces that could be inserted were there at the start. That force was pretty much annihilated, which is why the lightfighters are marching down. There are pockets that haven't been overrun just yet, mostly skyscrapers like the one you're in, but nothing with no real organization behind it. We understand the mayor and his staff are still at the Office of Emergency Management, but most of the police and emergency services are history on Manhattan island. No locals will be able to help you. Over."

"You're just full of the good news tonight, Rapier." McDaniels readjusted his M4 and kept an eye on the stairway leading to the floor below. "The maintenance worker who's with us, he said there's an armored car downstairs in the basement garage. I have no idea if it's a true armored car or just a limo that's been made a little more ballistically tolerant, but it's something. If we had anyone with us who could fly a helicopter, maybe we could go back into the Park and see what we could find, but that's out of the question. We might be able to get out of the immediate vicinity, but we need somewhere to go. Are Queens and Brooklyn still open for business? Over."

"They are, but getting there's going to be tough, Terminator. The order's gone out to blow the bridges. We hear that the barricades on the Brooklyn and Manhattan bridges have been overrun on the Manhattan side, and that means the stenches are going to hit the ones on the other side of the spans. Over."

Fuck! "You're not making this any easier, Rapier. Maybe you should hold off on that activity. We might be able to get across. Over."

"It's not us, Terminator. It's the CinC who made the decision. Air Force is going to carry it out, probably with JDAMs or something from really high up." There was a pause. "Terminator, stand by for a moment."

"Roger, Rapier. Doesn't seem like I have a lot else to do at the moment." More silence on the other end of the radio, and

McDaniels did another visual recon of the roof. The glow from the fire was definitely diminishing, and as he watched, the lights of several midtown skyscrapers flickered and went out. Most notable was the Empire State Building, which until then was still illuminated in red and white lights. Now it was just a dark sentinel towering over everything around it. McDaniels' mouth went dry. As bad as things were, they could only get worse in the dark. Yes, his building still had power... but for how long? Even though he and the rest of the military men had all been trained in night operations and all carried night vision devices that made up for the lack of light, the prospect of fighting the dead in total darkness was somehow quite terrifying.

"Terminator, Rapier. Back with you. We were just checking some of the boards, and we might have something for you. You're about what, a mile from the East River?"

"Give or take a few hundred feet, roger that. What do you have, Rapier?"

"A Coast Guard cutter, off the coast of southern Long Island. The ship was on its way back to its home port in Boston when this op started. We grabbed it just in case, and it looks like we're still holding onto it. We're going to try and get that ship into the East River, and if we can, we might have something to work with sooner rather than later."

McDaniels considered that. He didn't care if the old Cousteau research vessel *Calypso* showed up with some leaky dinghies, anything was better than what they had right now.

"Rapier, Terminator. I like it a lot better than a burning MV-22. Can you find out how long it will take for the ship to get here? We have some preparations to make, and we still have to verify the presence of the vehicle. Over."

"Understood, Terminator. We're reaching out to the ship's commander now. Stand by for us."

"Roger that," McDaniels replied. Not that there was anything else he could do.

***

"Skipper, District One HQ on the encrypted channel."

Commander William Hassle had just stepped off the bridge of the USCG *Escanaba* no more than fourteen minutes ago and returned to his small, single cabin for a quick nap. He hadn't done more than hit the head and wash his face before the intercom buzzed, bringing with it this latest news.

"I'll be right up," Hassle said. There was no point in bitching to anyone about the fact he hadn't closed his eyes in over twenty hours, not when so many of the *Nob*'s crew had been awake for just as long. Besides, the commanding officer of a ship didn't bitch. It was just unseemly.

Hassle was back on the bridge of the ship known informally to her crew simply as the *Nob* in less than two minutes. He returned the duty officer's salute and came to a halt beside him. Lieutenant (junior grade) Petersen was ready to brief the *Nob*'s boss.

"We've got a tasking, relayed to us by HQ. Comes from Special Operations Command," Petersen said, sounding reasonably impressed. "They need us in the East River, somewhere around East Seventy-Ninth Street."

Hassle picked up the headset for secure comms and identified himself as the *Escanaba*'s master. As he spoke, he looked at the chart on the plotter before him. Without waiting for any further details, he plotted a course to where Petersen had said they needed to go.

The operator at District One—the *Escanaba*'s usual command authority—put on the special operations guys right away.

"*Escanaba*, this is Rapier. We're the component command running the operation in question. We show you as being off the coast of East Moriches, is that correct?" the voice on the radio asked, absolutely butchering the name of East Moriches.

"Rapier, this is the *Escanaba*. Roger, we are off the coast of southern Long Island. I understand you have a need for us to move into the East River and position ourselves in the vicinity of East 79th Street. Is this correct? Over."

"You have it right, *Escanaba*. We have a team in the area that needs to be evacuated, and they have with them a very high profile customer who has been deemed a national asset. We need to recover all souls as soon as humanly possible, over."

Hassle tapped the chart before him and looked at Petersen. "Let's get this in the plotter and see what kind of times we can give these guys," he said. Petersen nodded and set about it.

"Rapier, *Escanaba*. Understand all. But uh, isn't Manhattan a containment zone? Over."

"*Escanaba*, that is correct, but we still need you to move your vessel into the East River. Over."

"Rapier, understand that we do not have a helicopter onboard, so whoever needs to be picked up is going to have to try and make it to us. We can pick them up at the shoreline, but we don't have the kind of manpower to go in and get them if they're inside the city. Over."

"*Escanaba*, Rapier. Understood. How long will it take you to get into position, over?"

Hassle checked the electronic chart plotter's LCD display, then compared it with his own plot. There was only a few minutes difference between the two. It would be a 52 nautical mile jaunt, and the *Nob* could make about 22 knots flat out. But the seas were hardly glassy at the moment.

"Rapier, *Escanaba*. Given the current sea state, it's going to take us about four hours to get into position, more if we hit anything unforeseen. We understand air attacks might be launched against the bridges... is that to bring them down completely, or just leave a hole in the span? Over."

"*Escanaba*, Rapier. The word is the Air Force is only going to blow holes in the bridges so the... the OPFOR can't cross them. We're hoping this will still leave you enough room to navigate, but the attacks should be concluded in an hour or so. We'll get back to you with the battle damage assessment and let you know if your course will be blocked. Over."

"Roger that, Rapier. *Escanaba* is on the way. We'll report our status once we pass Governor's Island and the Brooklyn Navy Yard. Will this frequency be good? Over."

"Roger, *Escanaba*. This frequency is good. We'll look forward to hearing from you at zero one hundred hours, over."

"Helm, steer course two six three, call for twenty knots," Hassle said.

"Sir, steer course two six three at twenty knots, aye aye," the helmsman said. The *Escanaba*'s twin diesel engines picked up, and the large white vessel surged into the rising seas.

"Rapier, *Escanaba*. Talk to you at zero one hundred. *Escanaba*, out."

18

"So the Coast Guard is going to save our bacon, huh?" Gartrell shook his head. "My God. What has the world come to?"

McDaniels had to grin a little at the first sergeant's total deadpan delivery. He had joined Gartrell in the kitchen, where both of them smoked cigarettes they had liberated from poor Earl Brown.

"Seems like the Coasties are the only show left in town," McDaniels said. "They should be out in the East River in about four hours."

"All we have to do is get out to East River Drive and throw ourselves into the river, and the Coast Guard will take care of things from that moment on, is that it?" Gartrell took a long drag off his cigarette. When he pulled it away from his mouth, he held it before him and examined it thoroughly. He exhaled smoke from his nostrils.

"We've got maybe eight hundred rounds of various types of ammunition. And there are maybe a hundred thousand zeds between us and the East River. Total piece of cake, major."

"Why, First Sergeant Gartrell, do I detect the tremor of fear in your voice?"

"What you hear is eager anticipation. All we need to do is get down below, secure the vehicle, and figure out how we're going to make all those stenches line up in nice neat files so we can kill eight at a time with one shot. Once we clear those hurdles, well hell, I might just break out my teddy bear and security blanket and take a nap." Gartrell looked at McDaniels directly. "What's the word on our families?"

McDaniels slowly shook his head. "Nothing yet. But four zeds were shot on Normandy Drive, near the middle school. Fort Bragg is in lock down."

Gartrell looked back to his cigarette. "Yowza. You know, I'm thinking one or two of those beers might taste pretty damned good right about now."

McDaniels finished his smoke and tossed it into the sink. "I think they'll probably taste a hell of a lot better on the *Escanaba*," he said. "That's the name of the cutter."

"Well, then. Let's pack some of the brewskis up and get them ready for transit. Looks like we should get down to the garage and scope out this so-called armored car."

McDaniels nodded. "It does indeed."

Gartrell finished his cigarette and tossed it into the sink next to McDaniels'. "You know why it takes twelve Coast Guardsman to hold a burial at sea?"

"Do tell."

"Six to dump the deceased overboard, and six to jump up and down on the casket to push it under the mud."

McDaniels chuckled. That was a good one.

**

"Earl, tell us more about the garage. How big is it? Is there usually someone down there? Is it usually closed up, or can people get into it easily?" McDaniels asked. He and Gartrell had taken Earl to one of the tables in the far corner of the cafeteria so they could talk to him more easily. McDaniels didn't want to upset Earl's youngest daughter any further; Zoe was still having a difficult time coping with the fact that she had just seen six people die.

"Well, it's almost always closed... only reason the door ever went up an' down is if'n someone was leavin'," Earl explained. "The security guys would have to open the gate. No remotes or anythin' like that. Sometimes, the big guys would park their personal cars down there, but not too many a those. Not enough room, really."

"How would you get there?" McDaniels asked.

"Either the freight elevator, or the normal elevators to the garage level. Me, I always use the freight elevator to get around, almost no one else uses it 'cept us maintenance guys if there ain't a delivery."

"When was the last time you were down in the garage?" This came from Gartrell.

"Oh, this week, maybe. Friday night, dumpin' garbage in the dumpster."

"So you haven't been down there since? Which means you don't know if the garage door is open or closed."

"That's right, I don't know for sure."

"And what kind of vehicle is it?" Gartrell asked. "You said it was an armored car. Did you mean like the kind used when money is delivered to a bank, or an up-armored limousine?"

"Neither," Earl said. "It's like a... van, I guess. It's white, but no windows. Seats inside, though. I guess you'd have to see it to know what I'm talkin' about." Earl paused, then added, "It's made by Ford."

"A white Ford van. Okay, that should be easy enough," Gartrell said. He looked at McDaniels. "We should scope that out ASAP, sir. I'll take Rittenour with me, you and the deaf guy can stay up here."

McDaniels chuckled, but Earl frowned.

"That's not nice to say that," he scolded Gartrell.

"Sorry, Earl. Sorry."

"Earl, do you happen to have any rope around here?" McDaniels asked. Gartrell looked at him quizzically, but the major ignored his unspoken question for the moment.

"Sure. We got 'bout five hunnert feet a nylon rope on every floor, next to where the emergency packs are kept." He pointed off into the darkness. "There's a coil in the closet over there. Why you want it?"

"The city's starting to lose power," he said, looking at Gartrell as he spoke. "I figure if an elevator gets caught between floors, then the rope might come in handy. What do you think, first sergeant?"

"I think you're exactly right, and that we should probably get our hands on as much as we possibly can. No telling when we might need it, but if we get into a jam, I'd rather we had it as opposed to just wished for it."

McDaniels nodded. "Then take it with you. We'll see if there's a way to get the coils from some of the other floors later, if possible." He rose. "I'm going to go check on Finelly and Derwitz. You go ahead and hit the garage, I'll leave Leary up here."

"Roger that, sir." Gartrell practically leaped to his feet, obviously happy to have something constructive to do.

***

McDaniels left Sergeant Leary on the 27th floor with the civilians after ascertaining he was fit for duty ("I can hear now sir, really," the Special Forces soldier assured him) and entered the fire escape stairway. He found Derwitz had taken a position on the 26th floor landing, and Finelly was one floor below. Both were discharging their duties as vigilantly as possible, which essentially meant they were standing around waiting for something to happen. Neither soldier reported any unusual activity—no stenches, no noises, no nothing.

"It's kind of boring duty, sir," Finelly admitted. "But you know, it's a *good* kind of boring, when you think about the alternatives."

McDaniels smiled and clapped the tall soldier on the shoulder. "You guys are doing all right. Keep up the good work. You're doing some real good, here." Both men kept their voices low, mindful of the echoes the stairwell would cause.

"Thanks, major."

McDaniels nodded and looked down between the stairway handrails. Far below, darkness loomed. McDaniels listened as intently as he could, but heard nothing. Had the zeds left? Gartrell had reported they were massing on the ground floor, but McDaniels heard nothing from the 25th floor landing. If there was much commotion going on down there, he was sure he would have been able to hear it, especially since the stenches were hardly stealthy by nature.

He turned back to Finelly. "Go tell Derwitz to return to the cafeteria. Have him inform Sergeant Leary he's to take your position, and you fall back to the landing on twenty-six. We can't really communicate effectively since our radios are different, and Leary will be able to talk to myself and Gartrell if something goes down." He pulled the sat phone from its holster and handed it to the tall soldier. "And keep this with you. Without the booster relay at the assembly area, it's the only way we can communicate with Rapier. Move out, troop."

Finelly nodded, and walked up the stairs, where he had a whispered conversation with Derwitz. A moment later, McDaniels heard Derwitz's footsteps as he climbed up the stairs to the 27th floor. Finelly waited on the 26th floor landing, looking down at McDaniels, his MP5K held in both hands, his NVGs pushed back on their helmet mount.

McDaniels looked back down to the ground floor. Still nothing but a small patch of blackness.

Leary appeared, walking down the stairs as quietly as he could. He looked at McDaniels with a raised brow, and McDaniels leaned toward him.

"Sergeant, are you sure about your ears? If you were to get a call on the net, would you be able to hear it?"

Leary nodded. "Yes, sir. Only a slight buzzing in my ears now, nothing like it was before." As if to prove this, Leary kept his voice low, barely above a whisper.

"Okay. I'm going to head down and check things out. I want to see what the deadheads are up to. Things are pretty quiet, and if OMEN is back in the zone, that's probably not a good sign."

Leary looked over the railing and peered down the gap. "You think Mr. Keith's got something going on?"

"Won't know that until I see it for myself."

"I dunno, sir. Those things aren't really intellectual heavyweights. They might have forgotten all about us by now, since there's no way for them to get to us. But if they see you, that might change things. Again." As he spoke, Leary his eyes focused on the darkness below.

"I'll do my best to keep things as cool as possible," McDaniels said.

Leary straightened and reached into one of his pockets. He pulled out a plastic tube that was perhaps an inch and a half long, and handed it to McDaniels.

"IR chem stick," he said. "When you get down there, activate it and drop it, then use your NVGs. Ambient light might not be sufficient to see everything that's going on. It'll last for about three hours, and I doubt the stenches can see in the IR spectrum, right?"

McDaniels nodded and took the chem stick. He put it in a pocket on his body armor and started off.

"Major?"

McDaniels turned back. Leary looked at him then down through the handrail again.

"Long walk down, and a long walk up. Hope your legs are up for it if something goes down. And if that happens, what are your orders?"

"Stay here. Defend the civilians, and report to Gartrell. If I'm gone, I'm gone. Your job is to zero as many of those zeds as possible, until Gartrell gives you something else to do."

"Roger that. Does the first sergeant know you're doing this?"

McDaniels smiled and started down the stairway.

***

The elevator ride to the garage level was as smooth as silk, which is how Gartrell liked it. His primary fear wasn't that he and Rittenour would be mobbed by a raging tide of hungry stenches once the door slid open (though they were ready for that with weapons cocked and locked), but that the building would suddenly lose power and leave them stranded between floors. To that end, they had already checked to ensure the elevator had a maintenance hatch in the roof; it was accessible to them once they removed the panels covering the fluorescent lights on the ceiling. They also had the heavy coil of rope Gartrell had taken from the cafeteria, and it lay in one corner on the elevator floor. Of course, its utility would be in going down, not going up, but Gartrell was something of a pack rat when it came to items that might be of use. He had also squirreled away some sandwiches and bottles of cold water in his back pack, just in case they were in for a longer stay in the elevator than they had planned for.

Ding. The elevator came to a halt, and both men took deep breaths. Gartrell had the point position with the AA-12 at the ready. Rittenour had his Heckler & Koch Mk 23 pistol clasped in both hands as he stood off to the side. Both men had their NVGs powered up but raised; if the doors opened and total darkness was on the other side, they could flip them down and be operational in a split second.

The heavy stainless steel clad door slid open, and Gartrell tensed, his finger on the AA-12's trigger. Rittenour flipped the safety switch that locked the elevator in place.

The elevator didn't open into the garage directly, but into a dimly-lit, glass-walled vestibule that was in the garage's center. Gartrell stepped out and spun left while Rittenour covered the area to the right. The garage was illuminated by several lights, yet it was hardly a bright affair; there were still more shadows than either man liked, but the ambient light was too strong for the NVGs to be effective. Glass doors were on either side of the vestibule, and both were closed. Gartrell motioned for Rittenour to follow him. He slowly pushed the door open, then eased out into the garage proper. Rittenour followed, both moving as stealthily as possible.

The garage door was closed, as was the personnel entrance beside it. Two vehicles were parked inside. One was a black Audi A8, and its lustrous paint gleamed even in the garage's meager light. The second vehicle was much larger, a Ford E350 van. Gartrell ignored it for the moment, electing to do a full search of the garage. There was a ripe, pungent aroma in the air, and he exchanged a glance with Rittenour. There were only two things Gartrell could think of that would emit that odor: rotting food, or a zed.

It turned out to be garbage. There was a dumpster in the garage, which Earl had told them about, and it hadn't been emptied. As such, its contents were quickly going south. Both men made a quick but thorough search of the garage. They were alone.

Gartrell returned to the van and examined it critically. It was a monster, all right, something he hadn't expected to see in the middle of New York City. White in color, the only windows were up front; there weren't even windows in the double doors on the back. It rode high on a heavy duty suspension and slightly oversized tires that sported an aggressive tread. Gartrell moved to the front and found the vehicle was outfitted with a brush guard to protect the grille and a heavy duty bumper. He knelt and peered underneath the vehicle's nose. A transfer case bulged between the front tires. The van had been converted into a seemingly-hardy four wheel drive vehicle.

Gartrell straightened and looked at Rittenour. "Well, someone was certainly planning to be able to get out of here." His voice seemed loud in the garage's close confines.

Rittenour nodded. "I guess they wanted to make sure no one was stuck here during a blizzard. I'll tell you, the thing looks tough. A guy in another ODA has something like this at Fort Bragg. He uses it when he and his buddies go hunting." Holding his pistol in his right hand, Rittenour walked toward the van and pounded on its side with his left fist. He was rewarded with several solid thumps. "Wow, definitely up-armored. I'll bet this thing's going to be a total pig to drive."

Gartrell tried to open the driver's door, but it was locked. He and Rittenour tried all the doors. No luck. The van was locked up tight. Gartrell sighed and looked around the garage.

"All right, let's find the keys to this thing. I hope they're down here somewhere."

19

The farther he descended, McDaniels became less certain that going down alone was a great idea. While he'd encountered no difficulties other than a growing ache in his knees and lower back, the lower he went, the more uncomfortable he became.

And then, there was the smell.

As he descended, a decidedly unpleasant odor wafted up from below. A fetid breeze moved through the stairway, venting upward like a draft through a chimney. The dead were down there, that was for sure. They hadn't grown bored or otherwise left the building. But what they were doing was another matter entirely.

10th floor.

9th floor.

8th floor, and the air was foul.

7th floor, no improvement.

The 6th floor, and it was difficult not to gag.

McDaniels stopped on the 6th floor landing. Chunks of shattered concrete and cinderblock crunched beneath his boots. He kept motionless and just listened, breathing as lightly as he could. He heard movement from below, but exactly how far, he could not tell. A scrabbling sound, cloth moving against cloth, the occasional crackle of rubble being displaced. The stairway leading to the fifth floor was gloomy, as some of the lights had been blasted out when Rittenour triggered the charges. McDaniels reached up to his helmet and switched on his NVGs, but left them in the stowed position. He firmed his grip on his M4 and slowly walked down the stairs, keeping his back against the wall as he moved. He took it step by step, moving slowly and stealthily. A keen sense of dread filled his chest, but his training maintained supremacy... for now.

There were bodies on the fifth floor landing, as he had known there would be. Above the stench of rotting corpses, he could still sniff out traces of gun powder and the residue of the explosives. A few shell casings littered the ground. The door leading to the fifth floor offices was bent and misshapen, as if

Thor had struck it with his mighty mallet. McDaniels gingerly stepped around the corpses and flipped down his night vision goggles. Carefully choosing his footing, he slowly descended the final stairway, the one which led to a chasm of darkness. Before easing himself toward the edge, he slung his assault rifle and pulled his pistol. He held it in his right hand while clenching the remaining hand rail in his left. If nothing else, it was still solidly set into the wall. Ignoring the stench as much as he was able, he took a breath and leaned over.

The dead were rising.

It took a moment for him to realize that he was looking down onto an undulating mass of twisted, decrepit bodies that roiled and fell like some ungodly ocean. Ruined faces turned toward him, unblinking eyes gleaming dully through the light intensification provided by the NVGs. The heap of bodies flailed this way and that as zed after zed added itself to the pile and struggled to climb over its fellows in an attempt to get to the top of the heap. As he watched, the top of the pile fell away from McDaniels as the mountain of dead collapsed. It reformed again as the zeds, fixated on feeding, merely started over. For sure, those at the bottom were crushed beneath the weight of the hundreds of bodies above, but the dead would not be denied. McDaniels was horrified. The pile reformed and surged upward yet again. It grew and grew and grew, rising closer and closer to the stairway where he stood, transfixed.

Then one of the zombies moaned, reaching for him even though it was still dozens of feet away. It was joined by another, and another, and another. The cacophony was jarring, almost as overwhelming as the grotesque sight below. McDaniels heard a voice through his headphones.

"Six, this is Leary. We hear the zeds, are you in trouble? Over." Leary's voice was professional, mechanical. McDaniels envied him for it, but he knew that practiced veneer would fracture and crack against a visage such as this one. There was no way a man could look at a scene like the one McDaniels faced and not go a little mad.

"Six, this is Leary, come in. Over."

Static crackled over the radio. "This is Five, what the hell is going on up there? Six, what's your pos, over?"

"This is Six," McDaniels said finally. "I'm on the fifth floor. Gartrell, we'll need to find out if that vehicle exists and if we can use it. Over."

"Six, this is Five. Is someone with you? Over?" The transmission was marred by static, doubtless due to the fact that Gartrell was encased in a tomb of concrete down in the garage.

"Terminator Five, did you find the van? Over."

"Roger Six, we have found the vehicle and are looking for keys to get inside. This is a new Ford, I doubt we can hotwire it and drive off... it's all computerized. Over."

The pile of the moaning dead collapsed again. Their laments seemed disappointed, desperate, and forlorn as the bodies crashed against each other, bouncing off the cinderblock walls with enough force to snap bones and rip away skin. But the zombies did not pay their injuries any heed. They merely rebuilt their pile, dozens of them climbing over each other, trying to reach McDaniels.

"Gartrell, find them. Quickly. The dead are piling up in the stairwell. Hundreds, probably thousands of them. They're climbing over each other trying to reach the stairwell. And eventually, they'll make it. Over."

There was a brief moment of silence before Gartrell came back. "Roger that, Six. We're searching for it. We'll find it and get ready to get out of here. Maybe everyone should come down to the garage, over."

The pile grew with a sudden lurch, as if it were some sort of inflating balloon. Spindly, pale arms encrusted in dried blood reached upward, and finally, a pair of hands grabbed onto the twisted rebar sticking out of the bottom of the last stair. A small face appeared in the gloom, mouth open, eyes wide. The zombie released a dry, hitching hiss as it pulled itself away from the others on arms that seemed to be no thicker than kindling. It was a child, a girl, maybe five or six years old, wearing a blood-stained Dora the Explorer T-shirt. The zombie's knuckles had been flayed open, and bone gleamed dully in the light.

My daughter, please take my daughter!

The ghoul's dry hiss turned into something approaching hiccupping laughter as it pulled itself up onto the stair, reaching for McDaniels' boot.

McDaniels put a bullet in its head. The gunshot was as loud as thunder in the stairwell, and the flash threatened to overpower the NVGs. But McDaniels saw the small skull explode into fragments, scattering ropey goo across the stairs, his boots, and the writing dead below. As the corpse fell back into the pile, it disappeared as dozens of the zombies pawed their way over it, shoving it deeper and deeper into the undulating mass of bodies.

"Major! Six, what's going on? Report back, over!" Leary's voice was still professional, but wearing. McDaniels shot two more zombies, then a third, before he could answer. He holstered his pistol and reached for one of the grenades strapped to the side of his body armor.

"I've got to knock this pile down before they get up here. A few of them almost made it, had to go to guns on them. Listen up, I'm releasing a grenade right now. Stand by."

McDaniels pulled the pin and hurled the grenade into the growing pile of bodies beneath him, then turned and ran up the stairs. At the landing, he spun back and drew his pistol. Hands flailed in the darkness beyond the stairs, groping for them, missing them by millimeters. And then a muffled *whump!* echoed throughout the stairwell, more felt than heard due to the mass of bodies surrounding the blast. But the grenade did its job; the zombies fell away from the stairway as the pile collapsed, this time blown out from somewhere near the center. McDaniels scuttled down the stairs again and lobbed another grenade, then retreated to safety. The device went off, and the effect was much like the first. McDaniels visually verified the heap had imploded, and indeed it had. The topmost zeds had collapsed onto those beneath them, crushing them into the bottom of the stairwell, blocking the fire door at the bottom with a stinking pile of shattered, broken bodies that still writhed and twitched. McDaniels' throat burned, and he realized he had been screaming during the grenade attack. The terror had finally overwhelmed him, albeit temporarily.

"Major McDaniels, what do we have going on down there?" Leary's voice was all business. "I'm on floor eighteen, on my way down to you, over."

"Negative! Stay upstairs, I need you there so we can communicate with the Night Stalkers." McDaniels felt around his body and took a quick inventory of his grenades. Three left. It was a good thing everyone had manned up with ordnance before jumping out into the city, and McDaniels had Gartrell to thank for that.

"Six, you sure about that?" Leary asked. "What about you? Over."

"I'll keep an eye on things down here for a while," McDaniels said. "If things get too hot, I'll pull back. But if I go off the air, presume the worst. Get the civilians, most especially Safire out of here. His safety takes full priority. Over."

"Good copy on that, Six. But uh, what about the kids? Over."

McDaniels reached into one of the pockets on his body armor and pulled out the chem stick Leary had given him and shook it vigorously, twisting it between his fingers. To the unaided eye, nothing happened. But through the NVGs, it was as if a floodlight had been switched on. He tossed the chem stick into the pit below him, then grabbed his M4 and pulled it tight against his right shoulder. He activated the laser targeting system on the barrel, and used it to mark targets below as the zeds flailed about, struggling to reconstitute the pile.

"Leary, Safire is the primary objective of this mission. The kids are... the kids are nonessential to mission success. Over."

"Understood, sir." If Leary felt any other way about it, it didn't register in his voice. (*My daughter, please take my daughter!*) "I'll be heading back upstairs then... are you sure you don't want me to send one of the Night Stalkers down to give you some cover? Being a separate operation right now probably isn't that smart, over."

"Understood Leary, but this is how it's got to be. These things are stupid and slow, but they're starting to pull themselves together again, forming another pile. I'll keep knocking it down as quickly as I can. I'll stay down here until the first sergeant can get that vehicle ready, or until I start running out of ammo. Break. Terminator Five, SITREP, over."

"Still looking for those keys," Gartrell said through the static. "Six, maybe we ought to relocate everyone down here. Might be wiser, with those things trying to go up if we were to come down. Over."

McDaniels shot a zombie through the head, then another, and another. He didn't rush; he took aim and fired as methodically as he could. The stenches fell back into the pile, and the dead (*Re-dead?* he wondered idly) bodies were eventually flung to the side of the heap.

"Negative on that last, Gartrell. The last thing we want is for these things to hear the elevator and maybe have OMEN figure this shit out and come hunting for us. Over." McDaniels fired and sent two more zombies back to the bottom of the heap.

"Understood, Six. Still looking for keys. Over."

"Roger that. Break. Leary, have Finelly contact Rapier and tell them the current circumstances—I left the sat phone with him. We might be forced to boogie sooner than we'd liked. Get an update on where that Coast Guard boat is, and find out if our radio gear is compatible. At some point, we'll need to talk to the Coasties, and I want to make sure they can hear us. Over."

"On it, Six. You want more grenades? Over."

McDaniels fired again, dropping a zombie back into the flailing pile, dark ichor spurting from its ravaged skull. "Negative, Leary. Just relay the information. McDaniels, out."

For a moment, McDaniels stood at the edge of the stairway to nowhere and looked down at the mound of dead below him. The zombies continued to moan, and they stared up at him with those soulless, dead eyes, their mouths open, exposing teeth and blackening tongues. McDaniels stared back at them in disgust.

"Fuck all of you," he muttered, then raised his assault rifle and patiently fired aimed round after aimed round.

20

Regina Safire no longer flinched every time she heard the distant *crack!* of a single gunshot every minute or so, but the soldiers hadn't really told them what was going on. The soldier Derwitz—Maxi, she remembered they called him—had told her that Major McDaniels was establishing a safe zone down below. He had been evasive when she pressed him for a more definitive answer, and had basically fed her some double-talk and was generally unconvincing when he told her she had nothing to worry about. Regina wasn't certain about that at all.

She tried talking it over with her father, but he was generally noncommittal. His eyes were downcast, contemplating nothing farther away than the tabletop before him. Regina understood why. All his life, Wolf Safire had been a man who had kept his emotions strictly contained. His forte was science, nothing but science. Though he had tried to improve himself, every time he stepped outside of Wolf the Research Scientist and tried something else—Wolf the Caring Father or Wolf the Attentive Husband, for instance—his efforts ended in dismal failure. The fact was he was spectacularly unsuited to carry forth with anything else but science. Regina had resented that as a young girl, but by the time she was in med school at Johns Hopkins, she no longer viewed her father's simplex existence as a deficiency. She had grown to find his emotional makeup actually admirable. Anything beyond the realm of the sciences wasn't for him, and he found that acceptable. After a time, so did Regina. Her mother had never grown accustomed to it, however. She had divorced Safire in 1978, and had been awarded custody of Regina. She saw her father only intermittently throughout the years until she graduated high school. It wasn't until she started looking at various universities that Safire had come back to her, advising her on which program she might be best suited for, and at which university. That she should choose his alma mater was practically a foregone conclusion, though both Harvard and Yale were equally attractive. But as she grew older, Regina found that she very much wanted to win her father's attention. Though her mother had been the one who guided her through life and assisted her in navigating its treacherous currents as a young girl in middle and high schools, Regina found herself courting her father's interest once she was a junior in high school. This had doubtless wounded her mother, but if so, she merely suffered in silence. At that time, Regina was already becoming more and more like her father; she was less interested in personal relationships, and more aware of the callings of science. Oh, she knew all about boys of course, and had sought out experiences with them whenever it was convenient, but at the end of the day, they proved to be more of a distraction than anything else. Studies were what fulfilled her, and dispatching the challenges posed by well-heeled instructors who felt their silly tests and quizzes were the sole measure of a student's scientific merit. By her senior year in high school, she had enrolled in every advanced placement course available to her, and where there were none, she merely took their college equivalents.

By then, of course, she had transformed completely into the closest approximation of a "daddy's' girl" as she could. Her mother suffered in silence, and the damage Regina had caused in her filial defection remained today.

If her mother was still alive, of course.

She reached across the table and squeezed her father's hand. He looked up at her slowly and gave her a wan smile that did nothing to reassure her. Regina smiled back with as much strength as she had and scooted out of the booth. Safire grabbed her hand suddenly.

"Where are you going?" he asked, finally breaking his long-standing silence. They were the first words he had spoken to her in over an hour.

"Just to take a look outside," she said. "I won't go far."

"You need to be careful," he said. "We're very close to a tipping point here. The military won't tell us that, but of course we can't really trust them to tell us everything."

Regina didn't know how to respond to that. The sudden anti-establishment streak her father had displayed since all of this began was a bit disconcerting. So she just shrugged, nodded, and slowly extricated her hand from his. Safire let her go and returned to his intense study of the Formica tabletop before him.

Regina walked across the darkened cafeteria, nodding to Earl and his family. The youngest girl was finally asleep, which was a godsend; seeing the tiltrotor airplane or whatever it was called crash had been horrifying for her. For all of them actually, but for her young mind watching several people meet their death was powerful stuff. Sleep was the best thing for her. She leaned against her father's chest, wrapped up in his arms. Earl's eyes were closed as well, his head tilted back against the booth's backrest. The oldest daughter was still awake, and she returned Regina's nod. Regina continued toward the windows, hands in the pockets of her jacket. She peered outside, resting her forehead on the cool glass as she looked down at the storm-torn street below.

Below, totally ignorant of the driving rain and wind, the dead had massed around what would be the front of the building. Forty, fifty, maybe even sixty deep. The sight of so many zombies collecting in one area was significant, she thought. It meant New York City had a much larger problem than the one she had heard on the late night news, where the sightings of the dead were sporadic at best, nothing to worry about, the NYPD could handle them. Contrasting that with what she saw now, not even thirty-six hours later, made it difficult to ignore. New York City, if it hadn't fallen already, was within hours of doing so. And the gathering zombies outside meant they were still hungry.

And we're the food.

Earl's oldest daughter joined her at the window. She looked down at the gathering dead, her face mostly expressionless. Regina wondered if that was because she was too young to be frightened by things like this, or if it was because her life had been much harder than, say, her own. Maybe she had already developed a tough shell, and a vista like the one below them just wasn't strong enough to penetrate it.

"That's whack," she said.

Regina nodded. "Yeah. Yeah, it definitely is."

The black girl stepped back from the window and shoved her hands into the pockets of her jeans. She wore them low on her hips, and Regina noticed the protuberances of her hipbones standing out in stark relief against her dark skin.

"I'm Kenisha," she said by way of introduction.

"Hi Kenisha. Regina."

"Why are you with these soldiers? I mean, it doesn't seem like you just hooked up with them like we did. Looks like they came for you and your pops, right?"

"Yeah."

"Your father, he's an important guy?"

Regina shrugged and smiled. "Not in the big scheme of things, no."

"Then why are you with all the soldiers?"

Regina ran a hand through her dark hair, then rubbed her eyes tiredly. "He's done research that might be important. It might be something that can help put a stop to this."

"No shit? What kind of research?"

Regina shrugged again. "Something to do with the infection vector. He might have come up with a way to stop it from turning live human hosts into... well, into *them*." She pointed down at the shambling figures in the street.

"Really. You mean he might have a way to kill those things for good?"

"No, not exactly. Only a way that would keep humans alive after they've been attacked by the dead. You know, if you get bitten by one, or get any of their body fluids in a cut or your eye or your mouth, whatever the virus is that's in them will kill you. And then you'll become one of them, and run around looking for people to eat."

"Damn. For real? If that's the case, then your daddy's going to be saint, or something." Kenisha turned and looked back at Safire, sitting alone in the semi-darkness, his back to them. "He's a little unhinged, though. Guess I can't blame him."

"My father isn't as strong as yours," Regina said with a sigh.

Kenisha turned back to her, a wan smile lighting up her face. "My daddy? Strong? That's a joke. He's afraid of his own shadow."

Regina shook her head. "I doubt that. He managed to keep you and your sister safe all this time. If we hadn't shown up, maybe you'd *still* be safe."

"Maybe. But for how long? Until the food and water runs out? Who would be looking for us? Who would even *bother* to come for us?" Kenisha looked back at Safire. "If your father has some important stuff to pass on, then the government will come for him. That's the only way we're getting out of here. Otherwise, we'd be here until those things finally got to us. Or until we just died ourselves." A hard cast descended upon the girl's features, and Regina saw that she'd had more than a little bit of time to think about it. Regina realized that she hadn't. She'd always just assumed that McDaniels and his people would be able to save them. Even after seeing the aircraft crash on the roof, she'd blithely believed that she and her father would be rescued somehow, some way. But looking down at the malignant mass of former humanity that was growing around the building like a cancerous tumor attacking healthy flesh...she was no longer convinced. Maybe this was going to be their last stand.

More gunshots rang out, tinny and distant, but still audible. Kenisha turned toward the sounds.

"They're in the building, aren't they?" she asked.

Regina realized that no one had really briefed the Browns on anything since the MV-22 had crashed. She sighed and nodded.

"It looks that way. They blew up one of the stairways to keep them from getting to us, but they must have found another way. But Major McDaniels is apparently taking care of them for the moment."

"'For the moment'. So I guess that won't last forever. How many bullets can one guy have?" Kenisha nodded to the street below. "He'd need hundreds of thousands. Maybe millions."

Regina had nothing to say to that. The girl was right, of course. But admitting it aloud might very well capture Fate's attention and seal their doom, and she wasn't about to do anything rash. Though she had never been a superstitious person, the events of the past few days had duly informed her that there were things that overshadowed her previous religion of science.

21

McDaniels found he could take the time to take a drink from his canteen on occasion, or even enjoy a small snack if he was willing. He'd gotten used to the stench, so eating was something he might be able to contemplate. It was funny what a person could get used to, and in the short order. He'd found the stink of the rotting dead to be overpowering at first, then merely rank, and now it barely classified as plain old strong. Either he was made of stronger stuff than he'd thought, or his brain had short-circuited his sense of smell in an attempt to save him from going mad.

The dead still formed their abominable pile below as gray-white figures clambered over each other with a greedy single-mindedness. McDaniels was no longer amazed—or depressed—that the pile reformed every time he knocked it down. He likened the ghouls below to single cell organisms. There was no true complexity to them or their actions, just the most rudimentary of instinct. They needed to feed. Why they needed to feed was unknown to McDaniels, since they were already dead, but at least the reanimated corpses were consistent. He would not have been overly surprised if they suddenly started shouting *"Brains! Braaaaaaaaaaaains!"* like in the old zombie movie he had seen as a freshman in high school.

So when the pile rose to a sufficient height and the ghouls grew nearer to the stairway he stood on, he raised his M4 and fired a single round through each grotesquerie's head, sending the corpses sliding down the pile, knocking away others who sought to climb to the top. The mound would disintegrate again, and it would take some minutes for it to reform. McDaniels did some calculations, and figured he had fired off almost sixty rounds since taking up his firing position. To the best of his recollection, he had only missed twice. That was hardly a personal best—he had gone through thousands of rounds without missing a target at the gunnery range—but given the current threat's rather low velocity, it was forgivable. He lowered the assault rifle after repulsing the latest zombie advance and stepped back from the edge. Cartridges clinked and clattered beneath his boots as they rolled off the edge and into the black maw below.

"Terminator Five, this is Six. It's been a while, first sergeant. What do we have? Over."

"Still searching, major. No joy as of yet, over." The static was still bad, and McDaniels had to work to ensure he understood every word of Gartrell's transmission.

"You've got to try and do better, first sergeant. Have you looked for a lock box where keys might be kept? What about an office or something down there? Over."

"Done it all, major. Going through the entire garage, looking for a hiding place. Over."

God damn it. McDaniels knew they were missing something here. Finding the keys to a vehicle shouldn't have been so hard, unless they were on a person who was offsite. But then what was the point in having such a vehicle if the person who had the keys wasn't in the area? It made no sense, but this was the civilian world. Nothing had to be codified in the thick volumes that spelled out Army regulations.

"Understood, Five. I'm keeping the zeds occupied for the moment. Over."

"Roger, Six. We were able to bust into the Audi that's down here, but no keys in it, either. Over."

McDaniels thought about that for a moment. An Audi? Then he remembered the single ghoul he and Finelly had taken out up on 27. Earl had said it was the company president, a diehard workaholic who had... well, died hard at work, apparently. McDaniels doubted the man had been anything other than a Type A personality. And Type A personalities were usually over-controlling more often than not...

"Roger that, Five. Break. Leary, come in."

"Six, Leary. Go ahead, over."

"Leary, check that corpse we bagged. Go through its pockets, find what kind of keys it has on it, over."

There was a momentary pause, then Leary came back on the net. "Roger that, Six. Understand you want me to go through the pockets of the dirty, stinking stiff whose head you blew off and look for car keys. Over."

McDaniels checked the situation below. The dead were massing again. He shouldered his rifle and waited.

"That is correct, Leary. Report your findings, over."

"On it, Six. With the corpse now, stand by."

McDaniels watched the undulating pile of the dead rise higher and higher by irregular increments. Sometimes, it grew with almost startling rapidity; other times, it would grow to two or three stories and then collapse as the flesh and bone that made up its underpinnings failed beneath the load. He had no idea how many corpses were at the bottom of the mound, but he was certain they had to be nearly liquefied by now.

"Six, Leary. Got one key ring. Has two integrated remote keys on it. One for an Audi. The second is for a Ford. Over."

McDaniels stepped back from the edge of the stairs, trying to ward off the building sense of anticipation that was rising in his breast. "Leary, any way to know if this is the key we're looking for? Over."

"Only way to find out is to try it, Six," was Leary's deadpan reply.

"Six, Gartrell. You want us to come up and take that key? Or do you want to send someone down with it? Over."

McDaniels mulled it over for a moment. "Gartrell, Six. I'm getting worried that these stenches might hear the elevator motors and get curious. Remember, at least part of OMEN is onsite. Over." As he spoke, McDaniels kept his voice pitched low. The zeds could still hear, so there was no need to give OMEN any additional information... if they could still comprehend spoken words.

"Understood, Six. So what's the option?" Gartrell asked over the static-marred channel.

McDaniels peered over the edge of the stairway. The pile was getting to be about the right size now. He raised his rifle to his shoulder and fired, taking down one zombie. Its demise did not have the desired effect, so he waited for a suitable candidate to appear, then sent that one back to hell. That did the trick, and the pile imploded suddenly, filling the air with the sounds of snapping bones and bodies striking cement.

"We're pretty much out of time, altitude, and ideas on this one, Gartrell. I say we take whatever God throws our way and roll with it. And right now, he's given us a key that says Ford on it, so let's get everyone downstairs and check it out. If it's not the right key, then we try and come up with a Plan C. Over."

"If we give up the high ground now, we might not be able to take it back. Over."

McDaniels kept his eyes on the massing zeds below and tried to keep the irritation out of his voice when he replied. "Like I said earlier, first sergeant, we don't exactly have a bonanza of options. If the zeds hear the elevator machinery and figure out what it is, then we'll get very few opportunities to use it before they come crashing in. If you think there's a better way, now would be the time to let me know. Over."

There was a long pause before Gartrell finally responded. "Negative Six, no better alternatives come to mind, over."

"Roger that. Break. Leary, have one of the Night Stalkers go roofside and contact Rapier. We need an update on that Coast Guard cutter. Notify them that we'll be moving out relatively soon, and it would be simply stellar if the Coasties could get the lead out. While that's underway, you and Finelly get everyone organized and ready to roll. Over."

"Roger that, Six."

"Thanks, Leary. Break. Gartrell, Leary will tell you when to send up the elevator. And make sure you send the ropes up as well. If something goes wrong, we might need them. Over."

"Six, Gartrell. Ropes are in the elevator. We'll key in and send it up as soon as we get the word. Over."

McDaniels started to respond, but a different sort of activity caught his attention down below. He adjusted his night vision goggles very slightly with his left hand, his right still clutching the pistol grip on his M4 assault rifle. A figure still wearing almost all the accoutrements of a United States Army Special Forces soldier had pushed its way inside the stairwell down below and had turned its pale face upward. Flat, lifeless eyes locked onto him from behind the clear plastic dust goggles it still wore; of course, the Special Forces troops had donned their goggles before boarding the Black Hawks back at the assembly area in Central Park. McDaniels didn't know the soldier's name, but he—it?—had been a member of OMEN.

McDaniels was surprised at the sudden shock he felt. He thought he had prepared himself for this, since he knew that at least some members of OMEN had reanimated and had been responsible for breaching the lobby. But to actually *see* one of the Special Forces troops as a zed was something else entirely.

What wasn't lost on him was the M4 the zed carried in both hands. Slowly, the ghoul brought the weapon to its shoulder and peered through the scope.

Holy mother of —

The M4 barked once, and a puff of concrete dust erupted from beneath the stairway McDaniels stood on. McDaniels stepped back as the rifle cracked again, and he was pelted with concrete chips as the bullet immolated itself against the bottom of the stairway over McDaniels' head. The shot was more wild than aimed; the ghoul with the weapon was constantly being jostled by the other dead as they hauled themselves back onto the pile, and that made the shooter ineffective.

"Holy fuck," McDaniels gasped. His heart was pounding a mile a minute as he slowly edged back toward the ledge. *Crack!* Another bullet slammed into the concrete overhead, leaving a three inch pockmark in its wake. McDaniels shouldered his rifle and fired off three shots in rapid succession. The rounds found their target, but his aim was off. The first round hit the dead soldier's helmet, but the Kevlar must have turned it. The last two struck the zed in the body armor and sent it tottering back through the lobby door.

"Six, everything all right down there?" Leary asked. "I just heard several shots. It sounds like you're in a gunfight, over."

"Six, hit us back with your status, over," Gartrell broadcast immediately, stomping on McDaniels' first attempt to reply. McDaniels kept his stance, scanning the roiling mass of dead for any sign of the OMEN trooper. He caught a flash of something in the glare of the chemstick, infrared light reflecting off metal. He had just enough time to make out the outline of an arm protruding from the pile. Gripped in the hand at the end of the arm was an Mk 23 pistol, its muted surface dully reflecting the light. He waited for a moment, his sights trained on the arm as he searched for a face. He found it as a zed shifted to one side, and Sergeant Larrabee's lifeless eyes met his. McDaniels fired a round through the zed's face, right below the rim of its helmet. The pistol fell from the outstretched hand, and the corpse sank back into the heaving mass of the dead.

"All, Six has just been engaged by two zeds from OMEN. I think I bagged one, but the other got away. Both used their firearms. Gartrell, you and Rittenour had better be ready for company. Looks like OMEN means business, over."

"Roger that, Six. Odd that they would try and shoot you. If they can remember that stuff, surprised they wouldn't remember they aren't supposed to shoot superior officers, over." It was meant as a half-hearted joke, but McDaniels ignored it.

"I think they want to drop me since I'm interrupting their plan to get to the rest of the group," he replied. "Looks like they're willing to sacrifice one meal in order to get into the a la carte line, over."

"Sounds like OMEN's operating at a different capacity than the rest of the stenches, Six," Gartrell said. "I'll bet Safire could confirm that, but that's a discussion for a different day. What's the op now? Are we still a go with the transfer to the garage? Over."

McDaniels thought about it long and hard for a moment as he watched the dead mound reform. He knew he had only eight more rounds in his current magazine, and after that, he had only eight mags left. Not a hell of a lot. It was time to go.

"We're on, Gartrell. Once I break station here, the stenches will eventually gain access to the stairs and make their way upstairs, so let's be damned quick about it, over."

"That's a great big roger," Gartrell said. "I never liked New York all that much before, so getting the hell out of here is music to my ears. Elevator's on its way up with the key and ropes, over."

Below, the pile of the dead grew once again with single-minded ferocity, the corpses moaning as they added their bodies to the column of twisting, necrotic flesh. There was no sign of any of the OMEN troopers, but he did catch flashes of battle dress in the rancid heap. Other soldiers from the assembly area, or perhaps from the blockades, had joined the mass of ghouls in their attempt to overrun the building.

"Roger that, Gartrell. I've got to hold these things back for a little bit longer, but I'll be up. Break. Leary, hold the elevator for me unless there's another incursion. If the twenty-seventh floor is threatened, get the hell out of there, over."

"Ah, roger that, Six."

"Will see you in about ten. Six, out."

McDaniels raised his M4 to his shoulder and squeezed off a round, blasting apart a zed's skull and sending it tumbling down the pile. He pulled a grenade from its mount, yanked the pin free, and hurled it into the midst of the swarming dead. It exploded, sending a shock wave throughout the stairwell. McDaniels heard a sudden crack, and felt the stairway he stood on shift to the right. With a muted curse, he turned and bolted to the safety of the landing as concrete gave way and rebar twisted. Brass cartridges rained down on the ghouls below as the remains of the stairs nosed down into the pit of the dead. The entire stairway followed a moment later, twisting and tumbling as it tore free of the landing and fell with a loud thud, flattening the mound of zombies beneath its weight. A great cloud of dust rose into the air, and McDaniels coughed. Then the landing trembled and shook, and he jumped over the bodies there and ran up the next stairway. He stopped on the sixth floor and looked back as the fifth floor landing tilted crazily. It didn't collapse, but it continued to shake and tremble on overstressed rebar supports. As he watched, the painted concrete cracked and crazed beneath the strain. One of the dead zombies slid across its surface and disappeared into the dark abyss below as cement chips zipped through the air and bounced off the cinderblock walls. Finally, the landing came to a rest, tilted downward. The first few steps on the stairway leading to the sixth floor landing were badly cracked as well. McDaniels figured it wouldn't take much to get the landing to tear free and tumble down below. If the zeds down there had any capacity left for surprise, they'd likely realize it when the huge slab of concrete fell their way.

There was nothing more to do. McDaniels turned and hurried up the steps, on his way back to the 27th floor.

22

Surging along at twenty knots, the ride aboard the *Escanaba* was uncomfortable as all hell, for the ship kept taking rollers over the bow. As she steamed into a quartering head sea, the twenty foot waves hit her 270 foot long hull with all the tenacity of a relentless prizefighter seeking to score a knockout. But the *Escanaba* was no lightweight. She pushed through the seas, taking all the punishment they could muster as her white steel bow sliced through each advancing wave, then dove down into the trough on the other side.

Commander Hassle and the rest of the crew on the *Nob*'s bridge grabbed onto anything that would support them so they wouldn't be knocked sprawling across the deck. As they drew closer to the mouth of New York harbor, called Lower Bay, the sea state began to diminish thanks to the terrain on either side. Ahead and to the left of the *Escanaba*'s bow lay the New Jersey shoreline and Staten Island. To the right was the western portion of Long Island. The land masses were mostly dark, punctuated here and there by the orange blaze of raging fires. Occasionally, the glow of smaller lights—headlights, Hassle thought—would break through the shroud of blackness, but the *Nob* was too far to offer any refugees even a glimmer of hope if they happened to catch sight of her running lights. They were on their own.

For her part, the *Escanaba* had the sea lanes to herself. Other ships were in the water, but most of them were dark, unlighted. Many were at anchor; others, like the six hundred foot container ship to the *Nob*'s port, were adrift. Hassle and others looked at the vessel through the FLIR systems mounted on the ship's mast. Dark figures stumbled across the container vessel's decks, looking toward the *Escanaba*'s lights as she drew past. The figures on the ship's decks had long ago stopped paying any attention to the driving rain or raging wind that battered their vessel. The container ship belonged to the dead now.

Jesus Christ, Hassle thought.

Coney Island slowly came into view, its carnival rides forever at an end. The great rollercoaster, the Cyclone, was a skeletal presence in the obsidian night, the remains of some great beast whose passing had gone mostly unnoticed. Hassle did not turn one of the FLIR scanners in that direction, for fear he might see a legion of dead tottering through the remains of the amusement park. He had happy memories of summers spent at Coney Island, and he did not want them violated by images of the dead claiming their new kingdom.

More and more boats became visible through the radar and the FLIR as the *Escanaba* rounded Coney Island and Sea Gate and propelled her way into the waters of the Upper Bay. The Port of New Jersey was dark, desolate, illuminated by only the battery-powered buoys that marked its harbor lanes. Governors Island was similarly nondescript, a lump of darkness against the gray waters as it slid off to the ship's portside. To starboard, lights still gleamed in Brooklyn, but there were fires as well. Beacons strobed in the water ahead as NYPD launches maneuvered against the weather. *Escanaba*'s radio operator contacted the launches and briefed them on their mission.

The response was terse: "Do what you gotta do and get out."

"Guess they won't be helping us out," said Lieutenant Commander Miles Sullivan, the ship's executive officer.

Hassle shrugged. There was nothing else to do.

Then, Lower Manhattan lay before them, an inferno of flame and smoke and windblown sparks that flared and despite the storm. The skyline of the city was different; the Woolworth Building as no more, apparently the victim of a collapse. The half-completed Freedom Tower stood in high relief against the glowing backdrop of flame, a testament to dreams unfulfilled. As the *Escanaba* drew nearer, the smell of acrid smoke reached Hassle's nostrils. Off to port, the Statue of Liberty stood silent witness to the fall of the Greatest City in the World. The crew standing watch on the *Escanaba*'s bridge surveyed the destruction from inside the safety of the pilothouse. No one spoke. There wasn't much that could be said.

"Stay sharp for surface contacts," Hassle warned. "No telling what's in the water now."

The lookout called then from his position at the bow. "Con, Bow... got people in the water, a *lot* of people!"

"Bow, Con. Do you mean actual people or bodies?" Hassle asked over the intercom.

"Ah... Con, Bow Lookout. A lot of 'em are moving, so it's tough to say. No one's screaming for help, but they're trying to swim toward us. Don't really know what to say."

"All lookouts, Con. Report on bodies in the water," Hassle ordered. The reports came back immediately. Many bodies were motionless and severely damaged, missing limbs and suffering from what Hassle supposed were severe deboning injuries from the reports. But a good portion of these bodies were still moving. Not swimming, exactly, but reacting to the presence of the *Escanaba* as she pushed past them. Several of them made to climb aboard, but with only a smooth steel hull available, there were no handholds.

Sullivan looked at Hassle, his face composed and calm in the red light that illuminated the bridge. "I'm thinking we might need to issue some weapons to the lookouts, just in case. From everything we've heard, we do *not* want one of those... zombie things... to get on board."

Hassle nodded. "Agreed. Get it done."

Sullivan picked up the ICS and issued the order for the lookouts to be armed. Hassle reminded the bridge crew to be vigilant for waterborne obstructions, and advised them to not respond to anything that was not a clear signal for help from actual, live human beings. And even as he said this, he found his gaze continually straying to the great city that lay to port. Using light-intensification binoculars, he scanned the ports and shoreline of Manhattan. The East River Drive was packed solid with abandoned vehicles, from the Financial District to as far north as he could see. Several vehicles were on fire, and silhouetted against the flames, the walking dead slogged through the wet night. Hassle watched as zombies standing along Peck Slip took notice of the *Escanaba*'s passage and literally climbed over the pier guardrails and flung themselves into the river, in what he believed could only be a vain attempt to get to the ship. New York City, the Big Apple, was essentially a giant graveyard filled with the walking dead.

This is unbelievable. Just totally, completely unbelievable. Hassle was a rational, educated man, a skilled sailor who was a permanent cutterman in the Coast Guard, and a more-than-just-competent officer. He believed that an open mind and a personal flexibility to challenges were the cornerstones of a successful career in the U.S. Coast Guard. But what he saw now simply blew those things away. He and his crew were able to zero in on drug runners and illegal aliens trying to gain entry into the United States, and they had all been recalibrated to serve as one of the most potent lines of defense against terrorism. But nothing in their experience or training could prepare them for this. Nothing.

But he kept his best commander's face on, and never let his true feelings show. For the sailors and officers aboard the USCG *Escanaba*, he was totally calm, cool, and in control. Under his watch, the ship would prevail. They would succeed in their mission.

There was simply no alternative.

Ahead, great flashes of light strobed across the dark waters of the East River, illuminating everything for miles. Sparking explosions besieged an entire span of the Brooklyn Bridge, which lay only five hundred meters ahead of the *Nob*'s bow. Revealed in the sudden light were dozens of small boats, and floating in the swollen, windswept river, hundred—maybe even thousands!—of bodies, some of which clumsily pirouetted in the water to regard the explosions with dead eyes. A startled rush went through the bridge crew, and the ICS went wild with shocked reports from the lookouts.

"Helm, slow to eight knots!" Hassle said as he trained his binoculars on the span ahead. He watched as a huge section of the Brooklyn Bridge slowly collapsed, great chunks of concrete and steel and asphalt slamming into the water with incredible force. Plumes of water shot up even higher than the bridge itself, showering it with muddy river water.

"Eight knots, aye sir!" The helmsman manning the con grabbed the engine throttle levers and pulled them back to the required setting, and the white-hulled *Escanaba* immediately slowed.

"Christ, you think they would have waited until we'd passed!" Petersen said from his station at the radar console. As he spoke, more explosions tore through the night as the Williamsburg and Manhattan Bridges were also attacked.

"Everyone take it easy!" Hassle said, his voice sharp-edged. "We knew this was going to happen, and we knew the Air Force had orders to bring down the bridges. It sucks that we have to pick our way through the mess, but this is what it is. Now everyone cut the chatter, and get back to doing your jobs!"

The bridge crew did as they were told. Some merely shrugged off the attacks as something to be expected. Others took longer to refocus on what they had to do, but they did it, one by one. Hassle watched this from his position on the bridge, and felt a stirring of pride in his chest. No matter what happened, the crew of the *Escanaba* were professionals, and they would see things through.

Sullivan grabbed the shipboard ICS handset. "Lookouts, Con. Stay sharp, we're going to have to pass through those debris fields. Watch out for anything that's lying right below the surface. Additional crews topside, we need all eyes on deck now."

Hassle raised his glasses back to his eyes and surveyed the destruction ahead. The Air Force attack had been precise; only one section of the Brooklyn Bridge had been rendered impassable, which mean the debris in the water would be fairly localized. He gave the helm bearing and speed directions, and the *Escanaba* shifted her position from the center of the river and moved more toward the Brooklyn side. Her forward speed reduced to five knots, so slow that her hull barely produced a wake as it sliced through the water. More crewmen emerged on the main deck, clad in foul weather gear and holding large flashlights. Searchlights were powered up on either side of the ship and directed downward toward the water. Even though they were looking for debris that could penetrate the ship's steel hull—or much worse, destroy her running gear—the lights revealed countless reanimated corpses floundering about in the river. They turned toward the *Escanaba* as if of one mind and thrashed toward the slowly-moving vessel. The vast majority of them had suffered violent, painful deaths. Even from his position on the bridge, Hassle saw many were missing limbs, or trailed their guts behind them like streamers. It was madness, total and complete madness, a horror show on a stage so vast that it was incomprehensible.

How are we going to survive this? Hassle asked himself. His thoughts weren't about his ship or his crew, but about the human race itself. How could humanity survive what seemed to be a plague of the dead?

Knock it off. You have a job to do. Let echelons above reality figure out the big stuff. You just need to pick up some people before they become... non-people.

The *Escanaba* slowly picked her way past the debris zone around the Brooklyn Bridge, then crept past the smaller one surrounding the Manhattan Bridge. As they slid past the bridge's stout pilings and emerged on the other side, something slammed to the foredeck, collapsing into a pile next to the *Nob*'s 76-millimeter main gun. Hassle heard a distant *thump* as something else landed on the pilot house. He immediately put down his binoculars and bolted for the port exit.

"Sullivan, you have the con!" he barked as he undogged the hatch and stepped out into the storm-torn night. Without pausing to zip up his coat, he scurried down the steps, made slick by rain despite their anti-skid coating. As quickly as he could, he made his way to the bow, moving from handhold to handhold as the big ship wallowed slightly in the wind.

By the time he made it to the bow, several crewmen stood around the figure lying next to the bulbous shape of the Mk 76 gun turret. They shined their flashlights on it. Whatever their beams exposed, it had completely captivated their attention. No one even looked up when Hassle pushed his way toward them.

The zombie was broken and battered, its legs snapped like kindling. Its body had been torn open by the impact, and a grisly black gruel leaked out from its punctured chest cavity. One eye bulged from its socket, and the left side of its face was crushed inward. Despite the incredible damage it had suffered, the ghoul still moved. It emitted a gurgling whine as it tried to right itself and crawl toward the clutch of Coast Guardsmen surrounding it. Its one good eye moved from man to man as it slowly inched along the rain-slick steel deck, using its one good arm to drag itself along.

"Holy fuck," whispered one of the crewman, a female Guardsman clutching an M16.

"Never seen anything like that in my entire fucking life," said another crewman, a short, slight kid Hassle knew came from Michigan. He didn't seem to be repulsed by what he saw, which Hassle thought was odd. Hassle was at least twenty years older, and the sight of the oozing corpse slowly writhing on the deck like some sort of demonic snake almost sickened him.

"Somebody shoot it through the head," Hassle said, raising his voice above the wind. When no one moved, he reached for his pistol and pulled it from its holster. Thumbing off the safety, he gingerly stepped toward the zombie as it crawled toward him. It hissed again, fixing him with its one good eye.

Hassle fired two shots through its head, and the zombie fell to the deck, motionless.

More gunfire from overhead caught his attention, and he looked up. A Coast Guardsman waved to him from the railing on top of the pilot house.

"One zombie dead up here, sir!" the crewman shouted.

From the rear of the vessel, where the helipad was located, came more gunfire. Hassle stepped back from the zombie he had shot and slapped a crewman on the shoulder, hard, getting his attention.

"Get a gaff and throw this thing off the side! Do *not* touch it! No one touch the thing with your hands, just gaff it and throw it over the side!"

The crewmen muttered their acknowledgements and Hassle sprinted to the aft section of the ship. Two more zombies had come aboard, but the crewmen there had dispatched them with shots to the head. No one had been bitten. Hassle repeated his orders to toss the corpses overboard without touching them, then returned to the bridge.

"We need to keep alert to make sure we take these things down the second they land," he told Sullivan. He described how the crewmen at the bow just stood around watching the zombie before he had intervened and killed it. "Someone's going to get bitten by one of these things if they're not careful, and we can't have that."

"Understood. Connolly took out the one topside, and he and some of the other guys tossed it. They were smart enough to use gaffs. But we should check everyone, just to make sure. Just in case someone might be... you know, infected." Sullivan clenched his teeth together after he had said that last part, his face hard set.

Hassle nodded slowly. "Have the medics check over everyone who was involved in handling the bodies. And have the chief of the boat put together a detail to dispose of anything that makes it aboard. And no matter what, those things get shot immediately!"

"Aye, sir," Sullivan said. He saw to the arrangements as the *Escanaba* bore down slowly but relentlessly on the Williamsburg Bridge. The center section of its span was missing, and its suspension cables supported only empty air. But figures still milled about in the darkness, figures that occasionally slipped and fell into the dark water. Most were on the Manhattan side of the bridge, and as he watched, Hassle saw flashes of light wink in the darkness on the Brooklyn side. Petersen noticed them too and trained his binoculars on them.

"Muzzle flashes," he said. "Looks like the National Guard and NYPD are taking out the zombies on the Brooklyn side of the bridge."

"Good on them. The more they kill, the fewer will try to get to us." Hassle ordered the helmsman to steer the *Nob* closer to the Wallabout Channel, which lay on the Brooklyn side of the river. The helmsman repeated the order and executed it flawlessly, bringing the cutter to within one hundred feet of the entrance to the Brooklyn Navy Yard. Despite its name, the Yard was not a Navy facility and its piers and moorings were mostly vacant. Anyone who had a boat and who could get to it were long gone. The *Escanaba* plowed on at five knots, barely moving. It passed underneath the Williamsburg Bridge without any incident, and Hassle ordered the ship to mid-channel and an increase in speed to ten knots. The *Escanaba*'s diesel engines roared in response when the power was added, as if they had chafed at the mere five knots they had delivered for the past hour and half. As the ship left the shattered bridges behind, the crew seemed to sigh in unison.

Then the lights of Manhattan winked out, as if the entire city had suddenly died in its sleep.

23

By the time he made it to the cafeteria on the 27th floor, McDaniels was severely winded. His thighs were on fire, and his quadriceps spasmed and twitched, complaining at the demand placed upon them. Sweat poured off his face, and he coughed several times. He tasted blood in the back of his mouth.

Well, I guess I never should have stopped going on those fifteen mile road marches after all...

Finelly met him at the door. He took a moment to size him up, then said, "You look like shit, major."

"At least try and sound respectful when you say that," McDaniels replied, breathing hard. "Is the elevator here?"

"Yes, sir."

"Did one of you guys contact Rapier?" McDaniels turned and leaned over the handrail and peered down into the stairway below. He didn't see anything down below, couldn't hear anything, but he knew the dead were coming. And OMEN was leading them.

"We did. That Coast Guard boat's approaching the East River now. They must've had a hell of a ride getting up here. Air Force just hit the bridges all around Manhattan, so we're pretty much cut off."

"Makes my day," McDaniels said. He still looked down the staircase, waiting, watching. Finelly suddenly walked up and put a hand on his shoulder and pulled him away from the railing.

"We really need to get inside and button this place up, sir."

"They'll be coming up."

"And we'll be going down, sir. We can't stay up here with a couple of hundred rounds each and shoot every stench in the city. Time's up."

McDaniels removed his helmet and leaned against the handrail, listening. He heard nothing but the wind slipping past the ill-fitting door above them and the slight sounds of machines doing their thankless labor. An army of the dead could have been marching up the stairs, but if they were, Cord McDaniels couldn't hear them at the moment.

He straightened and nodded to Finelly. "Okay, let's get this show on the road before a bunch of dead people try to freaking eat us."

"Best plan I heard all day, sir. You want me to stand watch out here?"

McDaniels shook his head and pointed to the door. "Negative. Inside the hallway would be better, but we won't be staying for all that long. Come on." The two men left the fire stairs and closed the entry door behind them. After they tied it off with the fire hose, they set out in search of the others. They were waiting for them in the cafeteria's dining room, standing near the freight elevator entrance.

"What's going on down there?" Safire asked. It was a legitimate question, not a shrewish demand. Clearly, the scientist was finding a way to moderate himself, which suited McDaniels just fine.

Mindful of the young people, McDaniels quickly explained that they were in danger of being overrun from below. He turned to Leary and asked for an update.

"Coasties can talk to us on our frequency," he said, tapping his radio earphones. "They won't be in position to pick us up for another hour or so, but they're on the way. They'll hold the ship off the northern tip of Roosevelt Island, which is right across the river from us. Been doing some recon from the roof, and it looks like all the north-south streets are full of traffic, but a lot of the smaller cross streets were kept clear so official traffic could move cross-town. Still some abandoned vehicles, but we can make it around most of 'em."

"What about the ones we can't?" McDaniels asked, voice low.

Leary shrugged. "Deal with that when it happens. I'm thinking we could push them out of the way, if what the first sergeant says is true about that van down there. But there is a barricade at the end of Seventy-Ninth"—he turned and pointed out the windows, but McDaniels couldn't see anything through its rain-soaked surface—"with a couple of fire department tanker trucks. Before I joined Special Forces, I was on a fire team. I can drive one of those things and blast a path clear for us if that's what it takes."

McDaniels nodded slowly. "Yeah, that sounds great, Leary. We'll worry about that when it comes, like you said." He grabbed the shorter soldier's elbow and guided him toward the rest of the group. "But we've got to work on getting the hell out of here, because those things are on their way up here. And OMEN is leading them."

"Is it Keith?" Leary asked.

"I didn't see him, but I saw some of the others. And there are other soldiers in the mix now, too. Saw some uniforms down below. If any of them remember even a tiny percentage of their skills..."

Leary got it. "Yeah, maybe we ought to get the hell out of here. But where are we going to go? If that boat isn't in position yet..."

"Maybe we can find another boat and head out to meet them. Or maybe just push off the shore and wait for them in the river. I don't know what, but we sure as hell can't stay here for much longer. Let's go, folks," he said to the rest of the group. "Who's got the keys to that truck down there?"

"I do." Leary pulled the keys out of his pocket. McDaniels nodded as he stepped toward the waiting freight elevator. Its fluorescent lights shined brightly in the murky atmosphere of the cafeteria. He pushed Safire toward the elevator.

"We've got to move smartly folks," McDaniels said. As the rest of the group moved into the elevator, he keyed his radio's microphone. "Five, this is Six. You ready for us down there? Over."

"Ready as we'll ever be, Six. Over." The static still messed with the communications, but McDaniels could make out what Gartrell said without having to think about it too much. He was the last aboard the elevator, and he stabbed the button marked G. The door began to slide closed.

Then the lights went out.

Someone screamed—it wasn't the youngest girl, it was her older sister, Kenisha. A thrill of fear went through everyone, and both McDaniels and Leary reached out and grabbed the edge of the elevator door. It was within millimeters of sliding closed when the power failed, and there was just enough of a gap for them to get their fingers inside. They pulled, and the door slowly retracted back into its recess with the greatest of reluctance.

"Five, this is Six... we just lost power up here, over!"

"Roger that, Six. Same down here, in case you were curious. Are you trapped in the elevator? Over."

"Negative, we're still on twenty-seven. Give me a second to figure this out, over."

"Roger, Six."

"Everybody out," McDaniels ordered. He reached behind him and grabbed the front of Safire's jacket and hauled him out of the elevator.

"Major, do you mind?" Safire snapped, not happy with the roughness of McDaniels' actions. McDaniels ignored him and flipped down his night vision goggles.

"Troops, go NVGs," he ordered. Leary already had his in place. Finelly and Derwitz snapped their goggles down over their eyes and shouldered their weapons. They looked at McDaniels, waiting for orders. McDaniels didn't keep them waiting.

"You two, guard the corridor outside. Watch the fire exit. Don't get too close, some of our guys are with the dead, and they know how to use their weapons, including grenades. Once I figure out how we're getting out of here, I'll recall you."

"Got it, sir," Finelly said. He and Derwitz turned and headed for the hallway outside. McDaniels returned to the elevator and pressed the G button again. The door did not move, and only the meager emergency light was on. The call panel was completely dark. The elevator—like the rest of the building, and the entire city McDaniels saw through the rain-slick windows—was dead.

He fell to his knees and pushed and tugged at the tile floor. There was no hatch he could detect. Earl stepped toward the elevator then and looked down at him, his hands in his pockets.

"Ain't nothin' in the floor there, major. What, you think they'd put somethin' there that people might be able to fall through when they're a hunnert feet off the ground?" he asked, the puzzled amazement plain in his voice.

McDaniels pushed himself to his feet, smiling ruefully beneath his helmet and night vision goggles. "I guess not," he said. "Is there any other way off this floor, without having to go down the stairs?"

"Naw, this is —" Earl stopped himself and put a hand on his chin. He stroked it thoughtfully. Leary watched them from behind his night vision goggles, then opened his mouth to say something. McDaniels waved for him to be silent.

"Earl," he said softly, "if you have something, you got to tell us now, man."

As soon as he finished, a thin sound cut through the sudden silence. It was a long, drawn out moan. Leary shouldered his M4 and darted toward the door that led to the corridor, but McDaniels didn't need any confirmation. The dead were making their way up the stairs.

"The dumb waiter," Earl said. "It goes down to the twenty-sixth floor board room—"

"Where is it?" McDaniels said.

"The kitchen. Follow me," Earl said, and he hurried across the dark dining room.

"Where are we going?" Regina asked.

"Follow him," McDaniels said, waving the others to follow. Regina did that, a hand on her father's arm, towing him along as she hurried after him and Earl.

"Yes, I heard about the dumb waiter, but what good is getting to another floor going to do if we can't get to the basement?" she asked.

"We can get to the freight elevator from there and climb down the shaft," he told her as he followed Earl into the kitchen. The emergency lights were brighter here, and he flipped up his goggles, falling back to using the good old Mark I eyeball.

"You think we're going to be able to climb down the *elevator shaft*?" Safire asked, the incredulity plain in his voice.

"We sure as hell are," McDaniels said.

Earl looked around the kitchen for a moment, then found what he wanted. A single stainless steel door was mounted in the wall, approximately three feet high by three feet wide. He grabbed its handle and yanked it open. On the other side was a small elevator with shelves for plates of food.

"Yeah, here it is!" he said, not even attempting to hide his simple delight at the discovery. McDaniels fancied that in his mind, Earl had saved them all. That was very probably close to the truth.

"It's a good step in the right direction, but with the power off, how do we get down?" McDaniels asked. "It uses electricity, right?"

Earl reached inside and plucked a rope with one hand. "Naw, this is part of the original equipment! This thing was here when the building was put together, and no one really paid much attention to it unless there were dinner meetin's and things like that. No sense in puttin' an electric motor on it, you know?" He let go of the rope and reached inside the elevator and pulled out one of the shelves. He placed it on the floor. McDaniels reached over Earl's shoulder and pulled out another shelf. Within moments, the elevator was clear. McDaniels immediately tried to climb inside, but even with the shelves removed, it couldn't hold him and his huge backpack. He shrugged it off and tried again. It was a tight fit, but he made it.

"Earl, describe the board room to me. And what else is on the twenty-sixth floor?"

"Board room's got a big table, with about twenny chairs. Dumb waiter opens up on the wall facing the windows. Only one door leading out to the hall, but there are glass windows overlookin' it. It's all offices, only a few cubes that the secretaries would use. I know they're all gone, no one on that floor other than the boss, and we know what happened to him."

"Which way to the freight elevator from the board room?"

"Left out of the board room, end of the hall. Here, I'll send you down. Be careful and try not to move around too much, major. I don't think this thing was built for people, you know?"

McDaniels clutched his M4 and nodded. "Got it."

Earl pulled on the rope, and the dumb waiter hitched and jerked as it made its way down to the next floor. It hit the bottom of the landing with a tinny *clunk* and came to a full stop. A small push bar was on the door, placed there just in case someone happened to get trapped inside. McDaniels pressed it and slowly pushed against the door. It swung open on well-lubricated hinges. Slowly, McDaniels unfolded himself from the dumb waiter's tight confines. A long credenza was right below the door, and he stepped onto its lacquered surface gingerly, his M4 clutched against his side. Getting out of the dumb waiter was awkward and cumbersome, and he wondered how well the much bigger Finelly would handle it.

The floor was just as Earl had described it. McDaniels exited the board room and turned left, his rifle at the ready, his NVGs in place across his eyes. He moved quietly but quickly, his boots whispering across first carpet and then travertine tile. The freight elevator was in a room similar to what was in the cafeteria, which made it easy to locate. Using the fire key, he was able to force open the sliding door. The elevator shaft was completely dark, but his NVGs revealed it was also empty. There were no zeds in it, and the elevator was still parked at the floor above where McDaniels stood. He shoved a nearby trash can between the door and the frame to hold it open.

"Leary, this is Six." McDaniels spoke softly into his headset microphone. "Let's start sending everyone down. Get the rope from the elevator up there and bring it along. We're going to need it."

"Roger that, Six."

24

It took some time to get everyone relocated to the 26th floor, as stealth had to be maintained. As they descended one by one in the dumb waiter, McDaniels kept a close watch on the fire escape door, located down an adjacent corridor from the freight elevator. If the zombies tried to get to them, the attack would come through there.

The moans grew louder in the stairwell as the dead climbed higher and higher. It would not be long until they were right outside the 26th floor fire door. The question was, would they continue on to 27? And if so, how long would they remain there before coming back down? He decided that all depended on just how much of their collective tactical faculties OMEN team retained. If they were only running on so-called "muscle memory", then so long as they were quiet and especially mindful of what they were doing, then they could make it to the basement without incident.

If not, of course, then things would probably go to hell in a fast sports car.

Leary was the last to leave the 27th floor. As he lowered the dumb waiter with all of their gear loaded inside—none of the soldiers could withdraw with all their packs and weapons on them, as the dumb waiter was just too small—he reported he heard pounding on the fire escape door. It was hardly news to McDaniels, who heard the same thing from the 26th floor board room. Time was up. McDaniels pulled all the gear out of the dumb waiter and sent it back up.

"Let me know when you're inside, and I'll pull you down," he said over the radio as he yanked downward on the rope. The dumb waiter ascended on its well-lubricated rails.

"I'm inside, and the outer door is closed," Leary said a moment later. Just as a finished, a terrific crash echoed through the 27th floor, its sound reaching McDaniels through the dumb waiter's shaft. He pulled on the rope, bringing the dumb waiter down.

"What was that?" he asked over the radio. He was alone in the board room. Finelly and Derwitz were with the civilians in the freight elevator vestibule, rigging the ropes they had with them. While he hadn't expressly told Safire and the others what the plan was, it shouldn't come as any surprise that they were going to have to climb down to the basement parking garage.

"Sounds like the zeds are on the floor," Leary said calmly. "Probably so many of them they just popped the door out of the frame. Better watch out down there, sir... same thing might happen."

The dumb waiter arrived and McDaniels helped Leary climb out. "Let's hope not," he said, and led him to the freight elevator vestibule.

***

McDaniels was pleasantly surprised to find that Gartrell and Rittenour had tied their rappelling gear and gloves to one of the ropes, and Finelly and Derwitz had recovered them without hassle. They had then tossed the rope back down the elevator shaft.

His surprise at finding resistance from Wolf Safire was not quite as pleasant, however.

"I'm sorry, major. I simply can't climb down a rope for three hundred feet," Safire said. There was no acrimony in his voice when he spoke, or even fear. He merely stated what he believed to be a fact as he peered into the elevator shaft. To him, without the aid of night vision devices, it would be a pitch black maw yawning into hell.

"Why is that, doctor?" McDaniels asked.

"I'm sixty-seven years old, major."

"Age has nothing to do with this, doctor. But don't worry about a thing. You'll be strapped to my back." Underlining the urgency of the situation was the noise from overhead. It seemed that hundreds of zombies staggered around the cafeteria now, brushing against tables and chairs, knocking things over. There was a tremendous crash as dinnerware shattered against the floor. The zeds were tearing up the place looking for them, and McDaniels didn't want to depend on the zombies' total stupidity to keep them safe long enough for him to have a calm, rational conversation with Wolf Safire.

Safire must have thought McDaniels was joking. "I can't make it. I have a severe rotator cuff injury that was never successfully repaired, as well as significant arthritis in my hands and shoulders. I would love to do it, major. I have no desire to become food for the zombies, but I just can't." He put his hand on Regina's arm. "Please take my daughter and the rest of these young people out ahead."

"As far as this mission goes, they're non-essential personnel. You are the mission objective. You go first."

Safire's face clouded. "I don't think —"

There was a steady pounding from outside as first one zombie, then another and another and another started working on getting past the 26th floor fire door. Leary leaned into the corridor outside, then turned to McDaniels.

"They're at the door. I'm going to go pull the batteries from the emergency lights. Should slow 'em down a bit," he said, then disappeared as he stepped out of the vestibule and closed the door behind him.

McDaniels shrugged off his backpack and opened it up. He pulled out a loose association of black nylon straps, carabineers, and a piece of metal that looked superficially like a figure 8. He also pulled out several long plastic quick-ties which he shoved into a trouser pocket, then quickly slipped on the straps. Finelly snorted.

"Guess you Green Beanies don't go anywhere without your rappelling gear," he said.

"Can you and Derwitz rappel down?" McDaniels asked.

"Hooah," Finelly said.

McDaniels keyed his radio button. "Five, this is Six. How's it looking from down there? Over."

"Six, all clear in the shaft. I can see you guys up top. It's about two hundred and seventy feet to the bottom, so you have a hell of a climb down. Lots of supports to use as hand- and footholds, but they're about ten feet apart. Hope you've got enough gloves to go around."

"Roger that, thanks. We'll be coming down shortly." McDaniels handed his back pack to Finelly. "You look strong as an ox, Finelly. Can you carry my gear?"

Finelly lifted the pack and after assessing its weight, nodded silently. McDaniels handed him the quick-ties, then crouched before Safire.

"Hop aboard, doctor. Make it quick."

Safire looked scandalized by the proposition. "I don't think now is the time for a *piggyback ride*, major!"

"Get on, you pompous ass!" McDaniels snapped. "No one's leaving here until you do, including your precious daughter, so snap to it!"

Safire started to refuse, then thought better of it. With a heavy sigh, he slowly climbed onto McDaniels' back. McDaniels hefted him into position and twisted about slightly until he felt the scientist was about as well balanced as he could be. He nodded to Finelly.

"Strap him up," he said.

Finelly used the quick-ties to secure Safire to McDaniels as well as he could. McDaniels pulled a spare pair of gloves from one pocket and handed them to Regina.

"Put those on, you'll need them. Earl, you have gloves?"

"Yeah," Earl said, his voice thin and unsure. "You really think we gotta climb down the elevator shaft? I mean, there ain't no ladders or nuthin' down there —"

"Hear all that pounding, Earl? That's what's going to have you for dinner. Climbing down is the only chance you have of getting out of here alive. Finelly, strap his youngest kid to his back. Kenisha, Regina, you guys are on your own. Kenisha, you look like you're in great shape, can you do this?"

"I was a gymnast in high school," she said. There was a nervous quality in her voice that McDaniels wasn't sure he liked, but there were a thousand zombies trying to get at them. What wasn't there to be nervous about?

"You'll do fine. Take a set of gloves." He hopped upward slightly, adjusting the load on his back. Safire groaned at the indignity of it all, and McDaniels felt his breath on the back of his neck. McDaniels grabbed the secured rope in both hands and yanked on it, testing the strength of the knot Finelly and Derwitz had tied.

"Here, I have some extra gloves." Derwitz handed them to Kenisha, and she smiled vaguely as she pulled them on.

"They fit," she said.

"Be glad I got small hands," Derwitz said.

"Maxi's always wanted to be a woman," Finelly added.

"Blow me," Derwitz said. "Oh, sorry about that," he added for Earl's benefit, glancing quickly at his young daughter.

Leary stepped back inside the vestibule. McDaniels couldn't see much of his face behind his NVGs and radio microphone, but he didn't look happy.

"We gotta boogie, major. Those things are going to get through that door pretty quickly. I pushed a file cabinet up against it, but it's not going to do more than slow them down for a second or two."

"On our way. Get your rappelling gear ready." As Leary pulled his rappelling harness out of his backpack, McDaniels keyed his radio transmit button. "Five, we're coming down. Over."

"Roger that, Six, and I advise you to get a move on. Over."

"Brace those doors," McDaniels said to Leary, then hauled himself and Safire into the elevator shaft. He cinched the rope through his rappelling gear and pushed off the edge of the open elevator door. Safire gasped even though the hop was a small one, just a quick experiment to ensure both he and the rope had what it took.

"Take it easy," he said to Safire. "Just enjoy the ride—it won't take very long."

And it didn't. Though it had been a while, McDaniels rappelled down the length of the elevator shaft quickly and efficiently, even with the extra weight on his back. For his part, Safire clung to him like a frightened child but he remained utterly silent during their bounding descent. Overhead, the second rope tensed as Finelly clambered onto it and began his own descent.

Gartrell's voice whispered in his headset. "Fifty feet now, major. Looking good, almost there. We're right here waiting for you..."

And with that, McDaniels was pulled backward as Gartrell and Rittenour grabbed Safire. They hauled both men out of the elevator shaft and into the darkened parking garage. As Rittenour ducked back into the shaft to spot Finelly, Gartrell cut Safire free. Some of the plastic ties had cut into his skin despite Finelly's careful placement. Once he was free, the elderly man practically collapsed to the cement floor. Gartrell half-caught him and cushioned the impact.

"Easy there, doctor," he said.

"Thank you... thank you," was all Safire could say as McDaniels turned and helped Gartrell ease him into a sitting position.

"No problem. You sit there and rest," McDaniels told him.

Finelly joined them a short time later, red-faced and slightly out of breath from the hard work ferrying McDaniels' loaded back pack from the 27th floor. McDaniels allowed himself a brief smile. Even though Finelly was at least a good fifteen years younger, McDaniels had made it down with more weight on him and more breath in his lungs.

Derwitz was next, and he shrugged off his pack after alighting. "Someone has to go back up and help the civilians come down, major," he said. "I'll do it."

"Sergeant Leary will see to that, Derwitz."

"They'll be blind. There's not much light in there, and they don't have NVGs. I'll only go up a couple of stories, talk them down if they need it."

McDaniels considered this for a moment, then nodded. "All right. Thanks for volunteering."

Derwitz headed back into the elevator shaft and clambered up the rope.

Safire slowly rose to his feet. "My daughter?" he asked.

"She should be making her way down shortly. Specialist Derwitz and Sergeant Leary will assist her in her descent," McDaniels said. That wasn't strictly true. While both soldiers would doubtless cheer her on, there was nothing they could do for any of the civilians now. They were on their own now.

"Leary, how's it going up there?" McDaniels asked.

Leary's response was a muted whisper. "They're in the hallway outside, major. I've blocked the door with as much stuff as I can, but if they decided to crash through, there's not a lot I can do about it."

"Roger that. Are all the civilians off the floor? Over."

"Yes sir, all are on the rope now. Over."

"Then get the hell out of there and close the elevator doors behind you, ASAP. Over."

"On it."

McDaniels left Safire where he lay and returned to the elevator shaft. He glanced up and saw the figures slowly climbing down the rope. They still looked tiny, so very far away.

Gartrell joined him. "This is going to take a while." He grabbed a hold of McDaniels' arm and pulled him away from the shaft. "Better step back, major. No one wants to be looking up when... well, you know."

McDaniels nodded and did as Gartrell asked. He handed the keys to the senior NCO and motioned toward the van in the center of the garage.

"Maybe you should see about getting that vehicle squared away, first sergeant."

"On it, sir." With that, he spun on his heel and hurried toward the waiting van. McDaniels stepped back toward the open elevator shaft. He couldn't help himself, he was drawn to it as if by some gravitational force. He looked up and watched as Derwitz hauled himself into position several floors above, speaking to the descending civilians in hushed tones that nevertheless echoed throughout the elevator shaft. Far overhead, Leary did the same, his voice soft but encouraging.

Then something echoed through the darkness, something loud and cacophonic.

"What's going on up there, Leary?" McDaniels asked.

"Zeds at the elevator door," Leary replied. "We're probably about to get the sharp end of the stick, sir. Over."

"How are the civilians doing, over?"

"So-so. It's plenty dark in here, and it's a long way. Earl's doing okay, I think. Not so sure about the others —"

A brief shriek cut him off. McDaniels' heart leaped into his throat as he saw a figure tumbling through the elevator shaft.

Oh God —

The figure bounced from side to side, and the sounds were horrifying as each impact forced a tiny, breathy exhalation from the body. The sounds echoed throughout the elevator shaft as the body tumbled and spun like a disjointed rag doll. Derwitz swore and pressed himself against the concrete wall as the body slipped past him, bouncing off a support. McDaniels was jerked backwards suddenly, and Rittenour's voice was in his ear.

"Get out of the way, major!"

And then, the body slammed to the bottom of the elevator shaft with a wet slap that carried with it the sound of bone being compressed past the stage of breaking. Something dank and fetid filled the air, and McDaniels pushed away from Rittenour and leaned back inside the shaft.

Kenisha Brown still breathed slightly through an open mouth. Her tongue was bloodied, and more blood trickled from her nostrils. One side of her face had been crushed inward, and the eye on that side was distended, the orb sticking out from the ravaged socket like some sort of glutinous marble. Her limbs were bent askew in several places, and her skull had been parted on one side. Brain tissue peered out, rendered in ghostly green and white by the night vision goggles.

And then, she stopped breathing.

Rittenour joined McDaniels at the elevator door and grimaced. "Jesus Christ. Poor kid..."

"Is it Regina?" Safire asked from behind them. His voice was weak and tremulous.

"No," McDaniels said over his shoulder, "it's not."

Safire said nothing in response, but McDaniels heard him weeping as silently as he could. McDaniels knew how he felt. If he had time, he'd weep himself.

More banging and slamming from above. McDaniels and Rittenour looked up the shaft as light flared and gunshots echoed through the building. Brass cartridges tinkled as they fell down the long tunnel, bouncing from wall to wall.

"Zeds are forcing open the door, major!" Leary reported. "They got us!"

"Sir." Rittenour pointed down at Kenisha Brown's body as it slowly stirred, writhing in place as its skeleton had been so severely damaged during the fall that it couldn't provide its muscles with a solid framework on which to generate real motion. The zombie's blood-filled eyes rolled this way and that, and the one good eye left in its head focused on McDaniels' left boot, some four feet above. It reached for him with a flopping arm. McDaniels pulled his pistol and fired a single round into its head.

"Come on people, you have to move now, and move quickly!" McDaniels shouted. "Regina, Earl—you have to hurry!"

"I'm trying," Regina said, and her voice was breathless.

Earl only muttered something, and McDaniels realized his words were for his surviving daughter, not for him.

"Easy does it, Regina. But as quickly as you can." Into his radio: "Leary, how bad is the incursion?"

"They're still fiddling with the door, but they know where we are," Leary said. "Expect them to be dropping in anytime now, if you'll pardon the pun. I'm trying to hold them back, but there are so many of them, they might just pop the doors open from sheer mass alone, over."

"Major." Gartrell hovered behind McDaniels' shoulder. He looked at Rittenour and jerked his head to one side. Rittenour fell back and joined Safire, who crouched on the cement floor beside the van. Finelly stood nearby, his weapon at port arms. Gartrell grabbed McDaniels' arm and pulled him away from the elevator shaft once again.

"Major, listen to me. We're ready to go. We have Safire, and we have transportation. Let's do the right thing and boogie, sir. We've ridden this as far as we can."

McDaniels looked at Gartrell as if he were an alien creature. For his part, Gartrell endured the major's derisive look as stoically as he could.

"You mean just abandon these people, first sergeant?" McDaniels said.

"I would call it resuming the mission," Gartrell said, his voice as hard as stone. He flipped up his night vision goggles, and glared at McDaniels through the gloom. "But you can call it whatever you like, major. It doesn't make a bit of difference to me."

"We're not running out on these people, first sergeant. They need us, we are soldiers of the United States Army, and this is our job."

Gartrell walked up on McDaniels then, got so close that their faces were only inches apart. McDaniels flipped up his own NVGs and half wondered if the altercation would get physical. If it did, he had no doubts he would be the victor.

"Now you listen to me, you two-bit loser," Gartrell said, his voice deep and raspy, the voice of a senior NCO who was used to being in charge of hundreds of troops and instilling fear in them with just a look. "I've been in This Man's Army for over twenty-five years, and you don't think for a *second* you know better what it takes to wear this uniform. You officers are all used to giving orders, but you have absolutely no fucking idea what it takes to translate those orders into results. And you're demonstrating the same bullshit you shoveled out in Afghanistan, McDaniels—you're the wrong guy for the job, because the *mission* is always second to you."

And with that, Gartrell unholstered his pistol and placed it squarely under McDaniels' chin. There was a click as he thumbed off the safety, and McDaniels was certain that his day had just come to an end.

"One chance. One chance only," Gartrell said, and his voice was barely above a throaty growl. "Get in that vehicle, or die right here. This is a no-shit circumstance, son. I am not allowing you to fuck up another mission when it is in my power to prevent you. Not this time."

"Drop that weapon, first sergeant." Finelly had taken a firing position several feet away, and his MP5 was shouldered. Its barrel was fixed on Gartrell's back. McDaniels didn't doubt that Finelly intended to shoot if he had to, and he also didn't doubt that Finelly would hose him as well.

"Hey, what the fuck is going on here?" Rittenour asked. He had his M4 in his hands, but it wasn't pointed at anyone... yet. "Finelly, put that down. First sergeant, you too. What the fuck, we don't have enough shit going down already?"

"Rittenour, get Safire into the van," Gartrell said. "Do it now."

"What the fuck for?" Rittenour asked.

"Don't bother with asking what the fuck for, just do it, troop!"

"First sergeant, put down that weapon!" Finelly said again, this time with panic-tinged conviction in his voice.

"Make me," Gartrell said. "The major's been a grade-A fuckup ever since I've known him, and now you're going to throw in with him, Finelly? I should've guessed, you aviation dilettantes are all alike." Gartrell kept his eyes on McDaniels as he spoke. When Finelly failed to respond to his jibe, he said, "What's wrong, Finelly? Can't man up enough to shoot a fellow American in the back?"

There was movement in the elevator shaft. "Help me, someone," Regina Safire called. "I can't get in by myself!"

"She's right there, Gartrell. An American citizen, who needs help. Going to turn your back on her?" McDaniels kept the iron in his own voice.

"Help her out, Ritt," Gartrell said. To McDaniels: "Next time, we won't have this conversation. You get me?"

"I get you, first sergeant."

Gartrell returned his pistol to its holster in one swift, fluid move, then snapped his NVGs back over his eyes. He turned and looked at Finelly, who still stood nearby, feet planted apart, MP5 at his shoulder.

"Secure that weapon, troop. And get that man loaded into the van," he said, pointing to Safire. "You'll be driving, I have shotgun." He patted the AA-12 slung across his chest. "No pun, of course."

He then stalked past McDaniels without looking at him and joined Rittenour at the elevator door. McDaniels reached up and dropped his NVGs over his eyes, and was surprised to see his hand wasn't trembling. Was it because he doubted Gartrell would shoot him?

No. It was because he knew that when a man like David Gartrell had his mind set on something, it took an act of God to get them not to follow through. And God had apparently acted through the core of decency Gartrell was wrapped around, and that prompted him to finally decide to save the civilians.

Even though the mission was by far more important.

25

"Don't look down," Earl begged his youngest daughter as he slowly climbed down to the end of the rope. "Just keep your eyes closed, baby, keep 'em closed." Zoe said nothing as she clutched her father's shoulders with her hands, her thin legs wrapped around his waist. She didn't respond when Gartrell and Rittenour reached up and grabbed the man and his daughter and guided them to safety. Earl caught a quick glimpse of what was left of his eldest daughter, and he stifled a sob in his throat.

"All right, Derwitz, Leary... get the hell out of there," McDaniels commanded. Derwitz scampered down the rope like a monkey from his perch on the fourth floor, and he swung over the corpse at the bottom of the elevator shaft with a deft agility that McDaniels admired.

"Coming down fast," Leary broadcast over the Special Forces soldier's net. "These things are about to pop through the doors on a couple of different floors, they're probably working their way downstairs now, major. Over." The rope shuddered, and McDaniels looked up to see Leary rappelling down its length as quickly as possible, barely stopping to push off from the wall after each bound. After a hundred feet or so, he was practically fast roping, sliding down the rope as if it were a fire pole.

Finally, they were all assembled in the parking garage, and not a moment too soon. The zombies succeeded in shoving open the doors on a higher floor. The impacts made by the bodies slamming to the bottom of the elevator shaft was pure cacophony.

"Time's up, we're out of here!" McDaniels said.

"Leary, get on the door! There's a pull-chain there that'll open it up. When the van pulls past, you hop in the back!" Gartrell said, asserting himself without any deference to McDaniels. Leary bolted across the garage while Gartrell and Rittenour shepherded the others into the waiting van.

"I've got shotgun, major," Gartrell said when McDaniels climbed into the front right seat.

"Think again, first sergeant." McDaniels slammed the door shut and buckled himself into the seat next to Finelly. Finelly gave him a quick grin and a thumbs-up as Gartrell oversaw the rest of the loading. McDaniels ignored both gestures.

"You know how to drive this thing?" he asked instead.

Finelly nodded. "Yup, drive something similar at Campbell. This one even has an automatic transmission and fulltime four wheel drive, so it's gonna be a breeze." He turned the key, and the big motor under the center cowling roared to life. Finelly nodded appreciatively when he heard the engine's song.

"Ten cylinder engine, gas burner. Two tanks, both full. Damn major, this thing's loaded for bear."

"Let's hope it's what we need."

Gartrell slammed the van's side door closed and pulled open the rear doors, then ran to the garage door. He stood opposite Leary, and nodded to him.

"Ready?"

"Ready, first sergeant." There was a furious pounding from the elevator door. The zombies were getting too close. Again.

"Van, ready?" Gartrell asked over the radio.

"Good to go here, first sergeant. Rittenour has security in the back of the vehicle, over," McDaniels said.

Gartrell pointed at Leary. "Crack it open! I'll secure the zone!"

"Here we go!" Leary yanked the chain downward, and the solid garage door rose slowly a foot at a time. Gartrell fell to his knees and peered under the slowly rising door. Beyond the door, darkness reigned, slashed by wet rain.

"Good so far," he reported. When the door had raised enough for him to duck under it, he darted out into the wet night, his AA-12 at the ready. "No zeds on the street just yet, but I can see 'em gathering at the corner, must be where the entrance to the building is. They can't hear the door being jacked open. Street's empty, most of the traffic was already cleared when the barricades went up, so haul ass out of there as soon as you can and turn hard right."

McDaniels relayed the information to Finelly, who stomped on the brake and dropped the van into drive. He didn't flip on the headlights, relying instead on his NVGs. The door rattled and shook as Leary cranked it up, his expression all hard lines as sweat rolled down his face. McDaniels mentally urged him on as the banging noises behind them became even more furious.

"Things're gonna get through, man," Derwitz said. He aimed his MP5 out the back of the van, mirroring Rittenour's stance. The Safires and the Browns were buckled up in the bench seats in the van's windowless interior, and young Zoe had her face buried against Regina's breast. Regina cooed to her as comfortingly as she could, though her eyes were wild, full of fear. In direct counterpoint, Earl and Safire were almost pictures of calm, the former still stunned by the sudden death of his firstborn, the second probably too terrified to display any meaningful emotion. McDaniels knew how they both felt.

The din outside the van reached a crescendo, and Rittenour epitomized it with two words: "Fight's on."

He started shooting. Zoe shrieked and buried herself against Regina as McDaniels spun in his seat. Through the van's open rear doors, he saw the stenches push open the elevator doors. Dozens of them boiled out of the dark shaft, zeroing in on the idling van. Their pallid skin reflected the red glow of its brake lights. Rittenour fired his M4 on semi-automatic, cracking off head shot after head shot that left zombies collapsing to the oil-stained concrete floor. Derwitz was less precise, squeezing off bursts from his MP5 that did little to stop the advancing horde. McDaniels yelled for him to flip to semi and go for head shots, but if he heard, Derwitz did not comply.

"We're attracting some attention from outside," Gartrell reported.

"Gate's up!" Leary cut in suddenly. "Major, get that fucking dumbass cowboy to jump on it!"

McDaniels looked at Finelly and found his attention was rooted to the vision of zombies swelling in the driver's side view mirror. He slapped the big man on the arm mightily, jarring him out of his shocked silence.

"Finelly! *Drive!*"

Finelly snapped out of it and stomped down on the van's accelerator. Rubber screeched as the four-wheel drive vehicle's knobby tires spun across the smooth concrete for a moment before developing enough purchase to send it hurtling out into the rain-filled night. He cranked the wheel hard to the right just outside the garage, almost scraping the van's side against the rear bumper of a car parked at the curb. As the vehicle came around and ground to a halt, McDaniels saw the car had a mass of parking tickets trapped beneath its windshield wipers, tickets that would go forever unpaid.

Gartrell and Leary sprinted for the van, the former firing several rounds from his AA-12 into the garage as he backpedaled through the rainy darkness. Leary launched himself into the van, then turned and grabbed the collar of Gartrell's body armor and hauled him inside. Gartrell scooted backwards and sat inside the van's cargo area, his legs hanging over its raised bumper.

"Go!" Leary shouted, as the first of the zombies came around the van's open rear doors. Its head disappeared into an explosion of visceral goo as Gartrell blasted it with the automatic shotgun. Finelly slammed his foot on the accelerator once again, and the van fishtailed as it surged down the street. But not before a ghoul could grab onto Gartrell's left boot, almost yanking him out of the van as it pulled away.

"Motherfuck!" Gartrell let go of the AA-12 and braced himself against the sudden weight as Leary grabbed onto him with both hands. The zombie held on as it was dragged behind the vehicle and bit down on the tip of Gartrell's boot. It shook its head back and forth like a dog playing with a chew toy.

"Leary, hold on to me!" Gartrell shouted as his right hand reached for his holster. He pulled his pistol and fired at the zombie trying to devour his foot, steel-toed boot be damned. He missed with the first shot, and succeeded only in hitting it with a graze with the second. But the impact was enough to make the zombie open its mouth and reach upward with one hand. Gartrell raised his free leg and kicked the abomination in the face with his right foot. Bone crunched beneath the heavy sole of his boot, and the zombie slid away, rolling across the wet street. Leary and Rittenour hauled Gartrell inside and slammed the van's rear doors shut. Gartrell leaned against the back of the seat the Safires and Browns sat on and wiped the rainwater from his face.

"Now *that*," he said, "is what I call entertainment."

***

The *Escanaba* reached her intended loiter station north of Roosevelt Island at almost three in the morning. There was no way to drop a hook to hold her position, due to the occasional dead floating in the dark waters. Hassle instructed the sailor manning the con to maintain station using the boat's diesel engines, something every swabbie had been trained to do if he was going to helm a vessel of any size in the Coast Guard. It was still a tall order; while the river current was generally north to south, the wind was pushing the *Nob* from the aft starboard quarter, and the air pressure was enough to make the ship's stern swing out. The helmsman was adroit enough to feel the ship slipping out from under him, and he increased the output from the starboard engine to bring it back in line. It was a repetitive process, but Hassle was glad to see the job was being handled competently.

"All lookouts, keep sharp. Watch for any of those things that might be trying to get aboard," he told the bridge crew. "Let's give those Special Forces guys a call on their frequency and let them know we're here, and find out how long they're going to make us wait in this crap."

***

The van bolted down 79th Street, heading east as fast as Finelly could make it go. The wide thoroughfare was hardly vacant, despite the military and police blockades that had been designed to force evacuees onto only the north/south avenues, like Lexington behind them and Third Avenue ahead. But Finelly was able to weave the big van around the vehicles that had been halted on the street, including one bus which had crashed into a storefront, its long length blocking most of the road. To get around that, Finelly merely steered the vehicle onto the sidewalk, smashing through a pile of garbage bags as he did so. The windshield wipers snapped back and forth, slapping out a furious tempo as they fought to keep the windscreen clear.

"This thing's got power, but it handles like a pig," Finelly said. "It really must be armored, feels heavy as hell!"

As if to prove that, a zombie stepped in front of the van, its mouth open, its arms raised. McDaniels felt only the slightest shudder as the van crashed into the zed at thirty miles an hour.

"That worked out well," Gartrell said from the back. "Keep doing that whenever you have the opportunity, Finelly."

"You got it, first sergeant."

A voice came over the Green Berets' radio headsets. "Terminator Six, this is the *Escanaba*. We're in position and waiting for you to get to the shoreline. We're looking for an ETA, over."

McDaniels smiled when he heard the voice on the other end of the radio link. "*Escanaba*, Terminator Six. We're en route now. It's going to be a while. Can't give you an ETA, but I hope to God you're going to wait for us, over."

"Roger that, Terminator. We'll hold station until you arrive, we've got plenty of fuel and hot coffee, over."

"Save some for us, *Escanaba*. Got to go now, we're about to try and cross Third Avenue. Terminator, out." McDaniels said. "That was the Coast Guard boat. They're on-station and waiting for us. All we have to do is get there," he told the rest of the van's occupants.

Finelly slowed the van as it approached Third Avenue. The barricade there had been deserted, but shapes still moved in the gloom. Several zombies turned toward the van as it hurtled up the street, their faces pale and drawn, eyes casting about wildly in their skulls. McDaniels realized they were almost entirely blinded by the night and the storm, but they still sensed a meal ticket coming their way. Beyond the ghouls and the barricade, Third Avenue was choked with traffic, but there had been some sort of accident just south of the barricade, and that had let some of the traffic in the intersection thin out a bit before things went to hell in a hand basket.

"We going to be able to push our way through that?" McDaniels asked, pointing toward the intersection ahead.

"No way to know other than to give it a shot," Finelly said. "Those zeds'll be able to get all over us though."

"No gun ports to shoot through," McDaniels said, "and maybe it's better if we don't. The noise'll bring every zombie in the area on top of us, even in the storm. Just do your best, Finelly."

Finelly brought the van toward the intersection as quickly as he dared. The zombies stumbled toward the white vehicle, their moans overridden by the storm-driven wind. They slapped at the van, their fists bouncing off the reinforced metal. One of them managed to grab the handle on the driver's door and yanked on it repeatedly, but the door locks had engaged automatically once the van's speed increased over ten miles per hour. McDaniels told the soldiers in the back to ensure the rear doors were also locked.

Finelly pressed the van's brush guards against the rear fender of a yellow taxi cab and gunned the engine. The van slowly pushed the taxi to one side, opening up the intersection just enough for the van to squeeze through. Finelly backed up a bit, ignoring the ghoul standing outside the driver's door with its face pressed against the glass. He cut the wheel and brought the van around, then accelerated through the opening he'd created. The zombies howled as the van slipped away from them, and the one clinging to the driver's door was torn away from the van as it brushed against the taxi.

"Well, that wasn't so bad," Derwitz said, just before a rapid hammering sound came from the rear of the van.

"What was that?" Safire asked, suddenly coming alive now.

McDaniels checked the side view mirror and saw sparking flashes in the murk behind the van. The mirror suddenly exploded into shards of glass and plastic, and he flinched instinctively as debris ricocheted off the bullet-resistant window. The van's rear end dipped and bounced on its suspension as one or both of the rear tires failed.

"Small arms fire," McDaniels said. "Looks like OMEN is onto us."

26

"How're we doing, Finelly?" McDaniels asked.

"Feels like we've got a flat," Finelly said as he goosed the accelerator, pushing the van past another abandoned car. "Having a bit of trouble keeping to a straight line."

"This crate's got run-flat tires," Rittenour said from the back.

"Yeah, but they ain't designed to drive up on stopped vehicles and provide enough traction to push 'em out of the way," Gartrell said. "Major, we're going to need something else to help us get through. Maybe some of us could dismount and push some vehicles out of the way...?"

"Sergeant Leary, you remember our discussion earlier?"

"Yes, sir." Leary's voice was flat and emotionless. "If we can find a fire engine or a snow plow or something, I'll use it to push through the gridlock. You guys will have to keep the zeds off me long enough to get it done."

"I think I see an NYPD tow truck up ahead at the next barricade," Finelly said. "One of those six-by-six deals. There's a fire truck, too."

McDaniels leaned forward and saw the vehicles through the rain-swept gloom. He was not surprised to see figures moving among the abandoned vehicles, and they slowly turned toward the van as it bore down on the intersection.

"Second Avenue up ahead. Okay Leary, you're on. Finelly, stop about fifty yards from the barricade. Leary and I will advance, clear the area as quickly as we can, and secure the tow truck. Leary, I'll do my damnedest to keep the zeds off you while you do your thing. Don't fuck around, make it quick and dirty."

"Hooah," Leary said, and McDaniels heard him shifting around in the back of the van.

"Rittenour, Gartrell, Derwitz—you dismount as well and provide security for the van until it can move again. Exit through the side door, and remember, OMEN's at our rear.

Expect to be engaged, so don't just stand around and make yourselves a target. Reduce your silhouette as much as possible."

"I think we all remember our basic soldiering skills, major," Gartrell said.

"Prove it to me," McDaniels said as Finelly brought the van to a halt. He unfastened his seat belt and pushed open the passenger door, his M4 at the ready. Behind him, the rest of the troops piled out of the side door and found themselves confronted by two zombies that stumbled toward them from the sidewalk. Leary fired two shots and dropped them in their tracks with practiced efficiency. As Gartrell led the other soldiers to the rear of the van, McDaniels and Leary sprinted toward the barricade. There were six or seven zombies between them and the tow truck. McDaniels shouldered his M4, flipped on the laser designator, and fired on them, taking his time to ensure each shot resulted in a kill. The zombies obviously knew they were there, but the driving rain and the total darkness had them at a disadvantage, whereas McDaniels and the rest of the soldiers had night vision devices that gave them more than just a slight edge. Bodies fell to the wet pavement with almost metronomic regularity. In seconds, the path to the tow truck was clear.

"Cover me," Leary said, and he advanced toward the dark rig with his sidearm in both hands. If something went down, the pistol would be more useful in close-quarters combat. McDaniels shadowed him, and took down two more ghouls as they stepped around a police cruiser.

From behind him, more gunfire rang out. A distant assault rifle chattered on full automatic, and McDaniels heard projectiles slam into the idling van.

"Six, OMEN is advancing on us," Gartrell reported over the radio. "A block back, but they're using full auto fire to fix us in place. I count four shooters, two of which are using NVGs. I'm popping smoke, but it's not going to hold them back for long. Move your ass, Leary!"

Leary did not answer as he ran to the tow truck and threw the driver's door open. McDaniels scanned the area for more targets, his M4 at the ready. He heard a faint moan over the wind, and was surprised to find a zombie had closed to less than three feet from him. As he spun to deal with it, the ghoul lunged forward and grabbed his arm. McDaniels let go of his rifle and slammed his gloved fist into its face with all his strength. The sudden burst of adrenaline gave the punch substantial authority, and the ghoul's head snapped back as it fell to the street. McDaniels put a boot on its chest and fired a single round through its head, blasting its skull apart. He turned back to the tow truck and saw Leary had hauled himself into its cab. Three zombies advanced upon the vehicle. McDaniels took out two of them, but hit the third zed in the shoulder—a wasted shot. It came around the truck's open door and clambered onto the running board as Leary searched about the cab's interior. McDaniels found he no longer had a clear shot.

"Leary!" McDaniels shouted.

Leary responded immediately. He put his left hand against the zombie's chest and brought his pistol up in his right. The single round he fired left a deep furrow through the ghoul's skull, and it toppled off the running board.

"Damn it major, keep these things off me!" Leary said over the radio.

Before McDaniels could reply, the tow truck's diesel engine chattered, then caught. Even above the storm, it was loud enough to be noticeable. McDaniels knew it would be the next best thing to a dinner bell. The rig's backup alarm sounded as its reverse lights snapped on, and the truck shuddered into motion, backing up toward the sidewalk. Leary cut the wheel hard to the left, swinging the vehicle back onto the street as its reinforced rear bumper slammed into a mailbox and ripped it off its mounts. The tow truck straightened out on the street, then shuddered to a halt. At the same time, several more zeds shambled toward the vehicle. McDaniels fired on them with his M4, dropped them to the wet street.

"Ready here, major," Leary said over the radio net.

From behind him, more automatic gunfire broke out, followed by two sharp, loud explosions. Someone was using grenades.

"We gotta boogie, major," Gartrell reported. "The smoke's slowing 'em down a bit, but there's so many we can't hold them for long. And OMEN is hanging back, not engaging us directly. Even dead, they're still smart bastards."

"Leary, you're good to blast open that intersection. Break, Gartrell, you and the rest of the troops fall back to the van and get ready to pull out. Set up a tight perimeter to keep the zeds off it, over."

"Roger, done that," Gartrell said.

The NYPD tow truck surged forward, its tires spinning on the rain-slicked street. McDaniels fell back, keeping his eyes on the tow truck as it slammed into the vehicles choking the intersection ahead. Metal crumpled and glass shattered as the rig's thick bumpers and push bars crashed into the cars and shoved them aside. The backup alarm sounded, and the tow truck reversed up the street, then surged forward again, colliding with the abandoned cars and trucks, shoving them aside as metal screamed and fiberglass fractured.

Something landed on the street off to McDaniels' right, and he glanced over to see a zombie writhing about on the curb. A moment later, another one slammed to the ground beside it, followed by another, and another. The impacts were horrific, and some of them did not survive the engagement with gravity as their skulls burst open. But many of them did, and even though the plunge splintered their skeletons, they still tried to crawl toward him, mouths open, lifeless lips drawn back, teeth exposed.

"We got window divers on scene," he told the rest of the team. "Pick it up, Leary, we're attracting a lot of attention here."

"Almost done," Leary said. "Tough to get traction on the wet ground." As he spoke, the tow truck rammed into the mass of vehicles again. Its engine roared as its tires spun, and McDaniels smelled the diesel exhaust despite the wind. More corpses slammed to the ground. McDaniels fell back to the van. A group of zombies came around the corner, their attention fixated on the roaring tow truck. One of them must have caught sight of McDaniels moving in the gloom, and it shuffled toward him on stiff legs. The rest of the group followed. McDaniels fired his last two rounds and dropped two of them in their tracks, then busied himself with changing out his spent magazine.

Something slammed into him from behind and knocked him sprawling across the rain-slicked street. McDaniels tried to roll with the impact, but his back pack got in the way, leaving him lying on his side. His night vision goggles were knocked askew, rendering him effectively blind as he blinked against the rain and the wind. The darkness of the city street worked against him now; he couldn't see his attacker, but he certainly felt it as it gripped him with strong, cold hands. McDaniels responded immediately and lashed out at his assailant. His left hand closed around a human wrist, and before he could stop himself, he yanked it toward him as his combat training took over.

It was a female zombie, a black woman with close-cropped hair. Instead of fighting against McDaniels, the zombie lunged toward him, jaws spread wide. McDaniels barely had enough time to get his hand around the zed's neck to hold it at bay. There was no way he could use his rifle in such close quarters, so he pulled his pistol instead. He thumbed off the safety while wrestling with the moving corpse, then placed the weapon under its chin and fired. The sound and fury of the gunshot left him momentarily dazzled, but he recovered quickly and shoved the now-motionless corpse off him.

"Six, we've got a problem back here," Gartrell said over the radio.

"On my way. Break. Leary, do you need me to provide security? Over."

"Negative, major. I'm almost through here, you guys should have a pathway in just a second," Leary said over the crash of metal and the squeal of tires spinning out on wet pavement.

McDaniels grabbed his rifle, charged it, and ran to the rear of the van. As he came around the vehicle's rear, a bullet slashed through the upper surface of the sheet metal, and tore a long gouge through the white paint before it flattened against the armor underneath. There were several such impact points all along the rear of the van.

He found Derwitz was down with a bullet wound to the thigh. He was tended to by Rittenour, and the Night Stalker continued to fire his MP5 at the approaching zombies, backing up Gartrell by zeroing any which happened to get through his field of fire. For his part, Gartrell wasn't playing nice, nor was he wasting time trying to line up the AA-12 for head shots. He was firing low, blasting the legs off the zombies as they stumbled through the windblown smoke emitted by the smoke grenades he had thrown.

"Gartrell, hit them in the head!" McDaniels shouted.

"Negative, major. If I can blow their pelvises to jelly, they won't be able to make up that much ground before we're out of here!" Gartrell kept blowing the legs off the zombies. There was already a good amount of them down on the ground, slowly crawling toward him on their bellies.

And in the near distance, muzzle flashes lit up the night. McDaniels automatically returned fire, trying to zero the OMEN zombies before they could advance further. It didn't work; they moved just enough to prevent him from lining up for head shots, and the rounds that struck their bodies didn't slow them at all. Not only were they wearing ballistic armor, they also happened to be dead. 5.56mm bullets to the body were no longer effective.

"Ritt, how's Derwitz?" he asked.

"Busted femur, losing a hell of a lot of blood," Rittenour said. "Can't treat it well. Bad shot, combat gauze isn't doing what it should."

"I can still fight, sir!" Derwitz's voice was pinched from the pain, but he continued pumping rounds downrange, killing stenches that got too close to Gartrell's position from outside his field of fire. McDaniels admired the small soldier's chutzpah, but enough was enough.

"Let's fall back! Leary's almost got a path made for us, so load Derwitz into the van and get ready to get the hell out of here."

"Roger," Rittenour said, and without further comment he scooped up Derwitz and ran back to the idling van twenty feet away. Derwitz made a complaining noise, but there was nothing else he could do. As McDaniels assumed guard duty and kept the zeds off Gartrell, he caught a glimpse of Derwitz's face as Rittenour carried him past. Even through the night vision goggles, he didn't like what he saw. Derwitz must have been in a remarkable amount of pain.

"Gartrell?" McDaniels fired a quick burst at one of the OMEN zeds as the four of them advanced, two on either side of the street. He hit it, for the zombie stumbled to its knees. It wasn't hurt, of course; the impact of the bullets against its chest armor had only knocked it off balance. McDaniels seized the moment to go for a head shot as it slowly clambered back to its feet, ignoring the return fire of the other OMEN zombies. He was rewarded with at least one bullet striking true, and the OMEN zombie wilted to the ground and lay still.

"I heard you major, you want us to fall back to the van. You have me covered?"

"You're covered, first sergeant."

"Hooah." Gartrell rose and fell back, keeping low as more rounds zipped past. "Good shooting there," he said as he moved past McDaniels. McDaniels didn't answer, just kept pouring on the heat on semiautomatic, trying to keep OMEN pinned. But what he saw moving behind the dead Special Forces soldiers sent a stab of fear lancing through his heart.

Thousands of zombies filled the street behind OMEN team, drawn to the commotion like bees to honey. They surged forward in a single mass, as if they weren't individual corpses but one huge, integrated creature. And at their head was OMEN team.

A bullet struck McDaniels square in the chest, and he stumbled backward. Another zipped by his ear—*crack!*—as loud as a firecracker and infinitely more lethal. McDaniels gathered his footing and fell back to the van as the smoke from the grenades finally petered out.

And then, the rain stopped.

27

"Leary, move it! We're about to be overrun!" McDaniels shouted over the radio as he ran back to the van.

"You're good to go, major," Leary said. "I just blasted my way through the intersection and am moving down the street to clear the next one, over." As he spoke, McDaniels heard the NYPD tow truck's diesel engine winding out, growing distant.

"Roger that!" McDaniels threw himself toward the van as Gartrell helped Rittenour load Derwitz inside. With the vehicle to his back, he turned and fired at OMEN as they advanced, sending a fusillade of bullets ripping into one soldier and several other zombies behind it. The salvo did nothing to stop them, but did slow them for a moment.

"Major, let's roll!" Gartrell said over the radio.

McDaniels broke from his position and returned to the front passenger seat of the van. He slammed the door shut as a mottled corpse crashed against it and tried to pound through the reinforced, bullet-resistant glass. Finelly didn't need anyone to tell him what to do, he put his foot on the pedal and the van accelerated away. Bullets struck the rear of the vehicle.

"We're going to catch up to the tow truck pretty quickly," Finelly said.

"We'll do what we did last time," McDaniels said. "No other choice. But we might need you to dismount and fight, if Derwitz can't."

"I don't think he can," Rittenour said.

"I can fight, major," Derwitz said weakly.

McDaniels turned in his seat and looked into the back of the van. Earl and his daughter clung to each other. Safire and Regina sat side-by-side, holding hands, their expressions tense and frightened. In the very back of the van, Rittenour and Gartrell worked on Derwitz, but McDaniels exchanged a quick glance with the first sergeant. He knew then that Derwtiz was bleeding out.

"Finelly, we'll need you outside," McDaniels said, turning to face front again. "Earl, can you drive this van? Aggressively, like Finelly, but not wreck it at the same time?"

Earl's voice was soft and subdued, the terror of the situation blunted by the pain of his eldest daughter's death... and the potential for his surviving daughter to follow suit. "I can do whatever you need me to do, major. You need me to drive, I can drive. I drove trucks bigger than this before, and in all kinds of cities."

"Any of those cities overrun by zombies?" Finelly asked.

"You think that's funny or something, kid?" The disapproving scowl was audible in Earl's voice.

"No, sir. Not funny at all. Sorry."

"I can drive this truck, McDaniels," Earl said.

McDaniels nodded. "When we stop at the intersection ahead, take the driver's seat. Leary, how is it up ahead?" McDaniels asked over the radio.

"Wet with the occasional flesh-eating zombie, but at least the rain has stopped," Leary said. Over the transmission, McDaniels heard more rending metal. "I'm already blasting through this intersection, but be careful when you guys pull up, the zeds are starting to get a bit thicker on this side of town... don't know why. Over."

"It's the FDR Drive," Safire said quietly.

"Doctor?" McDaniels prompted.

"It's the dead from the FDR Drive on the east side of the city, major." Safire's voice was plain and direct, almost scholarly. "All those people who were caught by the dead, or who... expired... by other means. They've reanimated, and there were doubtless thousands of people there, as that was one of two main escape routes from the city."

"Understood. Thank you."

"You'll have to fight through them, major. There could be thousands of them."

McDaniels jerked a thumb toward the rear of the van. "It's no longer novel, sir. There are thousands of them right behind us."

"Second Avenue, coming up," Finelly said. "The tow truck's almost through the intersection already—" As he spoke, a zombie jumped in front of the van. The van crashed into it, and the zombie flew over its snub nose and slammed across the windshield before it fell to the pavement. Regina shrieked, and McDaniels swore.

"Sorry sir," Finelly said. He hadn't even hit the brake.

"No problem. Troops, we'll do it as we did before. Uh, Doctor Safire"—McDaniels turned and looked to Regina—"could we impose upon you to attend to Specialist Derwitz after we exit the vehicle? He *is* wounded, after all."

Regina looked at McDaniels with a confused expression, then suddenly turned and looked behind her. It was as if she had just realized there was a wounded man present. She turned back to McDaniels and nodded quickly.

"Of course. I'm sorry I wasn't... wasn't already doing something."

McDaniels faced forward as Finelly slowed the van to a halt. "Let's go, troops," he said, and bailed out the door. Finelly put the vehicle into park and did the same. McDaniels glanced back into the van and saw Earl climb into the driver's seat as he slammed the door closed. At the same time, something moaned behind him, and he whirled to find several zombies moving toward him from the corner of 79th and Second Avenue. They had doubtless been called to the scene by the ruckus Leary was making, and the sight of an actual person got their attention in a major way. Of course, as the person in question, McDaniels was far from flattered.

He dropped them all with careful, precise shots. When the last one hit the pavement, its fingertips brushed the toe of McDaniels' left boot. He looked down at the corpse through his night vision goggles.

My, that was close.

A sudden explosion of gunfire from the rear of the van captured his attention. He remained where he was, keeping watch over the front right corner of the van as the tow truck continued to bash its way through the traffic that choked the intersection.

"Leary was right, major. There are more zeds down this way," Gartrell said over the radio. He wasn't kidding. No sooner had the first sergeant's words filtered into his ears through the radio headset he wore, McDaniels saw yet another gaggle of zombies approaching the van, moving amidst the abandoned vehicles choking Second Avenue.

"Leary, this is Six. Watch out for the zeds at your three o'clock position, over."

"Roger that, Six. I don't intend to stop moving long enough for them to get to me, over."

"Finely, you have activity on your side of the vehicle? Over."

"Roger that, major, got stenches all over the place, just ranging them out now..." An MP5 spoke from the other side of the van, and McDaniels gathered that Finely had gotten a bead on his targets and was servicing them with all possible dispatch. He raised his M4 to his shoulder and started plinking away at the advancing zombies on his side of the vehicle while they were still among the cars on Second Avenue. He was able to terminate almost all of them before they mounted the sidewalk.

"Gartrell, Rittenour, any sign of OMEN? Over," he asked as he took care of the remaining zeds.

"Negative, no contact. Which is a little spooky. Over."

"Roger that."

"Major, route is clear, you'd better get on it." Gunfire came from the other side of the intersection, and McDaniels looked away from his work long enough to see Leary firing his pistol at a group of walking dead on the eastern corners of 79th and Second. He saw figures moving along the tow truck's bed.

"Leary! You have zeds on your vehicle!"

"I know that, major. Can't do anything about them right this second. I'll see you guys at the other intersection, and maybe you can help clean them off. Over."

With that, the big blue NYPD tow truck charged down 79th Street, heading for the next intersection. It left a cloud of foul-smelling diesel exhaust floating in the air behind, and the sudden pungency of the scent was surprising to McDaniels.

"Team, mount up!" he shouted, and the soldiers returned to the waiting van. As he hauled himself into the front passenger seat and slammed the door shut, Finely chased Earl out of the driver's seat.

"Thanks for keeping the seat warm," Finely said.

"Man, you're lucky it ain't wet," Earl said.

"Go, Finelly!" McDaniels said once Gartrell and Rittenour were aboard. Finelly stomped on the accelerator, and the van bounced slightly as it drove over several bodies. Many of them were still moving.

"Major McDaniels?" It was Regina Safire, from the rear of the van.

"Go, Miss Safire. How is Derwitz doing?"

"I'm... I'm afraid he's dead, major. He's... he bled out. There was no way I could stop the bleeding. His femoral artery had retracted back into his leg, and I have nothing I could have used to cut open the thigh to find it and clamp it." She stopped for a long moment, then added, "I'm terribly sorry, major."

McDaniels nodded curtly. "Understood, ma'am. First Sergeant Gartrell, at the next stop—"

"I'll dump the body after removing all the valuables, sir," Gartrell said.

"Thank you, first sergeant."

"It's part of the job, major."

McDaniels nodded again and concentrated on the route ahead. He suddenly remembered Finelly and Derwitz served in the same unit, and he turned to look at the big, blond-haired soldier driving the van.

"Finelly, are you—"

"Good to go, sir. Losing Derwitz sucks, but it's not like we were tight buddies. But I think he did pretty damn well today, didn't he?"

"I'll be putting him in for a silver star, for damned sure."

Finelly nodded and drove on silently. McDaniels took the time to examine his M4 before they arrived at the next intersection. He wanted to ensure it was 100% operational before stepping out of the van. He heard Gartrell and Rittenour doing the same, changing out magazines and cycling the weapons to make certain their actions weren't getting fouled.

Ahead, a barricade separated the street from the intersection The NYPD tow truck smashed through it at well over forty miles an hour, sending wooden saw horses and sand bags flying. The rig hurtled into the intersection on the other side, sending a police cruiser pinwheeling away. The tow truck continued on and slammed into more vehicles, knocking them askew. The rig's reverse lights snapped on, and the vehicle rolled back for another run. Through his NVGs, McDaniels saw the zombies stumbling toward the truck from the various shops and alleyways. Dozens of them. He heard Earl gasp from the bench seat behind him, and he guessed the janitor caught a glimpse of the shapes in the reverse lights' glow.

"Leary, you've got about forty zeds closing on you from the rear, and you still have at least two holding onto the back of the truck. Recommend you bash the shit out of everything in your way and get the hell out of there, over."

"Workin' on it, major," Leary responded. "It would be awesome if you guys could hold them off me while I'm doing my job, over."

"Finelly, stop here," McDaniels said. Finelly tapped the brakes and brought the van to a halt two hundred feet from the intersection.

"Am I parking, or just waiting for a moment?" he asked.

"Park it. Earl, get in the driver's seat. Ritt, come forward with me. Finelly, stand guard at the rear with Gartrell. Everyone out."

The soldiers exited the vehicle and slammed the doors shut behind them. Rittenour joined McDaniels at the front of the van while Finelly faded back and positioned himself with Gartrell.

"What's the op, sir?" Rittenour asked.

"You get to show me how good a sniper you are with an M4. Take those zeds off Leary's back."

Rittenour raised his NVGs on their mount, then looked through the night vision scope atop his M4. McDaniels kept an eye out for any zombies in the immediate vicinity, but the racket caused by the tow truck had captured the attention of every zed in the area. None of them were looking toward the van.

Yet.

Rittenour lined up for a shot, then fired one round. Downrange, one of the zombies riding in the bed of the tow truck toppled into the street. It had only been steps away from the rig's cab, and Leary. McDaniels saw several of the zombies at the rear of the pack that was descending upon the tow truck slow and turn. They peered in the van's direction, but in the darkness they apparently couldn't see it.

The muzzle flash will change that, McDaniels told himself.

And right he was. Rittenour fired again, and the other zombie in the tow truck fell face first into the bed. The stenches that had been staring in the van's direction saw the flash of Rittenour's weapon, and several of them shambled up the street. Yet most of the horde remained fixed on the dark shape of the tow truck, its brake lights flashing on and off as Leary horsed the mammoth vehicle into the intersection.

"We really should have done something about those tail lights," Rittenour said.

"We really ought to do more about the zeds headed our way," McDaniels suggested. Following his own advice, he raised his rifle to his shoulder and prepared to fire. "Gartrell, what's the SITREP from the rear? Over."

"All clear for the moment, Six. Some zeds heading our way, but not enough to get panicky over. No sign of OMEN, though Finelly and I are on the lookout, over."

"Roger that. We're about to go loud up front." To Rittenour: "I'll take targets on the right side of the street, you take ones on the left."

"Roger that. Tell me when."

"Now."

The two M4s cracked as the two Special Forces soldiers fired single shots at the zombies as they advanced up the street. With each shot, a zed crumpled to the wet pavement, its skull ravaged and torn; it was rare for one of the men to miss their intended target, though it did happen on occasion. The zombies approached mindlessly, completely ignorant of the fate that awaited them, exposing themselves openly to the weapons fire. That was the most frightening thing for McDaniels. This enemy was truly unyielding.

But after a few moments, more zombies turned away from the tow truck, attracted by the crackling gunfire. Moaning, they advanced up the street as quickly as their dead legs could carry them. From behind the van, McDaniels heard the rattle of Finelly's MP5, followed a moment later by the throaty roar of Gartrell's AA-12. Both elements were in contact now.

"Reloading," Rittenour said, and he pulled the empty magazine from his rifle. McDaniels only grunted an acknowledgement and kept up the fire, taking down zed after zed as they surged toward the idling van. Beyond them, the tow truck continued battering its way through the clogged intersection, backing over zeds as Leary reversed the rig for another run. It didn't render the zeds completely ineffective, but it did make it much more difficult for them to harry the Special Forces sergeant as he did his work. That gave McDaniels an idea.

"Ritt, how much do you think that van weighs? Three, four tons, maybe?"

"About four and a half tons, maybe," Rittenour said absently as he slapped another magazine into his M4 and charged it up. He shouldered the weapon and resumed firing as McDaniels' weapon went dry.

"Reloading," McDaniels said, and went through the process. "Leary, let me know when you're done with that intersection, over."

"Almost done, Six," Leary responded.

"Six, we're getting a hell of a lot of attention back here. Over," Gartrell said over the radio.

"Roger, first sergeant. Have Finelly return to the van, over."

"On it, over."

"Crossing over," McDaniels said to Rittenour, and Rittenour lifted his M4 so McDaniels could slip by in front of him. Once the major was clear, he dropped the weapon back into position and resumed firing. McDaniels slipped slightly on the expended cartridges littering the street.

"What's up, sir?" Finelly asked as he ran to the driver's door and pulled it open. Earl immediately vacated it.

"I want you to blast a path through those zeds with the van," McDaniels told Finelly as he climbed into the vehicle's cab. "The rest of us will follow on foot and keep the zeds at bay as best as we can, but right now, we need to bull a path through those things. This van ought to be heavy enough to do it."

"Roger that," Finelly said. "You want me to go now?"

"Rittenour, get out of the way!" McDaniels yelled, then nodded to Finelly as Rittenour did as instructed. "Do it, we'll be right behind you."

Finelly closed the driver's door, dropped the van into gear, and took off. Gartrell turned, startled by the vehicle's sudden departure.

"Don't worry, first sergeant—no one abandoned you," McDaniels said. "We need to use the van as a weapon now to bull through these zeds, otherwise we're going to run out of ammo. Let's follow the van to the intersection."

"Got that," Gartrell said, firing one last blast at the zombies advancing from the rear. "Still no sign of OMEN, which has me fairly perplexed."

"Understood. Rittenour, ready? Let's go!"

The three soldiers sprinted after the van as it slammed into the zombies in the street. It was a horrific sight; bodies flew everywhere, and the van bucked up and down like a bronco that refused to be broken, crushing bodies beneath its knobby tires. Other zombies threw themselves at the vehicle as it passed them, but they merely bounced off the vehicle's sturdy frame and crashed to the street. The soldiers following the van made short work of them, eliminating them easily as they slowly clambered back to their feet. From behind, more zombies massed, but even the most fleet of them were unable to match the pace of the living. Just the same, Gartrell dropped back every now and then to take down those ghouls which managed to get too close.

"Major, I'm through the intersection up here," Leary said. "But I'm not too confident about the next one. I've beaten this rig to hell, and it's about to go tango uniform, over."

"What's the problem, Leary? Over."

"Busted radiator, Six, and a definitely messed up front end. Don't worry though, I'm not going to baby it. Let's just get rolling, over."

"Hold up for us for as long as you can, we're still dismounted. The van is almost at the intersection, we're on foot about a hundred feet behind it. Will be on board in about sixty seconds, over."

"Six, I can't sit here for sixty seconds, there are too many of these zeds around me. Gotta roll, over."

"Understood, you're good to relocate. We'll be right behind you, over."

As the trio ran up the dark street, firing at any zeds which posed even a remote threat, McDaniels heard the tow truck's diesel engine roar as it accelerated down the street toward the intersection with First Avenue. After that, there were only two more intersections left to clear, York and East End avenues. They were getting there.

We might just make it out of here yet.

As Gartrell fired another salvo to their rear, he made a puzzled sound over the radio. McDaniels glanced back, and saw the first sergeant staring back the way they had come.

"Gartrell, move your ass!" he barked.

"Roger. Thought I saw something back there, just wanted to check it out."

They made it to the van and climbed in. As they did, Rittenour noticed Derwitz's body, still lying in the back.

"Shit, we forgot to dump Derwitz," he said as he climbed over the dead trooper.

"We'll do it at the next intersection," Gartrell said. "Take his weapons and gear, we're going to need everything he's got."

"Roger that," Rittenour said, slamming the rear door closed just as a zombie hurled itself against them. The van bounced on its shock absorbers as several of them attacked the vehicle, pounding on it with their fists.

"Let's go, Finelly!" McDaniels said.

The van's tires spun as the vehicle accelerated forward, running right over those zombies standing before it. McDaniels bounced up and down in his seat, and grabbed onto the rollover handles with both hands to keep from being thrown against the dashboard. Finelly fought with the steering wheel, his teeth clenched, his eyes hidden behind his night vision goggles.

Ahead, the tow truck accelerated down the street, trailing a plume of steam. It also left a wake of damaged, twitching bodies, scores of zombies that had tried to stop the vehicle by throwing themselves in front of it. McDaniels wished more of them had the opportunity to do so, for even zeds couldn't move that fast with broken backs and legs. The van bounced again as it rolled over the jerking corpses. From behind his seat, McDaniels heard someone retch, and a moment later, the sickening reek of vomit filled the van. Gartrell swore.

"I'm sorry," Safire said. "I'm claustrophobic, and the motion of the van—" He broke off and vomited onto the van's floor again. His daughter patted him on the back, murmuring comforting words.

"Rittenour, have you stripped Derwitz's body of his gear?" McDaniels asked, just to keep his mind off the smell of the vomit and the fact that it made him want to puke as well. He couldn't even roll down a window to get some fresh air inside. As if reading his thoughts, Finelly flipped on the fans.

"Almost done with that, but haven't had the time to go through his pack," Rittenour said.

"He's got MREs, spare NVG batteries, ten clips of nine millimeter for his MP5, another four clips for his pistol, an IR strobe with spare batteries, a flight helmet..." Finelly recited every item as if he were reading from a shopping list.

"Make sure you get his goggles and give them to Earl," McDaniels told Rittenour. "And hurry the hell up, we don't want him turning while he's still in the van!"

"That's a no shit circumstance, major," Rittenour said.

"Six, I'm at the intersection of First Avenue," Leary announced over the radio. "I'm working it now, over."

"Roger that, Leary. We'll do the same thing as before, deploy a bit behind you and try to draw the zeds off, over."

"Much obliged, major." Anything else Leary said was drowned out by the rending crunch of metal that blasted over the radio link before Leary ended his transmission. Ahead, McDaniels watched the tow truck surge into the intersection. And as before, stenches practically popped up everywhere, rising from behind dead vehicles, stumbling out of shops, or falling out of the sky. McDaniels had no idea how many of them there were, but counting those to the rear of the van, it must have been thousands.

This is going to get worse before it gets any better.

"Halt here. Troops, dismount," he ordered, and he threw open his door. He did not take the time to conduct a proper scan, and for his trouble he was immediately attacked by a zombie that rushed the van from the sidewalk. In life, the zed had probably been a healthy teenage boy. In death, it was just another vile scarecrow looking for a meal. McDaniels swore and grappled with the ghoul as it slammed into him, driving him back against the van. His feet slipped out from under him, and he crashed to the asphalt on his butt. It was cold and wet. As he struggled to get his M4 turned on the grotesquerie, he felt its teeth scrape across his helmet as its hands raked across his face and tore away the night vision goggles. From the rear of the van, there was a shout from Rittenour, and then a scream from Regina, followed by a pealing cry from Earl's daughter. McDaniels ignored it and concentrated on getting his feet back under him, then launched himself upright like a jack-in-the-box. At the same time, his hand came up behind the ghoul's neck, and its jaws parted wide, exposing a slash of blackness that McDaniels saw even without his goggles. He spun and slammed the zombie into the side of the van face-first with all his strength. As the ghoul rebounded, McDaniels stepped back and drew his sidearm. He double-tapped the corpse in the head at extremely close range. The zombie collapsed to the ground like an uprooted telephone pole.

There was a single gunshot from the rear of the van, and McDaniels ran to the rear to see what the situation was. He was shocked to find the bullet-pocked doors were closed and locked. Where the hell were Gartrell and Rittenour?

"What the hell is going on in there?" McDaniels said over the radio.

The doors opened and McDaniels stepped back, snapping his NVGs back into place. Derwitz's body rolled out of the back of the van and slammed to the asphalt. The back of his head was missing. Rittenour stepped outside, followed by Gartrell.

"What the fuck happened?" McDaniels asked, glancing at the men before scanning the street for threats. And they were there, ghouls skulking along the sidewalks, advancing toward the idling van. Apartment buildings stood like gigantic, silent sentinels all around them, dwarfing the van. In the near distance, the tow truck's engine bellowed as the rig slammed into cars.

"Derwitz reanimated before we could dump him," Gartrell said.

"And he fucking *bit* me," Rittenour added, a slight edge of panic in his voice. He ripped off his left glove and held up his hand before his NVGs. He groaned.

"Skin's broken," he said, his voice barely more than a whisper. "Holy fuck, I could be *infected*..."

"You're going to be dinner if you don't man up and soldier, troop. Stay here with Gartrell, and zero some stenches!" McDaniels turned and ran back to the front of the van. He took his position off the front right fender and glanced to his left, visually checking to ensure that Finelly was in his assigned position.

"Zeds coming in from the left," Finelly reported.

"Coming in from the right, too. This is a residential area. More deadheads knocking around. Shit, I thought everyone had evacuated this far up." McDaniels shouldered his rifle and started firing. The rest of the soldiers did the same.

There was nothing else they could do.

28

"Boats are ready to go in the water, skipper," Lieutenant Petersen told Hassle.

"We're not ready for anyone to go ashore just yet," Hassle told him. "Until we hear from the Army guys, no Coastie goes into the water."

Petersen nodded. "Understood. Just wanted to keep you up to date. We're ready when you give the word."

"Anything from the deck lookouts?"

"Only that there are bodies in the water, and that some of them are still moving. Every now and then, one bumps into the boat and tries to get aboard, but of course, they can't." The *Escanaba*'s sheer line was almost ten feet above the waterline, and the waves in the East River weren't sufficient to propel any of the zombies onto the cutter's aft deck.

"Captain, we're attracting a lot of attention." Lieutenant Commander Sullivan pointed to the flat screen displays that carried the FLIR feed. Hassle looked down at the screens. Sure enough, packs of the dead were growing all along the riverside. The fence on the FDR Drive kept most of them back, but there were more than a few lurking around the pilings and piers below the cement breakwaters.

"Amazing how they don't read that well through the FLIR. I guess a lot of those people have been dead for a long time. No body heat left, they're all just ambient temperature." Hassle shook his head. "Poor bastards."

"It's the lights," Sullivan said. "They can see our running lights, and the deck lights where the boat crews are working. It seems to me that's going to make it much more difficult for those Army people to get to the shoreline, sir."

Hassle nodded, and turned to Petersen. "Where's the deck force department head?"

"Overseeing the small boat ops right now, sir."

Hassle nodded. That was where First Lieutenant Herve Castillo would do the most good, keeping watch over the men on the deck.

"Very well. Once the boat crews have finished preparing the RHI and the rescue boat, tell them to extinguish all deck lighting except for whatever is essential for crew safety. I want more men on the fantail with NVGs, just in case one of those zombies comes aboard. If there's any way to do that, it'll be from the stern, unless these things can climb up steel like Spider-Man. When you go back outside, gently remind Castillo that his men have to stay sharp. Even though there's almost no chance one of those things can get aboard, anything's possible. And with the weather getting better, I don't want anyone thinking they can slack off."

Petersen got the message. "I'll go tell him now, captain." He zipped up his foul weather coat and exited the pilothouse. Hassle watching him bolt down the gangway outside.

"Wind is tapering off," Sullivan noted. "Should make launch and recovery of the shore teams easier."

Hassle nodded as he rubbed his eyes. The entire crew was bushed. The run in from their holding area in the Atlantic had been thrilling but rough, and their arrival in New York City waters had been nothing short of traumatic. Hassle had seen more than one man lose his balance as the *Escanaba* heeled in the wind, or trip over the hatch combings of the watertight doors on the lower decks. The crew was being driven into the ground, but there was nothing he could do about it.

"Lord knows we need a little bit of easy right now," he said.

Sullivan grunted. "You really think those Army guys have someone who can stop all of this from going on?" he asked, waving an arm toward the darkened expanse of Manhattan.

"I don't know," Hassle said after a long moment. "But if they do, I hope to God we can get them out of there."

"Here's hoping you have a direct line to the big guy."

Hassle snorted. "Not in a hell of a long time, XO. He ignores me pretty much routinely these days—"

A sudden flash to the north caught his attention, and he turned away from the darkened city. A rustle went through the bridge crew, audible over the rumbling of the engines and the whisper of the fan-cooled electronics. Another flash from beyond the northern horizon reflected off the low-hanging clouds. It looked like someone was shooting fireworks into the sky.

"What the heck is *that?*" Sullivan asked.

"Artillery," Hassle said after another moment's observation. "Looks like someone with some serious firepower has made it to the Bronx, and they're lighting it up."

Sullivan shook his head slowly. "I've never seen anything like that. Makes our 76 look like a pea shooter."

"Excuse me, sir?" This was from the young, pimply-faced port lookout, who stood on the left side of the bridge. He peered into the darkness beyond the port windows through light-intensifying binoculars.

"Yes, what is it, son?"

"Movement in the streets, sir. Maybe a half mile away from here."

"More zombies?"

"Negative, sir. I think it's Army. And they're using a tow truck to bash through all the dead traffic in the street."

Hassle hurried over and took the binoculars from the crewman. "How long have you been observing them?"

"Just now, sir. With the extra illumination from that light show, you can just barely make them out. Right up that street there," the young man said, pointing out the direction.

Hassle raised the binoculars to his eyes. Black night was instantly rendered in varying shades of green and white. At first, he saw nothing more than the mouth of the street the crewman had pointed out to him, that and what seemed to be a zillion zombies lining up against the fence, staring at the *Escanaba* with mindless, hungry eyes. The artillery explosions flashed on the horizon, and the low cloud cover reflected more light into the area. The additional illumination revealed much more the Upper East Side than the binoculars could on their own. Hassle saw the crewman was right; someone was using a big, battered tow truck to shove aside cars and trucks on what seemed to be First Avenue, only a thousand yards or so from the *Nob*.

"XO, slew the FLIR to port. Zoom in on that area right there," Hassle said, pointing out the window.

Sullivan nodded to the crewman manning the electronics station, and the crewman grabbed the FLIR's control yoke. After aligning the unit with the street in question, he slowly zoomed in while Hassle and Sullivan watched the displays.

"That'll do it," Hassle said, and the zoom stopped. Framed within the confines of the display, he and Sullivan could very plainly see two large heat sources. Both were vehicles, the tow truck the lookout had mentioned, and behind that a van of some sort.

And around the van, people-shaped silhouettes blazed in dull white fidelity as a horde of dimmer shapes advanced upon them. But the Special Forces troops weren't going down without a fight; already, there were dozens, maybe even a hundred, inert bodies strewn around the area.

"God damn," Sullivan said under his breath.

"Tell Castillo to launch the boats," Hassle ordered.

"Will do. But what about the zombies at the waterfront? How're those Army guys going to get past them? I mean, we're talking a couple of thousand deadheads, at least!"

Hassle nodded slowly. "Weaps!"

The weapons officer looked up from his position on the bridge. "Sir?"

"Make the Mark 75 ready for firing. I'll want you to deliver a tight grouping of shells against that line of zeds when I give the order."

"Aye aye, sir," the weapons officer said as he immediately set about following his captain's orders.

"You're going to blast those things to pieces?" Sullivan said.

Hassle shrugged. "I don't know how effective it'll be, but at least we might be able to give those Army guys a path to drive down. Comms, get me the Special Forces team commander. He and I should have a chat."

"Aye aye, sir!"

29

The tow truck managed to clear another path through the clogged intersection at First Avenue. McDaniels ordered the rest of the troops back to the van, and they retreated while fighting a rear action. The zombies were so numerous now that the bodies were really beginning to pile up, and they continued to attack even as the van drove off. They pounded against its sides with their fists, moaning and wailing.

McDaniels checked his M4 ammunition. He was running out. He asked the others to report their ammo status, and was unsurprised to discover the rest of the soldiers were in the same predicament.

"We better start using grenades," Gartrell said. "You can use your M203 to keep them back a bit, major. Not the best weapon for use against dead people, but it's about all we have. We have to keep them back."

"Agreed," McDaniels said. "We should use the smokers again, too. The zeds are thicker in this area, it's more residential."

"Terminator, this is *Escanaba*. We have you in sight. Are you in the van following the tow truck? Over."

"Roger that, *Escanaba*. We're using the tow truck to clear a path through the intersections. How's it look on your end? Over."

"Terminator, not so hot—there are zombies all along the waterfront. We're going to open up on them with seventy-six mike mike, but we'll have to let up once you're in the zone. We'll try and clear a path to the water, and our boats will be waiting for you. How many souls in your party? Over."

"*Escanaba*, Terminator has nine souls, five shooters and four pax, over."

"Roger that, Terminator. You'll be met by two small boats, but the rigid hull inflatable is the one you'll be boarding. There will be four guardsmen aboard, armed with rifles and shotguns.

The other boat will stand off as a rescue platform should the RHI have an incident. The *Escanaba* will not dock, over."

"Roger, *Escanaba*. We'll be looking for the boats. Hope they can move in quickly, we're deep in Indian country. Over."

"They'll be in faster than you can blink, Terminator. Don't delay, once the boat is there, jump in right away. Over."

McDaniels smiled despite himself. "*Escanaba*, Terminator. Believe me, if we have to, we'll walk across the water to your boats, over."

"Understood, Terminator. Coffee's on and it tastes like shit, but it's all yours when you get here. Over."

"Roger that, *Escanaba*. We've got to go to guns on the deadheads now, will contact you when we're on the move again. Terminator Six, out here." McDaniels updated those who couldn't listen to both sides of the conversation. "Coast Guard's on station and waiting for us. They'll meet us at the river in two boats, but we'll board the rigid inflatable. Safires and Browns, you'll follow us and do exactly as we say, understood?"

"Yes," Safire said.

"Just get my daughter out of here," Earl mumbled. "I'll do anything you say, just get her someplace safe."

"We're going to do just that, Earl. Ritt, how you holding up back there?"

"I'm all right, but this bite... well, it hurts like hell." Rittenour's voice was barely audible above the roar of the van's big V-8 engine as Finelly charged after the tow truck. Then: "Doctor Safire... can you maybe help me?"

"Of course," Regina said.

"I meant your father."

McDaniels looked back at Safire as he sat on the bench seat behind him. He looked even more pale and drawn, his gray hair plastered to his head, his face covered with a sheen of sweat as he fidgeted on the seat, the puddle of stinking vomit lying between his feet. Safire did not turn around to face Rittenour, and he avoided meeting McDaniels' gaze.

"No," he said finally. "I only have research and a template for treatment. I don't have anything here that can help you. If we were in a good research hospital, perhaps. But not here."

"How long does he have?" McDaniels asked.

"It's... it's difficult to say."

"Coming up on the next intersection," Finelly reported. The van began to slow. "Check out the sky... something going on, looks like arty."

McDaniels ignored him. "Then give us your best estimate, Safire." He was in no mood to allow Safire off the hook.

"Between twenty-four and forty-eight hours. The fever will come first, then the sickness as certain tissues become... necrotic." Safire risked a quick glance at Rittenour, who sat behind him. "I'm sorry, Rittenour. If we can get out of here soon and get you to a suitable treatment facility, then you might have a chance. That's really the very best I can do."

Rittenour snorted and shook his head. "This fucking sucks," he said.

"Don't give up, troop." Gartrell slapped Rittenour on the shoulder. "We'll be aboard that boat in no time, and then we're out of here. We'll get you looked after, I swear to God."

Rittenour nodded silently.

McDaniels faced forward again. He slid a 40mm grenade into the M203 grenade launcher mounted below the M4's barrel, and clicked the launcher closed. He heard similar sounds from behind as Rittenour and Gartrell readied their weapons for combat yet again.

"Six, this is Leary—the stenches are fucking thick up here, but listen... I see that Coast Guard boat in the river! It's a beautiful sight. Over." There was no mistaking the excitement in the staff sergeant's voice.

"How's the truck holding up? Over."

"Six, the engine's shaking like it's a vibrator turned up to eleven and the temperature's through the roof, but it'll get the job done. Over." Already, there was the sound of crunching metal accompanying Leary's transmission.

"Roger that, keep doing what you're doing, we're about to dismount. Six, out." To the others: "Okay, we know the drill. Let's get to it."

Finelly braked the van to a halt thirty yards from the intersection. The big NYPD tow truck was back in action, slamming into the stalled traffic in the intersection, its tires smoking now that the pavement was beginning to dry. McDaniels was out of the van before it had come to a complete halt, his boots landing on the street sure and square. Finelly had been right, there was definitely something going on; the clouds overhead were illuminated by distant, stroboscopic lights, and above the crashing of metal, he heard faint explosions. He slammed the door closed behind him just as the first zed lurched toward him from the sidewalk. He dropped it with one round, then took out another and another. Most of the zeds were fixated on the tow truck, and they swarmed toward it like some sort of single-minded amorphous beast. But that didn't mean the van had gone unnoticed. As McDaniels attempted to pull a smoke grenade from the clip on his vest, another zombie heaved toward him, moaning. The stench of it made his stomach roil. He fired the M4 into its face with one hand while pulling the grenade from its clip with another. He let the rifle hang across his chest by its patrol strap and ripped the pin from the grenade, then tossed it in the tow truck's direction. The grenade rolled along the street before its fuse ignited with a visible flash. White smoke billowed into the air, turning the zombies into vague shadows even through the NVGs. McDaniels raised his rifle to his shoulder and fired at the specters, dropping them one by one. From his left, he heard Finelly's MP5 bark in a measured, single shot cadence.

"Grenade!" Gartrell shouted, and a moment later, a tremendous explosion tore through the night. The explosion was followed by the *crack-crack-crack!* of Rittenour's M4, backed by the throatier roar of Gartrell's AA-12. McDaniels saw a clutch of ghouls shamble through the wafting smoke and head toward the van from the sidewalk. He reached for the trigger on the M203 and fired a 40 millimeter grenade at them, but his aim was a bit high; the round passed through one ghoul's chest before it armed, knocking the animated corpse off its feet and slamming it into its companions. The grenade traveled on until it struck the wall of the apartment building behind them and exploded in a flash of fire and fury, sending chunks of concrete façade whirling through the air. The shrapnel pelted the zombies, but it did not deter them; they only clambered back to their feet, ignoring the damage done to their bodies, dripping viscous ichor onto the sidewalk and street. The one which had taken the grenade to the chest was among them, and it tottered toward the van, trailing a rope of gray-green intestine behind it. McDaniels fired round after round, dropping the zombies as quickly as he could, but there were many, so many. He found himself on the retreat, backing up step by step, his heart hammering in his chest.

Christ, how much worse can this get?

As if in answer, his rifle stopped firing after the twelfth shot. It was either a misfire or a jam, but he didn't have the time to troubleshoot it. He pulled his pistol from its holster and, holding it in a two-handed grip, resumed firing at the zombies as they closed in on him. One of them was so close that it fell against him after he had shot it, jellified brains leaking from its ravaged skull.

"Reloading!" Finelly shouted, seemingly far too soon.

"Finelly, I'm decisively engaged here and my weapon has jammed!" McDaniels shouted, an edge of panic in his voice. He kept firing with his pistol while backpedaling—*bang! bang! bang!*—but every time a ghoul collapsed to the street, two more took its place. And then, his pistol ran dry.

Oh fuck!

Suddenly, the zeds exploded. McDaniels cowered as Gartrell's AA-12 salvo slashed through them, blasting them to pieces. Body parts flew across the street as Gartrell advanced, firing the AA-12 on full automatic in brief, controlled bursts. But as withering as the weapon was, the zombies kept coming, crawling on their elbows or hobbling along on shattered legs, uncaring that they had been disemboweled. But the violence of the attack did substantial damage, and the damage slowed them enough so McDaniels could regain his composure, reload his weapon, and resume shooting. Most of the zeds had been reduced to crawling along the ground, and they made for much easier shooting.

"Major, if you get into a tight spot, don't be afraid to ask for help," Gartrell said, as McDaniels finished off the remaining zombies with perfectly placed headshots.

"I'll do that, first sergeant. Thanks for the assist."

Gartrell nodded then faded back to the rear of the van. Rittenour continued firing at a metronomic pace, apparently unfazed by the swelling ghouls. Or perhaps, after being bitten, he just no longer cared.

There was a note of curiosity in his voice when he said over the radio, "What the hell is a *taxicab* doing coming toward us?"

"Say again?" McDaniels said. Finelly resumed firing on the left side of the van, and more figures swam through the smoke grenade's milky obscurant, stumbling toward the idling van. McDaniels pulled back on the M4's charging level, but the weapon was jammed so severely he couldn't take the time to clear it. He holstered his pistol and pulled his MP5 from its tactical carry harness on his right thigh.

"Ritt's right, there's a taxi coming down the street, mowing down the zeds," Gartrell said. "I'm not digging this, major."

McDaniels fired at the zombies emerging from the smoke screen. "Could be other survivors, first sergeant."

"Fuck if it is!" Gartrell said, and his AA-12 spoke again, diminishing but not supplanting the rising roar of an engine running flat out. "It's OMEN, OMEN, *OMEN!*"

"Look out!" Rittenour shouted, his M4 firing on full automatic now.

There was a tremendous crash, and the van rocketed forward, sliding into the smoke amidst an explosion of glass and metal. McDaniels narrowly missed being sideswiped by the white vehicle as he dove for the pavement, rolling across the remains of the zombies he and Gartrell had cut down. Slipping and sliding in the disgusting filth of dark ichor which leaked from their finally inanimate bodies, he struggled to his feet as the roaring engine clattered and quit in a puff of smoke. A yellow taxi had slammed into the back of the van at high speed, demolishing the vehicle's heavy duty bumper and flexing the rear clamshell doors partially open. Smoke and steam boiled out from beneath the car's crumpled hood. Its entire front end had been destroyed, and its windshield was a spider web of cracks. Its engine cut out with a raucous clatter.

Inside the car's dark interior, shapes moved across the front seat.

Shapes in uniform.

McDaniels lifted his MP5 and fired a burst into the open passenger window as the figure there lifted its own weapon. McDaniels beat the zombie on the draw, and sparks flew as his bursts raked the taxi's door and the ghouls inside. All his attack really did was throw off the zombie's aim. Its return salvo slashed across the apartment building behind McDaniels, shattering windows.

McDaniels advanced toward the taxi, firing short, tight bursts. The zed sitting in the passenger seat was definitely one of OMEN Team, though McDaniels couldn't remember his name. As the zombie tried to return fire, one of McDaniels' bullets struck its MP5, ripping the weapon from the ghoul's grasp. That was all McDaniels needed, and he leaned it, clicked the fire selector on his weapon to SEMI, and fired a single round into the dead trooper's skull. Even the Kevlar helmet on its head couldn't save it, and the zombie slumped forward in the seat.

The driver of the taxi wore night vision goggles, and raised its sidearm. Before McDaniels could do anything, the gun went off. McDaniels felt a heavy punch to his sternum shove him away from the wrecked taxi. One of his feet slipped in the gore on the street, and he fell just as another pistol round whipped past his head. He hit the ground hard, and his wind left him in a rush.

The zombie in the taxi shoved open the driver's door and slowly pulled itself out of the wreckage. McDaniels rolled over onto his side, struggling to take a breath, but his diaphragm felt as if it had been paralyzed. He pushed himself to his knees as the zombie hurried around the taxi as quickly as its dead legs could carry it. It fired at McDaniels twice while on the move, but both shots missed. McDaniels raised his MP5 and fired back a quick burst. All the rounds stuck the zombie in its ballistic armor, causing it to stumble, but did no damage. McDaniels shouldered his weapon and fired again, just as the zed did the same thing. A round ripped past McDaniels' head. The zombie took McDaniels' shot right below the nose, and its head rocked back beneath the force of the impact. It collapsed to the street in a heap and lay unmoving.

Except for its mouth, which continued to open and close. As McDaniels' breath suddenly returned to him, he realized his shot had only severed the cervical vertebra that connected the zombie's barely-functioning brain to its body. In essence, it was now paralyzed.

McDaniels sent it to hell with a round to the head.

"Gartrell! Rittenour!" He turned in a quick circle, looking for both men. Gunfire continued from the front of the van, and he saw Finelly and Rittenour were keeping the zombies engaged as they stepped through the smoke barrier.

"Rittenour and Finelly are good to go," Rittenour said.

"Gartrell!" McDaniels repeated. Two zombies shambled toward him. He dropped them before they got within thirty feet.

"Here," Gartrell said, kneeling on the sidewalk as he changed out his AA-12's ammunition drum. Another member of OMEN lay face down nearby in a spreading puddle of viscous ichor. "This was Sanchez, and those two are Meltser and Warner. That leaves Keith and whoever else might still be... well, not alive, but you know what I mean."

"You all right, first sergeant?"

"Fine. Are *you* all right, major?" Gartrell rose to his feet and scanned the direction the taxi had driven in from. A swelling wave of zombies advanced toward them, only a block away. Gartrell and McDaniels studied them closely for a moment.

"I don't see any uniforms in that," McDaniels said.

"Same here. But they're out there—"

The squeal of metal and the shriek of a woman captured their attention. They turned to see several zombies had crawled on top of the wrecked taxi and were now trying to force open the van's crumpled clamshell doors. McDaniels lifted his rifle and capped off three of them immediately. The remaining zombies turned toward the sound of the gunfire and advanced upon McDaniels and Gartrell hungrily. McDaniels took them down, one by one.

"Leary, SITREP!" he asked over the radio.

"Almost through, Six. You guys should move forward now, and hurry it up! I've got zeds all over me! Over!"

"Roger that." To Gartrell: "Let's go." The two men ran back to the van, pausing momentarily to liberate some ammunition from one of the fallen soldier-zombies.

McDaniels called to the other soldiers. "Finelly! Rittenour! Mount up, we're leaving!"

"About time! These things are—" Finelly's retort was cut off by a single gunshot. The big trooper yelped and fell to the ground as CW3 Keith, the leader of OMEN team, stepped around the front of the van. The walking corpse wore night vision goggles and carried an M4, and it walked directly toward Finelly. Finelly backpedaled away from the approaching ghoul, his mouth hanging open in shock.

McDaniels, Gartrell, and Rittenour all fired at the same time, and Keith's upper body disintegrated beneath the firepower's onslaught. McDaniels and Rittenour's shots pulverized the former soldier's head, whereas Gartrell's rounds defeated its body armor and shattered bone and turned tissue in jelly. The corpse was flung away from the van and crashed spread eagle to the sidewalk.

"Fuck me," McDaniels said.

"Major!" Finelly shouted as he sat up on the street. McDaniels turned as several more stenches emerged from the smoke screen and lurched toward them, arms outstretched, fingers curled into claws. They regarded Finelly with dull, hungry eyes, and McDaniels wondered if they could somehow smell blood and fear.

Gartrell wasted no time in opening up, blasting each ghoul in the chest with near mechanical precision. The zombies fell back into the smoke, but beyond them, more shapes loomed, their silhouettes made visible from the flashing artillery explosions far to the north. Rittenour engaged targets slightly further out with measured semi-automatic fire.

"Major, we've got to di-di," Gartrell said, using slang from a war he had been too young to fight in.

"Hold them back!" McDaniels slung his MP5 and grabbed Finelly under the arms and hauled him to his feet. The big soldier tottered on one foot, and McDaniels saw why. There was a spreading stain of blood on his BDUs.

"Where are you hit?"

"The thigh, sir... just like Derwitz. But it didn't hit the bone, I'm good to go!" Eager to prove this, Finelly hobbled toward the van and pulled open the front passenger door. It squeaked on its hinges, and the big trooper hauled himself inside. McDaniels pushed him in, forgetting all about Finelly's injuries. A zombie shambled around the edge of the van, behind Gartrell and Rittenour. McDaniels lifted his MP5 and fired, but the round was low and succeeded only in blasting away its jaw. The zombie emitted a burbling moan as red-black fluid seeped from the injury and continued forward, reaching for Gartrell. McDaniels' second shot took care of it.

"Leary, what's the SITREP?" he asked over the radio. Inside the van, Finelly gingerly exchanged places with Earl.

"Almost through!" came the terse response. "I think I need you guys up here! Over!"

"We're on our way, troop—hang tough!" McDaniels fired at a group of zombies, dropping two before the MP5 ran dry. The rest didn't even slow down. "Gartrell, we're leaving!"

Gartrell fired at the oncoming group of ghouls, blasting away limbs and chunks of their bodies, then turned and pulled open the door in the van's side. "Let's go!" he shouted as he shoved a dazed-looking Wolf Safire across the seat, then pushed Rittenour inside. He then crouched in the doorway and resumed firing as McDaniels hopped into the front passenger seat and yanked the door closed. Only then did Gartrell slam his own door shut.

"Love the smell of cordite and puke," he commented. His boots were planted squarely in Safire's vomit.

"Finelly, you good to drive?" McDaniels asked. He reached for his backpack and pulled out a package of combat gauze.

"Good to go," Finelly said, but his voice was tight. "Could use a drink if someone can give me a canteen." As he spoke, he dropped the van into gear, cut the wheel, and accelerated into the smoke. The van jerked and trembled, and something made a grinding noise from the rear. An arm reached in through the gap between the back doors, and Zoe screamed.

"They're getting in, they're getting in!"

"Cover your ears, sweetheart," Rittenour said, moving to the rear of the van. He pulled his pistol and fired two rounds between the doors. The zombie fell away as the vehicle sped up. It shuddered even more the faster it went.

"This thing's kind of fucked up," Finelly said. "Feels like the axle might be bent." He gasped as McDaniels leaned over and cut open his right trouser leg with his knife, exposing the gunshot wound.

"You're right, the bullet didn't hit the bone. Looks like it missed the femoral, too. Don't worry Finelly, you won't be checking out like Derwitz did." McDaniels tore open the combat gauze packet and applied the dressing to the wound. Finelly gasped through clenched teeth, but didn't say anything further. The van bucked as it slammed through a clutch of zombies, sending their bodies flying. McDaniels was pitched into the plastic dashboard, but he kept on working.

"Is everyone else all right? Doctor Safire? Earl?"

"We're fine," Regina said.

"Speak for yourself," Earl muttered. McDaniels heard Zoe whimpering above the roar of the van's engine. He finished dressing Finelly's wounds as best as he could, then straightened up in the passenger seat and reloaded his MP5. Once that was completed, he quickly assessed if his M4 was salvageable; he decided it was not, so he pulled the magazine from it and tossed it aside.

The van charged through the wafting smoke and hurtled down the street. It blasted through any zombies in its path like a bowling ball mowing down pins in a perfect strike, sending them flying through the air. Finelly gripped the wheel tightly, keeping the van tracking as straight as he could despite its damaged rear end.

Ahead, the tow truck hitched and bucked as it pulled through the intersection, billowing a thick cloud of exhaust. A half dozen zeds clung to it, riding in its bed or standing on its running boards. Something flashed inside the tow truck's cab, and one of the ghouls fell to the ground.

"Leary, how are you making out?" McDaniels asked.

"Not so hot, Six... this pig is giving up on me, and I'm a hundred percent danger close!"

"We're right behind you, Leary. Just keep going as far as you can, and—"

Just across the intersection, the tow truck visibly shuddered. McDaniels heard its diesel engine screaming as if in dire agony as the van dashed through the intersection, its knobbed tires kicking up debris left in the wake of the tow truck's passage. As it bore down on the bigger rig, the tow truck jolted to a sudden halt. Thick smoke boiled up from beneath its hood.

"Leary, get out of there!" Gartrell said over the radio.

The zombies swarmed all over it the tow truck and smashed at the doors and windows with their hands, as lethal as Great White sharks in a feeding frenzy. As the van drew nearer, they heard gunfire as Leary frantically sought to defend himself. Several of the zombies turned at the sound of the oncoming van, and they threw themselves at it, grabbing onto the brush bar assembly covering its grille.

"Help me help me help me!" Leary screamed over the radio.

A zombie, then another and another appeared outside McDaniels' window, pounding on it with their hands and their heads as they hurled themselves against the door. McDaniels leaned away from the window and pulled his pistol. More zombies tried to reach for Finelly, their clawed fingers scrabbling across the smooth glass.

"We have to do something!" Rittenour said, the terror in his voice plain and clear to everyone.

"Drive!" Safire shouted at Finelly, suddenly animated now that the only thing separating them from certain, gruesome death was a collection of glass and metal that now seemed far too insubstantial. "Just *drive!*"

"Do it, Finelly," McDaniels said quietly.

Finelly made a strangled sound in his throat and goosed the accelerator. The van bulled through the collection of ghouls, mowing several of them down. As it pulled abreast of the tow truck, the mass of the dead succeeded in finally ripping open the driver's door. Leary was hauled out by scores of unfeeling hands and thrown screaming to the pavement. McDaniels looked on, totally horrified as Leary's screams came across the radio.

The horde descended upon him like a feral pack, tearing into him with teeth and fingers, his microphone dutifully transmitting every sound of his death.

"Fucking Christ," Rittenour said from the back, his voice a near sob. "Fucking Christ, I've known that guy for five years—!"

"*Go!*" Regina screamed suddenly, and she slammed her fists into the back of Finelly's seat, her voice taut and ragged. "Stop waiting, or we're going to *die* here! Go!"

Finelly needed no further prompting. He mashed the accelerator to the floor, and the van sped down the street.

30

Hassle and the rest of the bridge crew silently watched as the soldier was hauled from the tow truck. He disappeared from view, and neither the FLIR systems nor the night vision binoculars had enough fidelity to show every detail of his demise, but everyone on the deck knew what was happening. They heard it all on the radio.

The man was torn apart and devoured.

"Dear sweet Jesus," Sullivan said, his voice barely a whisper as he watched the FLIR display. Hassle could only nod. There simply wasn't anything that could be said.

"The van is moving again, sir," the port lookout reported. Even though the young guardsman saw everything through his night vision binoculars, his voice was flat and neutral. Solid stuff, this one.

Hassle tore his eyes away from the screen. "Weaps, let's light those things up and try to clear a path for those people."

"Aye, sir." The weapons officer spoke into the intercom and ordered all weapons to prepare to fire. Hassle turned to the communications engineer.

"Comms, contact the LEDET and tell them we're going to fire on the zombies. They're to keep their heads down and wait until we let up before they proceed to the shoreline."

"Contact LEDET and inform them we're going weapons hot and hold their pos until we let up. Aye aye, sir."

"All weapons ready, sir," the weapons officer said.

"Fire for effect," Hassle ordered.

A moment later, the night was further torn asunder as the *Escanaba*'s firepower joined that of the artillery barrage to the north.

***

The van approached the intersection of East 80th Street and East End Avenue. It was choked with traffic, just like all the other intersections had been. As the van rolled on, McDaniels tried to think of a good tactical plan. How would they get through the intersection with the van?

The answer was not comforting. *We don't.*

"Terminator, this is *Escanaba*. We're firing on targets now, over."

A bright, sparking explosion from up ahead momentarily overwhelmed McDaniels' night vision goggles. It did the same for Finelly, who swore under his breath and slowed the van slightly. Any zombies in the area turned toward the raucous din. The explosion's flash lit their slack faces and made their dull, stupid, lifeless eyes gleam for an instant. As McDaniels' NVGs cleared, he saw fainter, but more constant flashes from the Coast Guard cutter holding station in the middle of the East River. Muzzle flashes, and big ones, too. Then another sparking explosion blossomed into being at the very end of the street. Zombies were framed against the sudden illumination. Hundreds of them.

"Major, we're not going to be able to make it across that intersection in this thing," Finelly said, pointing out the obvious for everyone.

"I know that," McDaniels said. He scanned the street ahead, from left to right. It was—had been—a very tony residential area, with high-end apartment buildings lining both sides of the street. Scaffolding covered the majority of the left side of the street, as the facades on a block of buildings had been receiving face lifts before the zombie terror struck. The right side was clear, unobstructed.

"But it doesn't really matter." Safire's voice sounded weary. "Right across East End Avenue, there's a dead end, which we have to deal with whether the intersection is clear or not. Then we have to cross the East River Drive. There's at least a ten foot drop off separating the south- and northbound lanes. And then, we would have to get across the northbound lanes and wait to be picked up by the Coast Guard."

"Doesn't sound like you have much faith, doctor," McDaniels said.

Safire had nothing to say.

McDaniels pointed out the windshield. "Finelly, I want you to coast to a stop right there, where that mailbox is... see it?"

"I see it," the big soldier said.

"Rittenour, how are you doing back there?" McDaniels asked.

"Feeling kind of out of it, major. And this bite is really bugging the hell out of me."

"One more run, and then we're out of here. Finelly, how's the leg?"

Finelly shrugged as he guided the van toward the left curb. "It hurts, but I'm not staying here, sir."

"Very well. All right folks, we're going to have to make the last four hundred feet or so on foot, which means we run like hell. Everyone gets a partner: Safire, you're with me. Regina, you're with Finelly. Earl, you're with Rittenour. Zoe, First Sergeant Gartrell will take care of you."

"I want to stay with my daddy," Zoe said quietly, her voice small and childlike.

"He won't be far from you, hon. We'll make sure nothing happens to either of you, all right?" That was a total lie. McDaniels knew that if the shit has going to hit the fan any harder than it already had, then he would heft Wolf Safire over one shoulder and run straight for the river. They were out of time, and the mission had to be completed. Had to be.

"Anyone have any issues with their assignments? Shooters, are you ready? I want smoke dropped behind us the second we stop and dismount. Everyone stay with their partner, and we move together, shooters on the outside, civilians on the inside. Civilians, grab on to our belts. Shooters, leave everything that you can't use in a fight. If we can't make it to the boat, we're not going to need it anyway."

There was a muted chorus of hooahs from the soldiers, and McDaniels heard Gartrell and Rittenour shrug out of their heavy packs. Gartrell tapped him on the shoulder with something hard, metallic. McDaniels turned, and saw three magazines of nine millimeter in his hand.

"They were Derwitz's," he said. "You'd better take them. Also have some more pistol ammo for you as well." Gartrell handed over another three magazines, and McDaniels pocketed them.

The van glided to a halt, and Finelly slammed it into gear.

"Let's go," McDaniels said, and he snapped the door open and jumped out into the night.

The rain had stopped completely some time ago, and now the wind was abating. Overhead, the clouds thinned, and McDaniels saw they formed a spectral halo around the moon. He reached behind him and yanked open the van's side door. Gartrell emerged, and behind him, Wolf Safire regarded the dark street beyond with blinking eyes. McDaniels reached in and grabbed his arm as Finelly hobbled around the van's battered and bloodied grille. Safire stepped out into the night, his head snapping this way and that like a bird's. Nearby zombies shuffled along, their attention focused mostly on the ship in the river as it fired on the shoreline. That wouldn't last for long, McDaniels knew. He was eager to get going, but he waited for Regina to get situated with Finelly and Zoe to be parted from her father by Gartrell. Everyone worked silently. No words were spoken. It didn't take very long for the group to get organized. McDaniels nodded once and led them toward the sidewalk that was covered by the scaffolding and blue-painted plywood. It was quite dark under the scaffolding's cover, and he intended to use the darkness to their advantage.

As he walked, he contacted the *Escanaba* and informed the Coast Guardsman on the other side what the plan was.

"Got that, major. The captain says he'll halt the attack the second you give the word."

"Roger that. Six out." Behind him, Safire shuffled along, his fingers wrapped around McDaniels' belt. McDaniels panned his head from left to right and back again at regular intervals, as the NVGs had only a 40 degree field of view. This was the only way to remain aware of what was going on around them and avoid developing tunnel vision at the same time.

As McDaniels led Safire toward the corner of 80th and East End, a zed shuffled around the corner and moved toward them. Through his goggles, McDaniels saw the ghoul was unaware of their approach; its face registered none of the usual excitement they exhibited whenever the opportunity to feed presented itself, and its eyes were mostly fixed on a point somewhere in infinity. It tottered toward them, dragging one foot behind the other, its jeans and denim shirt speckled with black droplets. Blood. McDaniels took a deep breath and raised his rifle to his shoulder.

Not for the first time, he wished the suppressor at the end of the MP5's barrel worked exactly like they were supposed to in the movies: a gentle spitting sound, and then the zombie would simply collapse into a heap. None of the other ghouls surrounding them would ever know a thing. Unfortunately, it didn't work that way.

More ghouls milled about in the street, slowly walking toward the pyrotechnics caused by the *Escanaba*'s barrage. McDaniels quietly spoke into his headset's boom microphone.

"*Escanaba*, Terminator Six... I need you to start hitting the intersection with your big guns, can you do that? We're about twenty meters west of it, over."

"Terminator, *Escanaba*. We can shift fires that way, but we need to reposition the boat. In the meantime, you'd better fall back, over."

"No time, *Escanaba*." The zombie approaching the group stopped suddenly. It moaned and shambled toward them as quickly as its stiff legs could carry it. Other stenches in the street turned toward the sound, their interest obviously piqued. Behind him, McDaniels heard the rest of the soldiers raise their weapons and prepare to engage. Safire's grip tightened on McDaniels' belt.

"We need that to happen right now, *Escanaba*, or we're dead. Six out." McDaniels raised his MP5 and sighted on the zed hurrying toward him. It moaned again, its hands outstretched, fingers wiggling as it groped about in the darkness, searching for the human it knew was nearby.

Crack! The zombie's head exploded when McDaniels fired. It collapsed to the sidewalk, twitched once, then lay still.

That was all it took. The rest of the ghouls surged toward the group, moaning and shrieking like banshees.

"Fight's on!" Gartrell said, and the roar of his AA-12 drowned out the ululations of the dead.

***

"Conn, let us drift backwards about fifty yards so the 76 can service the targets!" Hassle ordered.

"Aye sir!" said the helmsman, and he dropped the *Escanaba*'s big diesel engines into idle. The current did its job, and the 270-

foot cutter lazily drifted out of its station keeping position, gently rolling from side to side despite the stabilizer fins that were supposed to keep the vessel steady even in heavy seas.

"Weaps, let us know when you can put steel on target," Hassle said. "And notify the gunners that the .50 should maintain its firing pattern!" he added when the big machinegun on the port side of the ship fell silent, likely in response to the vessel's sudden relocation. The command was given, and the .50 started up again, firing into the night, raking across the zeds standing along the shoreline. The .50 caliber rounds made short work of the targets, blasting them into chunks of disassociated necrotic flesh.

"Ready for firing!" weaps reported.

"You're clear to fire. Do it!" Hassle said as the *Escanaba*'s engines growled back to life, holding the vessel steady in its new position.

***

"This isn't my idea of a hot date!" Gartrell said as he blazed away at the approaching mass of ghouls, dropping them to the street as quickly as the AA-12 could fire. The other soldiers poured it on, hitting zombies in the head, adding their again lifeless bodies to the pile that grew around the group.

"Continue the advance!" McDaniels said. "We can't get trapped here. Form up on me!" As he spoke, McDaniels moved, blasting a path through the zombies that approached him on the sidewalk. Safire moved with him, whimpering beneath the gunshots and the cries of the dead, his hand clenched around McDaniels' belt. Gartrell and Rittenour stayed on the outside, blazing away at the zeds that approached them from the street, dropping them as quickly as possible. Finelly used his own MP5 to secure the rear. He stumbled over the corpses left lying on the sidewalk, and narrowly avoided the clutches of a ghoul that managed to get past Gartrell and Rittenour. He shot it in the face at point-blank range, blasting skull and dead brain matter all over the blue scaffolding.

Then the night was torn apart by the first of the *Escanaba*'s 76 millimeter rounds.

The intersection lit up as the high explosive round slammed into it at a slant, decimating the cars and trucks there as it essentially vaporized the zombies standing nearby. The shock wave of concussive force radiated outward at speeds over 200 miles an hour, carrying with it shards of glass and chunks of metal. Flames blossomed into existence as fuel tanks exploded; the fire hungrily consumed everything it could, gasoline, rubber tires, vehicle upholstery, anything that would support it. Even the zeds themselves turned into walking pyres, thrashing about before the flames consumed so much of their tissue that they could no longer move. Thick, black smoke roiled into the sky. Then another round hit. And another. And another. Shock waves raced through the intersection, intensifying as they were channeled up the streets, carrying with them a fusillade of shrapnel. Safire went down with a cry, pulling McDaniels with him. McDaniels hit the sidewalk hard, but maintained enough presence of mind to keep firing at the approaching zombies as they themselves stumbled and fell from the force of the attack. In the intersection, more cars exploded, and anti-theft alarms wailed. Another round hit, and the windows of every building facing the intersection finally shattered, stressed beyond their limits. Window unit air conditioners fell into the street, and one crashed through the plywood roof of the sidewalk scaffolding, crushing a zombie's skull in the process. Dozens of ghouls still shambled about in the street, their primitive minds overwhelmed by the fury of the attack, blinded by the bright flames and the thick, acrid smoke. The soldiers concentrated their fire on them, dropping them one by one by one.

Until finally, the immediate vicinity was secured. For the moment.

"*Escanaba*, Terminator Six! Check your fire, check your fire!" McDaniels shouted into the radio.

"Roger, Terminator Six—fire mission cancelled, over."

"Daddy?" Behind McDaniels, Regina Safire's voice was barely audible over the crackle of raging fire and the moaning of distant zombies. Farther away, the .50 caliber machinegun on the *Escanaba* continued to chatter. McDaniels pulled himself into a kneeling position and took the opportunity to recharge his weapon. More muted clicks and snaps told him the rest of the soldiers were doing the same.

"*Daddy!*" Regina said again, her voice building into a ragged shriek.

McDaniels turned. Wolf Safire lay on his back just behind him, his face paler than usual, his eyes unfocused and glassy. Clearly visible in the glow of the firelight, a dark stain spread across the front of his white shirt. It grew larger and larger with each second. McDaniels gasped. A long shard of glass protruded from Safire's chest, right where his heart would be.

No, no, no, no, no—

"Regina." Safire's voice was muted, barely audible. "My little Reggie-girl..."

Regina threw herself to the sidewalk beside her father's prone form, already going to work. "Don't move, Daddy. Don't move. I need to look at this." As she gently pulled open Safire's shirt, she looked up at McDaniels. "Help me, God damn it!"

Gartrell finished reloading his AA-12, and he looked down at Safire quickly. "Fuck," he muttered, then went back to work. Rittenour joined him a moment later.

McDaniels knelt beside Regina, weapon still in hand as tendrils of smoke drifted over them. He was no doctor, but he had seen his share of battlefield injuries, and this one looked serious. As Regina pulled the blood-soaked shirt away from her father's chest, he saw more blood pump up from around the large splinter of glass in Safire's chest. That his heart had been pierced was beyond questioning. Regina wept as she tried to wipe away the blood with her sleeve.

"McDaniels." Safire's voice was soft and dry but still audible, his words perfectly enunciated. "McDaniels, my daughter..."

"We'll get her out," McDaniels said. "And you too."

"My jacket pocket. It's in my pocket. Hurry."

McDaniels reached past Regina and searched the man's jacket. He found the pocket and reached inside. He pulled out a thick, silver IronKey thumb drive, and held it up to where Safire could see it.

"This?"

Safire nodded slightly. "I lied. All the data... it's on that. Password protected. It's 'Regina Marie 1971'. That's the password."

"Regina Marie 1971. Your daughter's birth date?"

"Yes."

Gunfire rang out, and Gartrell said, "More zeds inbound, major. We've got to get moving."

McDaniels pocketed the thumb drive and reached for Safire. "Come on, doctor. Let's get you out of here."

Safire slapped his hand away with surprising strength, then turned toward Regina. "My Reggie-girl... you always stood by me."

Regina cried openly now, still wiping at the blood on his chest. The flow had diminished remarkably in just the last few seconds. It was clear to McDaniels that his heart was giving out.

"Daddy," she said, her voice full of emotion.

Safire's fingers touched her cheek. "My little Reggie-girl... how I lo—"

His hand fell away, and the light left Wolf Safire's eyes for good.

Regina wailed. Earl sidled over and put his arm around her, tears brimming in his own eyes.

"I'm so sorry, miss," he said. He reached out and put his other arm around Zoe. The young girl was crying too.

"Major!" Gartrell's voice was sharp and hard-edged even above the gunfire. McDaniels nodded and grabbed a hold of Regina's jacket as he hauled her to her feet.

"We have to go! Let's get moving!" He pulled Regina down the sidewalk, but she screamed and fought against him.

"No! No! We can't leave him to become one of *them!*" she cried.

McDaniels dropped a naked, singed zombie that advanced toward them, its flesh burned almost black by one of the car fires. It fell to the street, wisps of smoke rising from its seared flesh.

"Come on!" he said, pulling harder.

Regina ripped his hand off her jacket and reached for his belt. Before he could stop her, she pulled his pistol from its holster and whirled back to face her father's corpse. Holding the weapon in trembling hands, she clicked off the safety as Earl pulled Zoe away, her face against his chest. Regina pointed the pistol at her father's body.

"Oh Daddy," she said, her voice barely a whisper.

She pulled the trigger, and the pistol bucked in her hands. A single round, right through Safire's forehead.

"Damn, if we'd known you could shoot we would have given you a gun earlier," Gartrell said. "Better let her keep it, major. And let's get the hell out of here!"

McDaniels grabbed Regina's arm and pulled her after him. "Okay, he's gone. Let's go. Hurry!"

He led them down the sidewalk, dropping any zeds that got in their way. Gartrell moved out into the street, extending their perimeter, and waited until the zombies were close enough to ensure they got head shots. McDaniels led them into the inferno of the intersection and picked his way through the morass of burning automobiles and trucks, coughing as the acrid smoke seared his throat and nostrils. A zombie wearing a fireman's uniform lurched toward them, half its face a scorched mass of smoking flesh. Regina fired at it, hit it in the neck, driving it back a step. Her second shot hit it right below its one remaining eye, and it collapsed against the hood of a crumpled taxi.

Suddenly, a group of zombies stepped around an overturned mail truck and surged toward the group, right behind Rittenour. He shouted warning and went to guns on them, but he was too late. Though one, then two zombies fell to the street, the rest hit him like linebackers for the Green Bay Packers and slammed him up against another car. He screamed as their teeth found his flesh.

"Get away from me!" he screamed to the others as Finelly backtracked, firing on the zeds. "Get away from me! *Grenade!*" McDaniels saw the grenade in Rittenour's hands, and he knew what was about to happen.

"Finelly, run! Run!" he said, obeying his own command as he reached back and dragged Regina with him. Gartrell pushed Earl and Zoe before him as Rittenour pulled the pin and dropped the grenade to the ground between his feet. Finelly hobbled away as fast as his injured leg would allow, a keening cry escaping from his lips. Rittenour collapsed, either by purpose or from the mass of ghouls, to fall across the grenade. It went off with a thunderclap, obliterating him and sending several tattered corpses cartwheeling through the air.

McDaniels kept pressing forward, ignoring the scalding heat of a nearby car fire that left him feeling baked. The heat and brilliant light overwhelmed his goggles, so he flipped them up on their mount. Just in time—separating itself from the inferno, a flaming zombie staggered toward him, too close for him to turn his MP5 on it. He lashed out with his left hand and punched it in its blackened face, driving it back a few steps until it tripped over a twisted bumper lying in the street. McDaniels ignored it and hurried across the shattered intersection.

Ahead, 80th Street came to an end, as proclaimed by a pair of twisted, bent signs that read DEAD END. The trees on the corner were awash with flame, their trunks cracking and splitting with firecracker-like snaps and pops. At the end of the street was an iron security fence, more decorative than anything else, that served to separate the street from the southbound lanes of the FDR. Beyond it, floating in the black waters of the East River, was the darkened silhouette of the USCGC *Escanaba*. Light flared from a point on its side as the .50 continuously fired at the mass of zombies that had been drawn to the shoreline. They stood three deep, despite the withering firepower being leveled against them.

This just gets better and better.

McDaniels glanced over his shoulder to make sure the rest of the team was with him, then flipped his goggles back over his eyes. "I'll go down first. Gartrell, you and Finelly help the others. The southbound lanes look clear." Without waiting for a response, McDaniels hauled himself over the fence and dropped down onto the bed of a pickup truck right below. The abandoned vehicle bounced on its shock absorbers, and for a split instant, McDaniels was afraid he would fall out of it. He regained his balance and looked around the vicinity, his MP5 in both hands. There were no zeds in the immediate area. Across the three lanes of dead traffic, the street seemed to disappear on the other side of the concrete guard rail. He knew the ten foot drop Safire had mentioned lay on the other side.

The truck bounced again as Regina Safire jumped into it and fell face first. She lost her grip on the pistol, and it clattered across the pickup's metal bed. Earl was next, landing on his ass right beside her. He jumped to his feet and extended his arms upward, waiting for Finelly to help Zoe over the fence.

McDaniels jumped out of the truck. "Get up, Regina," he said, raising his voice over the gunfire and the flames above. "I need you down here." She reclaimed the pistol and eased herself out of the pickup truck as Zoe fell into her father's arms with a small shriek. Both of them fell into the bed, and Gartrell jumped into it.

"Let's go, Sergeant Finelly!" he said, landing on his feet like a cat.

Finelly lifted his injured leg over the twisted iron fence, wincing at the pain. His wound was bleeding again, McDaniels noticed as he scanned left and right, waiting for the first zed to appear. And there they were... shuffling out from under an overpass several hundred feet to the north. In the glow of the fires above, they could clearly see the band of humans, and they accelerated toward them as fast as they could manage.

Finelly shrieked suddenly as five zombies attacked him from behind, pulling him away from the fence. Both Gartrell and McDaniels fired at them, but they were too late. Finelly was pulled away out of sight, but they heard his screams and one frantic burst of full automatic fire that ended almost as quickly as it had started.

"Run!" Gartrell pulled Earl to his feet. "Run now!"

Earl grabbed Zoe and flung both of them out of the pickup truck, with Gartrell right behind. And not a moment too soon; a literal wave of deadheads poured over the fence, collapsing into the pickup's bed like a grisly tsunami, moaning and writhing. Those below were crushed within seconds as the pile grew and grew. McDaniels pushed Regina ahead of him, then did the same with Earl and Zoe.

"Run down in that direction—we'll have to go down to where we can cross over into the northbound lanes!" he said, pointing south. There, the sloping southbound lane met the northbound where the ground leveled out, separated from each other by a thick concrete guardrail that was less than four feet high. As they passed him, he pulled his last smoke grenade and tossed it behind him in an attempt to obscure their retreat. Gartrell backed toward him, firing his AA-12 at the zeds in the pickup. As the smoker went off, Gartrell pulled a fragmentation grenade and tossed it into the pickup, then joined McDaniels. The two men sprinted down the lane, pushing past abandoned cars. Some of them were still running, engines idling. The frag grenade went off in a fiery flash, its retort muted by the scores of bodies that surrounded it. Shrapnel whirled through the area, bouncing off cars, shattering glass, and mutilating bodies that felt no pain.

"*Escanaba*, Terminator Six! We're running south to where we can cross over to the northbound lanes—concentrate your fires there! Give us a path!"

"Terminator, *Escanaba*—we're on it, you might want to hold up for as long as you can. Cover your ears, rounds out!" As the Coast Guardsman spoke, the 76 millimeter gun on the ship's foredeck spoke once again. Microseconds later, the powerful explosions ripped through the area in blossoming flashes of light and smoke. McDaniels and his group were pelted with all manner of debris, concrete, metal, plastic, pieces of deboned ghouls.

"Let me past! Let me past!" Gartrell shouted as he shoved his way past McDaniels. Behind, the first of the zombies stepped through the smoke screen. McDaniels fired two shots, dropping one. The zeds behind stepped over the body, stumbling and fumbling as they moaned, but still they came, ignoring the powerful explosions that ripped the night asunder on the other side of the retaining wall. Ahead, a ghoul suddenly appeared, right before Regina. She cried and stopped short, raising her pistol. She fired and missed. She fired again, but hit the zombie in the chest, which did nothing to deter it. As it advanced upon her, she raised the weapon higher, focusing on its head. But then Earl plowed into her from behind, and both of them went down. Zoe shrieked when she saw the zombie step toward them, its jaws spread wide. Its head disappeared in a pulpy flash of expanding tissue and fragmented bone as Gartrell fired a single shot over Zoe's head. He then pushed past the shrieking girl and leaped over Earl and Regina as they thrashed about on the roadway between the stalled cars.

"Get up! Get up!" McDaniels shouted to them. He turned and fired at the zombies behind them, dropping more ghouls this time as they emerged from the smoke. Earl and Regina got to their feet.

"*Escanaba*, Terminator—we're almost at the crossing point!" Ahead, Gartrell was already nearing where the lanes came together. "Cease fire with the big guns now, over!"

The 76 millimeter gun stopped firing a moment later, and the .50 caliber resumed, sounding tinny and ineffectual when compared to the ferocious roar of its bigger shipmate. Gartrell crossed over to the guard rail, then stopped short for a moment before shouldering his AA-12 and firing for all he was worth.

"Wait there! Wait there!" he shouted. As he fired, he backpedaled and reached into one of the cargo pockets on his BDU trousers. As a wave of walking dead suddenly crested the guard rail, he pulled out a long cylinder from the pocket. Running southbound now, away from McDaniels and the rest of the group, he jumped onto a car and fiddled with the cylinder. A bright purple-white flame sprang into existence. Gartrell had lit a flare.

Earl gave voice to the question McDaniels was asking himself. "What the fuck is that crazy man *doing?*"

He's leading them away from us, McDaniels thought.

"Come on, you dead motherfuckers!" Gartrell screamed, waving the flare over his head. "*Come on!*" He then set off to the south, bounding from car to car, pausing only momentarily to stop and shoot at the zombies closest to him.

"Gartrell!" McDaniels said over the radio. "Gartrell!"

"You're clear to cross now—get to it, it's not going to last! Find out where my family is, and make sure they're all right!" Gartrell's voice was breathless and rushed in McDaniels' headphones.

"Gartrell, you're committing suicide!"

"Things weren't exactly going my way before, major. You might want to take advantage of this and get your ass to the boat with that damned thumb drive." Gartrell paused to fire once again, then resumed running, the flare clearly illuminating him. "Besides, you always thought I was a pain in the ass anyway. If the meek are going to inherit this place, at least one of them has to live, and that's you!"

"Gartrell... Dave. Dave, thank you. Thank you."

"Just find my family, make sure they're safe," Gartrell said. "Terminator Five, out." Gartrell continued running, yelling and firing as he went, drawing the zeds away even as the *Escanaba* continued firing, picking them off one by one.

"Hole up somewhere!" McDaniels said. "We'll come back for you, Gartrell!"

There was no answer as Gartrell continued on into the night.

"*Escanaba*, we're coming across now! Send the boats in, and don't fire on us!" McDaniels switched on the infrared strobe clipped to his body armor, and it flashed brightly in his NVGs. "I'm illuminated with an IR strobe, over!"

"Terminator, *Escanaba*... roger that last, you are illuminated, over."

McDaniels grabbed Zoe and pushed her into Earl's arms, then shoved his way past them and Regina. He led them to where Gartrell had attracted the attention of the zeds, and leaned over the concrete guardrail. There was massive decimation on the other side, where the 76 millimeter rounds had done their job. Cars and trucks and buses were aflame, with great columns of fire reaching a hundred feet into the sky. Here and there, stupefied zeds tottered about. Some were smoldering, others were half blown to pieces; the .50 cal. on the *Escanaba* continued to chatter, raking the remaining zeds with tight, controlled bursts. Just the same, some rounds went wild, slamming into the concrete retaining wall.

"Let's go!" McDaniels led the group across the lanes to the south of the conflagration, staying clear of the engagement area. A zombie rose up from between two cars, and he gunned it down. Another appeared, this one much smaller, a girl in a frayed, blood splattered dress, clutching a headless teddy bear to its dead chest. Regina made a strangled sound in her throat as the small ghoul rushed toward them, moaning in hunger. McDaniels shot it through the head, straight and true.

"Hurry!" he urged them as he headed across the FDR. Another cement guardrail was ahead. McDaniels leaned across it, looking to the left and the right. A small group of zombies moved toward him from the south. McDaniels raised his rifle, but he needn't have bothered. Several muzzle flashes from across the water sent rounds that ripped through them, eventually bringing them down.

"Terminator! Over here!" came a voice.

McDaniels looked over and saw a small, rigid hull inflatable with a single outboard engine approaching the shoreline. Several armed Coast Guardsmen sat in it, all wearing night vision goggles. A stocky Guardsman with an M16 waved at him from the bow, holding an IR chem stick. McDaniels hopped over the guard rail and reached back for Zoe. Earl lifted her over the guard rail and handed her to him, then helped Regina crawl over. Behind him, a mass of ghouls boiled over the guard rail separating the north and southbound lanes.

"Holy shit, this again?" he muttered before flinging himself over the edge of guard rail, landing beside his daughter.

McDaniels charged toward the metal fence separating the shore from the river. "Come on, Coast Guard! We're next on the menu here!" Regina, Earl, and Zoe joined him at the fence. The river was perhaps five feet below.

"Don't jump in the water!" the Coast Guardsman said. "Zombies!" He pointed to a corpse floating nearby, slowly paddling its way toward where McDaniels and the others waited.

"Good God, when will this be over," Regina moaned.

The Coast Guardsman in the bow of the boat shouldered his M16 and fired a burst at the zombie. Though his aim was imperfect, at least one of the bullets struck the ghoul in the head, and it slowly sank beneath the dark water.

"Uh major..." Earl looked behind them. McDaniels turned and saw the first of what seemed to be a hundred zeds crossing the FDR, stumbling toward the other guard rail. It was the only thing that separated them from their hopeful next meal.

"Coast Guard, let's get a move on, we have about a hundred friends named zed showing up for dinner!" he shouted as the boat drew nearer.

"Keep your shirt on, Army," the Guardsman in the bow said. The boat stopped right below them, and McDaniels stepped away from the guard rail. He peppered the advancing ghouls with fire from his MP5.

"Earl, help the ladies into the boat, but be quick about it!"

Earl was already in the process of handing off Zoe. Regina turned and fired her pistol at the zombies, then vaulted over the railing and into the waiting boat. The .50 caliber aboard the *Escanaba* spoke, and several of the ghouls were blasted into pieces as the heavy rounds passed through them like exploding missiles. It didn't faze those who were not hit. The zombies made it to the guard rail and crawled over it, moaning, eyes flat and soulless in the firelight.

"Major!" Regina shouted.

McDaniels vaulted over the fence and crashed into the boat.

"Pull away!" the Guardsman in the bow yelled as he and another Guardsman pushed the boat away from the cement breakwater. Just in time; the zombies swarmed over the fence and plunged into the dark water, landing only a foot or two from the small vessel. A moment later, and the Coast Guard would have had a lot more company in the boat.

The Rigid Hull Inflatable's outboard engine roared, and the boat turned toward the waiting *Escanaba*.

31

Aboard the *Escanaba*, McDaniels turned and looked back at New York City. It was dark, dotted here and there with fires that continued to rage. He searched for any sign of Gartrell, but there was nothing. His radio calls went unanswered, and that was not a good sign. Even if Gartrell was in hiding, surrounded by zombies, he would click his microphone on and off to let McDaniels know he was still alive.

Which he likely wasn't.

"Did anyone see what happened to First Sergeant Gartrell?" he asked the deck crew. "The soldier with the flare?"

"He turned up that street there, 79th Street," said a tall Coast Guardsman about McDaniels' age. His nametape read HASSLE and his badges of rank were silver oak leaf clusters. A commander. McDaniels saluted automatically, and the captain of the *Escanaba* returned the salute, then stuck out his hand. "I'm Commander Hassle, skipper of the *Nob*. Welcome aboard, Army. Looks like you guys had a hell of a night."

"Cord McDaniels, and that we did. Any idea if he might still be alive, sir?" McDaniels asked.

"When his flare died, we lost sight of him. We were concentrating our attention on you and the civilians. I'm sorry." Hassle looked past McDaniels, where Coast Guardsmen were tending to Regina, Earl, and Zoe. "I don't suppose that black man is...?"

"Doctor Safire? No. He's dead. Back there."

Hassle looked shocked. "Oh, Jesus Christ. The man is *dead?*"

"Completely. But he's not forgotten." McDaniels stepped away from the rail and pulled the IronKey thumb drive from his pocket. "This is his research. All of it, right here."

Hassle looked at the thumb drive for a long moment, then smiled wearily. "For real?"

"For real. You think you might have a safe place for this?"

"How about the ship's safe? Fireproof and waterproof, and only I and the XO have the combination."

McDaniels nodded. "That'll do."

Hassle took the IronKey and smiled again. This time the expression was full of relief. "I'll notify my district command. They'll get word back to your superiors. Looks like you might have saved the day after all, Army." The cutter began to move then, accelerating into a slow turn that would take them around Roosevelt Island.

"We've been ordered back to Boston, our home port," Hassle said, responding to the unspoken question in McDaniels' eyes. "We'll probably transfer you and your party to another ship or an aircraft there." Hassle glanced back at the city. "How many men did you..."

"All of them," McDaniels said. His voice was a flat monotone.

Hassle looked at him for a moment, then nodded. There was nothing else to be said on that matter.

"Let me get you a cup of that crappy coffee you were promised," he said instead. "It won't taste very good, but it'll keep you on your toes for the next four days."

"I'd like that," McDaniels said.

Click. Click.

McDaniels whirled back to face the city. He pressed his radio's transmit button. "Gartrell! Terminator Five, is that you? Over."

Click. Click.

"Five, this is Six. Can you speak? Over."

Click.

"What is it? Your first sergeant is alive?" Hassle asked, amazed.

McDaniels was struck by the absurdity of the question, but it suddenly made sense to him in a way that it would never have yesterday. A lifetime ago.

"Five, this is Six. Are you somewhere on 79th Street? Over."

Click.

"Five, are you injured? Have you been bitten? Over."

Click.

"Five, stand by." McDaniels turned back to Hassle. "My first sergeant is still alive. We need to go get him."

"I don't have the manpower for that kind of operation," Hassle said. "I'm sorry, we can't do that. Besides, it's... it's suicide. I can't order my men into *that*." He jerked his chin toward the darkened city.

"You have got to be fucking kidding me," McDaniels growled.

Hassle didn't bend, and his eyes grew hard. "I'm not kidding you, soldier. And this ship has been ordered home."

"Captain, I don't give a flying fuck if the President himself ordered you back, you give me some men so I can go get First Sergeant Gartrell. We wouldn't be here if it wasn't for him!"

"Gartrell's alive?" Regina asked from nearby. She was draped in a thin blanket. A Coast Guardsman walked toward McDaniels and held another blanket out toward him. McDaniels ignored him and fixed Hassle with his best Special Forces Officer Glare.

Hassle looked away. "I'm sorry, major. We can't do that."

"So you're going to leave that man there, to die?" Regina asked incredulously. "After everything all of those men did for us, you're just going to leave him to *die*?"

"It's not my call," Hassle said. "I've been given a mission." He looked up at McDaniels, and true regret showed in his eye. "I *am* sorry, Major McDaniels. But I won't send my men in there. I won't send them in to die. They're Coasties, not Special Forces."

"Then give me a boat. I'll go myself. Or just get close enough to the shoreline that I can go ashore and find him myself."

"You won't be doing that, major. And any move by you to do such a thing will get you time in my brig. And trying to force the issue"—Hassle motioned toward McDaniels' MP5, hanging across his chest by its patrol strap—"will get you a burial at sea."

Unbidden, Gartrell's joke sprang to life in McDaniels' mind. *Why do Coasties need twelve men to bury someone at sea? Six to dump the deceased overboard, and six to jump up and down on the casket to push it under the mud.*

"You're despicable," McDaniels said.

"Lieutenant Castillo, take Major McDaniels' weapons away from him," Hassle ordered. "Use whatever force is necessary, but I want this man disarmed."

"Sir," Castillo said. He was the short, stolid man who had been in the bow of the RHI. Two of his Guardsman compatriots came forward while Castillo hung back, a hand on his sidearm.

"This is ridiculous!" Regina shouted. "*Ridiculous!*"

"No ma'am," Hassle said. "This is reality." To McDaniels: "You're not getting a boat, and this vessel is bound for Boston. Hand over your weapons. Now."

McDaniels turned and faced the city. He let the Coast Guard take his weapons, but slapped them away when they tried to take his radio. "First swabbie who tries to take my communications gear will walk away with two busted collarbones," he said.

"Leave the radio alone," Hassle said. "He's in contact with one of his men."

"Five, this is Six. The Coast Guard won't allow us to come ashore and rescue you. You have to find a place and hole up, over."

Click. Click.

"I'll be back, Gartrell. As soon as I can get some fellow legionnaires or even lightfighters, we'll be back for you. Over."

Click.

No? What the hell does that mean? "Five, this is Six. We'll be back for you. I'll bring you back to your wife and kids. I swear it."

Click.

"Gartrell... we'll be back, Gartrell. You know the code, we never leave our own behind."

There was no response.

"Gartrell? Five, this is Six. Come in. Five, come in, over."

The radio remained silent. McDaniels stepped back to the railing and watched as New York City slid past. The *Escanaba* turned to starboard, and the city fell away.

"Gartrell? Gartrell!" McDaniels repeated the calls, but the radio remained silent. As the Coast Guard cutter retraced its course to the open sea, McDaniels heard nothing further from First Sergeant David Gartrell.

The man he hated.

The man who had saved him.

The man who had saved them all.

The End

ACKNOWLEDGEMENTS

Just as no man is an island, no novel is written entirely by a single person. The Gathering Dead is no different. I'd like to thank a pack of fine folks who lent me their expertise, wit, and wisdom over the past several months it took to generate this book. They are:

Derek Paterson. For the past fifteen years, he's been sounding board, reader, editor, proofer, and all around great guy. My friend, thank you for being such a remarkable resource.

Fred Anderson, for all the good advice, and for sharing your own work. Seeing what you can do has made me brave enough to find new directions for my own efforts.

Joe LeBert, for his "every man" opinions and quick ability to detect what works and what does not. Even though you forget all about a book a week after you've read it, for those first seven days you're an excellent source of information.

Kevin G. Slater, for all the good stuff on life in the U.S. Coast Guard in general, and the USCGC Escanaba specifically. Any mistakes or errors found in this work are my fault, not his. And thanks for all the great parties over the past 30 years, Kev!

Special operators SFC Carlson and CPT Braedenton, as always, you are the total stud muffins when it comes to articulating the specifics of the Special Forces mission.

Residents of New York City's Upper East Side will not recognize the office building on the corner of Lex and East 79th, because it does not exist. It's a total fabrication, invented for the story. I've also taken great liberty with the topology of New York City where it suited the writer.

Errors regarding the excellent NYPD are my responsibility.

The same for errors regarding the U.S. Army's Special Forces branch, the greatest collection of fighting men ever assembled. These are multifaceted individuals who likely have a greater education than most of the rest of us who epitomize the very ideals of honor, of courage, of selfless sacrifice. Gentlemen, if my portrayal of you in this work is not accurate, please accept my most heartfelt apologies.

And a great big thanks to you, those who bought this book. I hope you enjoyed it.

Stephen Knight lives in the New York City area.

THE LIVING END

James Robert Smith

**One Hundred and
Fifty Million Zombies.**

Sixty Million Dogs.

**All of them hungry for
warm human flesh.**

**The dead have risen, killing
anyone they find. The living
know what's caused it-a
vicious contagion. But too
late to stop it. For now, what
remains of society are busy
shutting down nuclear
reactors and securing chemical plants to prevent runaway
reactions in both. There's little time for anything else.**

**Failed comic book artist Rick Nuttman and his family have
joined thousands of other desperate people in trying to find a
haven from the madness.**

**Perhaps refuge can be found in the village of Sparta or maybe
there is salvation in The City of Ruth, a community raised from
the ashes of Carolina.**

**In the low country below the hills, a monster named Danger
Man changes everything.**

**While watching over it all, the mysterious figure of BC, moving
his gigantic canine pack westward, into lands where survivors
think they are safe**

**And always, the mindless hordes neither living nor dead,
waiting only to destroy.**

There will be a reckoning.

WHITE FLAG OF THE DEAD
Joseph Talluto

Book 1: Surrender of the Living.

Millions died when the Enillo Virus swept the earth. Millions more were lost when the victims of the plague refused to stay dead, instead rising to slay and feed on those left alive. For survivors like John Talon and his son Jake, they are faced with a choice: Do they submit to the dead, raising the white flag of surrender? Or do they find the will to fight, to try and hang on to the last shreds or humanity?

Surrender of the Living is the first high octane instalment in the White Flag of the Dead series.

RESURRECTION
By Tim Curran
www.corpseking.com

The rain is falling and the dead are rising. It began at an ultra-secret government laboratory. Experiments in limb regeneration-an unspeakable union of Medieval alchemy and cutting edge genetics result in the very germ of horror itself: a gene trigger that will reanimate dead tissue...any dead tissue. Now it's loose. It's gone viral. It's in the rain. And the rain has not stopped falling for weeks. As the country floods and corpses float in the streets, as cities are submerged, the evil dead are rising. And they are hungry.

"I REALLY love this book...Curran is a wonderful storyteller who really should be unleashed upon the general horror reading public sooner rather than leter." – *DREAD CENTRAL*

The Official Zombie Handbook: Sean T Page

Since pre-history, the living dead have been among us, with documented outbreaks from ancient Babylon and Rome right up to the present day. But what if we were to suffer a zombie apocalypse in the UK today? Through meticulous research and field work, The Official Zombie Handbook (UK) is the only guide you need to make it through a major zombie outbreak in the UK, including: -Full analysis of the latest scientific information available on the zombie virus, the living dead creatures it creates and most importantly, how to take them down - UK style. Everything you need to implement a complete 90 Day Zombie Survival Plan for you and your family including home fortification, foraging for supplies and even surviving a ghoul siege. Detailed case studies and guidelines on how to battle the living dead, which weapons to use, where to hide out and how to survive in a country dominated by millions of bloodthirsty zombies. Packed with invaluable information, the genesis of this handbook was the realisation that our country is sleep walking towards a catastrophe - that is the day when an outbreak of zombies will reach critical mass and turn our green and pleasant land into a grey and shambling wasteland. Remember, don't become a cheap meat snack for the zombies!

BIOHAZARD

Tim Curran

The day after tomorrow: Nuclear fallout. Mutations. Deadly pandemics. Corpse wagons. Body pits. Empty cities. The human race trembling on the edge of extinction. Only the desperate survive. One of them is Rick Nash. But there is a price for survival: communion with a ravenous evil born from the furnace of radioactive waste. It demands sacrifice. Only it can keep Nash one step ahead of the nightmare that stalks him-a sentient, seething plague-entity that stalks its chosen prey: the last of the human race. To accept it is a living death. To defy it, a hell beyond imagining

CPSIA information can be obtained at www.ICGtesting.com
Printed in the USA
BVOW041311080112

280054BV00003B/8/P